What Readers Are Saying About Karen Kingsbury's Books

"Karen Kingsbury's books inspire me to be a stronger follower of Jesus Christ, to be a better wife, mother, sister, and friend. Thank you, Karen, for your faithfulness to the Lord's gentle whisper."

—Tamara B.

"It's as simple as this: God's heart comes off these pages—every line, every word. You can feel the love and redemption of Christ through every character's life in each book. The message is a message of hope, hope in the One who has saved us and reigns victorious!"

—Brenae D.

"Karen's books are like a personal Bible study—there are so many situations that can be applied directly to the truths found in God's Word to help strengthen and encourage me."

—Laura G.

"I have read many of Karen's books, and I cry with every one. I feel like I actually know the people in the story, and my heart goes out to all of them when something happens!"

—Kathy N.

"Novels are mini-vacations, and Karen Kingsbury's novels are my favorite destination."

—Rachel S.

"Recently I made an effort to find *good* Christian writers, and I've hit the jackpot with Karen Kingsbury!"

—Linda O.

"Karen Kingsbury books are like my best friends; they make me cry, laugh, and give me encouragement. God bless you, Karen, for using your talent for Him."

—Tammy G.

"Every time I read one of Karen's books I think, 'It's the best one yet.' Then the next one comes out and I think, 'No, *this* is the best one.'"

—April B. M.

"Karen Kingbury's books are fantastic! She always makes me feel like I'm living the story along with the characters!"

—Courtney M. G.

"Karen's books speak to the heart. They are timely, entertaining, but, more important, they speak God's love into hungry souls."

—Debbie P. K.

"Whenever I pick up a new KK book, two things are consistent: tissues and finishing the whole book in one day."

—Nel L.

"When I was in Iraq, Mrs. Kingsbury's books were like a cool breeze on a hot summer day, and they made the hard days a bit easier to bear. By the end of my tour, all the ladies in my tent were hooked!"

—Olivia G.

"These books are the *best*! I have bought every one of them. I love getting my friends 'hooked' on Karen Kingsbury!"

—Dana T. C.

"Not only do Karen Kingsbury books make you laugh and cry, they will leave you begging for more. I stay awake all night when a new one comes out, reading by flashlight while my family sleeps!"

—Hellen H.

"Reading a Karen Kingsbury book is like watching a really good movie. I just can't get enough of her books."

—Esther S.

"The lady who orders books for our church library shakes her head and laughs when I tell her, 'OK, Karen Kingsbury has a new book out! I get first dibs when you get it!'"

—Jeannette M. B.

"Each new Karen Kingsbury book is like a visit home. Nothing beats time with family and friends, which is just what Karen's characters are!"

—Erin M.

"As someone who has struggled with health issues over the last two years, Karen's books have been such an encouragement to me. They remind me that God is with me and will never leave me. Please keep writing; I need that reminder."

—Carrie F.

"Pick up a Karen Kingsbury book, and I guarantee you will never be the same again! Karen's books have a way of reaching the deepest parts of your soul and touching places of your heart that are longing for something more."

—Becky S.

"Karen Kingsbury's books make a way for God to get ahold of your heart and never let go!"

—Jessica E.

"Karen Kingsbury really brings fiction to life, and I'm longing to read the next segment. Real men really do read KK!"

—Phil C.

"God's love, mercy, and hope shine through every one of Karen Kingsbury's books. She has a passion for the Lord and it shows in every story she writes. She is amazing!"

—Kristi C. M.

"It is hard for me to walk out of a bookstore without a Karen Kingsbury book in my possession. I am hooked."

—Shilah N.

"Karen Kingsbury is changing the world—one reader at a time."

—Lauren W.

"Karen writes straight from the heart and touches each of her readers with every new story! Love, loss, family, faith, all the struggles we each face every day come to life in the characters she creates."

—Amber B.

More Life-Changing Fiction™
by Karen Kingsbury

STAND-ALONE TITLES

Between Sundays

The Bridge

Coming Home, The Baxter Family

Divine

Like Dandelion Dust

Oceans Apart

On Every Side

Shades of Blue

This Side of Heaven (with friends
  from Cody Gunner Series)

Unlocked

When Joy Came to Stay

Where Yesterday Lives

E-SHORTS

The Beginning

I Can Only Imagine

REDEMPTION SERIES—BAXTERS 1

Redemption   Book 1

Remember   Book 2

Return   Book 3

Rejoice   Book 4

Reunion   Book 5

FIRSTBORN SERIES—BAXTERS 2

Fame   Book 1

Forgiven   Book 2

Found   Book 3

Family   Book 4

Forever   Book 5

SUNRISE SERIES—BAXTERS 3

Sunrise   Book 1

Summer   Book 2

Someday   Book 3

Sunset   Book 4

ABOVE THE LINE SERIES—BAXTERS 4

Take One   Book 1

Take Two   Book 2

Take Three   Book 3

Take Four   Book 4

BAILEY FLANIGAN SERIES—BAXTERS 5

Leaving   Book 1

Learning   Book 2

Longing   Book 3

Loving   Book 4

KAREN KINGSBURY

THE CHANCE

**SIMON &
SCHUSTER**

London · New York · Sydney · Toronto · New Delhi

A CBS COMPANY

First published in the US by Howard Books, 2012
First published in Great Britain in 2012 by Simon & Schuster UK Ltd
A CBS COMPANY

This paperback edition, 2013

3 5 7 9 10 8 6 4

Simon & Schuster UK Ltd
1st Floor
222 Gray's Inn Road
London
WC1X 8HB

www.simonandschuster.co.uk

Simon & Schuster Australia, Sydney
Simon & Schuster India, New Delhi

A CIP catalogue copy for this book is available from the British Library.

Paperback ISBN: 978-1-84983-965-5
eBook ISBN: 978-1-84983-966-2

Printed and bound by CPI Group (UK) Ltd, Croydon, CR0 4YY

To Donald:

Another year behind us, and already Tyler has nearly finished his second year at college while Kelsey is coming up on her one-year wedding anniversary, married to the love of her life. I'll never forget watching you walk our sweet girl down the aisle. Hard to believe that precious wedding planning season has come and gone. Isn't our Lord so faithful? Not just with our kids but in leading our family where He wants us to be. Closing in on two years in Nashville, and it's so very clear that God wanted us here. Not just for my writing and to be near Christian moviemaking and music, but for our kids and even for us. I love how you've taken to this new season of being more active on my staff, and helping our boys bridge the gap between being teenagers and becoming young men. Sean and Josh will graduate in just a few weeks and I can only wonder— the way I've done so often along the way—where the time has gone. Now that you're teaching again, I'm convinced that we are both right where God wants us. Thank you for being steady and strong and good and kind. Hold my hand and walk with me through the coming seasons—the graduations and growing up and getting older. All of it's possible with you by my side. Let's play and laugh and sing and dance and together we'll watch our children take wing. The ride is breathtakingly wondrous. I pray it lasts far into our twilight years. Until then, I'll enjoy not always knowing where I end and you begin. I love you always and forever.

To Kyle:

Kyle, you and Kelsey are married now, and forevermore we will see you as our son, as the young man God planned for our daughter, the one we prayed for and talked to God about and hoped for. Your heart is beautiful in every way, Kyle. How you cherish simple moments, and the way you are kind beyond words. You see the good in people and situations, and you find a way to give God the glory always. I will never forget you coming to me and Donald at different times and telling us that you wanted to support Kelsey and keep her safe—and ultimately that you wanted to love her all the days of your life. All of it is summed up in one simple action: the way you look at our precious Kelsey. It's a picture that will hang forever on the wall of my heart. You look at Kelsey as if nothing and no one else in all the world exists except her. In your eyes at that moment is the picture of what love looks like. Kyle, as God takes you from one stage to another—using that beautiful voice of yours to glorify Him and lead others to love Jesus—I pray that you always look at Kelsey the way you do today. We thank God for you, and we look forward to the beautiful seasons ahead. Love you always!

To Kelsey:

My precious daughter, you are married now. I think about the dozens of books where I've written about you in these front pages, how you have literally grown up in these dedications.

The days when you were in middle school and high school, then college and engaged. All of it has been detailed in the dedications of my books. And now you are Kelsey Kupecky. Your wedding was the most beautiful day, a moment in time destined from the first thought of you and Kyle in the heart of God. Kyle is the guy we've prayed for since you were born. God created him to love you, Kelsey—and you to love him. He is perfect for you, an amazing man of God whose walk of faith is marked by kindness, integrity, determination, and passion. We love him as if we've known him forever. Now, as you two move into the future that God has for you, as you seek to follow your dreams and shine brightly for Him in all you do, we will be here for you both. We will pray for you, believe in you, and support you however best we can. With Kyle's ministry of music and yours in acting, there are no limits to how God will use you both. I rejoice in what He is doing in your life, Kelsey. He has used your years of struggle to make you into the deeply rooted, faithful young woman you are today. Keep trusting God, keep putting Him first. I always knew this season would come, and now it is here. Enjoy every minute, sweetheart. You will always be the light of our family, the laughter in our hearts, the one-in-a-million girl who inspired the Bailey Flanigan Series. My precious Kelsey, I pray that God will bless you mightily in the years to come, and that you will always know how He used this time in your life to draw you close to Him and to prepare you for what's ahead. In the meantime, you'll be in my heart every moment. I love you, sweetheart.

To Tyler:

It's hard to believe you're almost already finished with your second year of college, ready for the next season of challenges and adventures. Your blog, Ty's Take, is being followed by so many of my readers longing to know how God is working in your life while you're in college. What's incredible is how you have become such a great writer in the process. I know you are planning to make a ministry-related career out of singing for Jesus on stages across the world, but don't be surprised if God also puts you at a computer keyboard, where you'll write books for Him. Oh, and let's not forget your gift for directing. So many exciting times ahead, Ty. I can barely take it all in. I still believe with all my heart that God has you right where He wants you. Learning so much—about performing for Him and becoming the man He wants you to be. You are that rare guy with a most beautiful heart for God and others. Your dad and I are so proud of you. We're proud of your talent and your compassion for people and your place in our family. However your dreams unfold, we'll be in the front row cheering loudest as we watch them happen. Hold on to Jesus, son. Keep shining for Him! I love you.

To Sean:

You've almost reached graduation, Sean, and we see God's hand at work in your life constantly. You have taken up drumming, and most days you spend three hours perfecting your gift for music. I love your confidence when you say that you'll be the best drummer ever, and then a decade after that you'll open your own restaurant. Nothing like passion and a plan! You are growing up and listening to God's lead, and in the process you are taking your studies and your homework so much more seriously. God will bless you for how you're being faithful in the little things. Be joyful, God tells us. And so in our family, you give us a little better picture of how that looks. Stay close to us, Sean. Remember, home is where your heart is always safe. Your dream of playing drums as a professional musician is alive and real. Keep working, keep pushing, keep believing. Go to bed every night knowing you did all you could to prepare yourself for the doors God will open in the days ahead. I pray that as you soar for the Lord, He will allow you to be a very bright light indeed. You're a precious gift, son. I love you. Keep smiling and keep seeking God's best.

To Josh:

Soccer was where you started when you first came home from Haiti, and soccer is the game that God seems to be opening up for you. We prayed about what was next, whether you would continue to shine on the football field and the soccer field, or whether God would narrow your options to show you where He is leading. Now we all need to pray that as you continue to follow the Lord in your sports options, He will continue to lead you so that your steps are in keeping with His. This we know—there is for you a very real possibility that you'll play competitive sports at the next level. Even with all your athleticism, I'm most proud of your spiritual and social growth this past year. You've grown in heart, maturity, kindness, quiet strength, and the realization that time at home is short. God is going to use you for great things, and I believe He will put you on a public platform to do it. Stay strong in Him, and listen to His quiet whispers so you'll know which direction to turn. I'm so proud of you, son. I'll forever be cheering on the sidelines. Keep God first in your life. I love you always.

To EJ:

EJ, I'm so glad you know just how much we love you and how deeply we believe in the great plans God has for you. With new opportunities spread out before you, I know you are a bit uncertain. But I see glimpses of determination and effort that tell me that with Christ, you can do anything, son. One day not too far from here, you'll be applying to colleges, thinking about the career choices ahead of you and the path God might be leading you down. Wherever that path takes you, keep your eyes on Jesus and you'll always be as full of possibility as you are today. I expect great things from you, EJ, and I know the Lord expects them, too. I'm so glad you're in our family, always and forever. I'm praying you'll have a strong passion to use your gifts for God as you head into your junior year. Thanks for your giving heart, EJ. I love you more than you know.

To Austin:

Austin, you are now in high school, and I literally wonder every day how the time has passed so quickly. This past summer as you grew to six foot five, we learned about your high blood pressure, how your congenital heart defect had become congenital heart disease. But rather than grumble and complain, you listened and learned and worked with us to adjust every aspect of your life. You eat differently, sleep more, drink water all day long, and you know the fruits, vegetables, and supplements that lower blood pressure. The results have been amazing! From that first day you stepped onto the high school football field, you have given one hundred percent of your special heart to every single play, and we couldn't be more proud of you! Austin, I love that you care enough to be and do your best. It shows in your straight A's, and it shows in the way you are tackling your health. Always remember what I've told you about being a warrior. Let your drive and competition push you to be better, but never, ever let it discourage you. You're so good at life, Austin. Keep the passion and keep that beautiful faith of yours. Every single one of your dreams is within reach. Keep your eyes on Him, and we'll keep our eyes on you, our youngest son. There is nothing sweeter than cheering you on—from the time you were born, through your infant heart surgery, until now. I thank God for you, for the miracle of your life. I love you, Austin.

And to God Almighty,
the Author of Life, who has —for now —
blessed me with these.

THE CHANCE

Chapter One

Her mom didn't come home for dinner—the third time that week.

That was the first hint Ellie Tucker had that maybe her father was right. Maybe her mother had done something so terrible this time that their family really would break in two. And no one and nothing would ever put them back together.

Ellie was fifteen that hot, humid Savannah summer, and as the Friday afternoon hours slipped away, as six o'clock became six thirty, she joined her dad in the kitchen and helped him make dinner. Tuna sandwiches with a new jar of mayonnaise, warm from the cupboard. They worked without talking, her mother's absence weighing heavy in the silence of the passing minutes. The refrigerator didn't have much, but her dad found a bag of baby carrots and put them in a bowl. When the food was on the table, he took his spot at the head, and Ellie sat next to him.

The place across from her, the spot where her mother usually sat, remained glaringly empty.

"Let's pray." Her father took her hand. He waited for several beats before starting. "Lord, thank You for our food and our blessings." He hesitated. "You know all things. Reveal the truth, please. In Jesus' name, amen."

The truth? Ellie could barely swallow the dry bites of her sandwich. The truth about what? Her mother? The reason she wasn't home when the doctor's office she worked at closed an hour ago? No words were said during the meal, though the quiet screamed across the dinner table. When they were finished, her dad looked at her. His eyes were sad. "Ellie, if you would do the dishes, please." He stood and kissed her on the forehead. "I'll be in my room."

She did what she was asked. Twenty minutes later, she was still finishing when she heard her mom slip through the front door. Ellie looked over her shoulder, and their eyes met. Lately, Ellie felt more like the mother, the way a mother might feel when her kids were teenagers. Her mom wore her work clothes, black pants and a white shirt. As if work had just now gotten done.

"Where's your father?" Her mother's eyes were red and swollen, her voice thick.

"In his room." Ellie blinked, not sure what else to say.

Her mom started walking in that direction; then she stopped and turned to Ellie again. "I'm sorry." Her shoulders dropped a little. "For missing dinner." She sounded like someone Ellie didn't know. "I'm sorry."

Before Ellie could ask where she'd been, her mom turned and walked down the hall. Ellie checked the clock on the microwave. Seven thirty. Nolan had another hour in the gym, another hour shooting baskets. Then Ellie would ride her bike to his house, the way she did most nights. Especially this summer.

Since her parents had started fighting.

She dried her hands, went to her room, and shut the door behind her. A little music and some time with her journal, then Nolan would be home. She turned on the radio. Backstreet Boys filled the air, and instantly, she dropped the sound a few notches. Her dad said he'd take away her radio if she listened to worldly music. Ellie figured worldly was a matter of opinion. Her opinion was the Backstreet Boys' music might be as close to heaven as she was going to get in the near future.

The boys were singing about being larger than life when the first shout seemed to rattle her bedroom window. Ellie killed the sound on the radio and jumped to her feet. As much tension as there had been between her parents lately, neither of them ever really shouted. Not like this. Her heart pounded loud enough to hear it. She hurried to her bedroom door, but before she reached it another round of shouts echoed through the house. This time she could understand what her father was saying, the awful names he was calling her mom.

Moving as quietly as she could, Ellie crept down the hall and across the living room closer to her parents' bedroom door. Another burst of yelling and she was near enough to hear something else. Her mother was weeping.

"You'll pack your things and leave." Her father had never sounded like this—like he was firing bullets with every word. He wasn't finished. "I will not have you pregnant with *his* child and . . . and living under *my* roof." His voice seemed to shake the walls. "I will not have it."

Ellie anchored herself against the hallway so she wouldn't drop to the floor. What was happening? Her mother was pregnant? With someone else's baby? She felt the blood leaving her face, and her world started to spin. Colors and sounds and reality blurred, and she wondered if she would pass out. *Run, Ellie . . . run fast.* She ordered herself to move, but her feet wouldn't follow the command.

Before she could figure out which way was up, her father opened the door and glared at her, his chest heaving. "What are you doing?"

The question stood between them. Ellie looked past him to her mom, sitting in the bedroom chair, her head in her hands. *Get up,* Ellie wanted to scream at her. *Tell him it's a lie! Defend yourself, Mom! Do something.* But her mother did nothing. She said nothing.

Ellie's eyes flew to her father again, and she tried to step away, tried to exit the scene as quickly as possible, but she tripped and fell back on her hands. Pain cut through her wrists, but she moved farther away from him. Like a crab escaping a net.

It took that long for her father's expression to soften. "Ellie. I'm sorry." He stepped toward her. "I didn't mean for . . . You weren't supposed to hear that."

And in that moment Ellie knew two things. First, the horrible words her dad had shouted through the house were true. And second, her life as she knew it was over. It lay splintered on the worn-out hallway carpet in a million pieces. She scrambled to her feet and turned away. "I . . . I have to go."

Her father was saying something about how this was more than a girl her age could understand and how she needed to get back to her room and pray. But all Ellie could hear was the way her heart slammed around in her chest. She needed air, needed to breathe. In a move that felt desperate, she found her way to her feet and ran for the front door. A minute later she was on her bicycle, pedaling as fast as she could through the summer night.

He would still be at the gym, but that was okay. Ellie loved watching Nolan play basketball. Loved it whether the place was packed with kids from Savannah High or it was just the two of them and the echo of the ball hitting the shiny wood floor. With every push of the bike pedal, Ellie tried to put the reality out of her mind. But the truth smothered her like a wet blanket. Her mother had come home late again—the way she'd been coming home late since early spring. And today . . . today she must have admitted what Ellie's dad had suspected all along.

Her mom had been having an affair. Not only that, but she was pregnant.

The truth churned in Ellie's stomach, suffocating her until finally she had no choice but to ditch her bike in the closest bush and give way to the stomachache consuming her. One disgusting wave after another emptied her insides until only the hurt remained. A hurt that she already knew would stay with her forever.

Exhausted and drained, Ellie sat on the curb, head in her hands, and let the tears come. Until then, shock had kept the sadness pushed to the corner of her heart. Now she cried until she could barely breathe. Her mom didn't love her father, which meant she didn't love either of them. She wanted more than Ellie and her dad. There was no other way to look at it. Shame added itself to the mix of emotions because Nolan's mom never would have done something like this.

Ellie lifted her face to the darkening sky. *Nolan.* She wiped her face and inhaled deeply. She needed to get to him before it got any later, needed to find him before he left the gym. Her bike was old and the chain was loose, but that didn't stop her from reaching the school in record time. The sound of the ball hitting the floor soothed her soul as she rode to the back door of the gym. She leaned her bike against the brick wall next to his.

Nolan kept the door propped open in case a breeze came up. Ellie slipped through the entrance and took a spot on the first row of the bleachers. He caught the ball and stared at her, his eyes dancing, a smile tugging at his lips. "You're early."

She nodded. She didn't trust her voice, not when all she wanted was to cry.

A shadow of concern fell over his tanned face. "Ellie? You okay?"

No one could take away the pain like he could, her best friend, Nolan Cook. But as much as she wanted his comfort and understanding, she didn't want him to know. Didn't want to tell him why she was upset, because then, well, for sure it would be true. There would be no denying the truth once she told Nolan.

He set down the ball and walked to her. Sweat dripped from his forehead, and his tank top and shorts were damp. "You were crying." He stopped a foot from her. "What happened?"

"My parents." She felt her eyes well up, felt her words drown in an ocean of sadness.

"More fighting?"

"Yeah. Bad."

"Ahh, Ellie." His breathing was returning to normal. He wiped his forearm across his face. "I'm sorry."

"Keep playing." Even to her own ears, her voice sounded strained from all she wasn't saying. She nodded toward the basket. "You have another half hour."

He watched her for a long couple of seconds. "You sure?"

"We can talk later. I just . . ." A few rebel tears slid down her cheeks. "I needed to be here. With you."

Again he narrowed his eyes, worried. Eventually, he gave a slow nod, not quite sure. "We can leave whenever you want."

"When you're done. Please, Nolan."

A last look into her eyes, then he turned and jogged back to the ball. Once it was in his hands, he dribbled right and then left and took it to the hoop. In a move as fluid and graceful as anything Ellie had learned in her three years of dance, Nolan rose in the air and slammed the ball through the net. He landed lightly on both feet and caught the ball. Dribbled back out, juked a few imaginary opponents, and repeated the move. Ten straight dunks and he jogged to the drinking fountain and drank for half a minute. Next it was three-point shots.

Nolan played basketball with his heart and mind and soul. The ball was an extension of his hand, and every move, every step, was as natural for him as breathing. Watching him, Ellie felt her eyes dry, felt herself celebrating his gift of playing basketball, the way she celebrated it every time she had the privilege of seeing him play. Nolan's dream was as simple as it was impossible.

He wanted to play in the NBA. It was something he prayed about and worked toward every day. Every hour of every day. From the A's and B's he struggled to earn to the long hours he put in here each night. If Nolan didn't wind up playing professional basketball, it wouldn't be for lack of trying or believing.

When he'd sunk five shots from spots all along the arch of the three-point line, he ran to the water fountain once more and then tucked the ball under his arm and walked back to her. He used his shirt to wipe the sweat off his face. "Could it be more humid?"

"Yeah." She smiled a little and looked at the open back door. "Not much of a breeze."

"No." He nodded to her. "Come on. Let's go to my house. I'll shower, and then we can go to the park."

That was all Ellie wanted, a few hours alone with Nolan at Gordonston Park. The place where they had their favorite oak tree and enough soft grass to lie on their backs and count shooting stars on summer nights like this one. She still didn't say anything, not yet. They walked silently out the back door, and Nolan locked it. His dad was the Savannah High coach, and he had given his son a key a year ago. Too much trouble to open the gym every time Nolan wanted to shoot.

They rode their bikes to Pennsylvania Avenue and took the shortcut down Kinzie to Edgewood. Nolan's house was only half a mile from Ellie's, but they might as well have been in separate worlds for how different the neighborhoods were. His had fireflies and perfect front lawns that stretched on forever. Ellie's had chain-link fences and stray dogs, single-story houses the size of Nolan's garage.

The sort of house Ellie and her parents lived in.

She sat with Nolan's mother in the kitchen while he showered. Ellie's eyes were dry now, so she didn't have to explain herself. The conversation was light, with Nolan's mom talking about the new Bible study she'd joined and how much she was learning.

Ellie wanted to care, wanted to feel as connected to God as Nolan and his parents were. But if God loved her, why was her life falling apart? Maybe He only loved some people. Good folks, like the Cook family. A few minutes later, Nolan came down in fresh shorts and a T-shirt. He grabbed two chocolate chip cookies from a plate on the kitchen counter and kissed his mother's cheek.

Ellie blinked, and she realized, as she'd been doing a lot

lately, that Nolan was growing up. They'd been friends since second grade, and they'd walked home together since the first day of middle school. But somewhere along the journey of time, they'd both done something they hadn't seen coming.

They'd gotten older. They weren't kids anymore.

Nolan was six-one already, tanned from his morning runs, his blond hair cut close to his head the way it was every summer. He'd been lifting weights, so maybe that was it. The way his shoulders and arms looked muscled in the pale green T-shirt as he grabbed the cookies.

Ellie felt her cheeks grow hot, and she looked away. It was weird seeing Nolan like this, more man than boy. His mother turned to her and smiled, warm and genuine. "Come by anytime, Ellie. The door's always open. You know that."

"Yes, ma'am. Thank you."

Ellie and Nolan didn't talk about where they were going. Their spot was the same every time. The patch of grass, alongside the biggest oak tree in the park—maybe the biggest in the city. The one dripping with Spanish moss, with gnarled old roots big enough to sit on. They walked side by side to the spot.

Ellie and Nolan had come here to talk about life since the summer before sixth grade. Back then they played hide-and-seek among the trees, with the enormous oak serving as home base. During the school year, when it was warm enough, they'd do their homework here. And on nights like this, they would do what came easiest for them.

They would simply crack open their hearts and share whatever came out.

"Okay. Tell me." Nolan took the spot closest to the massive tree trunk. He leaned back, studying her. "What happened?"

Ellie had been thinking about this moment since she walked through the door of the high school gym. She had to tell him, because she told him everything. But maybe she didn't have to tell him this very minute. Her throat felt dry, so her words took longer to form. "My mom . . . she came home late again."

He waited, and after a few seconds, he blinked. "That's it?"

"Yeah." She hated postponing the truth, but she couldn't tell him yet. "My dad was really mad."

He leaned back against the tree. "It'll blow over."

"Right." She moved to the spot beside him and pressed her back lightly against the tree trunk. Their shoulders touched, a reminder of everything good and real in her life.

"One day when we're old and married, we'll come back to this very spot and remember this summer."

"How do you know?"

He looked at her. "That we'll remember?"

"No." She grinned. "That I'll marry you."

"That's easy." He faced her and shrugged. "You'll never find anyone who loves you like I do."

It wasn't the first time he'd said it. He kept his tone light, so she couldn't accuse him of being too serious or trying to change things between them. She would laugh and shake her head, as if he'd suggested something crazy, like the two of them running off and joining the circus.

This time she didn't laugh. She only lifted her eyes to the distant trees and the fireflies dancing among them. Good thing she hadn't told him about her mother, about how she'd run off with another man and gotten pregnant. That would change everything. Nolan would feel sorry for her, and there would be no more teasing about marriage. Not when her parents had made such a mess of theirs.

Ellie exhaled, hating her new reality. Yes, the news could wait.

Right now she wanted nothing more than to sit here beside Nolan Cook under the big oak tree at the edge of the park on a summer night that was theirs alone and believe . . . believe for one more moment the thing Ellie wanted more than her next breath.

That they might stay this way forever.

Chapter Two

With all she owned in an old suitcase beside her, Caroline Tucker stood in the dark night outside of her house on Louisiana Avenue and tried not to think about all she was losing. He would've killed her if she'd stayed. She felt certain. Either way her life was over, but for the sake of her unborn baby, she had to leave, had to find another way.

The hardest part was Ellie.

Her daughter was gone—to Nolan's house, no doubt. Which meant sometime tomorrow, when her husband wasn't home, Caroline would have to find a way back here from west Savannah without a car. So she could explain the situation. So Ellie wouldn't hate her.

Her friend Lena Lindsey pulled up in a newer model silver Honda and stepped out. For a moment she stood there watching Caroline. Just watching, their eyes locked. Lena knew the whole story now, every ugly detail except one. The fact that Caroline was pregnant.

Finally, Lena put her hands on her hips. "He found out about Peyton?"

"Yes." Caroline looked over her shoulder. Every light in the house was off. She kept her voice low. "He kicked me out."

Lena came close and hugged her. She was as black as Caroline was white, and even though it was 2002, for some people in Savannah, their friendship broke unwritten rules. She and Lena never cared what anyone thought. They were as close as sisters, and had been since high school.

"Come on." Lena opened the passenger door of the Honda. "We'll figure this out."

Lena and her husband lived on the west side of Savannah in an upscale two-story house with their three young sons. Her husband, Stu, was a dermatologist, and Lena ran his front office. When Lena and Caroline got together for coffee or manicures, there was no end to the stories they shared about the medical offices they ran. Another way the two friends stayed connected.

Not until they reached the highway did Lena turn to her. "You're pregnant, right?"

Caroline's gaze fell to her fingers, and she began twisting her wedding band.

"Heaven help us." The words came with a heavy sigh. "I told you to stay away from that man." Lena didn't hold back. "Famous country singer?" She shook her head. "Probably has a Caroline Tucker in every town." Her tone softened. "Sweet girl, why? Why'd you do it?"

It was one of the questions crashing around in Caroline's head. One she could actually answer. "I loved him."

Lena took her eyes off the road long enough to look at Caroline. She didn't need to point out that the guy had clearly never loved Caroline, never cared about her. Or that she'd been nothing more than another groupie. Another one-night stand on his nationwide tour. Lena didn't need to voice a word of it.

Her eyes said it all.

Over the past few months Lena had asked questions about how much time Caroline was spending at home. She even offered to find a counselor to help make things right between Caroline and Alan. But Caroline avoided Lena's attempts and denied the affair until a few days ago. Now they rode in a silence heavy with sadness.

Caroline stared out the window at the night sky. When had the trouble started? How had her life gotten so out of control? When she sorted through the places where she'd gone wrong, one event came to mind. The concert two years ago last January, the day Peyton Anders came to town for his *Whatever You're Feeling* tour. All of Savannah knew about the show. Peyton was that big. That year he was twenty-six. He had a ruggedly handsome face and a football player's build. By then he'd been the Country Music Conference's best male vocalist for three years running, and that spring he had just added Entertainer of the Year to his credits.

"You thinking about it?" Lena's voice interrupted her thoughts.

Caroline turned to her friend. "Trying."

"That's a start."

"Me and Alan . . . it's been bad for so long, Lena." Caroline's voice cracked, the hurt and heartache choking her. "He . . . doesn't want me."

"Do I look like a stranger, Carrie Tucker?" That's what Lena had always called her. Carrie. "I was there." She gave her a sidelong glance, then looked back at the dark road ahead. "Remember?" She paused again, but her intensity remained.

"Keep thinking, Carrie. Go all the way back and figure out the knot. So you can stand a chance at unraveling it."

"Yes." Caroline turned away. Fixing the mess wasn't an option, but she couldn't say that. Not to Lena. Her friend believed in staying married. Period. Even now, when Caroline's marriage to Alan was long dead.

She stared once more at the night sky. The concert that January had sold out, but Stu knew the concert promoter. The guy gave him a couple of front-row seats. Lena's husband didn't care for country music, so Lena had asked Caroline.

The invitation had been the highlight of Caroline's entire year.

Without warning, an image flashed into her mind. Her and Alan, walking down the aisle of a country church, in love and absolutely sure about forever. She was pretty and young back then, twenty years old with long blond hair and innocent eyes. In the early days, every moment with Alan had been marked with a hope deeper than the ocean.

The memory disappeared. There was no way to measure the distance between then and now. Who she'd been and who she'd become. Caroline felt tears sting at her eyes. Who they had both become.

She turned to Lena. "Alan and me. The mess we're in." She dabbed her fingers at the corners of her eyes. "It's my fault, too. I'm not making excuses."

"I hope not." Lena kept her gaze straight ahead. "Married to one guy, and you turn up pregnant by someone else?" She raised one eyebrow. "Not a lot of room in the car for excuses." She paused for a long while. Then she gave Caroline's hand a tender squeeze. "I'm sorry. I don't mean it like that."

"I know."

"It's bad right now." Lena tightened her hold on the steering wheel. She made a left turn into her neighborhood. "God loves you, Carrie. He wants you and Alan to figure it out."

Caroline nodded. It wasn't the first time Lena had said it. Lena was a Christian. The real kind. She never preached, but she wasn't afraid to call Caroline out on something. She had before. She loved Caroline that much.

They reached Lena's house, and as they got out of the car, a rush of guilt clawed at Caroline's determination. "I don't think we can work this out. It's over. It's been over for years, Lena." She paused for a quick breath. "Maybe I should go to a hotel."

Lena looked at her. "You about finished?"

Caroline hesitated. "I don't know what to do—"

"Carrie Tucker." Lena walked around the front bumper and put her hands on Caroline's shoulders. "Get your suitcase." She gave a single nod, then turned and headed for the front door. She didn't look back. "The guest room's made up."

The discussion was over. Caroline pulled her suitcase from the back of Lena's Honda and shut the trunk. Five minutes later, she was sitting on the edge of the Lindseys' guest bed. She was the most horrible wife and mother ever. The absolute worst. What would Ellie think? She would get home from Nolan's house and find her mother gone. Pregnant with someone else's baby. The thought made Caroline sick to her stomach.

Suddenly, she remembered something.

Her heart beat faster as she pulled her purse close and dug around the bottom, past the Walmart and Target receipts and gum wrappers until she found what she was looking for. A bottle of Vicodin. Twelve pills, at least. Earlier today a recovered patient had asked her to discard them. Instead, Caroline had slipped them into her purse.

In case she needed them to deal with her own pain.

But the pills could do more than that. Much more. They felt heavy in her hand. She took off the lid and brought them close to her face. Smelled the strength of them. Their bitterness. It wouldn't take twelve pills. She could chew a couple of them, and that would be that. No husband who didn't love her. No daughter ashamed of her. No baby about to be born unaware into an ugly world.

The sound of footsteps made her lower the bottle. She slipped the lid back on and dropped it into her purse. Her hands shook, and she couldn't draw a full breath. What was she thinking? How could she even consider killing herself?

"Hey, there." Lena stuck her head into the room. "Get settled. Stu and I will be in the kitchen." Her eyes looked softer than they had before. "Whenever you're ready to talk."

She left without waiting for Caroline's response. It wasn't whether Caroline wanted to talk but when. As long as she stayed here, Lena and Stu would do everything in their power to see Caroline and Alan reconciled. It was how they were wired. Caroline stood and dropped her purse in the far corner of the room, as far away as possible. She still loved Alan. The old Alan. She always would. If only they could find their way back.

Pray, Caroline. You have to pray. As soon as the thought hit her, she refuted it. She had prayed every step of the journey with Alan. Where had it gotten her? A random reel of moments played in her mind, times when she had asked for God's help, His wisdom and understanding. His comfort. But always her marriage had grown worse.

She closed her eyes and could see him again. Alan Tucker, the love of her life. Coming home from Parris Island an hour

away, walking through the front door of their apartment off
Forsyth Park in his marine uniform, grinning at her. "It happened! I'm a drill instructor! I start Monday."

Caroline's mind had raced, wondering what that meant for
her, for them. "Will the hours . . . be longer?"

Alan had hesitated, his expression clouded with sudden
confusion. "I'm a marine, Caroline. If it means more hours,
then I put in more hours."

For the first of a thousand times it occurred to Caroline that
she would never be most important in Alan Tucker's life. His
extra workload kept him on base Monday through Friday and
home only on the weekends. Somehow, though, his absence
caused *him* to doubt *her*. He would come home on Friday and
ask where she'd been, what she'd been doing. If her answer
took too long, his tone would grow impatient. "It's not that
hard, Caroline. Where have you been?"

He really meant what men had she been seeing. There never
were any other men back then, but Alan would remind her
almost every weekend that it was wrong for her to wear tank
tops or short shorts, or to look too long at a guy bagging her
groceries or taking her money at the car wash. "It's a sin to
make a man stumble, Caroline." He would smile at her as if
this were a perfectly normal conversation between a husband
and wife. "I'm glad you understand."

Caroline began to wonder about the man coming home
every weekend, and what he had done with the guy she loved.
Only when they were in bed did she see glimpses of that Alan.
His patience and tender touch made her feel crazy for doubt-
ing him.

The parade of memories continued. Months after Alan's
promotion, Caroline was bringing Ellie home from the hospi-

tal, and Alan was warning her that she'd have to do a lot of the work on her own. He was sorry. He wanted another promotion at Parris Island.

Wanted it at all costs.

The loneliness of missing Alan had been soothed overnight by the presence of her little daughter. As Ellie grew older, the two of them walked to the park every afternoon. Caroline would blow bubbles from a plastic wand into the wind while Ellie chased them, her little-girl laughter filling the humid Georgia air. They were together every waking hour. Caroline would read to Ellie each night, Dr. Seuss and then Junie B. Jones, until they both knew the stories by heart. Alan liked to remind them that they should be reading more C. S. Lewis and fewer frivolous books.

She could hear Ellie's long-ago voice: "Daddy, we *do* read those. *The Lion, the Witch and the Wardrobe* is my favorite." She shot a twinkle-eyed look at Caroline. "But Junie B. Jones makes us laugh, right, Mommy?"

Five years of happy moments with Ellie came in a rush, all of them marked by peanut butter sandwiches and afternoon naps and the smell of chocolate chip cookies baking in the oven. Disney movies and practicing letters and coloring together, every day as wonderful as the last. But then Ellie went to kindergarten.

At first Caroline had only the lonely mornings to remind her that Ellie was getting older. But a year later, Ellie was in school full-time. The first day of class, Caroline returned home alone, stared in the mirror, and, through teary eyes, asked herself one question: "What are you going to do now?"

Alan didn't take calls at work, and though he checked in every night, their conversations were matter-of-fact. Which bills had come, what accounts were paid, how was Ellie, what was she learning in school. Only the weekends were marked by an intimacy and joy between Caroline and Alan. They would take quiet walks along the river and sip exotic coffees at a café downtown. She was in love with Alan, even if they only had the weekends. But that didn't make her weekdays less lonely.

The single ray of light, the one that gave her a reason to get up on Monday mornings, was the time she still had with Ellie. Caroline volunteered at her daughter's school, helping out on craft days and field trips, and in the afternoons Ellie took dance and gymnastics lessons at the YMCA. The two grew closer with every passing year. She could hear Ellie's voice again, older this time. "You're my best friend, Mom . . . you and Nolan. No one gets me like you two."

But somewhere between the elementary grades and the start of Ellie's middle school years, the shared times between them became less frequent, and eventually, they happened only once in a while. The turning point came when Caroline took a job at Dr. Kemp's office, the year she and Alan realized they'd fallen into debt. Whether it was Caroline's time working away from home or Ellie's ability to sense the tension between her parents, the girl began spending most of her free time at Nolan's house.

And just like that, the parade of memories and moments came to a grinding halt.

No wonder Caroline had jumped at the chance to see Peyton Anders with Lena that January. The sameness of her life, the lack of interaction and laughter with either Alan or Ellie, had been driving her insane. A concert would give her a night to feel alive again.

That—and only that—was all Caroline Tucker ever expected.

She was a good girl from a good home. She went to church every Sunday with Alan and Ellie, even during the worst weeks. Never in all her life could she have imagined what was about to happen.

The thing that would change her life forever.

Chapter Three

Alan Tucker thought about getting in his car and finding Ellie, bringing her back from the place where she hung out with Nolan Cook. The park near the boy's house. But if he did that, she would know her life was about to change. In the end, that was why he didn't go. Ellie deserved one last night before the start of the rest of her life.

The one in a new location. Without her mother.

Tonight's news had changed everything. He would not raise Ellie in a town where people were forever talking about her mother, about her terrible affair and who she'd had it with. Tonight Alan finally had answers to the questions that had plagued him for so long. He still struggled to believe the reality. Peyton Anders.

Alan sighed, and the sound rattled through his aching chest. Of all people, Caroline had been cheating with a famous country singer. Worse, they'd been going behind his back for two years. He lay on top of the covers and stared through the darkness at the patchy bedroom ceiling. He wasn't sure which was worse—the fact that Caroline had cheated on him or the truth that she'd given her heart to the guy two years ago. Two years. He exhaled and rolled onto his side. He wanted only the best for his family. In all the years of spending weekdays at the base, he had never so much as taken a sip of alcohol. When the guys went out drinking, Alan stayed in his room and read his Bible or watched reruns of *Gilligan's Island* and *I Love Lucy*.

He had asked Caroline more than once who she was spending time with, but he never really expected this. That the only woman he'd ever loved would find someone else. Or that she would lie to him. Betray him so completely. His stomach churned, and he wondered whether he would ever feel good again. True, he and Caroline hadn't slept together in months, but before their intimacy waned, they'd had their good times.

Now, now he hated remembering even one of those moments. She would sleep with him at night and then flirt with Peyton the next morning from work. He never should have fallen in love with someone as beautiful as Caroline. Especially with his career as a marine. A few of his friends had warned him sixteen years ago, when he announced he was marrying her. Even his mother had been worried. "She's very pretty." She looked doubtful. "Does she understand you'll be gone a lot? Women like her . . . well, some of them can be self-absorbed."

Alan clenched his jaw. He had been angry at his mother for her comment back then. And now . . . He couldn't finish the thought, couldn't bring himself to rehash in his mind the truth about his wife. But this much was certain: Caroline would regret what she'd done to him. She would regret it as long as she lived. He already had a plan. Weeks ago his commander had told him about a promotion—one that would take him to San Diego's Camp Pendleton Marine Base. He would continue his work as a drill instructor, but for larger classes. If things went well, he would wind up working at the adjacent military brig, the one run by the navy.

The San Diego drill instructor position was open immediately. Until tonight, he hadn't really thought he'd do it. Ellie was a freshman at Savannah High, and Caroline had her job at Dr. Kemp's office. Life had a certain rhythm to it.

But all that had changed tonight.

Five minutes after Caroline pulled away, he called his commander. "How soon can I start in San Diego?"

"Next week." The man didn't hesitate. "Tell me when, and I'll set it up. They have temporary housing on base until you find something."

Alan did the calculations. He and Ellie could pack tomorrow and leave Sunday morning. If they put in long hours on the road, they could reach California in three days. "I could report Wednesday. Be ready to work that Monday."

"Done." The man sounded surprised. "They'll be glad. Pendleton's hurting for instructors." He hesitated a couple seconds. "You're the best, Tucker. Glad you're moving up, but I hate losing you."

If only his wife felt that way.

Yes, she would be sorry. He would move with Ellie and raise her by himself. Let her try to sue him or fight for custody. She wouldn't dare, not with the sordid details of her last few years. No, she wouldn't fight him. If she could do this to him and Ellie, then she didn't care, anyway. He wouldn't subject their daughter to a life of shame. Caroline didn't want to be a mother, not if she could do this.

His heart felt heavy in his chest. He still had to tell Ellie. She might be mad at first, but in time she would understand. She would miss Caroline, of course. But when she got old enough, he'd tell her the truth. How her mom had at one time been a wonderful person, kind and caring, the love of his life. But eventually she had chosen another man over being a wife to him or a mother to Ellie. Those future conversations would be heartbreaking, but Alan could see no other way. Ellie would have to understand. The only other person she wouldn't want to leave was Nolan. Her best friend. But eventually she would get over him, too.

San Diego would have a whole new world of friends for her.

Alan felt his determination harden like fresh cement on a summer day. Whatever Ellie thought and however upset she might be, they were leaving Savannah. There was no other way. He heard the sound of her bicycle in the driveway, and he looked at the clock. It wasn't quite eleven, Ellie's curfew. He listened as the front door opened and closed again. For a single instant he started to get up. Better to tell her now so she would have the right mind-set. More time to prepare.

But he stopped himself.

By now she would've forgotten her parents' fight. She'd probably had a great night with Nolan, talking under the trees and listening to music and being a kid. Ellie was entitled to a good night's sleep, entitled to sweet dreams. The news that her mother was pregnant with another man's child, that Ellie was moving to San Diego with her dad, would grow her up in a hurry. Alan ached for her. He would tell her tomorrow. He wouldn't interrupt the sanctity of the moment.

Her final night of childhood.

❦ ❦

The conversation with Lena and Stu was brief. They wanted Caroline to call a counselor in the morning. Seek intervention immediately so that somehow, by some miracle, her marriage could be saved. Caroline listened and nodded. But the talk was pointless. There was no way back. Alan Tucker would never love her again.

She retreated to the guest room and let the memories surface once more until they were in plain sight of her heart. And suddenly, she was there again, at that first Peyton Anders concert.

From the minute Peyton took the stage that night at the Savannah Civic Center, he seemed to sing to her alone. Their eyes met, and at first even Lena thought it was nothing more than harmless fun. Flirty interactions between an entertainer and a fan. The sort of thing a guy like Peyton probably did every night.

Caroline figured the exchange was something she and Lena would laugh about when they were old someday. The night the famous Peyton Anders had singled Caroline Tucker out of the whole audience and made her head spin.

But after a few songs, the brief looks became an occasional wink, and as the concert played on Caroline allowed herself to believe that she and Peyton were the only ones in the auditorium. Near the end of his set, he motioned for her to go to the side stage. At the same time, two guys from his crew appeared near the steps. They waved her over as Peyton took a brief break. He drank back half a bottle of water and then smiled at the audience. "They say Savannah has the prettiest ladies in the South."

Caroline remembered how she felt, her heart in her throat, as she waited near the side stage. Peyton was going on. "All night I've been noticing one very pretty little lady." He shrugged, his boyish grin beyond charming. Somehow he managed to look like a middle-school kid crushing on his friend's older sister. "What can I say? I can't sing this next song without her."

The crowd cheered, the sound deafening. By then the two men had led Caroline up onto the stage. She could still see herself waiting in the wings, dressed in a white blouse, her best jeans, and cowboy boots, her knees shaking.

"Come on, sweetheart, come on out here."

Caroline felt like she'd fallen into a dream. *This can't be happening,* she told herself. He was famous and eight years younger. She was a member of the PTSA, not the Peyton Anders Fan Club. But what could she do now? She came tentatively to him, the applause and howls rattling her nerves. When she reached him, he took her hand. "What's your name, darling?" He held the microphone out to her.

"Caroline." She blinked, blinded by the glare of the spotlight. "Caroline Tucker."

Peyton chuckled and looked at the audience. "Caroline Tucker, ladies and gentlemen. Is she beautiful or what?"

More cheers and applause. Caroline tried to exhale. She had to be dreaming. That was the only way to explain it. By then the kind words Alan once lavished on her had long since given way to functional conversation. How was Ellie doing in school? Why hadn't the laundry been done? When was she going to call the plumber about the broken drain in the bathroom sink? That sort of thing. Alan came home tired and distracted. Some days he barely glanced at her as he walked through the door, so it wasn't a surprise that she hadn't felt pretty in months. Old and weary, lonely and uncertain. Tired and used up. All of those.

But not beautiful.

One of Peyton's guys brought over a bar stool, and Peyton held her hand while she climbed onto it. Then he sang her the title song of his newest album. The song that had inspired the tour: "Whatever You're Feeling." The lights and crowd and applause faded away as Peyton sang and Caroline held her breath. Every line, every lyric, every word seemed written for her and this strange connection between them, a connection that had happened in as much time as it took her to breathe. Even now the lyrics were as familiar as her name.

Now that we're both here
Nothing left to fear
We could have it all
So let your heart fall
Here in this moment that we're stealing
Baby, I am feeling
The same thing you are feeling
Whatever you are feeling.

When he finished the song, he hugged her, and in a way no one could've detected, he whispered, "Give your number to my guys." Then he smiled at the audience. "Caroline Tucker, ladies and gentlemen."

She walked off the stage, dizzy and excited and sick to her stomach. Two thoughts consumed her. First, she'd committed what had to be an unforgivable sin: She had been attracted to another man. And second, nothing was going to stop her from rattling off her home phone number to one of the guys. Peyton Anders had that sort of intoxicating effect on her.

Before she could make her way back to her seat, Peyton finished his set and joined her in the dark cramped wings backstage. And there, among speaker boxes and electrical cords, sweaty and breathing hard, he came to her. He didn't hesitate. "That was amazing." He put his hand on the side of her face, and even in the dark, she could see the desire in his eyes. Still breathless from the show and without waiting another moment, he kissed her.

Peyton Anders kissed her.

She didn't have to say anything to Lena when she returned to her seat. Her expression must've given her away. The entire audience could probably tell. Lena scowled as Peyton's fans screamed for an encore. Over the deafening noise, she leaned in and shouted, "You kissed him, didn't you?"

Caroline couldn't lie. She also couldn't feel bad about it. Not when she'd just had the most amazing night in years. Maybe ever. She and Lena argued about it on the way home, and Caroline dismissed her actions. The blame was Alan's. He was the one who had stopped loving her. Besides, Peyton Anders wasn't a threat to her marriage. "He'll never call. It was a fan thing. Nothing more." She had felt herself blushing as she justified the kiss. "You know, caught up in the moment."

"You don't need a kiss from Peyton Anders, Carrie. You need marriage counseling."

Their conversation didn't end until Lena dropped her off. Caroline figured that was that, but she was wrong. Peyton's first phone call came at two in the morning. Caroline was awake, on the far side of the bed, reliving every minute of the concert. Since it was Friday night, Alan had been home. Caroline grabbed the phone and glanced at her husband. He was still asleep. She hurried out of the room and into the kitchen at the other end of the house. "Hello?" she whispered, looking over her shoulder. Even now she remembered being terrified Alan would wake up.

"Baby, it's me. Peyton." His words ran together as if he'd been drinking. "Tonight was heaven. When can I see you again?"

In a decision she would question until her final sunset, Caroline thought about Alan in the other room, about how she had once loved him and longed to be married to him. Then she thought of how he'd left her lonely so often. She clenched her teeth for half a second and rattled off a different number. The doctor's office where she worked. She told Peyton three things. First, he could call her only at work. Second, she was married, so they had to be careful. And third, she couldn't wait to see him again.

From that moment there was no doubt about their feelings. The intensity of their passion, the impossibility of it, brought them closer every time they talked. Caroline never could really believe Peyton Anders was calling *her*. He must've had dozens of groupies in every city. Why would he seek her out? She let herself be carried away by the thrill of it all, convinced nothing would come of it. The phone calls went on for a year until Peyton came back to Savannah the following January. Peyton arranged for her to be backstage during the show, and she said nothing about it to Lena. After the concert, Caroline and Peyton made out for half an hour in a private room backstage. Caroline remembered telling Peyton she needed to leave, that she couldn't lose control. It was one thing to flirt with the singer by phone, one thing to kiss him backstage. Those things were only a diversion for her otherwise nonexistent love life.

But she cared about Alan too much to have a real affair.

When she said good-bye to Peyton that night, he whispered, "One of these days I'll quit touring, and it'll be me and you. I'll move you to Nashville, and we'll start a life together."

Caroline only smiled. She never would have considered such a thing, but she didn't owe Peyton an explanation. The fascination with him was nothing more than a fantasy.

The next day at the office, Lena called. "You went to his show last night, didn't you? To the concert?"

"Lena, this isn't the time for—"

"Listen. You're gonna go destroy everything that matters, Carrie. Think about Ellie . . . and Alan. You promised that man forever." She waited. "You listening? "

"Yes." Caroline sighed. "How was your dinner with Stu?"

"Carrie."

"I don't want to talk about it. He left town this morning. He's just a friend."

"You can't lie to me."

And so it went. Later that spring when Alan told her he still loved her and that they should get counseling, Caroline felt a ray of hope. But six months later, they still hadn't found the time or the counselor.

On their next anniversary, Alan took her to dinner, but the whole night he looked defeated. She was sure her expression wasn't much different. "I feel . . . like I'm losing you." He sat across from her, struggling to make eye contact. "Like we're losing us." He reached for her hands, and for a moment they both seemed to remember how much they'd lost. "If I've been a terrible husband, Caroline, I'm sorry. I never meant to be."

She tried to smile. "I keep thinking things will get better."

"You deserve better."

Caroline thought about Peyton. Yes, she and Alan both deserved better. That night he promised things that made Caroline forget anyone but her husband. But come morning he was gone again, another week of work. A month later his promises were all but forgotten. By then, Ellie spent more time at Nolan's house than she did at home. Some nights Caroline looked at her wedding photos and cried for the love they'd had back then, the love they'd lost along the way. They were both to blame, and the answers didn't seem to exist.

The phone calls from Peyton continued, and when he came to town the next time—just four months ago—he insisted she come to the show early. They texted right up until she arrived and he met her at the backstage door. They stepped inside the arena and hugged for a long time. "I love you, Caroline. I think about you constantly."

His words frightened her. "Love, Peyton?" She drew back, searching his face. "This isn't about love."

"It is. I love you. I do." He looked hurt. "There's no one in my life like you, baby. You're on my mind every hour, every day." He kissed her, a dangerously passionate kiss that made her forget anything but the man in her arms. He stared at her, breathless. "You have to believe me, baby."

Over the next ten minutes, her defenses fell. She hadn't pictured this, never imagined it. But long before he took the stage, he convinced her he was telling the truth. She wasn't a diversion or a fantasy or a game. Peyton Anders actually loved her.

Then he dropped the news. "I have four days off." He raised his brow, nervous and tentative. He trembled as he looked deep into her eyes, straight to her weary soul. "I booked us a room."

"What?"

"A room." He moved closer to her. "Come on, Caroline. We can't stop this." He kissed her again, longer this time.

The combination of her ice-cold marriage and Peyton's passionate kiss pushed Caroline over the edge. She drew back, breathless and beyond her ability to reason. "After the show . . . take me there."

And so he did.

They found a routine. She spent every daylight hour with him and they never left his room, as if nothing and no one but Peyton existed. She called in sick and came home late each night. During her few hours at home she would make lunch for Ellie, and in the morning talk to her for a few minutes, as long as the shame would allow. Then she would head for the hotel.

It was just four days. She figured she would never get caught.

But that Friday, Alan returned from the base early and questioned Ellie. When he found out Caroline hadn't come home until ten o'clock for the last three nights, he took up his position by the front door. His eyes were the first thing she saw when she crept into the house that night.

He glared at her, his teeth clenched, and called her things that stayed with her like skin. Names she couldn't escape. And every day since then, they'd fought and thrown accusations at each other like so many hand grenades. Tension filled the house, and Ellie stayed away more than ever. She had grown up, and now she was a beautiful reminder of all that Caroline herself had been as a teenage girl. But the closeness they shared when she was little was as gone as yesterday.

Caroline turned her heart and hopes toward Peyton. With everything in her, she knew her actions were wrong, but she couldn't help herself.

He was no longer a diversion, a reason for getting up in the morning. He was her future. His calls continued, and she cared less and less whether Alan found out. For that reason she wasn't terribly worried when her period was three weeks late. If she were pregnant, she and Peyton could simply start their life together sooner. Not until she called Peyton to tell him did her world fall apart. He was silent for half a minute before he said something she'd never forget. "You could never prove it's mine. No one would believe you."

And just like that, the game between her and the famous Peyton Anders was over. She took a pregnancy test and stared at the positive results. In a blur of fear and terror and uncertainty, she couldn't remember how to breathe because the test stood for two things. The start of a new life.

And the end of her own.

Chapter Four

Ellie had never run so far or so fast in all her life. Anything to get away from the terrible news.

The backpack bouncing against her shoulder blades held everything she could ever need. Maybe she would never come back. Maybe she would go to Nolan's and say good-bye and keep on running. Until she stumbled into someone else's life. Anyone's life but her own.

Lightning flashed in the distance, and the air was hotter and more humid. Ellie's breathing came in jagged gasps, but she didn't care. With every stride, she felt herself move farther away from the terrible truth, her new reality. Her mom really was pregnant by someone else. Her dad wouldn't talk about the baby's father. But five minutes ago he'd told her the worst part.

They were moving to San Diego in the morning. Which meant she wouldn't get to say good-bye to her mom.

There had been no time to get her bike. As soon as Ellie understood her dad was serious and this was her last night in Savannah, Ellie grabbed her things and started running. She hadn't slowed since. Faster, longer strides. Her lungs hurt, but she didn't slow down. Maybe she should run across the city to Ms. Lena's house so she could at least hug her mother one more time and tell her good-bye. She had never loved and hated someone so much in all her life. Ellie felt tears slide onto her cheeks, and she slapped them away. Her mother wouldn't care. She had cheated on her dad. All those nights when she came home super late she'd been with . . . with the other guy.

When she could've been with Ellie.

She felt faint, like she might pass out and die on the sidewalk. So what if she did? She would go to heaven, and she could skip this nightmare, the one she couldn't outrun.

Finally she reached Nolan's front yard, just when she couldn't take another step. Half crying, half gasping for air, she went to his front door and knocked. She didn't think about how she must've looked or what his family would think. She only knew that she couldn't go another minute without him.

Nolan answered the door, and his smile turned to shock. He—if no one else—cared about her. "Ellie . . ." He stepped onto the porch and shut the door behind him. "What is it? What happened?"

Her gasps turned to sobs, and Ellie wasn't sure if she could catch her breath. She definitely couldn't talk. Instead, she wrapped her arms around his waist and held on to him, clung to him as if being here with him might save her.

"Shhh . . . It's okay." He stroked her dark blond hair and held her.

Ellie didn't want to ever let go. Even in the midst of the horror of that evening, she knew without a doubt that she would remember this moment forever. Sure, Nolan teased about marrying her one day, but they'd never hugged like this.

So even on the worst day of her life, she would always have this memory.

The way it felt to be in Nolan Cook's arms.

When she could finally talk, she stepped back and searched his eyes. "I'm moving. Tomorrow morning."

"What?" Clearly, Nolan's response was louder than he intended. He lowered his voice. "Tomorrow? Ellie, that's crazy."

"It's t-t-true." She drew in three fast breaths, the sobs still drowning her on the inside. "My mom . . . she's pregnant."

Nolan raked his hand through his hair and took a step back. He turned to the door and then back to her. "That's a good thing, right? I mean . . . she's not too old." His face was pale, and his words sounded dry. "You're moving because she's having a baby?"

Ellie hated saying the words, hated believing them. But it was too late for anything but the truth. "My dad's not . . . He's not the father."

The night air was absolutely still, not a bit of distant ocean breeze. A chorus of frogs provided a distant sound of summer, but otherwise, there wasn't a single sound between them. Nolan's eyes grew wide, and he came to her slowly. "You mean—"

"Yes." This time the tears that found their way to the corners of her eyes were hot with shame. How could this be happening? "She cheated on him. That's why we're moving."

Again Nolan stepped back, and this time he leaned against the house. As if he might drop to the ground if something didn't hold him up. "You mean . . . like you're moving to a new house. Away from your mom?"

"Nolan . . ." She felt her heart skip a beat, felt her head spin. "We're moving to San Diego. My dad and me. Tomorrow."

His eyes grew dark and angry in a hurry. He shook his head.

"No." He pounded his fist into the pillar that held up his front porch. Then he walked out onto the grassy yard and shouted it again. "No!"

She waited, her arms crossed, wiping at the occasional tear on her cheeks. "I . . . don't want to go."

"Then you can stay here." He came quickly to her, his breathing faster than before. "My parents would let you. You can finish high school, at least."

"Yeah." Ellie bit her lip and nodded. "Maybe." No matter what they decided or what she wanted to do, she couldn't stay. Her father wouldn't dream of letting her stay. He always came to get her if she wasn't home on time.

"San Diego?" His anger subsided, as if his plan was enough to convince both of them that somehow, come morning, they'd still live a few streets away from each other. "Why there?"

"Camp Pendleton. They offered my dad a job." She shrugged, and a chill ran down her arms despite the summer heat. "Even before he found out about my mom. He wasn't going to take it, but then . . ."

Neither of them said anything for a long while. Nolan put his hands on her shoulders, and they looked at each other. In his eyes she could see memories from nearly a decade of growing up together. He shook his head. "You can't leave, Ellie."

"I know." She shivered a little, unsure of her feelings.

"Come here." He held out his arms, and she came to him. Once more he hugged her, rocking her slowly, as if by holding on here and now, they could avoid what was coming. After a minute or so, he pulled back, and some of the sadness left his eyes. "I have an idea."

"What?" She looked down, wishing he would hug her again.

"Come on." He grabbed her hand. "Follow me."

The feel of his fingers around hers was all she could think about. That and the crazy way her mind raced, desperate to stop the clock. They ran behind the house and through a side door in the garage. Nolan flipped on the light. "Over here." He worked his way around a stack of boxes and file cabinets to an area of fishing poles and tackle boxes. Letting go of her hand, he dug around until he found an old metal container about the size of a shoe box. It was dusty, and a cobweb hung from it. Nolan grabbed an old newspaper and wiped it off.

"What is it?" Ellie held on to her backpack straps.

"My first tackle box." He grinned at her. "I used to take it everywhere." He kicked at a bigger red plastic chest. "I use that now. More room."

Ellie was completely confused. "Okay."

He looked around. "I need a shovel."

She spotted a small one on his dad's workbench. "There?"

"Perfect." He grabbed it and handed it to her. His eyes danced as he tucked the box under his arm, the way he always did with his basketball. He took her hand again. "Come on. Trust me."

He led her out of the garage, and together they ran to the front of his house. "Wait here." He set the box down on the porch and held up his hand. "Don't move. I'll be right back."

Whatever he was up to, it was helping. Ellie loved his sense of adventure, even on a night like this. She looked at the stars and tried to imagine leaving for San Diego in the morning. *Please, God . . . don't let this be the end. Please . . .*

He was back, and this time he had a pad of yellow paper, a pen, and a flashlight. He put them, along with the shovel, inside the box. Then he tucked the box under his arm, and with his free hand, he took hers once more. "Let's go."

She didn't have to ask where. He was taking her to their spot at the park, the place where they always wound up together. Edgewood Street was empty, and the road between his house and the park completely quiet. They crossed and entered through the old iron gate. The park was open only to locals, but Ellie and Nolan always felt it belonged to them. It just seemed that way.

He closed the gate quietly behind them, found the flashlight in the box, and flipped it on. Sometimes the moon was enough, but not tonight. The sky was darker than coal, and the stars dotting the black sky weren't enough to mark their way.

Like always they ran past the smaller trees to the biggest one in the park, thirty yards from the gate. Their tree. Nolan set the box and the shovel beside the largest root, the one they used as a bench. "Here's the plan." He was out of breath, probably because he was excited about his idea. Whatever the idea was. He sat down, turned off the flashlight, and positioned the pad on one knee. "We'll write each other a letter and put it in the box." He thought for a moment. "Today's June first. We'll bury our letters here by the tree, and eleven years from now"—he smiled—"on June first, we'll meet here and read what we wrote."

Ellie knit her brow, but she couldn't stay serious with that look on his face. Her laughter caught her off guard, soothing the desperation in her heart. "Why eleven years?"

"Because. In English we're reading this book called *The Answers*. It's about the future. It's sci-fi, and it talks about how in eleven years there's a weird convergence or something, and overnight all the answers happen." His words came fast, like they were trying to keep up with his racing mind.

"Answers to what?" She laughed again. She'd never seen him like this.

"You know." He looked around, trying to find the right explanation. "What color is the wind, and how deep is the ocean, and what causes dreams, and lots of stuff. Those kinds of answers." He paused. "I mean, only God has the answers." He gave her a silly grin. "I don't know. Eleven years seems easier to remember."

"Hmmm. Okay." She bit the inside of her lip to keep from laughing again. As crazy as he was acting, he was clearly dead serious. "So we write each other a letter . . . and we don't read them until then."

"Yeah." He hesitated, and his shoulders sank a bit. "Unless your dad changes his mind and doesn't move you to San Diego tomorrow."

Sadness tugged at the magic of the moment. "Eleven years, Nolan. That's so long."

"Well . . . I mean, we'll see each other before then. We'll write and call, and I'll come visit you. But . . ."

She could see where this was going. "Just in case . . ."

"Right." His enthusiasm waned, and his eyes grew damp. "Just in case. We'd still have this one chance."

She nodded slowly. One chance. Just in case. The idea felt so sad, she could barely stand up beneath it. She took off her backpack, dropped it to the ground, and took the spot beside him on the tree root. "What's the letter supposed to say?"

"Umm." He looked around as if grabbing ideas from the thick night air. Gradually, his eyes found their way to hers. Even in the dim light, she could see that he looked nervous. He held her gaze for several heartbeats. "Let's write how we feel about each other."

She narrowed her eyes. "You already know."

"Well . . . not really." He found his easy grin again. "I mean, you know how I feel. How I'm going to marry you someday." He winked at her. "But seriously. Just write how you feel, Ellie."

Usually, this was the part of the conversation when she told him he wasn't going to marry her. He would go off and be a famous basketball player, and she would write a bestselling novel. But tonight—with the minutes falling away much too fast—she couldn't bring herself to say any of it. She reached for the paper. "I'll go first."

"Okay." He looked relieved. He handed her the paper and pen. He flipped on the flashlight. "Here. Use this."

She propped the flashlight so that it shone straight on the paper. "Don't watch."

"I won't." He chuckled. "That's the whole point. We can't know what the letters say."

"Not for eleven years."

"Right." He looked satisfied.

Ellie stared at the blank paper. She glanced at Nolan and saw that he was looking up, staring at the stars through the Spanish moss overhead. *Okay,* she told herself. *How do I feel?* A whirl of emotions swept through her all at once, and she forced herself not to cry. Not here. Suddenly she wanted to write this letter more than anything else they might do tonight.

She positioned the pen at the top of the page.

Dear Nolan,

First, I'm only doing this because you won't read it for eleven years. Ha ha. Okay, here I go. You want to know how I feel about you?

She stopped and stared at the same sky. They weren't in a hurry. It was just after nine o'clock, which meant they had two hours. How did she feel? Her eyes found the paper, and she started writing again.

> *These are the things I know for sure about how I feel. I love that you're my best friend and I can come over here whenever I want. I love that you stuck up for me at recess in third grade when Billy Barren made fun of my pigtails. Sorry you got in trouble for tripping him, but not really. I love that, too.*
>
> *I love that you're not afraid to get mad, like when those jerks on the football team dumped their Cokes down that skinny kid's shirt. I love that you were the first one to bring him a bunch of napkins. Really, Nolan, I love that. And I love watching you play basketball. It's like . . . I don't know . . . like you were born to play. I could watch you on that basketball court all day.*
>
> *Let's see . . .*

She looked at him again and tried to imagine saying goodbye in a few hours. Tears stung her eyes. *Not now, Ellie. Don't think about it.* She sniffed and found her place on the paper.

> *Here's the part I could never tell you right now. Because it's too soon or maybe too late, since I'm leaving in the morning. I loved how it felt earlier tonight when you hugged me. It never felt like that before. And when you took me to your garage and then over here to the park, I loved how my hand felt in yours. If I'm really honest, Nolan, I love when you tell me you're going to marry me.*

What I didn't really understand until tonight is that it isn't only those things that I love.

I love being here, me and you, and just hearing you breathe. I love sitting beneath this tree with you. So, yeah, I guess that's it. If we don't see each other for eleven years, then I want you to know the truth about how I really feel.

I love you.

There. I said it.

Don't forget me.

Love,
Ellie

Not until she signed her name did she feel the tears on her cheeks or notice that one of them had fallen onto the paper. She dried it with her fingers, folded the page, and sniffed again. She handed him the paper. "Your turn."

He must've seen her tears, but he didn't say anything. Instead, he put his arm around her shoulders and held her for a long time. "We'll see each other. We will."

Her tears slowed. She nodded, because there were no words. Finally, he let go of her, settled against the tree trunk, and took the flashlight. He positioned it beneath his arm and started to write. She didn't want to stare at him, but whatever he was putting on the paper seemed to come easily. He stopped and grinned at her. "I've been waiting for a chance to say this."

She laughed, because that was the effect he had on her. His letter wasn't overly long. Most of one page, but he didn't take another break as he wrote. When he finished, he folded his the same way she had. Then he lifted the old tackle box to his lap, opened it, and held it out to her.

She felt a ripple of doubt. "You're not gonna come back and read it, right?"

"Ellie." He raised his brow. "We're burying it. Neither of us can dig it up for eleven years. No matter what."

She ran her thumb over the cool yellow lined paper and then dropped her letter in the box. He did the same, and then he shut the lid. Using the flashlight, he found the shovel and stood, staring at the ground. "How 'bout right there? Between the tree roots?"

"Where we usually have our feet."

"Exactly." He handed her the flashlight, got down on his knees, and began digging. She aimed the light at the spot where the hole was appearing. The ground was soft, and he had the hole dug in no time. "There." He stood and wiped the back of his hand over his forehead. "That's big enough." He set the shovel down and lowered the box into the space. It fit with five inches of room on top. "Perfect." He brushed the dirt off his hands. "You bury it."

Ellie passed him the flashlight. She took the shovel, slid it into the loose dirt, and dumped it on top of the box. With every shovelful, she tried to picture it. Digging up the box eleven years from now. She would be twenty-six, out of college, and on her way to a writing career. Maybe even an author by then. Gradually, she filled in the space around the sides and top of the box. When she was finished, Nolan pressed his foot into the fresh-packed dirt, and it settled some. Ellie added a few more shovelfuls, and they repeated the process until the ground over the box was solid.

They sat down, and Nolan turned off the flashlight. "I can't believe you're leaving."

"Me, either." The laughter from earlier was gone, the reality sinking in. For almost two hours they sat beneath the tree and talked about every wonderful memory they had shared. At last they stood and stared at each other, dreading what was ahead. He looked down at the ground. "What's in your backpack?"

She had almost forgotten. "I grabbed some things from my room. When I left." She released his hands, stooped down, and unzipped it. She brought out a small, worn plush bunny. "Remember this?"

His laugh interrupted the seriousness of the coming good-bye. "I won it for you . . . at the church carnival."

"It's been on my bed since I was in fifth grade." She handed it to him. "I want you to have it."

The lightness of the moment fell away again. He took it and brought it to his face. "It smells like you."

She rummaged around in the backpack and pulled out a framed photo, the two of them at eighth-grade graduation. "My mom had these made. One for each of us. I forgot about them until tonight."

Nolan took the picture. It was too dark to really see it, but that wasn't the point. He set the frame and the stuffed rabbit down on the tree root and took her hands again. "I don't have anything to give you."

"You already have." She felt her eyes blur again, felt the tears overflow from her aching heart. "That diamond ring you won me from the machine at Pete's Pizza. I kept that."

"You did?" He looked as happy as he was surprised. "I didn't know."

"I kept everything you ever gave me."

"Hmm." He took a slight step closer. The humidity was thick around them, the moss low in the trees, marking this magical place that had been theirs alone. "You have to write that novel. The one you always talk about."

She smiled even as a few tears slipped onto her cheeks. "I will."

When it was almost eleven, Nolan reached for her hand again. This time he slid his fingers between hers. The way he might if he were her boyfriend. "You know what I'm afraid of?"

"What?" She leaned against his shoulder.

"I play my best basketball when you watch." He looked at her, his eyes searching hers. "How am I supposed to win a state championship without you?"

"You have your dad." She smiled, but her heart beat fast again. They had only a few minutes. "You're the coach's son, Nolan. You'll always be the best."

"See." He still faced her, their hands joined. "You say things like that. Around you, I feel like no one can stop me. Like I'll play in the NBA someday."

"You will." Her smile fell away. "I . . . have to go."

He hung his head, and his grip on her hands grew tighter. As if he were angry at time itself for daring to take them from this place, this night. When he lifted his eyes to hers once more, he looked broken. "I *will* call you. When you get there, call me and give me your number."

"Okay." She knew his number by heart. That part would be easy. "But . . . how will you visit?"

"I'll get my license next year." He ran his thumbs along her hands. "It'll be fun. A road trip."

She didn't want to say it, but his parents would never let him drive cross-country by himself. Not at sixteen years old. But she only nodded, wanting to believe it because he said so. Because there was nothing else to do.

He paused, watching her, as if trying to memorize the moment. "Ellie . . . don't forget me."

She wanted to ask him if he was crazy. Because she could never forget him, never stop trying to find her way back, never stop believing he would find her again somehow. But she didn't want to break down, so she only fell slowly into his arms and put her head on his shoulder. "I don't want to go."

"I'll walk you back, since you don't have your bike."

The idea breathed a few more minutes into their time together. He slung her backpack over his shoulder, and they walked to his house across the street first, so Nolan could leave the shovel and flashlight, the paper and pen. Then he eased his fingers between hers once more and walked close beside her all the way to her house, their shoulders brushing, their steps slow and even.

The lights were off, but that didn't mean her dad wasn't waiting up. He would never stand for her being out past curfew. Even tonight. They stopped near a large bush, so if her dad was watching, he couldn't see her saying good-bye. Again Nolan pulled her into his arms. "I hate this."

"Me, too." She wiped at her quiet tears. "I have to go."

He put his hands on her shoulders the way he had earlier, and in the glow of the streetlight, they could see each other better. It was the first time she had ever seen Nolan's eyes full of tears. His hands found their way to the sides of her face, and without either of them talking about it or questioning it, he leaned in and kissed her. Not a long kiss or anything, like in the movies. Just his lips against hers long enough that she had a hint of what he might have written in his letter. A hint of how much he cared.

He held up one hand and mouthed, "Good-bye, Ellie."

Her voice was less than a whisper. "Good-bye."

As if each step physically hurt him, he backed away, and

then he turned and began running down the street, away from her and out of her life. Ellie dropped to her knees on the grass and buried her face in her hands. *God . . . how could you let this happen?* Her mother cheating, her father moving her away. And this last night with Nolan—when they could no longer pretend about being only friends.

Her tears came fast and hard, the sobs as strong as they had been when she first heard the news about her mom, about the move to San Diego. They would miss their freshman year at Savannah High together, and she wouldn't get to watch him play basketball. They wouldn't sit next to each other at the school's bonfires, and they wouldn't go to dances together. They wouldn't have another summer night beneath their old oak tree. It was all over, all behind them.

The one thing that gave her strength to stand and make her way into the house, the only reason she could draw another breath at all, was the old metal box buried between the tree roots. The box and the letters and the possibility that remained eleven years from today.

Their one last chance.

Chapter Five

When Ellie didn't come to his house the next night, he knew it had happened. She had moved to San Diego, and he could do nothing but wait for her phone call. But when a week passed and then another, and she hadn't called, Nolan began to worry.

"She knows our number." He and his father were shooting around at the gym, getting ready for the start of the season. Nolan felt his frustration grow stronger. "I don't get it."

"Maybe they don't have a phone yet. They're probably in temporary housing on the base. Until they get settled." His dad passed him the ball. "You'll hear from her."

"I hate that she's gone." Nolan muttered the words under his breath. He shot the ball, and it slipped easily through the center of the net.

His father caught it and held it, watching him. "I know you miss her, son. I'm sorry." He hesitated, his concern genuine. "If you don't hear from her soon, I'll help you find her." He looked at his watch. "Come on. Your mother's got dinner."

"I need another hour." He held his hands out for the ball. "Please, Dad." Basketball was his hiding place. The only way Nolan survived missing her.

For a few seconds, his father looked like he might insist. But then he grinned. "You're a coach's dream. You know that, right?"

Nolan smiled, because he'd won—and because every minute he pounded the ball against the parquet, each hour as he fired up one shot after another at the hoop, was another minute he didn't have to think about missing her.

Her first phone call didn't come until a week later. It was just before nine o'clock, and he was nearest to the phone when it rang. He picked it up, hoping it was Ellie, the way he always did lately when the phone rang. "Hello?"

"Nolan." She sounded relieved and nervous at the same time. "It's me."

"Ellie . . ." He took the closest chair and shaded his eyes with his free hand. "Why haven't you called?"

"My dad . . . He won't let me." Her voice fell to a whisper. "We don't have a phone."

Nolan's mind screamed for answers. "But you're getting one, right?"

"I don't know." Her voice broke, and she didn't say anything for several seconds. "I haven't talked to my mom, either. We never said good-bye. It's like she doesn't even care about me."

"Ellie . . . that's awful." Nolan felt the muscles in his arms tighten, felt his face getting hot. "Maybe my dad could talk to him."

"I don't know." Tears filled her voice. "Maybe."

"Where are you? Is he there?"

"We're at the store. I told him . . . I had to use the restroom." She sounded desperate and afraid and heartbroken. "I . . . I took some quarters from . . . from his nightstand." She caught a few quick breaths. "If he catches me . . ."

"Ellie, this is crazy." His voice was louder than before. "I'll talk to him. Go find him."

"I can't." Her voice got swallowed in her tears. "I have to go. I just . . . had to hear your voice."

Panic squeezed his chest, pushing him toward the door as if he could somehow find a way to her. "Is he . . . Are you in danger?"

"No, nothing like that." She was quick to respond. "I just . . . miss you."

They needed a plan. Nolan hurried through a handful of options. "Give me your new address."

"It's changing." She groaned. "We're in San Diego, on the base. My dad says we could get our permanent housing any day."

"Still, you can tell me. They can forward mail after you move. Hold on." He grabbed a piece of paper and a pen from the closest drawer. "Okay, what is it?"

She gasped. "Nolan, I have to go."

"Wait." His panic doubled. "You know my address, right?"

"Of course: 392 Kentucky Avenue, Savannah, 31404. How could I forget it?"

Relief came over Nolan like sunshine. "Okay. So you need to write to me, Ellie. Find a way. In the letter, give me your address. Then I'll write to you, and we can figure out how to call. Maybe a neighbor has a phone you can use."

"Nolan!" Her voice dropped to a desperate whisper. "I have to go! I miss you."

"I miss—" The phone went dead. Nolan hung his head and slowly put the receiver back. She must have spotted her dad. *At least we have a plan.* He exhaled, trying to feel good about it. She knew his address. Ellie was her own person. She'd find a way to write to him, no matter what her dad wanted.

The problem was he had no way to reach her until she did. Again one week became two without a word from her. Nolan spent the lonely days playing more basketball than he'd played in all his life. He would head home after school, check the mail, change into his gym shoes and shorts, and grab his ball. He wouldn't come home until nine or ten; then he'd do his homework, fall into bed, and the next day do it all over again. Week after week after week.

The season was about to start, and he still hadn't heard from her. Other than when he was on the court, he walked around in a constant state of worry. Fear, even. Ellie would've written, so what had happened? He had tried calling Camp Pendleton a few times, asking for a way to contact the Tucker family.

"That's private," he was told every time. "We don't give out personal information."

Tryouts came, and Nolan worked with a blind intensity. At the end of the three days, his name was on the list of varsity players. His father pulled him aside. "I set a higher bar for you than the other guys." He grinned. "And you just flew over it. Congratulations, son. I couldn't be more proud."

It was what Nolan had been working for since sixth grade—the chance to play varsity as a freshman. But the news fell flat against the reality of missing Ellie. "You think she's okay?" he asked his dad that weekend. "I mean, why wouldn't she write?"

"Maybe her letter got lost." His dad's tone was always kind; he felt sorry about the situation for sure. "I do think she's okay." He put his hand on Nolan's shoulder. "You'll hear from her. Let's see if we can find her after the season if you haven't heard from her by then."

Nolan nodded. Maybe his dad was right. They couldn't do much now. Besides, Ellie loved when he played basketball. If he played with his whole heart, he would feel her with him, in the stands, cheering for him, believing in him.

Almost like she was there.

The first contest of the season, Nolan lit up the scoreboard with twenty-two points and seven rebounds. The rhythm of the game, the motion of it, the speed at the varsity level were all as natural for Nolan as waking up in the morning. The win was only the beginning. One game blended into another, and he was the standout. But when the applause died down and the crowd went home, he would sometimes sit in the empty gym and feel her.

Just feel her there in the silence.

The way she sat at the edge of the bleachers when he played, leaning over her knees and cheering for him or standing, hands in the air, face intense. He could feel her tanned arm brushing against his as they ran along the edge of the river, hear her laughter and whisper in the summer night air beneath their oak tree.

Why won't she write, Lord? The question echoed through his mind, but there were no answers. No letters from Ellie. No communication at all.

One evening halfway through December, his dad hung around the dinner table after his mom and sisters had left. "Son . . . I'm worried about you."

"I'm fine." Nolan found his smile as a way of punctuating the point. "I'm thinking about my game."

"Your game's perfect." His father didn't laugh. "You're being too quiet. You're not the same." He waited. "It's Ellie, I know. We'll find her, Nolan. We will."

Nolan nodded, and when they stood, his dad gave him the kind of hug he used to give when he was a little boy. The kind that made the world feel whole and safe and right. But as Nolan walked upstairs for bed that night, he missed Ellie so fiercely he couldn't draw a full breath. Maybe he would get on his bicycle and start riding, head west. As far west as he could get. He actually stopped halfway up to his room and gripped the stair rail. The pull toward the front door was that strong.

Some days he thought about going to their tree and digging up the box and reading her letter so he'd know how she really felt about him. The temptation was never stronger than the night of the team's first loss. He had been in a funk, unable to hit even a simple layup in the fourth quarter.

Throughout his late dinner and homework up in his room alone, he couldn't stop thinking about her, even after his parents and younger sisters were asleep. He stood and walked to the photo Ellie gave him. The one of the two of them. *Where are you? Why won't you write?* Was she in high school on the base? Or was she at a private school somewhere nearby? Suddenly, he wanted to read her buried letter more than he wanted air. He crept downstairs, grabbed a flashlight and the small shovel, and jogged across the street.

But when he reached the spot where the box was buried, as he stooped down and touched the blade to the hard-packed earth, he stopped. He couldn't dig up the box, couldn't read her letter early. That wasn't the plan. Plus, they'd made a promise. If he broke it now, then what would happen to their meeting? He wouldn't have a reason to show up here in eleven years, and they might miss their one last chance.

He stood slowly, staring at the spot where the box was buried. He didn't need to read the letter to know how she felt about him. She loved him, same as he loved her. They might not have all the answers, all the details figured out. But there was no one they cared for more than each other. He would find her after basketball season, and they would write to each other. And when he got his license, he would drive out west, and they would laugh and take walks on the beach and figure out when they could see each other again.

Even if he had to wait eleven years to see her, he was sure of this much: He loved her. Time couldn't change that, no matter how much passed between now and the next time he saw her.

Nolan walked back toward home, and halfway there, he saw a shooting star. He froze, looking up. *Do you see it, too, Ellie? Wherever you are?* He sighed and kept walking. *God, please, let her know I'm thinking about her. Help me find her.*

He prayed that way often as the season continued. He turned sixteen in January and earned his driver's license just as play-offs were starting. Every day on the way to school, he felt compelled to get on the highway and head west. And every day, instead, he poured all his emotion and intensity and passion into playing basketball.

Savannah High made it past the first three rounds of play-offs with huge wins against the top schools in Georgia. The state semifinal game was a challenge, but Nolan's thirty-two points gave them the edge, and they pulled out a four-point victory in the final minutes. And just like that, they were in the state play-off game—the first time in fifteen years.

If Nolan hadn't been so busy perfecting his jump shot and

increasing his free-throw percentage, he might have been more concerned about the way his dad looked, how he seemed more tired and pale after practice. But Nolan's thoughts were consumed with hoops and Ellie, and he chalked up the changes in his dad to stress over the play-offs.

On the last day of February the team traveled to Atlanta for the state finals. Nolan sat by his dad on the bus ride. They talked about their opponent and ways to get around the other team's big man, tricks that would work best for defense. Halfway there, his dad turned to him and smiled, the sort of smile that came from deep inside his soul. "No father could ever be more proud of his son." He patted Nolan's knee. "I couldn't let today get away without telling you that."

Nolan let the compliment work its way through him. "Thanks." He grinned at his dad. "You, too. You're the best coach ever, Dad. I mean it."

His father elbowed him lightly in the ribs. "I had a little help, son. Your ability is God-given, but your work ethic is . . . well, it's unlike anything I've seen."

Nolan nodded slowly. He could credit at least part of his hard work this season to Ellie. He played so he wouldn't miss her. All the hours he otherwise would have spent with her amounted to more hours of practice than ever in his life. "I have a question." The other players were talking quietly, sitting in groups of two or three, game faces on, concentrating on the upcoming contest. No one seemed to notice Nolan and his dad caught up in their conversation.

"Shoot." His dad leaned against the window of the bus so they could see each other better.

"Do you think I have a chance? I mean to play in the NBA someday?"

"Son." His father smiled. "You *will* play in the NBA." He raised his brow. "You have it all. Talent . . . dedication . . . grades. And you have your faith."

Nolan felt the weight of every word. In that moment—in the bus on the way to the state championship—his father's certainty felt almost prophetic. Nolan nodded, unblinking. "Thanks." The bus seemed suddenly empty, as if he and his dad were the only two on board. "You make it feel possible."

" 'With Christ, all things are possible.' " The Bible verse had always been a favorite between the two of them. His dad put his arm around Nolan's shoulders. "One day everyone in the world will know about your gift. And you will use it for good, son. I know you will."

Nolan carried the conversation into the arena that afternoon, and when he stepped onto the court two hours before tip-off, he felt a chill run down his arms and legs. The pros used this court, the Atlanta Hawks. The scoreboards anchored to the end walls and hanging over the center of the court, the box seats, the multiple levels and concourses that ran around the venue. All of it felt like home to Nolan. Like he belonged here. His father was right. One day he would play in an arena like this, and he would use his game for good.

He glanced at the best seats, the ones courtside. The seats where Ellie would sit. Because he *would* find her, and they would figure out their feelings for each other, and he would marry her. Just like he always said he would. No, they hadn't talked or written letters, but they would. And when that happened, there would be no turning back.

Warm-ups that day were focused and intense, and Nolan felt invincible. The Savannah Bulldogs were ready to take their championship, ready to fight for it. And no one came readier to play than Nolan. During the National Anthem, he placed his hand over his heart and soaked in every detail of the atmosphere. The place was packed. Savannah High had sent six buses with cheerleaders and fans, and most of the rest of the community of Savannah had driven to the game. Nolan's mom and sisters were in the stands with the other parents, and his dad was at the front of the line of Savannah players, his eyes on the flag. Nolan stared at his dad. Something about his expression didn't look right. A little older or more tired. Maybe that was it. Whatever was wrong, everything would be right after they won this championship.

The 4A championship was entertainment to everyone who loved basketball, so Atlanta locals had come in force, too. The Hawks' regular season announcer was at the microphone for the contest, a tradition from years back. Everything about the pregame was like something from a dream. Vendors walked the aisles selling popcorn and Coke and hot dogs, and each of the two schools was represented with a section of fans in school colors. The Bulldog faithfuls had light blue and yellow towels, and as tip-off neared, they waved them in a frenzy, creating a dramatic show of the school's spirit.

Only Ellie was missing.

Nolan gritted his teeth. He couldn't think about her now, not with so much at stake. He started that night—the way he had all season. The Bulldogs won the tip-off, and against the backdrop of the roaring fans, they were off and running. Nolan hit two three-pointers in the first quarter, and combined with help from the team's forwards, they took a five-point lead into halftime.

The win was theirs, Nolan and his teammates could feel it. Nothing could stop them from claiming the championship they'd set out to win back in November. But Savannah High came out flat in the third quarter. Nolan's dad called a time-out, and the players huddled as he spoke. "Don't let up out there." His voice was loud and intense. "They want it, too. Come on, guys!" Sweat dripped down his father's face as he scribbled out a play on his whiteboard, a plan to keep the ball away from the leading scorer on the opposite team. "Everyone, do your part. This is our night, men. Let's get it done."

His father's plan was brilliant. As they hit the floor, Nolan was sure it would work. But instead of finding their rhythm, the Bulldogs followed the time-out with three straight turn-overs. When the fourth quarter started, Savannah was down by four. The minutes seemed to fly off the clock at double time. Nolan took over, but it was like trying to keep waves from hitting the shore. He worked harder than he had all season and, as the game wound down, the Bulldogs fought their way back to a one-point lead.

But then something happened.

Nolan looked at the stands. He looked at the place where his friends were cheering for him, and suddenly, all the noise and smells and the reality of being in the final minutes of a state championship basketball game faded. In their place was just one thing, one thought.

The way he missed Ellie Tucker.

Chapter Six

Her dad didn't talk to her, not the way her mom had always done back when they were a family. But that Saturday night, Ellie felt more restless than usual. She wasn't sure if this was the week, but she'd checked on the Internet at the library and found out that Nolan and the Bulldogs were in the state play-offs. If they won last week, then tonight they'd be in the final game. Winning a state title.

She sat on her bed cross-legged, facing the window. The base was crowded and noisy. Soldiers and uniformed people everywhere. Her father had enrolled her at the base school, but Ellie hated it. Only a handful of kids talked to her. Two girls in her history class were nice, but they had their own friends.

Her heart hurt as she stared at the night stars. Nolan in the state play-offs and she wasn't there? The truth made her so mad, she could've walked to Georgia. Day and night without a break—whatever it took to find him. She had sent him three letters, but he hadn't responded. At the bottom of each one, she had written their new address. She found stamps in one of the kitchen drawers, and she would always ride her bike across the base to mail them. So that nothing could get in the way of it reaching Nolan.

But he hadn't written back.

Ellie propped her elbows on the windowsill. Maybe he was too busy. Maybe now that she was gone, he'd forgotten her. All his attention must be on basketball. She sighed. Of course. That's what it was. He was starting on the varsity team. He wouldn't have time to think about writing to her. Not till after the season.

The longer Ellie thought about how much she missed him, the more images of her mother filled her mind. Her mom hadn't written, either. So was that it? Her mom didn't love her anymore? After all they'd been through, she could let Ellie leave without a fight? Tears spilled onto her cheeks. Maybe she would never see either of them again.

Her mom and Nolan.

She wasn't sure how long she sat there before a small rock hit the window. It made a sharp sound, and Ellie jumped back, her heart racing.

Who would . . . She looked out the window. She recognized the group of teens, the girls from history class and a few guys they hung out with.

Her dad was in the living room, the Lakers turned up loud on the TV. She eased her window open and stuck her head out. "Hey." She kept her voice to a loud whisper.

"Ellie, hi!" One of the girls giggled and came closer. "We're going to the beach. Come with us."

Ellie glanced over her shoulder toward the living room. Her father would never let her go. She looked at the kids. "When are you coming back?"

"I don't know." The other girl laughed. There were four of

them—the girls and two guys from the baseball team. "Maybe twenty minutes. Come on, Ellie!"

She hesitated, but only for a few seconds. Her dad could take her away from Nolan and haul her across the country to a place where she knew no one. He could ruin her life and spend his nights watching TV. But he couldn't keep her locked in her room.

Without saying another word, she found her tennis shoes and a light jacket and slipped out the window. She closed it halfway behind her and then set off with the group. The notion of disobeying and running wild on the beach with her classmates was exhilarating. The first time she'd felt alive since they moved to San Diego.

They didn't do anything bad or illegal. Thirty minutes of laughing and running on the beach. When she crept back into her bedroom, she could still hear the game on in the other room. Her father hadn't even noticed. As she fell asleep that night, she didn't pray like usual. Praying hadn't gotten her anywhere. It hadn't changed her father or prompted Nolan to write to her. So maybe this was better. The new Ellie would figure out life on her own—without God.

Because by now it was clear: God didn't care about her, anyway.

❧ ❧

The game raged on and Nolan tried to shake the feeling, tried to find the control he'd played with seconds earlier. But he felt half as fast, half as sharp as before. *Get it together, Cook,* he ordered himself. Time kept melting off the clock. *We have to do this . . . come on. Please, God . . .* Nolan made his usual pass, the one through the key to the Bulldogs' big guy. But this time the other team intercepted it. Before Nolan could turn around, they threw the ball full court and connected with a player streaking up the sidelines. Bulldogs down by one.

All season Nolan had pictured himself in this game, leading it, winning it. But now he couldn't stop missing Ellie, couldn't stop thinking about how nothing made sense without her. *Focus . . . you have to focus.* He glanced at the clock. Fourteen seconds left. He doubled his concentration and intensity and went in for a layup. Bulldogs by one. But the other team scored a three and grabbed a two-point lead. Time-out, Bulldogs. Again Nolan noticed his father. He looked pale, clammy. Something was wrong. Nolan would ask him about it after the game.

The time-out seemed to last only seconds, and Nolan walked back out onto the court, not sure what play they were supposed to run. Rage flooded his bloodstream. They weren't going to lose this game because of him. He wouldn't let it happen. His teammate inbounded the ball, and the five of them worked it around until only two seconds showed on the clock.

Nolan ran to his spot, the place where he'd hit more shots and won more games than any other. Left side, three-point line. He clapped his hands, calling for the ball, and it came flying to him from one of the Bulldogs at the top of the key. The basket was all Nolan could see as he set up and released the shot. But something didn't feel right. The way his thumb lay against the ball, maybe, or the slightest interruption in his concentration. Nolan held his breath, watching the ball. It was going in, it had to. When it mattered, Nolan always hit this shot.

The whole arena seemed to freeze as the ball arced and fell

toward the rim. But instead of slipping through the net, instead of even hitting the rim, the ball fell short and slapped against the gym floor. Air ball. Before the reality sunk in, the buzzer sounded. And like that, pandemonium broke out across the arena.

Red jerseys flew past him from every direction, players chest-thumping and jumping into each other's arms. Atlanta's East Jefferson High had won the state title. Nolan dropped to the ground where he'd missed the shot. Where he'd lost the game.

His teammates reacted the same way, covering their faces with their jerseys and shuffling back to the bench. Nolan pressed his fists to his eyes. How could he have missed that shot? The win was theirs. Savannah High was a better team. He shut out the sounds of celebration around him. This was his fault. All his fault. He clearly wasn't as strong as he thought, not as experienced. A true champion would've blocked out everything but the game. Especially in the final minutes.

He stayed there, crying angry tears, until he felt a pair of hands on his shoulders. "Son, come on." His father's voice spoke straight to him, louder than every other noise in the arena. "You did your best. Come on."

Nolan lowered his hands and dragged himself to his feet. Then, in a moment he would remember all his life, he fell slowly into his father's arms. "I let you down, Dad . . . I blew it. I'm sorry."

His dad didn't say anything, just let Nolan cry while he held him. Control came eventually, but until then, his father held on. His dad said only one thing before he released him: "I love you, son. There will be other games."

Together they walked back to the bench where the team sat, towels draped over their necks, eyes on the ground, cheeks tearstained. The huddle was another moment, a glimpse of the greatness of his father—both as a man and a coach.

"No matter what that trophy says, no matter that it won't sit on the shelf at Savannah High, you are champions. You played like champions; you won all season like champions. And today you lost like champions—fighting until the final shot." He nodded, looking each of them in the eyes. "We will be back here next year, and we will win it all."

Only two players were seniors. Nolan watched the look in everyone else's eyes go from utter defeat and despair to the first glimpses of hope. They would win next year.

By the time his father was finished talking to them, they all believed it.

Next year belonged to them.

The bus ride home was quiet. Nolan figured the guys were doing the same thing he was—trying to imagine starting over, summer workouts, a million jump shots and free throws, countless hours in the gym.

Back at the school, his dad talked to him again. "Nolan, we play as a team. We win or lose as a team. No one player can be blamed tonight." He sat beside Nolan on a bench in the locker room after everyone else was gone. "A true champion can't be defined by his wins or losses—except in life."

Another quote Nolan would never forget. "Thanks, Dad." He paused. If only he had one more chance at that last shot. "You coming home?"

"In a little while." His dad wiped his brow. "I have to wrap up a few things here."

Nolan had driven his mom's car, since she went to the game

with the neighbor. He helped his dad to his feet, and they hugged again. "You're the best coach in the world. You did everything you could tonight."

"We all did." He patted Nolan's shoulder. "See you at home."

"I love you, Dad."

"Love you, too."

His father's words rang through his mind on the way home and even after he'd showered and come downstairs to be with his mom and sisters. No one was ready to sleep just yet. He helped his mom make grilled cheese sandwiches, a late dinner. But thirty minutes became an hour, and still his dad didn't come home.

Finally, at the two-hour mark, his mom grabbed her car keys. "He isn't answering his cell." Her words ran together, and she kept her voice down. Nolan's sisters were watching a movie in the TV room. "I'm gonna check on him."

She never got that far. She found her purse and, as she headed for the front of the house, the doorbell rang. Nolan followed her, and as soon as she opened the door, they saw two uniformed police officers with their hats in their hands.

Nolan felt his heart stop, felt it skid into a beat he didn't recognize. What was this? What . . . what was happening?

One of the officers stepped forward. He identified himself and looked at Nolan's mother. "Are you Mrs. Cook?"

"Yes." Panic rang in her voice. "What is it? What's happened?"

"I'm sorry." He paused, but he didn't look at Nolan. Not once. "Your husband . . . he was found at the high school by the janitor. I'm afraid he had a heart attack. He didn't make it."

"Not my dad!" Nolan couldn't bear the possibility. "No, he didn't. No!" Whatever came next, Nolan didn't hear it. He ran past his mother, past the officers, running . . . running as fast as he could across the street and into the park. Through the trees to the place that belonged to him and Ellie. And there, with his back against the rough bark and his head in his hands, the sobs came. Deep sobs racked his body, and he let the truth fall down around him like deafening hail.

His father was gone.

The news was crazy . . . insane. Impossible. But it was true. There wouldn't be another chance to see him or hug him or play basketball for him. In that place beneath the old oak tree, in that single moment, he stood at the greatest crossroads he'd ever known. God had taken Ellie, and now he'd taken his father—his two best friends in all the world.

When he couldn't cry anymore, Nolan walked slowly back to his house, back to the place where the officers remained and where other cars were now parked along the curb and in the driveway. Before he reached the front door, Nolan realized something. He couldn't give up on God. Like his father, his faith was woven through him. He couldn't remove his beliefs any more than he could remove his DNA. Nolan stopped on the front porch. He was his father's son and he would survive. He breathed in and faced the rest of his life. In a few seconds his entire future had been reduced to two purposes.

Playing basketball for his dad.

And finding Ellie.

Chapter Seven

Spring 2013

Nolan Cook placed an extra pair of Nikes in his Atlanta Hawks bag and zipped it shut. He didn't need to leave home for half an hour, enough time to clear his mind, maybe figure out why lately the past felt like a dark cloud he couldn't step out from underneath. He sat on the edge of his bed and breathed in deep. *What is it, God? Why won't yesterday leave me alone?*

Sometimes Nolan wondered where the seasons had gone. One year had blended into two, and two somehow became a blurry decade. His life looked almost exactly as he had pictured it, how his dad had believed it would look. His Hawks were in the play-offs, and his role as leading scorer was one he had prepared for. He did what he could to help his community, and his faith still meant more to him than anything. Teams wanted to acquire him, kids wanted to be him, and girls wanted to marry him. After yesterday's game, the ESPN announcer told the TV audience that Nolan was the only pro player he knew with a heart bigger than his bank account.

All of that was great. His father would be proud, for sure. But for all that Nolan Cook had obtained, and for all that people held him up as someone who had it all, he didn't have what mattered most. He didn't have his dad. And he hadn't accomplished the only goal that really mattered.

He hadn't found Ellie.

Twenty minutes remained before his ride would be there. The one that would take him to the airport, to a private jet for the trip to Milwaukee. It was May 3, first round of the play-offs. The Hawks had already taken the first two games at home. They could advance by winning the next two on the road. He sat down on the plush bench at the end of his bed and looked out the window. He never tired of the view, of the rolling green acreage that made up his estate. He lived in a remote gated community out of necessity. Too many people clamoring for him.

At first it seemed a little pretentious. Too much for a kid from Savannah. But he'd come to this place. He could be alone here and then, in thirty minutes, be suiting up at the Atlanta Hawks locker room. Where he spent most of his time.

You should be here, Dad. You and Ellie.

A sigh rattled through his body. His father had been gone nearly eleven years, and still he missed him every day, every time he picked up a basketball. The whole world knew the story. If anyone had missed it years back, ESPN had done a feature on Nolan last week, how he played to honor his dad, and how he never left a gym without making the shot.

Left side, three-point line.

He pulled his Bible from beneath the bench, where he'd left it the day before. Without hesitating, he turned to Philippians, chapter four. The place he and his dad were studying the week of his death. The text was familiar even back then. But he didn't want to rely on memory. He wanted to see the words. He started at the beginning of the chapter and read past the greeting from Paul and the admonition to rejoice always. At all times. Past the verses about God's peace and right through to the thirteenth verse. " 'I can do all things though Christ, who strengthens me,' " he whispered.

It was a verse that had gotten him through the past decade, in moments when he was angry at God for all he'd lost and on days when he was ready to give up. Basketball had filled the empty spaces, and his faith had given him a purpose, but nothing had eased the pain of losing his dad. And nothing had helped him find Ellie Tucker.

He closed the Bible, stood, and crossed his room to the dresser with the mirrored hutch. Almost never did he allow himself a few moments to do this, but today seemed special. First time they'd made the play-offs since he'd been traded to the Hawks three years ago. He opened the narrow glass door and looked closely at the contents inside. A picture of him and his dad taken after they won the conference, weeks before the heart attack. The photo stood propped up, simple and without a frame. Slightly curled and yellowed around the edges. But Nolan kept it here, raw and untouched. The way he kept the image in his heart.

On the next shelf down was the stuffed rabbit. The one Ellie gave him the night before she left. He brought it to his face and breathed deep. Then he slowly walked to the window, the one that made up the far wall of the bedroom. He leaned his forearm against the glass and clenched the rabbit in his other fist. How could she still be missing from his life? With familiar ease he felt himself going back, slipping through the yesterdays to that spring.

Back to the days after his father's death. He was just a kid back then, so much growing up still ahead of him. Weeks passed before Nolan stopped heading to the gym to find his dad when school let out. A lifetime of sheer habit didn't break easily. Long after his dad's funeral and the touching show of sympathy from the whole school, Nolan would wake up certain his dad was alive. Somewhere, he had to be alive. He would sit there in bed, desperate and confused, and picture his father in his study down the hall. He had to be there, dreaming up defenses and outlining plays in his old notebook. Or reading his worn, cracked leather Bible the way he did every morning.

Over time, Nolan came to realize he would spend the rest of his days fighting against God or fighting for Him. Finding his own way or holding tight to the faith he'd claimed the day police showed up at his house with the news. He wrestled with the choice, desperate for one more day with his dad. Desperate to find Ellie. In the end, there was no real choice at all. His father's faith was his own. Period. He wouldn't fight against the one true God, the One who held both his father and his precious Ellie. He would serve Him all the days of his life, no matter what. He made the vow the first summer after losing his dad. He had never wavered on his decision since.

But a reality hit him that summer. As soon as school was out, it came over him like a Georgia heat wave. He was the man of the house. His dad was gone and he wasn't coming back, and his mother spent much of her time with his sisters. They were twelve and fourteen that summer, and they seemed to take most his mother's emotional energy. When she couldn't contain her tears another moment, she sometimes came to him. "Nolan, I'm turning in early. Can you get dinner for the girls?" He would hug her and agree to help however he could. With his dad gone, he was man of the house.

He wasn't about to let his mother see *him* cry.

When he was alone, he would sit beneath the old oak tree and think about his life, about what happened. And about how he could possibly find Ellie now that his father was gone. His dad had planned to help him find her that summer. Instead, all of them were trying to figure out a way to survive another day.

No letter from her ever came, something Nolan couldn't understand. Again he tried finding her by calling the base, but the calls turned up nothing. No one could help him. Some mornings he would get on the family's computer and search for her. *Ellie Tucker, Alan Tucker, San Diego, Camp Pendleton.* That sort of thing. The search never turned up anything. He even contacted Caroline Tucker. Ellie's mother broke down and cried on the phone as she admitted that even she didn't know where in San Diego Ellie lived.

"Her father's keeping her from me. Or maybe Ellie doesn't want me to know where she is."

Finally, the reality sank in. Finding Ellie wouldn't be as easy as his dad had thought. Short of getting in the car and driving to San Diego to look for her, Nolan was out of options. And when that became clear, he did the only thing he could do.

He played basketball.

His father was replaced by the assistant coach—Marty Ellison, an older man who loved Nolan's dad and understood the team like no one else. He arranged summer workouts and talked about winning the championship, the one Nolan's dad had believed in for them. Always, he was harder on Nolan than on the other guys.

One day Coach Ellison talked to him after practice. "Nolan . . . I'm sorry."

"For what?" Nolan was exhausted, the way he usually was after morning workouts. He had the basketball tucked under his arm. "For pushing me harder than everyone else?"

"Yes. I have no choice." Coach Ellison's eyes held a tenderness that surprised Nolan. "Your dad believed in your gift. He used to tell me he could see you playing in the pros." He put his hand on Nolan's shoulder. "I'm doing what he would've done."

"Yes, sir." Nolan was grateful for the explanation. It filled him and gave him a purpose he hadn't felt since losing his dad. Nolan shook the coach's hand. "Well, sir, keep it up. If he's watching from heaven, I don't want to let him down."

"Exactly."

By the end of summer, Nolan was twice the basketball player he'd been the previous fall. He played on a club team and everywhere he went he created a stir among college scouts. When the students of Savannah High returned to class, two things had happened. First, Nolan had appeared on a *Sports Illustrated* list of top ten sophomore players in the country. And second, he had come to realize something about Ellie.

She wasn't coming back. She wasn't going to call and she wasn't going to write. He would have to find her.

There were whole days that next year when all Nolan could think about was their one last chance, the letters buried beneath their old oak tree. Always he figured he'd find her somehow. But he never did. The years of high school flew by in a rush of basketball—club seasons, summer workouts, and high school games. They made the play-offs each year, but the team never qualified for the championship, never came as close as they had when he was a freshman. When his dad coached.

Winning a championship for his father became a goal he seemed unable to achieve. When the clock ran out on his last game as a senior, he found a quiet corner beneath the bleachers and cried. The first time since a month after his dad died, he let the tears come, because there were no more games left. The chance to win a state title for his father was gone.

That night he promised himself two things: Somehow he *would* find Ellie Tucker, and one day he *would* win it all. Maybe in college—since by then he had agreed to play on a scholarship at North Carolina University. Or maybe sometime after that. But one day he would have the perfect season and bring home a trophy for his dad.

The memories stopped there. Nolan returned the stuffed rabbit to the glass case and shut it. Better to keep thoughts of Ellie where they belonged—on a shelf where even he couldn't touch them. He looked once more at the photo of him and his dad. How quickly the years had gone. The blur of seasons at North Carolina and the two appearances in the NCAA Elite Eight round of the play-offs.

"Maybe this year." The words came softly. And in the silence that followed, he could hear his dad's voice, the tone of it, and he could sense the safety he felt when they were together. The man had been his coach and mentor as far back as Nolan could remember. The fact that he was taken out by a heart attack when he was just forty-one remained almost impossible to believe. He still caught himself thinking maybe there had been a mistake and his dad had moved to Portland, Oregon, with his mom and sisters. As if sometime in the next hour, Nolan might get a call from him, promising to pray and believing—like always—that no one would dominate the game the way Nolan would.

The truth was something altogether different.

Life had moved on. His mom was dating someone these days, a good guy. Nolan clenched his jaw and turned away from the hutch. He needed to check e-mail, something left-brained to get his mind off the past. If he was going to get his team through the play-offs, if this was the year he might win it all, one thing was sure.

He needed to stay focused.

🐾 🐾

They were thirty thousand feet over Tennessee or maybe Kentucky when Nolan woke up. The jet was a converted passenger plane, leather seats and footrests, the plane the Hawks used for away games. The ache in his heart from earlier had eased. His dad was with him. That would always be true.

He looked out the window at the topside of the clouds and beyond, at a narrow river cutting its way through the landscape. Every mile took him farther from Ellie. Where he last knew she lived, anyway. Nolan leaned back against the seat. How could more than ten years have gone by and he still hadn't found her? He had unlimited resources, after all.

In his senior year with the Tar Heels, they'd played the University of San Diego. Nolan caught a later flight home because he spent an entire day in a rental car, driving the perimeter of Camp Pendleton and canvasing the closest supermarkets, a Walmart, and a mall. He came home no closer to finding her than before. He realized then that it was pointless to search for her in San Diego. She could be living anywhere.

When MySpace and Facebook first surfaced, he had tried to find her online. At least once a week since then he searched for her and came up empty. By the time he was drafted into the pros, he wondered if she'd met someone in college and gotten married. If that was the case, fine. But he wouldn't rest until he had closure, until he could talk to her or look into her eyes and see for himself that she no longer cared for him.

The way he still cared for her.

Nolan's mind flashed back to the draft, how it felt to be taken third pick in the first round. They paid him $10 million for his signing bonus alone. He earned more per season than anyone had a right to. The day his first check cleared, he did what he'd wanted to do since the summer after his freshman year at Savannah High. He called a private investigator and explained the situation.

"Her name is Ellie Tucker."

"That's her name today?"

Nolan hated the question. "As far as I know."

"So you don't know her name." It wasn't a question. "What do you actually know about her?"

The questions caused one of his hardest moments since his father's death. Proof that he knew nothing about Ellie, that too many years had passed to be sure about what had happened to her or where she lived or what she was doing. Too many years to even know her name.

Still, he paid the PI and prayed—really prayed—that God would help him find her. Instead, for a heavy price tag, he was given a spiral-bound report that basically said the thing Nolan had feared most. Ellie Tucker—the girl who he was going to marry—was nowhere to be found.

He closed his eyes. That brought him to now. This week his manager was doing everything in his power to set Nolan up with a nice girl. The latest of many who had all amounted to nothing. This one was the daughter of a Christian singer, a

Grammy Award–winning solo artist whose voice was one of the best in any genre. Her daughter was twenty-one, a recent graduate from Vanderbilt University. Brilliant, beautiful, and ambitious. She ran a ministry for kids in Uganda, and already her efforts had resulted in the building of three wells that provided clean water to people who were dying without it.

His manager had called fifteen minutes before his ride picked him up earlier that day. "Nolan, I've got details."

"Details?" Nolan was reading e-mails, still trying not to think about how badly he missed his dad.

"About Kari Garrett."

Nolan didn't immediately connect the dots.

His manager chuckled. "You obviously weren't holding your breath for this call."

"No." Nolan felt himself smile. His manager didn't give up easily. "Who is she?"

"Kathy Garrett's daughter. The singer, remember?"

It had all clicked. "Of course. Sorry." Nolan pushed his chair back from the computer and rubbed his eyes. "What about her?"

His manager hesitated. "Remember? She wants to meet you. She's perfect, Nolan. You'll love her."

"Right. It's coming back to me." He wished he could feel more excited. "What's the setup?"

"The two of you and dinner in Atlanta the night after you get back from this run."

Nolan exhaled slowly. "Isn't that sort of awkward? Like I'm taking her on a date and I haven't met her?"

"It's not a date. It's a hang." He sounded confident. The plan wasn't going to change now. "Just get to know her. You'll thank me later."

Laughter found its way across the phone line. "Okay. Text me the specifics."

And like that, Nolan had a date with Kari Garrett. No matter what his manager wanted to call it. She wasn't the only setup who had come his way. One of the brass in the Hawks' front office was trying to pair him up with Tanni Serra, the nation's top pop star. A girl he wouldn't consider dating. Barely a week passed without someone trying to match him with a girl who otherwise would be untouchable.

"Man, what's that feel like? You can have any girl you want," his teammates teased him often.

"I don't want any girl." He would grin at them. Everyone knew the truth. Nolan Cook hadn't slept around, hadn't dated. He loved God, and he would one day find a girl who shared his faith. Still, the guys were right. He could have any girl he wanted.

Any girl except Ellie Tucker.

Never was he more deeply aware of the truth than on a trip like this, one that took him away from where he last knew she was living. In San Diego, California. The truth stayed with him as they arrived at the venue and stretched, and as they took the court to warm up. It stayed with him as they dominated that night, notching a third straight victory, and it stayed with him as he scanned the audience at every break, looking for her. The way he always looked for her. Just in case she'd moved to Wisconsin. The truth was this: If Ellie Tucker wanted to contact him, she could have. He was easy to find. For reasons he couldn't begin to understand, that could mean only one very sad thing.

Ellie had moved on.

Chapter Eight

She was Ellie Anne now.

The name change became official when she turned twenty-one—the best use of a hundred bucks Ellie had ever found. Her baby girl was two that year, and Ellie changed the child's name, too. She washed her hands in the backroom sink and dried them on her smock. She cut hair at Merrilou's, a few miles off Pendleton's naval base. Only once in a while did a client come in who remembered her as Ellie Tucker. The way her last client had.

Her next appointment was already here, so she'd have to take a break later.

Ellie returned to the front of the salon and smiled at her client. "You ready?"

The woman stood and smiled. "Another beautiful day." She was in her thirties, one of the more talkative ones.

"Always." Ellie glanced at the television. She had a clear view of it from her station, and since she worked the evening shift tonight, she couldn't resist putting on the game. Hawks versus Bucs, Game 4. If Atlanta won tonight, they'd advance to the second round and have a few extra days off to rest.

"Glad we can watch the game." The woman settled herself into the seat. She was a skinny bleached blonde with hair halfway down her back. She pointed to the screen. "I love that Nolan Cook. He's amazing, right? I mean, what guy is like him?" She caught a quick breath. "Tim Tebow, of course. They're both the same. Untouchable. Everyone's in love with them, and all they do is live for God and play ball for His glory. Right? I mean, it's amazing."

Ellie's eyes were on the screen. The game hadn't started, but the announcer was talking about Nolan. Her friend Nolan. The boy she had loved since third grade. Something about him averaging the most points in the league through the first round of play-offs, and how he had more steals than anyone in the Eastern Conference. The camera fixed on him, warming up, taking shots from around the arc of the three-point line, breaking for the basket and making a convincing layup.

Then the angle changed, and the faces of three kids filled the screen. The announcer was saying, "These are Nolan Cook's guests for tonight. Three kids from the local foster program. None of them have parents, but here, for the next few hours, they have Nolan Cook."

Ellie ran a fine comb lightly through the woman's hair. She was going on about how she wished she could set up a friend of hers with Nolan because there were just no guys like him and her friend was so great and . . .

Ellie only pretended to listen. Something she was good at after years of cutting hair. "Highlights again?"

"Yes." The woman used her hands to add emphasis. "Bright highlights. Something light blonde for summer." She sat a little straighter. "We have the Bahamas next week."

The salon was near the base, so the clientele was mixed. Some soldiers and soldiers' wives. But most people who came to Merrilou's lived high-end lifestyles and talked about their trips to the Caribbean or Hawaii or Europe. Their husbands held high positions at Morgan Stanley or UBS, one of the financial institutions in greater San Diego, where they made boatloads of money. Their wives enjoyed spending it and telling Ellie about the details.

Women like this one.

Ellie mixed the bleach and color in a small plastic bowl and kept her eyes on the TV. They were showing Nolan again, this time as he rallied his teammates into a fired-up huddle. The game was about to begin.

What are you thinking about, Nolan? Do I ever cross your mind?

The separation between them was her fault. She could have reached out to him. She'd known that years ago. When he was at North Carolina, she even wrote him a letter, took it to the post office, and then changed her mind and ripped it into a dozen pieces. Twice she had nearly dialed the phone number to the North Carolina basketball office, but both times she'd changed her mind. She'd thought again about contacting him when he was drafted by the pros. She researched his manager's name and office number. She still had it programmed into her phone.

Yes, she'd followed Nolan's life as far back as she could remember. How his father had died of a heart attack after losing the state final game the spring after Ellie moved to San Diego and how Nolan missed him. How he had poured all his passion and energy into basketball. He'd gotten exactly what he wanted back when they used to sit under their old oak tree. All of his dreams had come true.

All of his and none of hers.

And that was the one thing that had stopped her from contacting Nolan back when he was in college. It was the sad detail that still stopped her today.

Deep down, she didn't really want to find Nolan Cook. Didn't want him to see how her life had turned out. How she'd failed. Ellie felt the familiar ache in her chest. Her life was a sad mix of hurried choices and lifelong consequences. She'd rebelled against her father and fallen for a soldier when she was a senior in high school. Not long after, Ellie was pregnant. When the guy found out, he left her for another girl before being deployed. He was killed by a roadside bomb in the Middle East, and Ellie was raising their daughter by herself. She didn't talk to either of her parents, and hadn't in years.

How would she tell Nolan that?

The idea of Nolan seeing her now? Ellie shuddered at the thought. He would despise who she had become. She had missed out on college and instead spent her days cutting hair so she could feed her six-year-old daughter. Her dreams of writing that great American novel as gone as the summer nights under the old oak tree. She hadn't been to church in five years and had no plans to go. Not ever.

So why contact him?

What would she have in common with Nolan Cook, the man so public about his love for Jesus? Nolan wasn't looking for someone like Ellie. The right girl for Nolan would have rock-solid faith and a commitment to purity. She would be a role model for girls around the country, beautiful and innocent and strong in her convictions.

Ellie smeared the bleach on a square piece of tinfoil and wrapped it around a small section of the woman's hair.

Then she repeated the process. No, he wasn't looking for her any more than she was looking for him. Still, during basketball season, she couldn't help herself. She loved watching Nolan Cook play, same as she did when she was fifteen years old. The way he took control of a game and drove to the hoop, the way he could sink a three-point shot like butter through the net. His expression of determination and intensity.

She would never know him again, never seek him out. But when he played basketball on TV, for a few hours she could pretend once more that he was her friend and she was the only girl in his life. The way she pretended now.

"Did you hear me?" Tinfoil stuck over half the woman's hair. She pointed at the TV. "I said he's good-looking, Nolan Cook. Don't you think?"

Ellie smiled. She could see him the way he looked their last night together, when he took her in his arms and hugged her. He was just a kid back then. "Yes, he grew up to be very handsome."

The tinfoil pieces rattled as the woman looked over her shoulder at Ellie. "Grew up? You've seen pictures of him as a boy?"

"No." Heat flooded her cheeks. "Just . . . he's older now. I used to watch him when he played for North Carolina."

"Oh. Right." The woman turned back to the TV. "The guy breaks hearts every time he takes the floor."

Ellie nodded, her eyes on Nolan as she finished applying the bleach. "Time for the dryer."

"Make sure I can see the TV. I'm cheering for Nolan and the Hawks tonight."

Ellie led the woman across the salon and set her up beneath

the hot-air dryer in a place where she could see the game. The woman needed twenty minutes for her hair to process. Good thing. Ellie needed a rest from the chatter.

She returned to her station, her attention back on Nolan. A private smile tugged at her lips. No one would've guessed that Ellie had known him, that in another lifetime she and Nolan had been inseparable. She hadn't told a single person since the move to San Diego. Only her roommate. As if that part of her life had never happened at all.

The Hawks rolled out to a quick lead. Led by Nolan's fourteen points in the first quarter, they ran the floor like they were the team to beat. Same as they'd done the first three games in the series. Ahead by fifteen at the half, already the announcers were making predictions about who Atlanta would play in the conference final. As if they expected the Hawks to handle the next round as easily as they had handled this one.

Despite the lopsided score, Ellie kept the game on while she finished the woman's hair and then moved on to her next client. She didn't leave until nine o'clock, long after the game was over. On her way out, she turned left and walked to the end of the strip mall. The old bearded man was there, slouched against the brick wall and a pile of dirty blankets.

He scrunched himself a little higher as she approached. "Miss Ellie. How you be?"

"Good, Jimbo. Another beautiful day." She stooped down and pulled a donut from her purse. It was wrapped in a clean napkin. "One of the girls brought these." She smiled as she handed it to him. "I saved you one."

The man's eyes welled up. "Don't know why you're so good to me. I ain't never done anything this good."

"That's not true. You always tell me I look pretty."

"Aww, that's nothing." He brushed a gnarled hand near his face. "You're an angel, Miss Ellie. I'm . . . I'm nothing."

"Don't say that!" She wagged her finger at him. "Here. Tips were good today."

She handed him a twenty-dollar bill. He hesitated. His hands trembled as he took it. "I keep asking the good Lord what I ever did to deserve a friend like you." Tears slid down his weathered cheeks.

"Don't buy anything bad, okay?" She put her hand on his shoulder. "Promise?"

"Promise." He nodded fast, intent on his determination. "Only the good stuff."

"Like dinner." She stood and put her hands on her hips. "Okay, Jimbo?"

"Definitely. Thank you, Miss Ellie." He tucked the money into his shirt pocket, grabbed handfuls of his raggedy blankets, and pulled them close to his face.

"You'll feel better with a good dinner." The night air was cool for early May, but Ellie had a feeling that Jimbo was more embarrassed than cold. "You need anything?" Ellie had to get home to her little girl. But she had to ask.

"Nothing, Miss Ellie. I'm fine. I'm perfect. Thank you."

Ellie smiled. "Okay." She took a few steps back and waved. "See you tomorrow." Before she turned, she raised her brow at him. "Buy yourself dinner. You promised."

"Only the good stuff."

And with that, Ellie turned and crossed the parking lot to her car. The Dodge four-door was a decade old, and the left rear fender had been crushed in an accident by the previous owner. The car had logged over two hundred thousand miles, but it ran. Better than taking the bus.

Ellie climbed in, locked the doors, and headed home.

Her daughter was waiting.

🌿 🌿

Ellie named her Kinzie Noah Anne Tucker.

Since the name change five years ago, she was just Kinzie Noah Anne. Kinzie, after the street corner where Ellie and Nolan would meet before school each morning, the place halfway between her house and his. Kinzie Avenue. And Noah, the closest girl name to Nolan she could think of.

Kinzie met her at the door. "You're late." Her pale blond hair framed the frustration in her pretty blue eyes. "You said nine fifteen. It's nine twenty-five."

"Sorry, sweetie." Ellie set her purse down and swept Kinzie into her arms. The girl was still small enough to pick up. For a long time Ellie held her, and when she set her down, she bent low so they were eye to eye. "I missed you."

"Missed you, too." Kinzie's irritation turned to hurt. "I hate when you're late."

"I was talking to Jimbo." Ellie leaned in and brushed noses with her daughter. "He's doing okay."

"That's good." Kinzie smoothed out the wrinkles in her T-shirt and managed the first hint of a smile. "Did you tip him?"

"I did." She straightened and walked Kinzie to the kitchen, her arm around the child's slim, tan shoulders. "He promised to use it for dinner."

Kinzie turned her innocent eyes to Ellie. "You said he sometimes lies."

"Yes." Ellie nodded, serious. "I think he's working on it."

"I prayed for him last Sunday at church." Kinzie reached for Ellie's hand. "Come on. I made you dinner!"

88 🐾 KAREN KINGSBURY

Ellie stopped and looked at Kinzie, surprised. "You prayed for Jimbo?"

"A' course, Mommy. I pray for you, too. All the time."

"Oh." They headed for the kitchen once more. "That's nice of you." Ellie could thank her roommate, Tina, for Kinzie's recent obsession with faith. Tina's little girl, Tiara, was six also, and a few months ago they asked Ellie and Kinzie to join them at church. Ellie passed, but Kinzie jumped at the opportunity. Now Kinzie could barely talk about anything else. In a sweetly sad way, her daughter's love for God reminded Ellie of herself at that age. Eventually, she would know the disappointing truth. How God lost interest in kids once they grew up.

They reached the counter, and Ellie gasped. "Wow!" She walked closer to the plate of macaroni and cheese, carrot sticks, and toast Kinzie had made for her. "Look at you, Kinzie Noah. What a good little cook!"

Tina walked in and winked at Kinzie. Ellie's roommate had clearly given Kinzie a little help. This was their routine. Tina worked as a hairdresser, too, but she had the early shift. She picked up the girls from school at three every afternoon and made dinner with them. Ellie was in charge of breakfast and school drop-off each morning. Her schedule was worse. She had only an hour with Kinzie each day, then this little bit of time at night before bedtime.

And they had the weekends. Ellie's favorite time.

She ate beside Kinzie, captivated by the child's stories. She hadn't stopped talking since they sat down. "You know the bunny in our classroom, the one we rescued from the edge of the forest?"

"I do." Ellie took another bite of mac and cheese. "This is great, by the way."

"Thanks, Mommy." Kinzie giggled, completely recovered from her earlier disappointment. "Anyway, the bunny is so cute, Mommy. He looks like a stuffed bunny. And he can do this trick now where he wiggles his whiskers when he wants a carrot, and then sometimes he . . ."

Ellie stared at her plate, trying to focus. The bunny had done it. Triggered another wave of memories. Whatever Kinzie was talking about now, all Ellie could see was the stuffed rabbit, the one she had given Nolan the night before she moved. Did he still have it? Was it buried in a storage unit or thrown out in some long-ago bag of trash?

"Don't you think, Mommy? We should get a rabbit for our house?"

"Well." Ellie blinked and looked at Kinzie. "Rabbits are better off outside. Unless they need a little help. Like the one in your classroom."

Kinzie thought about that. "You're right." She sneaked a piece of macaroni off Ellie's plate. "Tastes pretty good, right?"

"It's perfect. You can open your own restaurant one day, Kinz. They'll line up around the block."

She giggled again, and it gave way to a yawn. "I'm sleepy."

"Me, too." Ellie finished her plate and set it in the sink. "Go brush your teeth. I'll meet you in the room."

The apartment had only two bedrooms, so Ellie and Tina shared rooms with their daughters. It was the only way to survive the cost of living in San Diego. She watched Kinzie skip off, and she tried to picture her own mother. Choosing a stranger over a relationship with her. Ellie's anger fanned the embers of a loss that never quite burned out.

She would die before she turned her back on Kinzie.

The thought tried to consume her, but she refused it. She

stuck her plate in the dishwasher and sat down at the computer. Savannah had been on her mind constantly. She typed the city's name into the Google search line, and a map appeared. Maybe she and Kinzie could drive there sooner rather than later. A few more clicks, and she had directions from San Diego to Savannah: 2,386 miles. A thirty-eight-hour trip.

She stared at the route. For a year she'd been saving, dreaming about the possibility. Dreaming about making the drive she had wanted to make since she was fifteen. She would go past their old house and walk the path from her house to Nolan's.

His mother no longer lived there. Ellie had read in *Sports Illustrated* that she moved to Portland to be near Nolan's sisters. Of course, he lived in Atlanta. So it wouldn't be about finding people. It would be about finding her way back, remembering a time in her life when everything was good and right and pure. A time when she believed. Nolan had moved on by now. The news had him paired off with another celebrity every other month. Even if he never actually dated them, he had choices.

"Mommy . . ." Kinzie called out from the bedroom. "I'm ready."

Ellie stood and pressed her hand into the small of her back, the place that always ached after a day on her feet. "Coming." She closed the map and walked to their room.

There was the other reason why she wanted to make the trip back to Savannah this summer. The most obvious reason, the one that was never far from her mind. She had a box to dig up. An old tackle box with two letters—one she wanted back in her possession and one she had wanted to read for eleven years.

Nolan would be in the play-offs, too busy and too far removed to think about the childhood promise they made that long-ago night. Too successful and in demand to remember their one last chance. She would be the only one who would make it back. But if she could figure out a way to get there, she would dig up the letters. She would do it on the day they agreed on, a time that was coming up in just five weeks. A date etched on her heart since she was fifteen.

June 1, 2013.

Chapter Nine

Peyton Anders was making a comeback in country music.

After five years without a tour, he had released an album last year that was once again tearing up the country charts. In any other situation, guitar player Ryan Kelly wouldn't have considered leaving the comfort of his home studio and touring. He'd done that for years, before he connected again with Molly Allen and married her, before he took a job working as a musician in Nashville.

Now he and Molly lived in Franklin, Tennessee. She ran a foundation that had transitioned from helping orphaned animals to teaching music to disadvantaged kids to granting the wishes of terminally ill children. Every night Molly came home with stories of lives changed. Between that and his studio work, Ryan loved everything about being home.

The opportunity with Peyton had come up a few months ago. His manager had contacted Ryan's. "He wants you and only you," the man said. "You're the best. Peyton knows that."

Ryan was going to turn it down until he talked to Molly.

"Peyton is searching, I really believe that." They'd met the country singer a year ago at a benefit dinner. Molly had thought then that he was looking for answers to the emptiness in his life. Now she looked thoughtful. "Maybe you're supposed to go."

He thought about the nights away, how much he'd miss her. They'd been married only a year. He could never have enough time with Molly. "Are you sure?"

"Yes. Go play for him." She framed her face with his hand. "You really are the best, Ryan. And maybe something big is going to come from it."

A week later, he was confirmed on the tour, and now they were a month into it. So far, Ryan couldn't think of a single redeeming reason why God would want him living out of a bus and playing guitar for the country star.

The guy was as bad as he'd always been rumored to be. He bragged about his drinking and he was reckless with the fans—hanging with girls in his private bus until they pulled out of a venue sometime in the wee hours of the morning. When they stayed overnight at a hotel—the way they were tonight—the girls didn't leave until checkout the next morning.

But this Saturday night something was different about Peyton.

Portland's Rose Garden was packed—Molly's old stomping grounds. Peyton was back on top as a performer, there was no doubt about that. But when the show ended, he pulled Ryan aside. "You busy tonight?"

Ryan would Skype with Molly for an hour, but otherwise he would be in his bus bunk, same as the rest of the band. "I have time. What's up?"

"I wanna talk." He looked nervous.

"Okay." They were just minutes off stage from the show. Ryan wiped the sweat off his brow and slung his guitar over his back. "We're here overnight. The hotel lobby?"

"I have a suite. How about there?"

Ryan knew Peyton was drunk as soon as he walked into the singer's room. A half-empty bottle of Jack Daniel's sat on the table, and Peyton leaned back in his chair, his eyes barely open.

"Sorry." Ryan hesitated at the door. "Maybe another time."

"No!" Peyton's answer sounded louder than he probably intended. He waved in broad strokes at the chair near him. "I've been waiting. I wanna talk. Seriously."

Ryan crossed the hotel room, pulled the chair close, and sat. For a long time he watched Peyton, wondering if the singer was sober enough to know how to talk. When it seemed like he might nod off, Peyton opened his eyes wide. "I got someone pregnant."

Ryan took the news like a kick to his gut. "On this tour?"

"No." He thought for a second. "Well . . . maybe." He hung his head for a long moment. When he looked up, defeat rang in his tone. "I'm talking . . . about Caroline." His words ran together. "Caroline Tucker. A girl in Savannah." He squinted at Ryan. "We're playing there soon. She's . . . on my mind." He looked straight at Ryan, and for a single breath he seemed sober. "I was her friend for two years. . . before we slept together. She was married." He shifted, unsteady. "I almost . . . loved her."

Almost loved her? Ryan was tempted to punch Peyton. How could the guy think like that? He gritted his teeth. "What happened to the baby? To Caroline's baby?"

"Don't know." Peyton downed half the liquor in his glass. "We didn't talk . . . after that."

Ryan stood and moved the Jack Daniel's from the table to a cupboard in the small kitchen. Peyton didn't seem to notice. Ryan grabbed a glass of water and swapped it for the one that still had a few ounces of liquor. "Drink that." He dumped the whiskey in the sink and hesitated, his eyes on the door.

Listen to him, my son . . . don't leave.

Ryan sat back down hard in his chair. The whispered words felt strangely like God speaking to him. *Okay, Lord, I'll stay. Help me hear what you want me to hear.* He rested his forearms on the table and leaned closer. "Tell me about her . . . about Caroline."

"She wasn't happy." Peyton swayed again. "Bad marriage." He hung his head for a long moment. "She worked at a doctor's office . . . Savannah, Georgia. I prolly shoulda given her some money."

"Peyton, man, are you kidding me?" Disgust filled Ryan's gut. "You don't even know whether the baby was born? You never followed up?"

Peyton narrowed his eyes as if trying desperately to form a sober thought. "That's why I asked you here." He looked embarrassed for the first time since Ryan had walked in the room. "Life's a mess." He leaned his head back and closed his eyes.

Ryan felt the slightest sense of purpose. Maybe this was why God wanted him on the tour. Peyton Anders wasn't exactly searching, but maybe he had reached the end of himself. "We can talk, but you need to be sober. Get some sleep."

Peyton didn't answer. He was already snoring.

🙢 🙢

Ryan placed the call as soon as he returned to his room. "I think God's showing me the reason I'm out here."

"I miss you." Molly's voice was marked by an endless sort of love.

He smiled. "Miss you, too."

"Had to say that first." Her smile sounded through the phone. "Okay, what happened?"

Ryan told her about Caroline Tucker, how she'd been unhappy and how she'd worked at a doctor's office in Savannah. "He told me he almost loved her. It's sad, Molly."

"Maybe we should find her. See how she's doing and if she had the baby." A discouraged silence settled between them. "We're taking a trip to Georgia, anyway." She laughed lightly. "Not sure if I mentioned it."

He loved her spunk. "Tell me."

"One of my foundation kids, a seven-year-old boy." Her voice fell a notch. "Everyone's praying for a miracle. He's very sick."

"He wants a trip to Georgia?" Ryan's heart filled at the thought of the sick child.

"Sort of." She breathed in deep, struggling the way she always did when she talked about the kids who came through her foundation. "He wants to go to a Hawks game. Wants to meet Nolan Cook."

"Mmm. I'm connecting the dots."

"Exactly." Her voice grew more enthusiastic. "We try to find this Caroline Tucker . . . see how she is, whether she kept the baby, and help our sick little guy meet Nolan Cook. All in one weekend."

"Perfect." They talked awhile longer, counting the days until they could be together. "No more tours after this."

"I agree." She laughed. "I love you, Ryan Kelly."

"I love you, too. We need a date night."

"Maybe read *Jane Eyre* out loud at The Bridge bookstore."

"Mmmm. Downtown Franklin. Like old times."

When the call ended, Ryan Googled the Hawks' play-off schedule. The team would likely have a home game two days into Peyton's tour break. The perfect time to go with the sick little boy and his family to Atlanta. Then they could take a trip to Savannah and try to find Caroline Tucker. So that maybe Peyton could apologize and change his ways. The singer might even find what he was really looking for.

A changed life.

Chapter Ten

Caroline Tucker put her arm around her young dark-haired son as they walked from church to the car. The afternoon sun felt warm on her shoulders. "How was Sunday school?"

"Fun." He put his arm around her waist and leaned in. "Teacher told us about Moses. How he needed all those years in the desert so he could learn to hear God's voice." He peered up at her, his brown eyes so like his father's she could barely focus. "God had to teach him that first."

"True." She kept her head high. Around them, other families crossed the parking lot, leaving church. Most of the families included a dad. She pictured Moses, years of living in the desert, learning about God and listening to His voice.

Caroline could relate.

"Can we stop at the store on the way home?" John's face lit up. "We need ice cream."

"Need?" She grinned. They reached the car, and she hit the unlock button. "We *need* eggs and milk."

"Okay." He laughed as they drove toward the exit. "Today's the basketball game with the guys, remember? After that, I really might need ice cream." He raised his brow. "Yes?"

Money was tight, but she was careful. She smiled, losing the fight. "Okay. We'll get ice cream."

"Yes!" He pumped his fist and stared out the windshield.

She caught his profile, and the reminder was as clear as the lines on the road. He looked just like Peyton. She loved her son more than her own life, but his looks were a constant reminder of her mistakes, her poor decisions. Proof that she alone had destroyed her family.

Caroline had named him John, which meant "gracious gift of God." Because at a time when she should be burning in hell for what she did, she was raising this beautiful boy instead. A boy whom she gave the last name Tucker, as if she could will her family back together by doing so. A boy who loved basketball as much as Ellie's friend Nolan Cook always had.

One who—by God's grace—had no interest in music.

As soon as John left the apartment with his basketball, Caroline found a piece of paper and sat down at the kitchen table, the way she did nearly every Sunday afternoon. It was time to write to Ellie. Caroline had no idea how many letters she had written to Ellie over the years. One a week, every week since her father moved them to San Diego. Alan had never given her a new address, so Caroline sent the letters to his mother's house. The one address she did have. Hundreds of letters. Her only way of reaching out to her daughter and letting her know how sorry she was. Over and over and over again. The letters never came back "return to sender," so Caroline hoped they were reaching her daughter. But not once over the years had Ellie ever written back.

She hesitated, her pen poised over the paper. From the beginning she had tried to find Ellie. The first few days after Ellie and Alan moved, Caroline had tried her mother-in-law's phone number, hoping to get Alan's new address. But the number had been disconnected. She and her mother-in-law hadn't been close. The woman might have changed her number years earlier; Caroline wouldn't have known. The truth that she had no real way to contact Ellie had sent a panic through her that remained to this day. She had immediately called the base, practically hysterical.

"My husband . . . he moved there with our daughter . . . I'm afraid they don't want to talk to me and . . . I need to reach them. Please." She could barely breathe. "It's an emergency."

The woman on the other end was kind, but she couldn't do anything. She informed Caroline that Alan hadn't reported for duty, but she promised to leave a message for him when he did.

But the hours had become days, and the days had become years, and still she hadn't had a single conversation with Alan. The man had turned Ellie against her for good reason, and now she was without options. She was a terrible mother, yes, but she deserved one last conversation with her daughter. She tried to get a loan so she could hire an attorney. The banks did everything but laugh at her. She was a single mother with a newborn baby. She had no money, no credit, no way of reaching her daughter except one.

Caroline stared at the paper. How many letters had she written? And how had more than a decade gone by? The weight of it pressed against her heart. There was no way to calculate all she'd missed. High school and homework, prom and graduation. Thousands of good nights and good mornings and everything in between. Her precious Ellie would be twenty-six now. All grown up. Years removed from the girl she'd been when she left Savannah. Through the open window, Caroline could hear the distant sound of the basketball on the pavement, the laughter of the boys as they played across the street at Forsyth Park.

Ellie must hate her. That was the only reason Caroline could think that her daughter hadn't written back. Not even to tell her to stop sending the letters. She planted her elbow on the table and rested her head in her hand, weary at the thought of pouring her heart onto the page one more time. Usually, she tried to spare Ellie the details of her life, the one she and John lived in Savannah. The tough times they'd faced. Instead, she'd usually pull out a memory from long ago, back when she and Ellie played at the park. When Ellie was her constant shadow and every day brought new adventures, new moments of laughter and love.

Today Caroline didn't feel like talking about the happy times. If Ellie wasn't going to write back, maybe she wasn't reading the letters. Maybe they went straight to the trash. She poised her pen at the top of the page. In case she did read them, maybe this was the time to be honest, to tell Ellie how it had been, what life had been like after her father moved them to San Diego. Ellie was hardly a child now. She could know at least a little of the truth.

Caroline summoned her determination and started to write.

Dear Ellie,
   Sometimes I feel like I should stop writing to you, and then I remind myself. I can never stop. This is one of those

times. I know you probably hate me, and I understand. What I did was terrible, unforgivable. But I have to write. See, usually I write about the old times, about how much I love you and miss you, and how badly I long for the years when you were a little girl. But today I want to go back to the days after you and your dad left. I moved in with my friend Lena Lindsey at first. I stayed with her until the baby came.

Once she started, the story flowed easily.

Lena and her husband, Stu, personified love—the sort of love Caroline and Alan had shared in the beginning. Caroline wrote slowly, so her words would be legible. While she lived with Lena and Stu, Caroline spent her nonworking hours doing one of two things—thinking of ways to find Ellie, and hating herself for sleeping with Peyton Anders.

Lena took her to church, a different church than the one she and Alan had attended. They met with one of the church's female counselors. By then Caroline was willing to try anything, willing to apologize and change, willing to get marriage counseling. But it was too late. Caroline worked at the doctor's office until the baby was born. When she tried to return, her position had been filled, and like that, she was without a job.

The story poured onto the page, a story Caroline had never shared in any of her letters before. With no way to fix her mistakes, Caroline had stayed with Lena and Stu, learning to forgive herself and trying to figure out a way to face life alone with her baby. Six months later, Stu and Lena moved to Atlanta, and Caroline took an apartment with a single mom she'd met at her new church. They shared a two-bedroom apartment, and Caroline found a new job at a doctor's office across town. Without her seniority, the pay was minimal. But it was a start.

Caroline reached the bottom of the page and took another piece of paper from the kitchen drawer.

> *Through all of it, I wrote to you, Ellie. And not once, not one time, have you written back. I'm not asking for your sympathy. I just want you to know I'm sorry. I've lived with my choices every day since you and your dad left. I miss you with every breath.*

It was true. After the first year, she had saved enough vacation time and money to buy airfare to San Diego. The thought of surprising Ellie terrified her, but still she would've gone. But that winter John caught pneumonia. They couldn't fly with the baby's poor health, and, despite her limited insurance, his medical bills wiped out her savings. By then it was clear Ellie didn't want to see her, anyway. Caroline wasn't sure she would have survived, but she had John to care for. John and her job and her renewed faith in God. As the years passed without word from Ellie, Caroline resigned herself to the truth: This was the only way. The letters she sent. Nothing could stop her from this Sunday afternoon routine. She would write to her daughter as long as she lived.

Caroline ended the letter by telling Ellie the same thing she always told her.

> *I pray for you every day, for the two of us. That God— in all His mercy—might bring you back to me. I'm sorry, Ellie. What I did to you and our family was inexcusable.*

It still is. I can only pray that one day you'll forgive me. I miss you. I love you.

Love,
Mom

With John still playing ball across the street, Caroline slipped the folded letter into an envelope, stamped and addressed it. Then she walked to the mailbox at the corner of East Bolton. And for the twenty-third time that year, she dropped the envelope through the slot and did what she did every time she sent a letter to Ellie. She begged God that somehow, some way, this time it might reach her. Really reach her.

Not just her hands but her heart.

Chapter Eleven

Alan Tucker kept one hand on his revolver as he strode down the cement hallway between the rows of the most dangerous inmates in the Pendleton brig. He needed to stay on his game, needed to focus. Last week the prisoners had rioted, and one of the guards was in the hospital because of it. Broken ribs and a concussion.

But if ever there was a day when he was distracted, it was this one. Today was Ellie's twenty-sixth birthday.

"Look at you, big man. . . . Think you're all tough out there." One of the prisoners grabbed the bars and slammed his face against them. Almost through them. "Watch your back, big man."

Alan kept walking.

He was good at this, good at ignoring them. Good at intimidating them. Same way he'd been good at intimidating his wife and daughter a decade ago. He did it because he was right. But somewhere along the life of knowing it all, it seemed, Alan Tucker had gotten things very wrong.

Because the only two women he'd ever loved were gone. Forever gone.

"Come here, pretty boy." The call came from the opposite side of the corridor. The prisoner cussed loud enough for everyone on the floor to hear him. "Tell you what, pretty guard. You come a little closer, and I'll trade your freedom for mine." He laughed like a crazy person. "Come on! I dare you!"

Alan stopped. He turned slowly and faced the man, squared up to him from his place ten feet away. "You must've forgotten, Joey. You'll never be free." He kept his cool. As if he had ice in his veins. "Never again."

From half a dozen cells along the hallway came laughter and more expletives. Joey backed up to the cell wall and charged the bars. "Watch your back, pretty guard." His words dripped venom. "You won't be free forever."

Alan stared at him. Just watched him for a full minute until the prisoner shouted more profanity and jerked away, turning his back to the cell bars. Alan walked away, satisfied. Another victory. More catcalls from Joey's neighbors, guys in for murder and rape and armed robbery. Joey had lost. They all knew it. Alan made it to the first of four steel doors and passed through them one at a time, using various keys and codes.

His shift was over. Another day of survival, keeping his prisoners in line. His supervisor patted him on the back as he grabbed his things from his locker. "You're good, Tucker. Very good."

"Thanks." Alan looked to the window. Somewhere out there, Ellie was celebrating her birthday without him. "See you tomorrow."

He kept his hand on his gun as he walked to his car. He didn't expect a problem, but he lived ready for one. It was what made him good at his job. That and the fact that Alan Tucker had a secret weapon. When he stared down a criminal on the Fourth Ward the way he'd just done to Joey, Alan did something he doubted any other guard did.

Alan prayed.

He prayed against the spiritual battle raging between them, and he prayed for God's mercy over the prisoner. He prayed it all in the name of Jesus Christ, not blinking, not looking away. And Alan knew, in the invisible places, in the spiritual realm, the demons in the cells and hearts of the Pendleton brig prisoners could do only one thing in response.

Flee.

Now if Alan could just get the prayers to work for himself.

The letters were killing him.

Alan Tucker stepped into his bedroom closet and took the oversized box from the top shelf. In a single motion he heaved it onto the end of his bed. Hundreds of letters. More letters than he could begin to count. Each of them weighed on his soul like so many bricks. Nearly eleven years ago, when his mother called to tell him Caroline had written to Ellie, Alan stopped by her house on the way home from work. He took the letters and hid them in his bedroom drawer. Five or six letters, and he figured that would be it. Surely Caroline wouldn't keep writing. But she had. She still did. The letters came like clockwork, some thicker than others, and over time he transferred them to the box in his closet.

At first he spent every weekend thinking of a way to handle the problem. He could contact Caroline and tell her to stop writing, or return the letters unanswered. He had no intention of giving them to Ellie. Their daughter had been hurt enough by her mother's betrayal, without a letter reminding her every week. Or he could read through them and see exactly what his unfaithful wife intended to tell their daughter.

Many times he considered throwing them away, burning them, or having them shredded, the way people did with boxes of old tax records. But always when he came close to doing that, he imagined Ellie—all grown up—and somehow finding out what he had done. Something in him could never go that far.

And so the tradition remained, week after week, year after year after year. He would swing by his mother's house on Friday after work and collect whatever Caroline had sent. Six years ago, after Ellie took up with the soldier and left home, Alan's mother began showing signs of dementia. Eighteen months later, she was diagnosed with aggressive Alzheimer's, and Alan set her up in a full-time care facility. He moved off base and into her house. The letters continued.

Once a week, at least.

He dipped his hand into the box, sorted through the mountain of envelopes, and pulled out one at random. In all the years he'd been collecting the letters, he had never opened one, never gone against his feelings that it would be wrong to do so. But today, on Ellie's birthday, he was at a complete and utter loss.

The envelope felt smooth in his hand. Maybe it was his imagination, but he could almost feel the words written across the front, the dip and swoop of Caroline's handwriting. The hope she must've felt in her heart as she dropped this very letter into a mailbox somewhere in Savannah.

What was wrong with him? How could he have cut her out of his life so completely? What sort of man was he to never check to see if she was surviving or if she'd kept the baby or if she'd found a way to exist on her own? He held the envelope close to his face and studied the postmark. March 2011. Two years ago. Always she included a return address, the same one for the last decade. So she at least had housing.

He ran his thumb over her name. Her married name, the one she still apparently went by. *Caroline . . . what happened to us? You were the only girl I ever loved.* Flashes from his past hit his heart like so many lightning bolts. The day he had met Caroline at a church picnic. She had been only nineteen, barely more than a child, and he was twenty-seven. Headed into a military career. Ten minutes into their first conversation, Alan had two thoughts.

First, he was going to marry her. And second, he would never love anyone else.

So what happened?

More flashes. Alan winced and tightened his grip on the letter. He could hear himself barking at her, using the same tone he used at work as a drill sergeant. *Caroline, why isn't the laundry done? Where were you all afternoon? Can't you make that baby stop crying? The Bible says a wife should obey her husband; keep that in mind.*

Phrases like that shredded his conscience and reminded him of a truth he couldn't escape. One that had surfaced a few months ago and had haunted him since then, hounding him and keeping him awake at night.

The truth was this: Caroline's affair was his fault.

The realization hit after his breakdown—the one that had sent him running to God for real, for the first time. He understood now. The faith of his youth was nothing but a hammer. A weapon he wielded against people to get them to fall into line. At work, he used his position of power to keep control over recruits. At home, he had used the Bible.

He'd made a mockery of Christianity, and now all that remained of his life were shattered pieces of a dream that had died long before Caroline slept with Peyton Anders. He thought about the prisoners at the Pendleton brig and the way Joey had glared at him, taunting him about being free.

Joey didn't know anything. Alan Tucker wasn't free. He was in a prison cell stronger than anything at the brig. Alan had no idea what it was to be free. Once more he looked at Caroline's words on the envelope, really studied her writing.

As he did, the flashes came again.

Caroline tossing back her pretty blond hair at their wedding reception, laughing at something he'd said. *I love being with you, Alan Tucker. I'll love it as long as I live.* The clock spun a few hundred times forward. *Alan! Come look.* She ran through their front door, her tanned legs flying beneath her. *The first fireflies of the season! The front yard is like a painting. You have to see it!* And he was taking her hand and celebrating summer with her in the front yard of their small home. More time passed, and she was dancing with Ellie in the living room, singing to her. And she was catching a glimpse of Alan in the doorway. *God has blessed us, Alan . . . My heart's so full, I can barely stand up under it.* Her smile lit up the room. *When we're old and gray, remind me of this moment.* And he had believed with everything in him that he would be that guy, there to remind her, just like she asked.

She was one of the happiest people he'd ever known. Only years of his harsh words, years of being left alone, could have killed the childlike love for life, the limitless joy, the wide-eyed innocence that once defined Caroline Tucker.

You were everything to me. He looked at the photo on his nightstand, the one of Caroline and him on their honeymoon. What sort of monster would suffocate the love out of someone like her? When had they stopped laughing and taking walks and watching stars in the sky? *Caroline . . . my love. I'm so sorry. I want you back the way you were.*

He would go to his grave wanting that, wanting to be at the other end of her smile. Wanting everything that could never be again. The picture of Caroline and him filled his senses, spreading despair through his body and soul. *Please, God, I need a miracle. Another chance.* His eyes shifted to a different photograph, the one next to it. A picture of Ellie in Savannah on her seventh birthday. The three of them had gone fishing that afternoon, but Alan remembered the laughter from that birthday more than any fish they caught. He squinted at the picture. His only child. The light from her spirit shone through her eyes, her smile proof that once, a lifetime ago, they had been a happy family.

If only he could call Ellie and wish her a happy birthday. Just that. The chance to tell his baby girl he was thinking about her. But they hadn't spoken in seven years. Seven full years. He closed his eyes and shut out the images. Otherwise his heart might stop beating from the sadness. The truth was, now that he'd found real faith, now that he understood his part in what had happened, he wouldn't mind if his heart stopped.

But he had work to do first.

Slowly, gradually, as naturally as one breath followed another, the answers came. God had already forgiven him, already set him free. If he lived in a prison of broken relationships and silent suffocating guilt, it was his own fault. The cell door was unlocked. He opened his eyes and stared at the pictures again. He would figure it out, find a way. Pray about what to do first and how to make a move toward his broken family.

The thought filled his heart. It swelled through his being until he felt wetness on his fingers. A dampness spreading across the envelope in his hand. What was this? His cheeks were wet, too. He breathed in deep and sniffed a few times. The sensation gave him a hope he hadn't felt since he left Savannah. Because for the first time since that day, he was doing the one thing he had never done before.

He was crying.

Chapter Twelve

It was the calendar, of course.

The reason Nolan couldn't stop thinking about Ellie, the reason she was on his mind every minute. The answer was as close and real as the date. Each time he looked at his phone, the numbers practically screamed at him. As he warmed up on the Hawks home court for the first game in the second round of the play-offs, he didn't need a countdown clock to know how many days there were until June 1, 2013.

Twenty-five. The shrinking number hit him first thing every morning, and stayed with him all day.

In a little more than three weeks, it would be eleven years to the day since the last time he saw Ellie Tucker. He hated that so much time had gone by. Back then, eleven years had sounded like a lifetime. Neither of them believed for a minute it would be that long before they saw each other.

The tackle box, the letters, burying them beneath the big old oak tree. All of it had been one big "just in case." Just in case they couldn't find each other . . . in case they lost touch. Just in case one year became three and three years became five and that turned into eight years, and then ten, without talking to each other.

Just in case all of that happened, they'd still have a chance.

"Cook, you with us?" Coach shouted from the bench. He didn't look worried, just intent. He clapped a few times and pointed to the clock. Four minutes till game time. He flashed a thumbs-up at Nolan. "You good?"

Nolan clenched his jaw. He had to focus. Had to be solid. Needed to find the zone. Never mind the calendar, this was *his* season, the one he'd prayed about since he was fifteen. Everything lined up, as if God had handed him the perfect scenario. A few trades in the off-season, and the Hawks had acquired him. With the talent already on the team, everyone believed they were set. This was the year they could win it all.

Nolan loved the Hawks. Some of the guys studied the Bible and barbecued together, and on their off days, they texted each other. They were like a band of brothers, and Nolan was the leader. At six-four he was hardly the tallest guard in the league. When reporters asked him to explain his success, he always said the same thing. A combination of God-given talent and extreme obsession.

The one caused by the losses of his sixteenth year.

He caught the ball, drove in for a layup, and ran to the back of the line. Dexter Davis was in front of him, Dexter who had been his best friend since freshman year at North Carolina. They inched forward in the rotation of the warm-up drill, and Dexter looked back. "You're thinking about her." It wasn't a question.

"Not really."

"You're lying." Dexter wiped the sweat off his brow. "Look, man. She's not here." He glanced at the arena. "Isn't that Kari girl coming to the game tonight?"

"Yeah. So?"

Dexter turned, caught the ball, shot a pretty jumper, and ran to the back of the line. Nolan did the same, hitting the shot. The moment he was behind Dexter again, his friend looked at him. "So . . . quit it." Dexter didn't have to spell it out. He knew everything about Ellie, how Nolan had tried to find her and how the eleven-year mark was almost here. "Quit thinking about her."

"Kari?" Nolan grinned.

"Don't mess with me, Cook."

"Who?" Nolan felt his intensity building. They moved closer to the front of the line. "That's my girl right there." He pointed to the ball.

Dexter flashed him a look. "Better be." He turned more fully toward Nolan and slapped his shoulders soundly with both hands. "Let's do this. Come on, Cook. Let's win it."

Two more minutes of drills, and the buzzer sounded. Through team introductions and the National Anthem, with every passing second, Nolan felt his mind clear, felt himself pushing back from reality, falling into the zone, the place where he'd spent most of the last eleven years. Where there was only God and the round leather ball.

Tip-off, and the game began. Nolan had no doubt they'd win. He could feel his teammates around him, sense their places on the court, anticipate their passes and rebounds and movements until they were playing in unison. Even at halftime with a fifteen-point lead, Nolan didn't let up. Dexter came up to him, right in his face. "Yes! I love playing with you, man. You're insane out there!"

Nolan didn't smile, didn't celebrate even on the inside. He grabbed a towel and wiped his face and arms. Then he shot a quick look at Dexter. "We haven't won yet."

Not until the game was over and the Hawks had notched a dramatic thirty-four-point win did he allow himself to see something other than the court and the game and the ball. His teammates gathered around him, celebrating, high-fiving and chest-thumping. They were on their way. This was their year. They could feel it.

Dexter found him after the team huddle and nodded to the stands. There, walking down the stadium steps, was a breathtaking brunette, tall and self-possessed and dressed like someone with the money to express it.

She smiled as their eyes met, and Nolan waved.

"Hmm." Dexter leaned close, his eyes on the girl. "Kari?"

"I guess." Nolan motioned for Kari to come closer. He kept his conversation with Dexter discreet. "We've never actually met."

"Well." Dexter turned his back to her, his eyebrows raised. "Want my advice?"

"Not really." Nolan still faced the girl, but he looked at Dexter. Teasing was part of their friendship. "What's your advice?"

"Tonight? Be in the moment." Dexter was six-eight, a dominating mountain of a man, but right now he looked like a kid on the playground. Three years ago Dexter had married a girl he met in college. The two had waited for each other, and now their faith and lives were a billboard for marriage. Dexter wanted nothing more than for Nolan to find love the way he had. He gave Nolan a light punch on the arm. "You hear me? Be in the moment."

"I will."

Dexter glanced over his shoulder at Kari and then back at Nolan. "Give the girl a chance."

Nolan couldn't promise anything. He could block out thoughts of Ellie for the game. But pushing away thoughts of her tonight, resisting the obvious comparisons? He wasn't sure he could do it. He had hardly dated, so his experience was limited. A few setups along the way, a publicity intern two years ago, a couple of chats over coffee. Nothing that stuck.

It was always easier to focus on basketball and believe he'd find Ellie. Now, though, he had to be realistic. She didn't want to be found. So maybe the time had come to move on. If only his heart would agree with his head.

"You're doing it again." Dexter gave an exaggerated sigh. "Come on, Cook. At least try."

"I will." Nolan laughed lightly. "Really." Tonight would be fun—at least he hoped it would be. But there was no getting around his deepest desire. How he'd rather go home and search Facebook or Twitter or Google.

Anything to find Ellie.

Nolan had no idea how he and Kari Garrett would spend the next few hours.

He showered and changed in the locker room while she waited. Small talk kept them company while they walked to his car, climbed inside, and headed out of the complex. Before the first awkward silence could hit, Kari turned to him. "Are you as good at bowling as you are at basketball?"

"Bowling?" He had figured they'd go for coffee or dessert. See if there was anything there. Bowling was a longer commitment.

She laughed. "I mean, let's be real. I can't take you at one-on-one, but I can hold my own in a bowling alley." Her long brown hair hung in layers over her shoulders and down her back. "Just saying."

Her tone, or maybe the look on her face, made him chuckle. The idea of bowling with the girl beside him sounded like fun. Something he hadn't done since college. "Actually, I *am* a decent bowler."

"Okay, then." Her brown eyes sparkled. "I know a place. Hold on." She pulled her phone from her purse and, after several seconds, she smiled at him. "Turn right at the next light."

Again Nolan laughed quietly. "Where are you taking me?"

"Trust. That's all you have to do." She settled back in her seat, holding her phone so she could see the map on the screen. "Trust and drive."

She wasn't Ellie, but she was fun the whole ride to the bowling alley. As they pulled into the parking lot, she looked at him and her smile faded. "Hey, Nolan, just so you know . . . I didn't want to do this."

"You don't want to bowl?" He found a spot near the entrance, killed the engine, and stared at her. She amused him, that much was certain. "You wanna do something else?"

"No." She laughed, her tone softer than before. "I didn't want this setup. My mom made it happen." Kari wrinkled her nose and rolled her eyes in the cutest way possible. "She does things like this."

"Really?" Nolan enjoyed the banter. "My manager told me it was your idea."

"Not at all." She gave a quick laugh, clearly embarrassed. "My mom means well. Once the setup happened, I didn't know how to back out."

Nolan thought for a moment. "My manager and your mom. That's hysterical."

"I figured we'd go bowling and make them both happy."

He liked her spunk. "I can take you back to your car." He raised one eyebrow. "I mean, I wouldn't want to force you into losing."

She studied him, her expression playful, confident. "That's okay. I mean, I *am* on a date with Nolan Cook, right? Like, what girl wouldn't want to be me right now?" She shrugged. "Of course, you're on a date with Kari Garrett. So . . . yeah."

"True." He liked her attitude. She could probably be a lot of fun if he got to know her. "What guy wouldn't want to be me right now?"

"Exactly." The shine in her eyes was brighter than before. "So . . ."

"So we might as well bowl."

"If you don't mind losing."

"We'll see about that." His laughter came easily. He climbed out of the car and opened the door for her. "I had no idea you were a pro bowler." She stepped out and easily fell in beside him. Their back-and-forth continued as they paid for two games and rented shoes. Nolan felt himself relax. He wasn't looking for a girlfriend, but this would be a fun night. He could feel it. They picked a lane at the end of the alley so they wouldn't be recognized, and he was still enjoying himself an hour later after she'd beaten him soundly two games straight. "Okay, okay. That's all." He raised his hands in mock surrender. "You destroyed me."

She gave a small curtsy. "My pleasure."

Something about the gesture, the way she moved or her tone, reminded him of Ellie. He forced the thought of her from his mind and grinned. "Let's get coffee."

"We don't have to." Her expression softened, and she looked

at him. Right through him. She smiled and slipped off her bowling shoes. "Really."

His answer was as honest as the good way he was feeling. "I want to."

As they left the bowling alley, two kids asked for his autograph. Nolan complied and smiled for a picture with them before he and Kari crossed the parking lot for his car. She looked at him, impressed maybe, or intrigued. "You handled that well. Very kind."

"Thanks. The kids are great." Nolan slowed his pace, in no hurry. "It's the adults, the ones who'll sell your signature. They take a little more patience."

"Hmm." Kari looked up at him. "I never thought about that."

"Doesn't happen often." He grinned at her. "I don't get out much."

She laughed. "That explains your bowling game."

He wore jeans and a black V-neck T-shirt, the sort of outfit that would blend in at most coffee shops. But his height gave him away, caused people to look twice, and sometimes that was all it took. They had barely ordered their coffee when a group of girls approached him, gushing over his win and asking him to sign their arms and the backs of their shirts.

Nolan complied quickly and then whisked Kari to the back of the coffee shop. Atlanta was home to most of the country's rappers and a great number of pop artists. A couple of hit TV series filmed here, too. Usually, the clientele at Breve didn't come undone over a celebrity sighting.

"Sorry." He set his coffee on the table and took the seat with his back to the rest of the café. "It's the play-offs."

"I love how you take it in stride." She sat opposite him.

"Yeah, well . . . tell me about you." He genuinely wanted to know. "You're making an album, right? That's what my manager said."

"I am." She sipped her coffee. Now that the conversation was more serious, the walls around her heart seemed to lower just a bit.

"Your mom can help."

"Yes and no. She's amazing. Everyone knows her music." Kari smiled. "The comparisons will always be there."

They talked about her determination to find her own way in music and her appreciation for her mother's help. The conversation remained easy as they sipped their coffees and as Nolan asked for her number. "You know." He winked. "In case I need to text you for bowling tips."

She laughed, and again Nolan thought that the moment felt real and comfortable. He wanted to stay here with this girl as long as she would let him, and for the next half hour no one bothered them. It took that long before she asked the question. "So, Nolan Cook. Is there a girl in your heart?"

If she'd asked any other way, he could've told her no. There was no girl in his life, no girl waiting at home for his call. No girl he was texting or calling. He stared at his half-empty coffee just long enough to give himself away.

She sat back, her smile still in place. "Tell me about her."

And like that, the conversation turned to Ellie. Nolan sighed. "I met her in third grade." He laughed easily, but he could feel his heart going back, traveling down the old familiar road in a way he was helpless to stop. "I haven't seen her in eleven years."

Kari's eyes showed her surprise. "She's the girl in your heart? And you haven't seen her since you were teenagers?"

"It's a long story." He wasn't sure how wise it was, talking to

Kari Garrett about Ellie. But he couldn't help himself. He liked talking about Ellie with someone other than Dexter. "We were fifteen when she moved away." He laughed, but only to hide his pain. "I was going to marry her. We . . . we didn't mean to lose touch."

"Oh." Kari looked like she wasn't sure what to say next. "That's sad." She took another sip of her coffee. "You tried to find her?"

"You could say that." He wrapped his hands around the base of his coffee cup and let his eyes settle on hers. "My dad died of a heart attack the spring after Ellie left. The two run together in my mind. I'm still trying to figure it out."

"Yeah." Her smile seemed forced. "I can see that." She breathed in deep and reached for her phone. "We should probably go. It's late."

Only then did Nolan realize that the walls she'd let down minutes ago were up now. Firmly in place. He'd said too much. Kari was fun and pretty, and she shared his love for God. He would've had fun hanging out with her again, but now . . . "I'm sorry."

"No, you're fine." She laughed, though there was nothing funny. This was the same Kari he'd climbed into his car with earlier that night. The one good at preventing awkward silences. "Thanks for tonight." She stood and grabbed her purse. "I had fun. Really."

"No, that was dumb." He laughed, too, but more out of frustration. "It's been eleven years."

As they left the coffee shop, Kari shifted the conversation back to their time bowling. "I should think about investing in a pair of shoes. You know, like the pros."

Even as she kept things light, Nolan silently chided himself for talking about Ellie. He had ruined things with Kari before they started. All because of a girl he hadn't seen since they were kids. Ellie could be married or living out of the country, for all he knew.

On the way to his car, a lone photographer stepped out of a dark doorway and caught a dozen pictures of them before Nolan put his arm around Kari's shoulders and hurried her across the street, away from the parking lot. They could walk around the block, take the long way. But by then it was too late. The guy had what he wanted, and an hour from now he would have sold the pictures to a handful of paparazzi websites and magazines.

Other NBA guys could avoid being fodder for the gossip rags, but not Nolan. When he and Kari were finally inside the car, he grabbed the steering wheel, glanced at her and groaned. "Sorry about that."

She laughed. "It's okay. People love a good story." On the drive back to her car, she entertained him with tales from her mother's recent tour. Conversation seemed to come naturally for her, and it made him realize again what a good night he'd had. As he pulled into the Hawks' facility, she grew quiet, and when he parked, she turned to him. "I had fun."

"Me, too." He still felt the tension between them, the reality that he had taken the talk about Ellie too far. "Back there, that stuff about the girl from my—"

"Nolan." She put her hand lightly on his shoulder, but only for a few seconds. "Don't apologize. She obviously still means a great deal to you."

"But it was so long ago. I just . . . I need to move on."

Again she allowed a bit of laughter. "You haven't heard from her in eleven years? Yeah. Probably move on." She opened the car door. "When that happens, I'd love to hang out again."

Resignation worked its way through him, and he sank back in his seat. "I'll call you."

She smiled, but her eyes told him not to make promises he didn't mean. "Those bowling tips. I'll be ready." She had a brilliant way of not being the victim. She ended their time together the way it had started, with laughter and lightness. He waited until she climbed into her car and backed up before he did the same. He followed her to the exit, the whole time wrestling with himself.

What was he thinking, talking about Ellie like that? He barely knew Kari. She wasn't wide-eyed and nervous around him, treating him like a celebrity, the way other dates had. He breathed out and let the sound settle in his soul. He didn't blame her for ending the night when she did. As long as Ellie could still fill his conversation that easily, no girl would want to invest time in him.

If only he could get past the next month, past the first of June. The play-offs would be winding down, and if Atlanta stayed in it, he would be home, right in the middle of a three-day break. He'd already looked. The date had been etched on his soul for eleven years. No wonder he talked about Ellie. What happened now came down to a simple truth. Wherever she was, whatever she was doing, did Ellie remember?

Or was he the only one who knew the significance of to-morrow?

Twenty-four days until June first.

Chapter Thirteen

Kinzie loved Sundays.

Tina had taken her to church since the start of first grade, and now she looked forward to Sunday all week long. Kids stayed for the first part of the service, and that was where she was right now. Sitting on the cool wood bench between Tina and Tiara, Kinzie listened to every word the pastor said.

"Sometimes it takes a while for people to find their happy-ever-after in Jesus." The man had nice eyes, and he never yelled. Mommy said once to Tina that she didn't want any pastor yelling at her about what she'd done wrong. So at first Kinzie watched for that, but so far the pastor only talked with kind words. Anyway, yelling wasn't why her mommy didn't go to church. Sundays were cleaning day, that's why.

"You go to church, Kinz," she would always say. "This is my time to clean."

Right now the pastor was talking about being nice to people who had hurt in their hearts. Hurt feelings, that's what he meant. Kinzie was pretty sure. She looked down at her pink-and-white tennis shoes. Something had happened that morning that she didn't tell Tina or Tiara. Mommy was at the computer, and she had her hands over her face. Kinzie watched her from the hallway, and she saw her mommy wipe her eyes. Her shoulders shook, too. So Kinzie knew for sure Mommy was crying.

She never cried in front of Kinzie, but sometimes when she didn't think anyone was watching, she would cry. This morning Kinzie walked up real quiet and put her hand on her mommy's back. "I'm sorry you're sad."

Real quick, her mommy sniffed and wiped the tears off her face. "It's okay." She turned around and hugged Kinzie. "I was just . . . wishing I could give you more. A different life."

"Why?" Kinzie leaned back and put her hands on her mommy's cheeks. "I like our life. I don't want something different."

Her mommy's eyes still held tears, but she smiled and kissed Kinzie's cheek and hugged her. "That's my girl. How did I get so blessed to have you?"

Kinzie smiled at her mommy. "Because Jesus loves you. That's what we learned at church."

Her mom looked away like she didn't really believe it. She hugged Kinzie again. "As long as *you* love me. That's all I need."

Lots of times Kinzie asked her mom to go to church. "You might feel better, Mommy."

"I know." Her eyes looked very sad. "But Sundays are when I clean the apartment. You know that."

The pastor was still talking about people who were hurt. "It's our job to love them, our job to show them the love of Jesus every day. And it's our job to pray for them."

Kinzie thought about praying for her mommy right now. *Dear Jesus, please be with my mommy and make her happy. I don't want it to take a long time for her to be happy. Thank you for listening. Love, Kinzie.*

When the kids went to Sunday school, Kinzie colored a picture for her mom, because maybe that would make her feel better. The picture was Jesus sitting on a bench next to her mommy, and they were eating ice cream and talking about summertime.

When they got home, Tina made lunch, and Tiara helped. Kinzie ran to the bedroom where her mom was vacuuming. She held out the colored picture, and her mommy turned off the machine. "What's this?" She took the paper and held it up. "Wow, Kinzie. You're such a talented little artist." Her mom sat down on her bed, and Kinzie sat beside her. "It's beautiful. Tell me about it."

Kinzie felt proud of her drawing, especially because her mommy said she was a good artist. She pointed to the people. "That's you sitting with Jesus. You're eating ice cream and talking about summer."

"Hmmm." Her mommy nodded. "Looks like we're having a nice time."

"You are." She stared up into her mom's blue eyes. "Pastor said some people take a long time to find their happy-ever-after in Jesus."

All of a sudden tears were in her mommy's eyes again. "I suppose that's true."

"But it doesn't have to take a long time, right?"

"Well, sweetie, it's complicated." She patted Kinzie's hair and stood. "I need to finish in here. Then I'll make pancakes." She hugged Kinzie, and she put the picture on the bed. "Thanks again for my drawing. I love it."

As Kinzie left the room, she felt sad, because maybe it

would be a long time before her mom ever went to church. But until then she would do what the pastor asked her to do. She would pray for her mommy.

That one day soon she would find her happy-ever-after.

🌿 🌿

Ellie had a feeling that tonight's bedtime routine would take longer than usual. She sat on the edge of Kinzie's twin bed and waited for her to brush her teeth. The day had been long and marked with emotion. Kinzie wanted so badly for her to go to church, and as always, Ellie got out of it by claiming she had to vacuum and do laundry. Sunday was cleaning day. But her daughter was learning more at Sunday school, learning about people who run away from Jesus. She was getting old enough to understand that cleaning could happen on another day.

Kinzie came in from the bathroom, her pink flannel nightgown swishing around her ankles. She smiled at Ellie, but as she folded back the covers and slipped into bed, her eyes looked troubled. Ellie ran her hand along her daughter's blond hair. "So, Kinz, you want to talk about anything?"

A serious look crossed her daughter's face. "Anything?"

"Sure." Ellie tilted her head, wanting desperately to connect. "Whatever you want."

"Okay." She blinked a few times, the way she did when she was nervous. "Did you ever believe in Jesus? When you were a little girl, like me?"

Ellie kept her smile. "I did." Her tone was kind, gentle. "Believing was part of my life back then."

"So," she paused, "now you don't believe?" She looked heartbroken at the possibility.

"Well." Ellie felt tears in her eyes. "Not like I used to."

Kinzie let that sink in. "Are you mad at Jesus?"

"Hmmm." She hadn't really thought about it before. "I'm not sure." Who was she mad at? Her parents, of course. And yes, maybe even Jesus. He could've prevented all this, right? Kinzie was waiting for an answer. "I guess life just got hard. With my mommy and daddy."

"When they broke up and your daddy moved you here?"

"Yes." Ellie had long ago explained why there was no grandma or grandpa in Kinzie's life. "It's hard to believe sometimes." Answering the questions was like walking through a minefield. Ellie breathed deep and remembered to smile. "Anything else, sweetie?"

For a long time Kinzie looked at her. The sweetness in her eyes was back. "I'm sorry, Mommy. That it's hard to believe." She sat up and kissed Ellie's cheek. "I'm praying for you every day."

"Thank you." Ellie searched her daughter's eyes, the innocence and faith there. "Keep praying. I know it helps."

"I will." Kinzie nodded and yawned at the same time. "I love you always."

"I love you forever." Relief flooded Ellie's soul. The exchange was something they'd read in a book once, and ever since then it had been their special way to say good night. She rubbed Kinzie's back till she fell asleep. Enough talk about faith and believing.

Ellie tiptoed out of the room and shut the door behind her. With everything in her, she wanted one thing—to pile the two of them into the car and drive east. As long and far as she could without stopping, just drive and play the radio and think and cry. It wasn't weighing on her only lately. Her birthday had made her think about her dad again. How he must have felt, living on his own, and how sad it was that the two of them hadn't talked. Other than Kinzie and Tina and Tiara, Ellie had no one. Her roommate was still awake, and Ellie found her in the kitchen.

Tina studied Ellie as she walked up. "Everything okay?"

"Just a long night." Now wasn't the time to go into it. She didn't want to talk about church or God or the reasons she struggled to believe. "I need to take a drive. Think about life."

"You're not doing it again, are you?" Tina gave her a look that demanded truth.

"What?" Ellie crossed her arms.

"You know what. Thinking about Nolan Cook." Tina shook her head. "You have to let that go. You were kids, Ellie."

"I know we were kids. It was a lifetime ago." Her tone was more defensive than she intended. She forced herself to whisper so she wouldn't wake up the girls. "Of course I still think about him. His name and picture are everywhere."

"I'm just saying . . ." Tina's expression was filled with compassion. "You can't move on while you're clinging to a fantasy."

Even Tina didn't know about the tackle box or the letters or the significance of June first. Ellie took her keys from the hook on the wall. "Thanks, Tina."

"Don't be mad." Tina followed her to the door. "I only want to help."

Ellie stopped and faced her friend. "I know. That's why I need to drive. So I can figure out why I haven't moved on."

"I'll pray for you. That you can figure out a way to let him go."

Ellie didn't want to hear that. Who did Tina think she was, offering to pray? Like she was better than Ellie? Her anger grew with every heartbeat. She needed to leave before she said something that would hurt them both. Not until she was in her car and halfway down the street did she think again about what Tina had said. Nolan was a fantasy . . . she would pray for Ellie to let him go. She tightened her grip on the steering wheel and her knuckles turned white in the moonlight. That's all Nolan was in Tina's mind? A fantasy?

She took a deep breath and exhaled with deliberate calm. Tina knew only Nolan Cook, the famous NBA player. If she'd seen Ellie and Nolan sitting under their old oak tree all those years ago, she would have understood. Nolan Cook was not a fantasy. He wasn't.

The thought shin-kicked at the edges of her conscience. Or was he? Who was she kidding? Nolan lived in a different world from the one they shared when they were fifteen. He was one of the most sought-after millionaires in the country. If he remembered her, it was probably only on occasion, and if he could see her now, a single mom unwilling to attend church with her little girl, Ellie knew exactly what he'd think. He'd be sad that life had changed Ellie Tucker, and then he'd wish her the best. He would probably offer to pray for her—like everyone else in her life—and that would be that.

No wonder Tina's comment hurt so badly. Regardless of what Ellie wanted to believe or what she sometimes let herself believe, the truth was blatantly obvious. Nolan Cook would never be interested in her now.

She was two miles away from her apartment before she realized she was headed toward her father's house. The one that belonged to Ellie's grandmother before she was moved to a nursing facility. When Ellie and her dad first moved to San Diego, they ate most dinners at her grandmother's house. The old woman never liked Ellie's mom; everyone in the family knew that much. Quickly, it became clear to Ellie that her grandmother didn't care much for her, either. It was the reason Ellie hadn't given Nolan her grandma's address as a way of keeping in touch. If mail came from Savannah, her grandma probably would have thrown it away.

Her grandma would talk about Ellie's mom and how terrible she was for walking out on her family and how she was too beautiful. Then she'd say that Alan had better be careful, because Ellie looked just like her mother. On and on and on her ranting criticisms would go. Back then every awful thing she said or alluded to forced Ellie to remember a different happy time with her mom, some special memory. Just so she wouldn't forget the way her mom really was. Or the way she had been before her affair.

But eventually, even Ellie's memories couldn't offer a defense for her mother's behavior. After a year when her mom didn't attempt to contact her, Ellie had no choice but to acknowledge the truth—her mother had changed. She no longer loved her the way she once did. First her grandma, then her mother, and finally her father all turned away from her. By the time Ellie walked out of her father's life, she had no one to call family.

No one but Kinzie.

Ellie kept driving, heading toward the little clapboard house. The one she had avoided for the past seven years. She wasn't sure what compelled her to drive here tonight. Whether it was the conversation with Kinzie, or the questions about why she didn't believe like she used to, or the eleven-year mark drawing close.

Whatever it was, she became more determined with every mile to see the house and maybe even park for a while. Watch for the man inside who had given up on ever reconciling with her. She didn't think about the absence of her parents every day, but the evidence was always with her. They had moved on, as if they'd never had a daughter. Sure, her parents' lives were messy. Her mom lonely, drawn to an affair. Her dad brokenhearted, controlling and dominating, always assuming the worst of Ellie.

But that didn't excuse them.

Suddenly, Ellie was consumed with curiosity. How did her father spend his nights, alone in the little house? Did he come home from a day of bossing people around and fall asleep in front of the TV? Or did he read his Bible all night and remind himself how right he'd been, how much he was a victim of his wife's unfaithfulness and his daughter's rebellion?

She turned down her grandmother's street, and as she neared the house, she killed her headlights. The closer she came, the slower she drove until she was parked in the dark shadows just out front. Sure enough, lights were on inside, and after Ellie watched for five or six minutes, her dad passed by the window. He carried a large box, and she watched him set it on the sofa in the front room. For a while he stood there, staring at it. Then he sat down and pulled something from it.

Ellie's heart raced, and her palms felt damp against the steering wheel. He still looked fit and handsome, a decade younger than most men his age. Fresh hurt and anger rushed to the surface. Why didn't he do something to fix their family? This was her father, after all. How did he live his life every day without trying to make things right with her, his only child? Or with his wife? A sick feeling came over her. She hadn't done anything to bridge the gaps, either. How did *she* live this way?

Her dad seemed consumed by the box and whatever it held. Ellie had no idea what he was doing, and she wondered at the timing that would randomly lead her here and allow her to see this scene play out. Maybe he was going through old pictures, something from his past. Their past. The box was too big to be bills or mail, but it might be full of scrapbooks or yearbooks or photo albums. She had a feeling the box held something purposeful, or he wouldn't have brought it out to the sofa to look through it.

Before they moved to San Diego, Ellie had spent years praying for her parents. That they'd stop fighting and get along the way they used to. That they'd laugh and love again. Night after night after night. She narrowed her eyes. What good had it done? Her mom still had the affair and her dad still lived in his bitterness. The two of them had let her go without a chase. Now she wondered if the box held some window to the past for her father. Ghosts from happy days gone by. Maybe the loneliness without his wife and daughter bothered him more than his silence let on.

She pictured him the way he'd been before they left Savannah. His hug at the end of a day, how he'd taught her how to ride a bike. Even when they moved—as badly as Ellie wanted to stay in Savannah, she believed she and her dad would be okay. And at first he was. His words were kind and helpful, encouraging. He listened to her talk about being let down by her mom and about missing Nolan.

Things changed when she started school. Instead of a hug, he greeted her at the end of the day with questions. A year later, the questions became accusations. *Who were you with? What does he want from you? Why were you out so late? You were drinking, weren't you? Let me smell your breath. If you're doing something with those boys, you need to tell me. You know what'll happen, Ellie . . . you'll wind up pregnant, just like your mother.*

Enough.

She ordered the battering memories to stop. If only he'd really known her. The way she never crossed a single line, never cussed or drank or did anything with boys, not until she graduated from high school. By then she felt guilty every time she was around her father, constantly compelled to prove him wrong.

At a James Taylor concert in the park that summer with her girlfriends, Ellie met C.J. Andrews, a handsome soldier six months from being sent to Iraq. He kept her out late at night and told her things she was desperate to hear. He was in love with her, and he'd waited all his life to meet a girl like her, and he would do anything for her. She was young and naive and inexperienced. On their fourth date, he took her back to his apartment and promised her they wouldn't go too far. The promises didn't stop until she had given him everything she had to give.

As soon as she got out of bed, she ran to the bathroom and threw up. Disgust and fear and filth crashed together inside her, and she demanded he take her home. He only flopped into a chair by his bed. "I'm not taking you anywhere."

Ellie had analyzed that terrible night a thousand times, and always she came to the same conclusion. C.J. really thought she'd stay, that he was some sort of gift she couldn't walk away from. But that was exactly what she did. She left his house that night and walked four miles back to her house. The whole time she couldn't think about what had just happened or how he'd lied to her or what she'd done.

She could only think about Nolan.

How much she missed him and how she wanted to find him in the worst way. She would tell him what happened and ask him to pray with her, to help her find her way back to the innocence of that Savannah summer. But she couldn't bring herself to call him.

When she got home that night, her father was waiting up, and for the first time, his accusations were right. *Only a harlot stays out this late, Ellie. Where've you been, and who've you been with?* Ellie only stared at him, blinking. Then she ran to her room and barely came out for the next two months.

By then she knew something was wrong. Her period was late, and she felt sick to her stomach in the mornings. She bought a pregnancy test, and as soon as she had the results, she told her father. There was no point in hiding it from him. She half expected him to kill her. And that would be that. Instead, he pulled out the Bible and forced her to listen to twenty Scriptures on sexual sin and giving in to the flesh. He told her she wouldn't be allowed out of the house until she could live a godly life.

His accusations and criticism made it impossible to breathe. That night she packed her things and—just like her mother— she left Alan Tucker for a new life without him. By then Ellie had already started classes at the same beauty school Tina attended. She walked to Tina's apartment and knocked on the door.

Her friend took one look at her and pulled her close, hugged her, and welcomed her in without asking questions. Twice, after she'd finished beauty school for the day, her father was standing outside waiting for her. Both times he admonished her, told her she needed to repent and get back into church if she wanted a chance at eternal life.

Every word came rapid-fire, and Ellie remembered the feeling. How her father didn't need a gun to kill her. He had the

Bible. After his last attempt to save her from hell, he stopped trying.

With Tina at her side, Ellie had her baby, and a few months later, she got word that C.J. had been killed. She didn't attend his memorial service. As far as she was concerned, the only part of him that mattered lived in the form of her baby girl. And so began the rest of her life. Through the constant missing of Nolan, Ellie had one reason to live.

Kinzie Noah. The baby girl neither of Ellie's parents had ever met.

Tears filled her eyes, and the image of her dad on the sofa next to the cardboard box grew blurry. She eased her car back onto the road and flipped on her headlights. Enough time in the past.

The ghosts were suffocating her.

Chapter Fourteen

Ryan Kelly had found her.

On his first day off from touring with Peyton Anders, he located the doctor's office where Caroline Tucker worked. It wasn't hard, really. He Googled Savannah and found a listing for every doctor's office. Sixteen calls later, he dialed a number and said the same thing he said every time someone picked up. "Caroline Tucker, please."

"She's at lunch." The voice on the end didn't hesitate. "Can I help you?"

"Uh . . ." The response had surprised him. "That's okay. I'll . . . I'll call back." When he hung up, Ryan pulled his notepad close and scribbled the doctor's name and contact information. He checked the tour schedule. They had a month left on the road, but tomorrow they were playing the Savannah Civic Center. Chills ran down his neck and arms as he went looking for Peyton.

Ryan knocked on the singer's dressing room door.

Peyton sounded distracted. "Come in."

Ryan opened the door and stepped inside. The singer had a

can of beer in his hand, and he was looking over a spreadsheet. He grinned at Ryan. "We're making a fortune on this tour." He held up the document. "Proof positive." He crossed the room and took a spot on one of the couches. "You need to talk?" He took a long swig of beer and stared at his spreadsheet again.

Ryan waited, allowing the moment the seriousness it deserved. "I found her."

Peyton kept his eyes on the numbers. "Who?"

"Caroline." Ryan watched for the singer's reaction. "Caroline Tucker."

Slowly, Peyton lowered the paper and set it on the coffee table. "I never asked you to find her."

"I wanted to." Ryan wasn't worried about Peyton's reaction. If things got bad between them, he didn't need the job. Studio work was waiting for him back home. "I haven't talked to her, but I'm going to see her when we're in Savannah."

Peyton massaged his temple and then the bridge of his nose. "I never should've told you."

"There could be a child involved." Ryan paused, containing his frustration. "If she had the baby, if she kept it, wouldn't you want to know?"

"Truthfully?" He lifted his eyes to Ryan. "No. I'll never see the child. Why would I want to know?"

Ryan took the couch adjacent to the one Peyton sat on. He sat at the edge of the cushion and lowered his voice. "You have an obligation."

"Yeah, well," Peyton muttered the words. "She should've protected herself." He took a drink from his beer. "It's not my fault."

Ryan felt sick. "I'd like you to go with me. I know where she works."

Peyton hesitated. Then he leaned toward a built-in drawer, jerked it open, and pulled out what looked like a checkbook. Without explaining himself, he took a pen from the same drawer and scribbled something fast and furious across the front of the top check.

He ripped it from the book and handed it to Ryan. A quick glance showed that it was for twenty thousand dollars.

Ryan folded it. "She may not want it."

"You can offer." For the first time since Ryan entered the room, Peyton's expression softened. "I'd feel better if she took it." He stood and pulled another beer from the small refrigerator. He looked over his shoulder at Ryan. "Want one?"

"I don't drink."

"Right." Peyton popped the top and returned to his chair. For a long time he didn't say anything. "You excited about the show? It's sold out."

"I'm still thinking about Caroline Tucker." Ryan stood and stuck his hands in the pockets of his jeans. "Maybe you should think about her, too." He walked toward the door.

"Wait."

Ryan slipped the check into his shirt pocket and looked back. "Yes?"

"Tell her . . . tell Caroline I'm sorry."

His words caught Ryan off guard. "I will." As he left Peyton's bus, Ryan was encouraged. God had put him on this tour for a reason.

He believed he would know why before the last show.

Five minutes before Caroline's lunch break, Ryan walked into the doctor's office where she worked and approached the front desk. Only one woman worked behind the counter, and Ryan guessed it was her. Even now, in her early or mid-forties, the woman was beautiful.

"Hi." He kept a professional demeanor. "Are you Caroline Tucker?"

"Yes." She positioned herself in front of her computer. "Checking in?"

"No." He wanted to explain himself quickly. He looked around to make sure no one was watching. "I'm a guitar player for Peyton Anders."

Her hands slowly fell from the keyboard. "Why . . . are you here?"

"Peyton told me about what happened. My wife and I . . . we wanted to find out what happened to you. Whether you were okay."

Shame colored the woman's face, and she folded her hands tightly together. She looked over her shoulder and then back at Ryan. "Could you wait outside? I have a break in two minutes."

"Definitely." Ryan walked outside and leaned against the redbrick wall. The woman must've been shocked. Peyton said over a decade had passed since the two of them had talked. A few minutes later, Caroline came outside. She was shaking despite the afternoon sunshine. Ryan spoke first. "Can I take you for coffee?"

She looked doubtful, afraid, even. "I'll drive."

"Fine." Ryan understood how the situation must've looked. A stranger walks into her office and asks about her affair with Peyton Anders? Of course Caroline was guarded. Ryan followed her to her car. *Lord, use me to help her.*

They drove in silence to a coffee shop a mile away. He paid for their drinks and sandwiches, and they sat at a table in the back corner of the room. She held her nervous hands in her lap and stared at him. "How did you find me?"

"Peyton said you worked at a doctor's office in Savannah."

She unwrapped her sandwich and took a bite. Then she folded her arms, hugging her elbows to her thin body. "What does he want?"

"Nothing." Ryan needed to get to the point. "Did you keep the baby, the one you had with him?"

Outrage sparked in her eyes, but it faded as quickly as it came. In its place was fear. "I have a son. He's ten."

Ryan felt his heart sink. "Peyton said your marriage . . . it was in trouble back then."

"Of course. My husband . . . he was the love of my life. We grew distant. We let things fall apart." A sound more cry than laugh came from her. "Peyton was a diversion. It . . . lasted two years." She looked more nervous than before. "Why is he talking about it now?"

"I don't think he told anyone else." Ryan had no proof, but he believed it, anyway. "My wife and I, we both prayed about you, about the situation. Peyton has a show here tonight."

"I know." Caroline looked down, her shame tangible. "I'm glad he didn't come see me."

Ryan wasn't sure what to say. When he finished his sandwich, he pulled the check from his wallet. "Here." He handed it to her. "Peyton wanted you to have this."

Caroline looked confused. Several seconds passed after she opened it before anger set in on her features. She ripped the check in half and in half again and dropped the pieces on the table in front of Ryan. Her eyes grew damp, and her hands shook harder than before. "The guy's a millionaire, and he thinks he can *buy* me off? For twenty thousand dollars?" She smoothed her hands over her black slacks. "You tell him he can have his money."

"I'm sorry." Ryan was angry with himself. Maybe he shouldn't have come. "Peyton wanted me to tell you he was sorry."

She lifted her chin, clearly trying to preserve whatever dignity remained. "My son and I are fine. You tell him that. We don't need his pity or his money." She breathed out and waited. Fifteen seconds . . . thirty. Gradually, he watched a calm come over her. "We have our faith in God. And we have each other."

Ryan felt his heart respond. "My wife and I, we're believers, too. Is there anything we can do, anything we can pray about?"

For a single moment Caroline looked like she might dismiss the possibility, deny needing anything, even prayer. But as she stared out the window, tears spilled onto her cheeks. She sniffed and faced Ryan again. "Please . . . pray for my daughter. I lost touch with her after . . ." A series of small sobs caught in her throat, and she covered her face with her hands.

The woman's torment was as real as the air between them. *You led me to look for her, God, to see if she was okay. Show me how I can help. . . show me my part in this.*

Ryan waited, and finally, she took the napkin from the table and pressed it to her eyes. "I'm sorry."

"It's okay. I have time."

She sniffed again and took a few sips of her coffee. "Thank you." Again she looked out the window. "My affair with Peyton . . ." Her eyes found his. "I lost my family over it. When I told my husband what happened . . . and that I was pregnant, he blew up. He kicked me out." She wiped at another couple of tears. "Two days later, he took our daughter and moved across the country to San Diego. She was fifteen." Caroline held the napkin to her face again. Seconds passed before she could find the rest of the words. "Ellie and I . . . we haven't talked since."

Ryan worked on his espresso. The weight of her confession settled around him like so many sandbags.

"My affair cost me everything."

Ryan had questions, but he wanted to wait, to give the moment the space it deserved. "I'm sure she misses you."

"I don't think so." Caroline seemed to gather herself, as if trying to find her way back to the controlled and collected woman she'd been at the doctor's office. But her tears kept falling. "I've written to her. A letter every week since she left."

"You know her address?"

"Alan's mother lives in San Diego. I send the letters to her house. They've never been returned. I have to assume Ellie is getting them." Caroline pressed the napkin to her face again. "She's never written back." The sounds of the coffee shop filled the moment. Caroline's grief looked like it could kill her. "Ellie lost a lot, too. She didn't have a choice about the move. Her best friend—" She stopped short. Almost like she didn't want to say too much. "He was a basketball player at their high school. They were very close. As far as I know, they lost touch, too."

Ryan searched his brain. How could he help her? And why had God placed him here? He didn't want to bring up the money again, but he had to ask. "Peyton's money . . . it would at least help you find Ellie."

"I don't want his money." She spoke the words as if they were poison, as if she couldn't wait to get them out of her mouth. Another few sips of her coffee, and she looked more composed. "I've been saving, but it doesn't matter. I've called around, searched the Internet for her." Fresh tears filled her eyes, and her fingers trembled again. "She doesn't want to be found." Caroline's voice faded. "It's not about the money."

He understood. They had run out of coffee and conversation. Ryan knew only one thing to do. "Can I pray with you?"

She folded her hands in her lap and hung her head. "Please."

Ryan leaned closer, his voice quiet. "Father, we ask for a miracle, that You would bring Caroline's daughter back into her life and that You would erase the years of hurt and loneliness and pain between them." He paused. "You know where Ellie is. Please use Caroline's letters to change Ellie's mind and bring her back. We ask for a miracle of reconciliation. In the powerful name of Jesus, amen."

Caroline didn't say anything, and as Ryan opened his eyes, he understood why. She was crying again, using the napkin to hide her face. As if an ocean of tears could never adequately express her sadness over losing her daughter. When Caroline could speak, she stood and thanked Ryan. Then she pointed to the restroom. "I need a minute. I have to get back to work."

"I'll keep praying. My wife and I. If it's any consolation, we both think God is working on Peyton."

"Pray that He'll work on my husband's heart." Tears shone in her eyes. "I don't want Peyton Anders. I want my family back."

Ryan understood. "I'll pray for that." He gave her his number. "If my wife and I can do anything, please call."

He left wondering about the past hour and why God had crossed their paths. Was Ryan supposed to help find Caroline's daughter? He called Molly on the way back to the venue. She had good news. A connection had been made between the Atlanta Hawks and the sick little boy whose family was working with her foundation. Since Peyton Anders had a four-day break after tonight's show, the boy's dream was set to take place in forty-eight hours—provided there was a Game 6 in the series.

Ryan would meet up with Molly and the boy and his family, and they would connect with Nolan Cook before the tip-off. Then the boy and his family would have courtside seats for the game. Ryan could hardly wait.

Especially after the heartbreaking coffee with Caroline Tucker.

Chapter Fifteen

The zoo day was Kinzie's idea, but Ellie was grateful for it. She needed a reason to stop thinking about her father sitting alone in his living room. A reason to get her mind off the first of June and how, in a few weeks, the date would pass and that would be that. Their last chance gone, the whole idea nothing more than silly kid stuff.

They set out on the path toward the lions, and Kinzie skipped beside her. She wore a white sundress with pink flowers to match her pink tennis shoes. "This is the bestest day ever, Mommy. Know why?"

"Why?" Ellie wondered if she should've worn shorts instead of the cropped pants she'd chosen. The morning sun was already hot on their backs.

"First, it's so sunny." Kinzie shaded her eyes. "Bestest days have to be sunny." She giggled and slipped her hand into Ellie's. "Second, we're on a 'venture. Because lions and tigers and bears is like *The Wizard of Oz,* and that's the number-one 'venture of all time."

The two of them had watched *The Wizard of Oz* last Saturday during a thunderstorm. Rain had kept the skies cloudy most of the week. "I think you're right." Ellie smiled at the blue sky. "This is a perfect day. Sunshine and adventure, and you know the best part?"

"What?" Kinzie had lost her right front tooth a few nights ago. Her grin was adorable.

"Being with you." Ellie swung her daughter's hand as they came up to the lion exhibit. "That's what I like best."

The lions at the San Diego Zoo had been in the news lately. One of the lionesses had given birth to three cubs, and the family was on display for patrons. People were gathered around the stone wall surrounding the rocky exhibit. Ellie and Kinzie slipped into an open spot. Sure enough, the baby lions were playing a few feet from their mother.

"Oooh." Kinzie put both hands on bars above the wall and peered over as far as she could. "They're so cute, Mommy." She blocked the sun from her eyes and looked from one side of the lions' area to the other. "Where is he?"

"Who, baby girl?" Ellie put her arm around Kinzie's small shoulders and followed her daughter's gaze. "Who are you looking for?"

"The daddy." She pointed to the lion cubs and their mother. "They're only half a family, see? The daddy's missing."

Her words cut straight to Ellie's heart. She tried not to react. "The daddy's around. He's probably sleeping in the shade."

"Oh." Kinzie stared at the cubs for a long time. "They look happy." She smiled up at Ellie. "Even without their daddy."

"I think so." Ellie could've dropped to the ground and cried. Kinzie rarely brought up their situation, how her life wasn't like that of many of her classmates who lived in houses and had a mother and father and siblings. The girl was happy and whole. She loved Tina and Tiara, and she didn't question what she didn't have.

But here the comparison was obvious.

After several minutes, Kinzie stepped back. "Let's find the tigers."

"Okay." They started walking, holding hands like before. "Kinz . . . did that make you sad, that the lion cubs didn't have their daddy around?" The walk to the tigers was halfway across the zoo. They had time.

"Sort of." Kinzie walked a little slower, the skip in her step gone. "Most kids have a daddy."

There it was. Ellie spotted a bench ahead, just off the path and shaded from the sun by an overgrown maple tree. "Let's sit for a minute."

Kinzie's smile didn't fade. "Okay. My feet are hot."

"Mine, too." Once they were on the bench, Ellie turned a little so she could see her daughter. "Do you ever think about *your* daddy?"

For a few seconds, Kinzie was quiet. "Sometimes." She squinted up at Ellie. "Is that okay?"

"Of course." She reached for her daughter's hand again. "Do you have questions about him?"

"Yes." She shrugged, her spirits visibly lower. "I don't wanna ask, because I don't want you to be sad."

Ellie felt awful. In her own frustration, she had created a silence in Kinzie, an inability to raise the questions in her heart about something as serious as her father. An idea took root in Ellie's heart. "How about this . . ." She smiled, despite the tears gathering on the inside. "Let's have today be a question day. We'll walk to the tigers and the bears, and along the way, you can ask any question you want."

A sparkle danced in Kinzie's eyes. "Really?"

"Really." Ellie stood and smiled. Her own heartache over the way she had failed Kinzie could wait until later. For now she wanted her daughter to feel as free as possible. "Any question at all."

They held hands and started walking again. Kinzie smiled, but the sadness in her eyes returned. "Anything?"

"Anything."

"Okay." Her tone was serious. Clearly, she had questions. "My daddy was a soldier, right?"

"Right."

"He died in the war?"

"He did." Ellie kept their pace slow. The zoo was getting crowded, and most of the visitors hurried past them. Ellie and Kinzie were in their own world. "He died a hero." It was the explanation she'd told Kinzie before. Her father was a soldier. He died fighting to keep America safe, and because of that, he was a hero. Until now that had been enough.

"Okay, Mommy. Here's my question." She slowed a little more. "How come you and Daddy never got married?"

Ellie wasn't sure she was up to this, but she owed it to Kinzie. No matter how she felt. *Keep it light, Ellie. Don't give her more than she's asking for.* "I didn't know Daddy that long. He had to go to Iraq a few months after I met him."

"But . . . you had a baby with Daddy."

Ellie wanted to do anything to steer the conversation away from Kinzie's father. If she believed in prayer, this would've been a good time to talk to God. Instead, she drew a deep breath and tried to find the right words. "Sometimes, Kinz, two people can think they love each other when really it's too soon to know if love is there or not."

"So . . . you didn't really love my daddy?"

"I thought I did."

Kinzie was quiet for a while. "Did you ever love a boy, Mommy?"

They were getting closer to the tigers, but they still had a lot to talk about. Again they sat on a bench in the shade. Ellie looked straight into her daughter's eyes. "I did."

"But not Daddy?"

"No, sweetie. Your daddy wasn't ready to love. He was . . . too young."

"Oh." Kinzie seemed content with that. "You loved a different boy?"

"Yes." Ellie wasn't sure how much to say. But if Kinzie asked, then she had a right to know. At least the broad strokes. "I loved him very much."

Conversations and voices from other visitors made it hard to hear Ellie's little-girl voice, but the moment seemed somehow protected, as if, in all the busy zoo, there were just the two of them. "What was his name?"

"Nolan." Ellie watched her daughter's face for a reaction. "Nolan Cook."

Kinzie stopped cold. She looked up at her mom, her mouth open. "Isn't he famous?"

"He is." Ellie stopped and ran her hand down Kinzie's light blond hair. "He plays professional basketball."

"That's what I thought." Her mind was obviously racing. "Two boys in my class talk about him all the time." She thought for a few seconds. "Does he love you, too?"

"Well . . . he might have." Ellie could see herself sitting beneath the old oak tree, feel Nolan Cook beside her again on that hot summer night. "A long time ago, maybe. We were only fifteen."

"Still . . . Does he love someone else? Like does he have a wife?"

"He doesn't." Ellie took her daughter's hand, and they started walking again. She never for a moment imagined they would talk about Nolan today. Maybe she shouldn't have said anything. "I don't know if he loves someone or not. But we haven't talked in more than ten years. He's got a different life now."

"Does he know where we live?"

"No." The questions came so quickly Ellie struggled to keep up. "I'd say for sure he doesn't know where we live."

"Mommy!" She stopped again, her eyebrows raised halfway up her forehead. "You should call and tell him!"

"Kinz, it isn't like that." They reached the tigers. "He doesn't remember me, baby. We can't talk about him, okay? No one knows about Nolan and me."

That concept was more than Kinzie could absorb: She made a confused face. "Other people talk about him."

"We can't tell anyone that I used to love him." Ellie used a sterner look this time. "Understand?"

Kinzie's enthusiasm fell off some. "Yes, Mommy."

"Okay, then." Ellie breathed deep and pointed. "Look! The tigers!"

For the next ten minutes, Kinzie forgot about asking questions, too caught up in the tigers and their stripes and how two of them seemed to want to fight. "They're the biggest cats ever!" Her eyes were practically round. "I didn't think they were this big in person."

"They're huge."

Kinzie tilted her head. "I wish I could pet one."

"Me, too." Ellie made a face. "Probably wouldn't be a good idea."

Kinzie laughed out loud. "They'd eat us up to pieces, Mommy. That definitely wouldn't be a good idea."

Eventually, they set off for the bears, and Kinzie started in again. "What about your mommy? How come you never talk about her?"

Here we go. Ellie pushed back the ocean of sorrow attached to the topic. Kinzie had no grandparents, none whatsoever. Ellie had never met C.J.'s parents. She didn't know anything about them. And since C.J. had wanted nothing to do with his daughter, Kinzie's birth certificate used Ellie's last name.

The child looked up at her, waiting. Ellie dug deep, searching for a strength she didn't feel; Kinzie deserved an answer. "My mom moved in with another family."

Alarm filled Kinzie's face. She had never asked about Ellie's mother before, and now there was no doubt the answer was troubling. "You mean she left you and became the mommy for someone else?"

Ellie thought about that. "Yes." Her mother had been pregnant with someone else's baby, so yes, that was true. "Something like that, sweetie. We didn't have a lot of time to talk about it. My mom moved in with another family, and two days later, my daddy moved me to San Diego."

"Here?" Kinzie seemed surprised. "So your daddy lives here?"

"Yes."

The questions on Kinzie's face were obvious before she put words to them. "Why don't we see him, Mommy? He's my grandpa, right?"

"He is. But he's mad at me." She smiled, trying to downplay the situation.

"Why?" Kinzie lowered her brow, clearly upset. "Why would he be mad? You're the best mommy in the world."

The compliment soothed the desperate pain inside Ellie. "Thanks, baby." She ran her hand down Kinzie's back. "He's mad because I had a baby before I got married."

"Oh." Again her expression sank. "So is he mad at me, too?"

"No, sweetie. Not at all." Ellie stopped and stooped down so that she was face-to-face with her daughter. "Never think that. This has nothing to do with you."

Kinzie was quiet, searching Ellie's eyes.

Ellie tried again. "He was mad at me, so I left. Once you were born, things got busy." Her mouth was dry. The moment was too important to get it wrong. "I guess . . . he should come and find me if he's not mad at me anymore."

Still more questions filled Kinzie's eyes, but it took her a little while to voice the one that must have been the most pressing. "What if I want to see him?"

Ellie grabbed at the only answer that worked. "Maybe you should talk to God about that. Then someday that might happen, Kinz."

Her eyes softened, and a smile tugged at her lips. "Okay, Mommy. That's what I'll do."

Ellie straightened again, and they walked to the bear exhibit. There were supposed to be four bears in the facility, but they could see only one. He was in a deep pond, batting at a ball floating on the surface of the water. They watched him for several minutes while he kept batting, trying to catch it in his enormous paws. Each time it spun away on the water's surface, elusive.

Kinzie stood next to her, resting her chin on the steel bar as she watched the bear in action. "Bears are like people, Mommy."

"How come?"

She lifted her sweet face to Ellie. "Because even if they try, they don't always get what they want."

"That's true." The comment hung on the walls of Ellie's heart for the next few hours as they moved on to the reptiles and primates. Kinzie seemed finished with questions, apart from another twenty or so about the animals and whether they liked living in cages—Ellie wasn't sure—and whether it was more fun living in the wild—Ellie guessed it might be.

Finally, they drove to a restaurant not far away. The place was packed, so while they waited for a table, they sat on stools near the window and sipped Cokes. A TV nearby was showing a basketball game. It took Ellie a few seconds to realize that one of the teams was the Atlanta Hawks.

Nolan's team.

"That's him." Ellie leaned closer to Kinzie and kept her voice low. "Nolan Cook."

"It is?" Kinzie squinted at the TV. "Oh, yeah! He plays for the Hawks! That's what the boys in my class said."

A foul was called, and Nolan went to the free-throw line. The camera captured a close-up of his face, the sweat and concentration, the determination. He bounced the ball a few times, and Ellie was instantly back in the gym at Savannah High, watching him play, mesmerized by his gift for the game.

"That's him, right?" Kinz looked from the TV to Ellie and back.

"Yes."

Kinzie grinned. "He seems nice."

"He is." Ellie smiled at her daughter. "He always was."

They watched him sink another free throw, and Kinzie took a long sip of her Coke. "I really think you should call him. You used to love him, Mommy."

"Remember? That'll just be our little secret, okay?"

She frowned, but her eyes danced. "Okay."

Their table was ready. Kinzie didn't bring up Nolan the rest of the afternoon, and Ellie was grateful. The day of open conversation had been good for them. Exhausting, but good. The problem was Ellie had the same questions as Kinzie. And no matter what words she found to pacify her daughter, when it came to Ellie's life, the truth remained.

There were no answers.

🌿 🌿

Nolan and Dexter were the last two in the locker room an hour after the Hawks' loss to Orlando. Atlanta led the series three to two, but today's game was the worst they'd played in the post-season. Nolan blamed himself.

No matter what he tried, he couldn't find the zone.

"You ever question God?" Nolan draped a towel around his neck and dropped to the nearest bench. His legs felt like rubber.

"Sure." Dexter leaned against the locker and stretched his feet out in front of him. "My wife's friend dies of cancer when we're barely out of college . . . a kid gets killed in a car accident . . . another soldier dies." He looked at Nolan. "I have a list of questions."

Nolan held on to either end of the towel. "I'm not supposed to wonder, right? I mean, I'm Nolan Cook." His soft laugh sounded sad even to him.

"You're human." Dexter took the spot beside him. He leaned forward and dug his elbows into his knees. "How'd it go the other day with the singer's daughter?"

"Kari." Nolan pursed his lips and exhaled hard. "Not great."

"Too bad." Dexter rubbed out a bruise on his left calf. "She looked nice."

"She was great." He ran the towel down one arm and then the other. "But I brought up Ellie. Like . . . it got away from me before I realized."

"Man, no . . . That's wrong." Dexter stood and paced the length of the locker room. He grabbed an ice pack from the freezer and brought it back. When he had it positioned over his calf he shook his head. "Ellie's a figment of your imagination. Call me crazy, but I don't think she wants you to find her. Otherwise she'd be leaving messages at the front office."

Nolan stared at the ground between his bare feet. Dexter was right. "I need to call her." He looked at Nolan. "Kari, not Ellie. Maybe after the play-offs."

Dexter nodded. "Yeah. After we win the title."

"Right."

"Why'd you ask about God? About having questions?"

"Just thinking about my dad."

"Mmmm. Yeah." Dexter sighed. "He should be here."

Several times when they were in college, Dexter's family had welcomed Nolan for Christmas or a few weeks of summer vacation. His teammate was one of eight kids from Detroit, and when his family got together, it was like a scene from a movie. "You're another son," Dexter's mother had told Nolan a number of times. She would pat his white cheek and Dexter's black one, and she would grin. "See the resemblance?"

Dexter's family got him through more tough times of missing his dad than Nolan could count.

"My dad would've loved this. The play-offs." Nolan noticed a bruise on his right arm. Even in a fresh T-shirt and shorts, he was still hot from the game. He might not have found the zone today, but he'd given it everything he had. He was glad they had a day off tomorrow. He stood and grabbed his basketball. "Come by later if you want. Bring your wife. The pool's ready for the summer."

"Okay." Dexter grinned. "Might take the sting off today."

"Yeah." Nolan dribbled the ball through the locker room, down the cement corridor, and through the tunnel to the court. He didn't want to tell Dexter, but finishing the play-offs had nothing to do with the timing of calling the singer's daughter. He had to get past the first of June. Maybe then he could put Ellie Tucker out of his heart for good. He dribbled to the edge of the court. Most of the lights were off, but that didn't matter. He jogged across the hardwood, found his place, and hit the shot on the first try.

Left side, three-point line.

For his dad.

Chapter Sixteen

Alan walked into Chaplain Gray's office and closed the door.

He'd been looking forward to and dreading this since he made the appointment a week ago. The two men had worked together for three years, but not once had Alan allowed the chaplain, or anyone else, to see into his heart, into the ugly, lonely reality that made up his life.

"Alan." Chaplain Gray stood and nodded. The man was military through and through, his words short and clipped despite his kind eyes. "Glad you came. Have a seat."

"Thank you"—he sat in the leather chair across from the older man—"for making time."

Chaplain Gray sat back in his seat, and for a long time he watched Alan, waiting. Finally, he folded his hands on the desk. "Tell me your story."

Alan had never thought of his messy life that way, like a story. He scrambled through the bitter details and found a starting point. The only place his story could start—at the church picnic where he met Caroline twenty-eight years ago. Alan wasn't big on flowery explanations, and he absolutely didn't want to break down. His tears had been close to the surface lately, but not here. He talked fast, so his emotions couldn't catch up. If his life were a story, he would tell the condensed version.

He caught the chaplain up to the current page in about fifteen minutes.

"A lot of broken pieces." The chaplain sat still, completely focused. "I'm sorry."

"Yes." Alan pictured Caroline and Ellie, wherever they might be. "Definitely a lot of broken pieces."

"Tell me again about the letters."

"The letters?" Alan imagined the box, the smell and heaviness in his hands. "There are hundreds."

"And Ellie knows nothing of them?"

"No." Shame burned his cheeks. What was the point, coming here and sharing this? Tears stung his eyes. He blinked. *Stay ahead of it, Tucker.*

"Have you thought about whether that's fair? To your daughter?"

Alan wasn't sure if it was the fact that he couldn't outrun his story any longer or the sound of the word "daughter"—a word he hadn't spoken or heard mentioned in reference to Ellie in years. Whatever the reason, his tears came. They flooded his eyes and flowed down his cheeks. He tried to remember the chaplain's question, but all he could remember was the word "daughter." His daughter, Ellie.

How could he have done this to her?

"Here." The chaplain's eyes softened more. He slid a box of tissues across the desk. "Do you have an answer? Is that fair to Ellie, keeping the letters from her?"

"Of course not." His words were small, trapped in the sea of sorrow filling his heart. "I'm the worst father. The worst man."

The chaplain waited a few seconds. "That's not why you came, to tell me that you're the worst father." He leaned his forearms on the wooden desktop. "You want to do something about it. Otherwise you wouldn't be here."

Alan nodded. He took a tissue from the box and ran it across his cheeks, quick and rough. He had no right to cry, no right to sympathy from himself or Chaplain Gray or anyone. Everything that had happened, all of it was his fault. He blew his nose and tried to find level ground once more. He blinked a few times and squinted. "Yes. I want to do something. I want to fix it."

The chaplain thought about that. He pulled a well-worn leather Bible closer. "Have you read John 10:10?"

Alan searched his memory. "Not lately."

"It reminds me of your story." He opened the Bible and flipped to the book of John. "It says, 'The thief comes only to steal and kill and destroy.'" He lifted his eyes to Alan's. "That's the first part."

Steal . . . kill . . . destroy. "The thief is the devil, clearly."

"Yes." Chaplain Gray frowned. "I see evidence of that throughout your story."

Evidence? Alan shielded his face with his right hand and closed his eyes. The awful words were written on every page of his life. The love he had for Caroline, the dreams they shared . . . his hope of being a loving, present husband and father . . . his relationship with Ellie . . . their family. All of it had been stolen, killed, and destroyed. When the parade of broken moments had finished filing across his mind, Alan looked at the chaplain.

The man seemed to be waiting. He looked at the Bible again. "The rest of the verse says, 'I have come that they might have life, and have it to the full.'"

Alan shook his head. "It's too late. Everything's ruined."

"You still have the letters." Chaplain Gray sat back in his chair, as if he'd said all there was to say.

"I told you. Ellie doesn't know about them."

"Maybe she should." He looked from the Bible back to Alan. "It's never too late with truth. It stands outside time."

Alan let the man's words run through him a couple of times. *Truth stands outside of time.*

Chaplain Gray seemed to see Alan's struggle. "The promises, Alan. Jesus has come to give you life to the full now. It's not too late if we follow His lead." The man looked like he could see straight through Alan. "What's God telling you to do?"

Again Alan closed his eyes. All he could see was the box of letters, the bulk of them, the enormity of them. Not telling Ellie about the letters. He wanted to think of something else God might be asking him to do. Extra prayer, maybe, or some act of service. He could join a mission trip this summer or lead a Bible study at the brig.

But deep down he knew that wasn't what God wanted from him. He winced. "You think . . . God wants me to give Ellie the letters?"

"They're hers."

Alan nodded, slightly dazed. "She'll hate me forever."

"She already does." The chaplain's wisdom was quiet and gentle, otherworldly. "Maybe God's asking you to write a couple of letters of your own."

A sick feeling grabbed at Alan's stomach. "To Ellie?"

"And Caroline." Chaplain Gray gave a light shrug. "What do you think?"

He couldn't imagine it. "What would I say?"

"Same thing you told me. How you made a mess of everything. How sorry you are."

"They would never forgive me. It's too late."

The chaplain put his hand over the open Bible. "'I have come that they may have life, and have it to the full.'" He looked at Alan for a long moment. "That's what it says. That's the truth."

Alan shook his head, and again he closed his eyes. It was impossible. Caroline was probably living a whole new life. She had rebelled against his heavy-handed faith, the way he wielded his controlling ways like a blunt sword at her and Ellie. She didn't seem to be dating Peyton Anders. At least not if the media was any indicator. And she wasn't remarried. She couldn't be, because neither of them had ever filed for divorce. Alan had never been able to go against God's plan and officially end things. The sick feeling grew worse. What a sad joke. He had gone repeatedly against God's plan for his marriage along the way. Certainly when he moved across the country from Caroline.

And every time he hadn't reached out to her since then.

What good would an apology do now? She'd think he was crazy. And if she knew about the letters, how he'd kept them from Ellie?

She'd wish him dead.

Suddenly, Alan knew as well as he knew his name that the chaplain was right. God was calling him to do everything the man had suggested. Write letters to his wife and daughter—the only women he'd ever loved. He opened his eyes and felt the resignation in his own expression.

The pastor looked subdued in an understanding kind of way. "You're ready?"

"No." Alan dreaded every aspect of what lay ahead. "But I'll do it."

"Okay, then." Chaplain Gray folded his hands. "Let's pray."

The letter to Ellie was short and to the point. Every word ripped at another piece of Alan's heart.

He sat at the dining room table, the one he'd been raised with. He had bought two cards for the occasion. A mountain scene for Caroline and a field of flowers for Ellie. Both of them blank on the inside. He held his pen over the middle of the flowered card.

> *Dear Ellie,*
>   *I should have written this years ago, and I am sure you'll hate me forever when you hear what I've done. But God has changed me, and He wants me to do this. I have to do it.*

He took a quick breath and then another. The walls were closing in. He kept writing.

>   *The box you now have contains letters from your mother. Hundreds and hundreds of letters. She's been sending them at least once a week since we left Savannah.*

His words took shape slowly, the force of them more than he could take all at once.

>   *All this time you've thought your mom didn't reach out to you. But she did, Ellie. Keeping these letters from you has been one of the worst decisions of my life. I have no*

excuses, none at all. I thought after her affair she might be a bad influence on you. That's what I told myself. But even that isn't the truth.

His heart ached, but he forced himself to move ahead.

The truth is, I felt hurt by what she'd done, and I wanted to hurt her because of it. But all I did was destroy any chance of reconciliation between us. I never took responsibility for my part in what happened, never thought about the reasons why your mother wasn't happy. I failed her, and I failed you. God has shown me that.

His tears made it hard to see. He stopped long enough to wipe his eyes.

Forgive me, Ellie. I'll be sorry as long as I live.
With a love I've never forgotten,
Dad

He put the card in the envelope, sealed it, and wrote Ellie's name across the front. Then he opened the card with the mountain scene, the one for Caroline. This letter would be harder. The harshness of his tone, the lack of concern for her tender heart, the years of leaving her alone . . . all of it pressed around his lungs. He might not survive the next few minutes.

The silence in the house gave way to the noise of his beating heart. His pounding, anxious heart. He held the pen over the white space.

Dear Caroline,

I should've written this letter a long time ago. But lately . . . well, lately, God has changed me on the inside. Changed me so that now I can see what a wretched man I've been, how terribly I treated you, and how I pushed you away.

Honestly, I don't know how I wound up here. When I look back, all I see is you and the joy and light in your eyes. You were so beautiful inside and out. I keep asking myself what sort of monster would berate you and control you and keep you locked away.

All at once the words came. He told her how the weeks and months had given way to years and how, over time, he didn't recognize who he'd become or the person he'd turned her into. He talked about Ellie and how he had controlled her, too, and then he reached the part about her affair.

I knew it was happening. You were gone so often, home late at night. I figured you had friends somewhere. But by then I saw you as one of my possessions, Caroline. I never dreamed you'd really choose someone else. Now I can't believe you didn't leave me sooner.

He wrote about being angry and wanting to pay her back and how the Pendleton offer had been on the table for weeks before she told him about the baby. With every line, he felt a layer of brick crumble from around his heart. Caroline had been the most fragile flower, tenderhearted and kind to a fault.

I wonder who you are now, Caroline, whether you've

*healed from the scars of my behavior. I pray that being
away from me helped you find your way back to the woman
you used to be. With everything in me, I want to believe
you're that girl again, the one you were before I ruined everything. I don't expect you to care about this letter or contact me. But I'm giving you my information just in case.*

The devastation of his actions, his meanness, felt like bags of
rancid trash heaped around him. Alan had no idea why he was
bothering with such a letter now. Like spitting at a forest fire.
Still, because it was what he felt God was calling him to do, he
wrote his phone number and address—the one she had been
using all along to write letters to Ellie.

Alan felt every muscle in his body tighten. The worst part
was coming. Once he wrote the next words, once she read
them sometime in the next few days, there would be no wondering whether he might ever see Caroline again or hear from
her. She would hate him. Period. He held his breath.

*I have an awful confession to make, Caroline. Something
I never should've done. Something that kills me to tell you.*

He exhaled. After a few seconds, he grabbed the slightest
breath.

*Ellie hasn't read any of your letters. From the first letter
you sent to the last and every one in between, I set them aside
in a box in my closet. I kept them from Ellie all these years.*

He couldn't breathe, but he didn't care. He didn't deserve to
live. He'd gone too far with his confession to stop now.

If you're thinking I'm a horrible man for doing this, I can only say you're right. But I had to tell you. I couldn't write you without letting you know what I've done. I don't blame you for hating me over this. But I can promise you one thing. By the time this is in your hands, Ellie will have the entire box. They belong to her. I assume the two of you haven't connected, because your letters keep coming. I can only pray, Caroline . . . maybe this will open doors between you. If that good thing could come from this, then it's worth having you hate me.

I'm sorry. I'm a changed man, and I have never stopped loving you. I don't know what else to say . . .

Forever in knowledge that I was wrong,

Alan

He read it over and wondered how she would feel, the inevitable shock on her face, her anger when she realized what he'd done with Ellie's letters. Picturing it was almost too much to take. His thoughts shifted, and he imagined Ellie's reaction when he gave her the box.

And he needed to give it to her.

His heart beat faster, and he felt faint. As if he might pass out and never wake up again. He had thought about giving her the box at the end of the week on his day off. He knew where she worked—at a salon not far from the naval base. It was the last step of completing all that God was asking him to do. Now that he'd written to Ellie and Caroline, he couldn't wait. He had to give Ellie the box of letters.

That Saturday, when she got off work, he would be waiting.

Chapter Seventeen

Ellie heard noises coming from the bedroom.

She had already gone through their nighttime routine, and usually by now Kinzie would be half asleep. But not tonight. Ellie stood in the dark hallway and peeked through her partly open bedroom door.

Kinzie was on her knees beside her bed.

A week had gone by since their zoo trip, and Kinzie hadn't missed a single night of praying. At least that's what she told her mother. But this was the first time Ellie had seen her daughter on her knees. Ellie tilted her head, touched by the scene. The wood floor had to feel hard beneath her nightgown. The window was open, but no breeze filled the room. The early summer night was hotter than usual.

Kinzie fixed the bottom of her nightgown so it wasn't bunched up. She didn't seem to have her eyes closed the way she usually did when she prayed at dinnertime. Instead, she looked up toward the window and the night sky. "Hi, Jesus." She sounded so confident that God was listening. "It's me, Kinzie. I'm back." Kinzie's voice was barely a whisper, but Ellie could hear every word. "Remember? I like to pray out loud when I'm by myself. Because it's just you and me." She adjusted her nightgown again. "I know you're with me, Jesus, because you put the stars in the sky right over my bed."

She giggled quietly and looked through the window again. "I keep thinking about Nolan Cook, the famous basketball player, and the way my mommy looked when she talked about him. If they used to love each other, then maybe they still do. Right?"

Ellie felt a chill run down her arms. Kinzie was thinking about Nolan? To the point of praying about him? She took half a step closer so she wouldn't miss a word.

"Anyway, I want to pray for my mommy." Kinzie's shoulders drooped a little. "Please help her life be happy. I know she's sad a lot. She doesn't have her family because everything is broken. And she doesn't have Nolan, either." She itched her elbow. "Most of all, Mommy doesn't have you. And that means she doesn't have her happy-ever-after."

Ellie blinked back tears. She had no idea her lack of faith mattered this much to Kinzie.

"That's all for tonight, Jesus. Thank you. Love, your new friend, Kinzie." She stood up, rubbed her knees a few times, and climbed into bed, probably satisfied with her prayer. But Ellie would never know that satisfaction, never share a moment like this with Kinzie. The fact that she couldn't join her daughter in faith and prayer was one more price she would pay for her messed-up family. Even though she didn't believe, she knew this much for sure as she finished the dishes and went to bed, and even the next day at the salon:

She would remember Kinzie's prayer as long as she lived.

❧ ❧

Ellie was on a break, organizing bottles of color on the back-room shelf, when she heard the sports announcer on TV say something about Nolan. She'd kept the channel on ESPN throughout the play-offs—especially on days like this, when the Hawks had a pivotal game. Atlanta took the series four to two over the Magic, clinching the win last week. The Eastern Conference Championship was tied at one game apiece, and today was the third game.

A win against the Celtics was critical.

Ellie dusted her hands on her apron and found an empty chair closest to the TV. Three sportscasters were lined up at a table, and the topic had turned to Nolan. "He's definitely got the nation's attention." The statement came from the older an-nouncer, a regular with ESPN for a decade.

The three bantered about Nolan's recent tweet. Ellie didn't follow him on Twitter or Facebook. She looked every now and then, but for the most part, it was enough to see him playing his heart out on TV without being privy to his thoughts and updates.

Nolan's tweet flashed on the screen.

> *I can do all things through Christ who gives me strength!*
> *Phil 4:13—Go Hawks!*

One of the announcers shook his head, clearly frustrated. "The thing is, Cook is a public figure. He has more support than any president in twenty years."

"He has haters, don't forget that." The reminder came from the older announcer.

"Haters aside, he has a great deal of support. I just think the sports field is no place for religion. Okay, sure, it's his private Twitter account, but he's got nearly five million followers. At that level, I think he should keep his faith to himself."

No one could doubt God more than Ellie, but even she felt angry at the comment. Nolan could say what he wanted on his own Twitter account. The other two announcers agreed with her. If the tweet had come from the Hawks' official account, that would be a problem. But not coming from his own.

"People don't have to follow Nolan Cook. That's their choice. You follow a celebrity in today's world because you want an inside look at his life, his feelings. A deeper look at what drives him and motivates him." The older announcer sat back firmly in his seat. He looked straight at the camera. "Nolan, you go right ahead and tweet about God. This is America." He chuckled and looked at his cohorts. "Last I checked, freedom of speech was still our right. If it's our right, then it's Nolan Cook's right, too."

The others laughed, too. None of them wanted to go too deep for too long on ESPN. Their job was to entertain viewers with details and stats about players and teams. Not veer into moral, ethical, or legal aspects of the athletes they covered. No matter how often those details became noteworthy.

"Got an inside tip that Nolan's bringing his new girl to the game tonight. Home contest against the Celtics in a crucial Game Three situation for Atlanta." The veteran tapped his pencil on the desk a few times and raised his eyebrows. "Hearts breaking wide open across America tonight. That's my guess."

Ellie felt her stomach drop and slide slowly to her feet. What was this? Nolan had a girlfriend? She moved to the edge of the chair, her eyes glued to the screen.

"Her name's Kari Garrett, daughter of award-winning Christian singer Kathy Garrett." The man pointed to the monitor, where a photo of Nolan and Kari flashed on the screen. The two were walking together on a city street at night. He had his arm around her.

They definitely looked like a couple.

Ellie listened for a few more minutes, long enough to hear how Nolan's manager had worked with Kathy's agent to set the two up.

"They seem like a perfect match, if you ask me." The youngest of the three sportscasters laughed. "With Nolan Cook off the market, the rest of us might have a chance."

The guys chuckled, nodding in agreement.

Ellie didn't move, didn't blink. Her eyes were dry, because the news was exploding like a hollow bullet through her chest. Nolan Cook had a girlfriend. She turned the channel to something else, anything else. The Food Network. Yes, that would work. She walked to the back room, her feet heavy. Her next client wasn't due for half an hour—good thing. Ellie couldn't face anyone right now, not until she had a few minutes alone.

She walked through the back door, across the parking lot, and found a spot on the curb. She planted her elbows on her knees and covered her face with her hands. He had a girlfriend? Okay, so that shouldn't surprise her. He was one of the most eligible bachelors in the country.

They'd lost touch eleven years ago. Of course he'd moved on. He must've had girlfriends in high school and in college. Not until recently had his every move been chronicled by the press. This girl might just be another in a string of girls. She let that sit in her soul for a long moment. No, that wasn't it. Nolan wasn't that kind of guy—dating one girl after another.

If he'd found a girl, if he were hanging out with Kari Garrett, then it wasn't a passing thing. It was serious. With Kari on his arm, there was no way Nolan was thinking of Ellie or wondering about their eleven-year mark. The news confirmed Ellie's greatest fears. For Nolan, she was nothing more than an old childhood friend. If he had ever tried to find her, she had made sure she wasn't available. Ellie Anne. The girl disconnected from her mother and father. The single mom.

What am I supposed to do now? She let the question blow in the drafty places of her heart. She'd been looking forward to June first, even if she hadn't admitted it to herself. It was the reason she'd been thinking about a road trip. Like maybe she and Kinzie would pile in her beat-up Chevy and head for Georgia and the tackle box buried beneath the oak tree.

No wonder she couldn't catch her breath or think straight or bear going back into the salon. She wouldn't watch another Atlanta game as long as she lived.

Somehow, against all logic or odds, she had come to believe that she wasn't the only one looking forward to the meeting. That if on the first of June she went to their old oak tree across the street from the house where he grew up, he'd be waiting. They'd dig up the box and share their letters and find out they weren't so different after all. And God Himself would smile down on the moment, and there would never again be a time when she and Nolan Cook lost touch.

Maybe the reunion between them would stop time, and all the questions Nolan had talked about that long-ago summer night really would be answered.

Somewhere in the storm cellar of her mind, she must have thought that could actually happen. And as long as the calendar didn't move them indiscriminately past June first, the idea was at least a possibility.

Until now.

❧ ❧

Her last client left just after nine o'clock. Ellie could hardly wait to get home. She had texted Tina a few times to make sure Kinzie was awake, and now if she hurried, she could read to her and hear about her day.

Ellie left through the front door. Two clients were getting their hair done, so she didn't need to lock up. She clutched a ten from her tip money in one hand and her new pepper spray in the other. One of the girls had been robbed by a couple of teens in the parking lot last week. Ellie wasn't taking any chances.

She spotted Jimbo curled up on the far end of the sidewalk. Poor guy. He looked terrible, his hair more matted than usual. She had invited him into the salon before to get his hair washed and cut. Something he loved. She would have to set up another appointment. Early next week, maybe.

The strange man popped out of the shadows on her left and slightly behind her. "Ellie."

Fear grabbed her and she spun around, her finger on the trigger of her pepper spray. His voice sounded vaguely familiar and his face—she gasped and her hand flew to her mouth. She took a few steps back. "Dad?" The word was a whisper, all that would come out.

His face looked older, but not much. He had no real wrinkles and the build of a man much younger. But there was something different about him. Something Ellie couldn't figure out. He held a large box in his arms, almost the same size as the one she'd seen him sitting next to in his living room that night a few weeks ago.

"Ellie . . . I had to come." Shame colored his eyes. He held out the box. "This . . . it's for you. It's heavy." He came a little closer. "Maybe I can carry it to your car?"

It had been seven years since she'd seen him, and he wanted to give her a box? No apology or explanation or questions about how she was? How her baby was? Anger ran cold through her veins. "What are you doing?" Her high-pitched tone gave away her sudden hurt. "How long have you been here?"

He leaned against the wall. For a few seconds he stared at the ground, and before he looked at Ellie again, he set the box near his feet. He seemed shaky, like he might faint. When he finally brought his eyes to hers, he looked ashen. "I came to tell you . . . I'm sorry."

Ellie hesitated. She was furious with him for showing up unannounced, for jumping out of the shadows. But nothing could minimize the impact of her broken-looking father apologizing to her. The way she had always hoped he someday might. She glanced down at the box and then searched his eyes. "What . . ." Her voice trembled. "What's in it?"

The question hung there for a few seconds. Her dad brought his hand to his face and pinched the bridge of his nose. He seemed to hold his breath before he exhaled and dropped his hand to his waist. "They're letters. From your mom."

Ellie felt her heart rate quicken. She looked down at the box, and this time she could see a fraction of what was inside. It was the size of a laundry basket, and it looked full to the top. She found her father's eyes again. "From my *mom*?" She swallowed, dreading the next question and instinctively knowing the answer at the same time. "For who?"

Her dad shook his head, and again his hand came to his face for a long moment. Finally, as if waging war against himself, he looked at her once more. "They're for you, Ellie. Every one of them."

Gravity ceased to exist. Ellie's world rocked hard off its axis, her ears buzzed, and she couldn't hear the rest of what he said. Her knees started to give out, and she could no longer feel the ground beneath her. What had he told her? Letters . . . something about letters. She squeezed her eyes shut, half bent over, her hands on her knees so she wouldn't collapse. If the box was full of letters . . . that her mom had written to her . . .

She stood slowly and stared at him. Her words came only with great effort. "She wrote me? All those letters?"

"Yes." His face had reached a new level of pale. Almost gray. "I'm sorry, Ellie. It was wrong of me to—"

"Since when?" Her lungs started working again, and the anger this time around was something she'd never felt before. Her voice rose, and she spoke through clenched teeth. "When did she start writing to me?"

"From . . ." He shook his head and looked at the box. His shoulders moved up a little in a pathetic shrug. "Ellie, she's been writing to you from the beginning. Since . . . since we moved here."

A tsunami of heartbreak consumed the landscape of her heart, wiping out all she had known or assumed or believed to be real over the last eleven years. Her mother—the one she thought had abandoned her—had been writing letters to her? If the box was full, then there could be a hundred inside. Maybe two or three hundred. Which meant . . . *You never gave up on me, Mom. You never stopped trying to find me.*

Ellie's anger washed away with the next wave of understanding. Tears filled her eyes, and she blinked them back. No, this couldn't be happening. She shook her head, desperate to fully grasp the revelation, searching her father's eyes. "Does she know? That you never gave them to me?"

His spirit seemed to be shattering in slow motion before her eyes. "No. She . . . she must think you've been getting them."

"All these years?" The words came loud and sharp and slow, despite the fresh tears on her cheeks. "All these years, Dad?" Her mouth hung open, anger once more taking the lead in the emotions pummeling her. "Why?"

Not even a hint of justification colored his expression. "I thought she'd be a bad influence on you." His shoulders dropped some. "It was wrong, Ellie. I know that now. God has shown me how much I hurt you and—"

"Stop!" She was shaking, no longer able to tell the difference between anger and gut-wrenching sorrow. Her world was spinning, but she couldn't back down. Not now. She pointed at him, every word slow and deliberate. "Don't you talk to me about God. Don't!"

"Ellie, I'm a different man now. That's why I had to—"

"Don't!" She shook her head. "I don't want to hear it." She stared at him, her heart slamming around in her chest. There was nothing else to say. She slipped her pepper spray into one pocket and her tip money into the other. Then she walked to the box, bent down, and heaved it into her arms.

"Here. I can help you."

She didn't respond, didn't look up. Instead, she took the box, turned her back on him, and walked to the end of the strip mall. Her father didn't follow. She set the box down and bent low, near Jimbo. "Hey, wake up." The smell of stale alcohol and sweat filled her senses. "Jimbo, it's me. Wake up."

He blinked a few times and squinted at her. "Ellie?"

She looked over her shoulder. Her dad was back near the salon, leaning against the wall, his head low. This had to be fast. She would break down here on the sidewalk if she waited another minute to get to her car. "Here." She pulled the ten from her pocket and pressed it into his hand. "Don't buy whiskey."

He took the money, his eyes welling up the way they always did when she finished a shift. "I won't."

"Not beer, either. Get milk and a burger, okay?"

"Milk and a burger." He nodded, scurrying to a sitting position and placing the money in his threadbare backpack. "Yes, ma'am."

"Okay." She stood. "See you later."

"Yes." He pressed his back against the wall, more awake. "You know what I do when I'm finished with my busy day, Ellie?"

She hesitated, feeling the urgency of getting home, getting to the box of letters. "What?"

"I talk to God about you." He dabbed at his eyes. "I ask the good Lord to bless you, Ellie."

Her heart felt his kindness in a way she needed. Especially with eleven years of her mother's letters sitting in a box at her feet. "Thanks, Jimbo." She put her hand on his shoulder. "That means a lot." She picked up the box again. "Be safe." She swapped a look with him, then crossed the dark parking lot to her car. The asphalt felt like thick sand, and she was breathing faster than she should have been. But she wasn't looking back. Not now or ever. She unlocked her car, slid the box onto the passenger seat, climbed behind the wheel, and slammed her door.

Was she dreaming? Did that really just happen? She let her head fall onto the steering wheel. How could he do this to her?

He had *lived* with her for five of those years. One season after another, her saying good morning to him over breakfast and walking past him in the hallway and wishing him good night before she headed off to bed. All without telling her the truth. How was that even possible? He'd kept her mother's letters from her all that time? The number of days and months and years screamed through her soul. Nearly eleven years? Hiding away letters her mother had written to her? How could he do that and not die from the guilt? *Breathe, Ellie . . . breathe. You'll get through this.* She lifted her head and looked at the box beside her. The large cardboard container filled with unopened letters her mom had been sending since they moved.

She started the engine and backed out of the space. And in that moment she suddenly understood why her father had looked different. It was his eyes. He no longer looked hard and angry, the way he had since they moved to San Diego. Ellie knew it with every loud, painful beat of her heart. She glanced at the spot where she'd been talking to her dad. She didn't plan to look. It just happened. The parking lot lights were bright enough that she could see him. He hadn't moved. As she drove past, she saw proof that she was right. The anger that had defined him for so long was gone. She knew because he was leaning against the wall, looking at her, and doing something she had never in all her life seen her father do.

He was weeping.

Chapter Eighteen

Nolan couldn't shake the picture, the one he'd seen in the e-mail. The eight-year-old boy should've had all his life ahead of him, but instead he had terminal cancer. His name was Gunner. Nolan couldn't remember his last name, just his first. Gunner. The kid and his family would be at the arena soon. Nolan pounded the ball on the hardwood and circled to the other side of the net. His teammates were serious, focused. Game 6 was two hours away and they were up 3–2. Beat Boston tonight, and the Hawks were in the NBA finals. Lose, and they'd be a game from elimination.

Nolan kept to himself, focused on the net. Ten quick jump shots and he made eye contact with Dexter, long enough to convey the obvious. They would do this. They would win it. They had to. One of the Celtics starters had spouted off on Twitter that they'd destroy the Hawks in Game 6. That Atlanta didn't have what it took, and Nolan Cook was overrated.

Overrated.

Nolan clenched his jaw. He wasn't losing tonight. God was with him. He would play outside his own strength and believe—absolutely believe—that when it came to basketball this season, the Lord wasn't finished with him yet. He had more ways he could shine for Christ. For Him and through Him, in His strength. Glorifying God. That was what mattered tonight.

That and Gunner.

The e-mail showed the small boy bald, with big brown eyes. The kid had two wishes. He wanted to play basketball for his high school. And he wanted to meet Nolan.

The first dream would never happen. Gunner had a month or two at best, from what his parents said in the letter. The second wish would come true today. Nolan sank a dozen free throws. The boy and his parents would be here in fifteen minutes.

So many sick kids. It was the hardest part of caring, of opening his heart and giving of himself. He wouldn't trade it. God had given him this platform, and Nolan would use it however he could. Hanging out with a sick little boy, bringing joy to a child who wouldn't live to see Christmas? Praying for him the way he would tonight? This was what playing basketball was really about. Caring was Nolan's absolute privilege.

But it wasn't easy.

Most of the kids he hosted were from Atlanta's foster care system. That or sick kids who still had a chance. So far this year he hadn't spent time with any terminal children. Not until tonight, with Gunner. Gunner, the boy who loved basketball. Nolan dribbled in for a layup, his heart heavier than the ball. It was wrong. The boy with the name that sportscasters would've loved wouldn't live to see next year's play-offs.

Nolan hit two jump shots. Tonight Gunner would give him another reason to win. Nolan was healthy, his body never better. He would play for Gunner today. God, his father, and Gunner. If that didn't give them the victory, nothing would. He shot around the three-point line, and in a blur of baskets, he heard their voices. The adults bringing Gunner in for his dream visit.

Most of his teammates had gone into the locker room to stretch and hydrate. He left the ball at the bench, toweled off, and turned toward the voices. Five people made up the group—two couples and the boy. Gunner moved slowly, but his eyes couldn't have been brighter.

"Hey!" Nolan jogged the rest of the way. He stooped down so he was eye level with the child. "You must be Gunner."

"Yes, sir." He shook Nolan's hand. "You're taller in person." He grinned up at the couple beside him. "This is my mom and dad."

"Hi." Nolan stood. Gunner's parents introduced themselves, and they all shook hands.

At that point the other couple stepped up. The blond woman was Molly Kelly, president of the Dream Foundation, and the man beside her was Ryan, her husband. In a couple of minutes, Nolan learned that Ryan was the guitarist for Peyton Anders and that he was on a short break from the current tour.

Nolan liked the couple. He wanted to find out more about Molly's foundation and how he could help. But all of that was second to the reason they were gathered here ninety minutes before game time.

A terminally ill little boy named Gunner.

Nolan walked beside the child as he showed them the training facility and weight room. A few other Atlanta players made their way out of the locker room. He introduced them, watching the child's eyes light up. Every moment that remained of his life, Gunner would remember this day.

Nolan tried to gauge how easily the boy tired, and by the time they returned to the arena, he felt confident Gunner could handle a little more. The boy's parents and Molly and Ryan trailed behind, and Nolan looked over his shoulder at the group. "Anyone up for a little ball?"

"Seriously?" Gunner spun around and looked at his parents. "Please! I'm not tired, I promise!"

His mother had happy tears in her eyes. She put her fingers over her mouth and nodded. Her husband took her other hand and coughed a few times; both of them were clearly touched. "Yes, he can play. He'll let you know when he needs to stop."

Nolan smiled. His throat was too thick to talk. He patted Gunner on the back while he found his voice. "You ready, buddy?"

"Yeah!" Gunner gave a few weak fist pumps. He ran for the ball by the Hawks' bench and dribbled it back. Nolan raised his eyebrows. The kid was good. "Look at you!" Nolan held out his hands for a pass, and Gunner bounced the ball to him. "Wow . . . you're really great!"

Gunner's dad beamed even as his eyes grew wet. "His first-grade coach said he had the ball-handling skills of a middle-schooler."

They would never know how good the boy might be or what could've happened if he hadn't gotten sick. Again Nolan struggled to find his voice. Never mind the future. Gunner had this moment, right here. That would have to be enough.

He cleared his throat. "Hey, I have an idea." He looked at Ryan and Gunner's dad. "How about two-on-two. You guys against Gunner and me." He high-fived Gunner. "Sound good?"

"Yes! Nolan's on my team!" Gunner did a celebration dance, both hands in the air, but just as quickly, he dropped them to his sides and his shoulders sank. He caught a few quick breaths. He was tiring, but his eyes stayed full of life. "Okay! I'm ready."

The contest lasted fifteen minutes, but in that time Nolan swept Gunner into his arms and lifted him high enough that he made two shots. Combined with six buckets from Nolan, the two of them were the clear winners. When it was over, Nolan crouched down to Gunner's level. "You're awesome, buddy!"

"Thanks!" An exhausted Gunner threw his arms around Nolan's neck. "That was better than the championship of the whole world!" He looked out at the empty court, seeing things that would never be. "I could probably even play for the Hawks tonight. That's how good I feel!"

His mother wiped silent tears, and Molly kept an arm around the woman's shoulders. Nolan knew one thing for sure. He would remember Gunner always. They sat down on the bench. Someone from the Hawks' office had delivered a tray of healthy snacks—grapes and string cheese and sunflower seeds. Gunner sat next to Nolan, replaying every moment of their brief game. After they ate, the boy left with his parents to get his next dose of medication.

When they were gone, Ryan talked about the timing of his days off and how glad he was to be here. "I drove in from Savannah. Had some important business there and then this. The timing was perfect."

"Savannah." Nolan could smell the summer air, feel the rough bark of the old oak tree against his back. "I grew up there."

"Really?" Ryan tilted his head. "I didn't know that."

Nolan felt the sadness in his smile. "I don't talk about it very much. The girl I was going to marry moved away when we were fifteen."

Ryan winced, but his expression said he wasn't sure if Nolan was serious. "That hurts."

"Yeah." He paused and looked down for a few seconds. "Later that year I lost my dad. Heart attack." He kept his tone light, because he barely knew these people. But he sensed that he didn't need to hide the truth. Especially with them. Pain was a part of life—something that people who worked with Molly's foundation absolutely understood.

"I think I read about that." Ryan lowered his water bottle and leaned over his knees. "Your dad was a coach, right?"

"He was." Nolan let his eyes drift to the court. Left side, three-point line. "He coached me until the night he died. I miss him every day."

"I'm sorry." Ryan reached for Molly's hand. They were both caught up in Nolan's story. "Your mom, what happened to her?"

"She's great." Nolan popped a few grapes in his mouth. "Lives in Portland near my sisters. They make it out to a few games every season."

"And the girl?" Molly smiled, her voice tender. She looked at her husband. "Sometimes someone moves, and the feelings never quite go away."

"Exactly." Nolan chuckled, but only because that was the expected response. He'd been fifteen, after all. "You sound like you know."

"Our story's a little crazy." Ryan reached for Molly's hand.

"I'd like to hear it. Maybe after the game. The front office is setting up an ice cream bar for all of you."

"Thank you." Molly's eyes shone with sincerity. "This means so much to Gunner."

"I can tell." Nolan nodded and stood, shaking their hands again. "I have to go. After the game, meet me at the bench." He had started for the tunnel when Molly called his name.

"You never said what happened with the girl."

"Oh, that?" Nolan hesitated, picturing Ellie, feeling her in his arms again. He found his smile. "She moved to San Diego with her dad. I never heard from her again." He waved. "See you soon."

And with that he reined in every emotion, every feeling and thought fighting for position in his head, and forced them into just one.

Beating the Celtics.

Chapter Nineteen

The question of Kari Garrett came up at halftime.

With the Hawks trailing by four points, three reporters asked him about her. Three sportscasters. As if they couldn't find some aspect of his game to talk about. Nolan didn't let his frustration show. Yes, she had planned to attend the game . . . no, they weren't officially dating . . . and no, she wasn't here. Something had come up.

His answers were kind but short. As he jogged to the locker room to join his team, one of his father's favorite lessons from Luke, chapter twelve, whispered through his soul. *To whom much is given, much will be expected.* A reminder his father referred to often. There was no room for grumbling or complaining. God had given him a dream job, a public place to shine for Him. He could be kind to reporters.

Inside the locker room, Nolan found his teammates looking exhausted, gathered around their coach. The man looked frustrated as he pointed at Nolan. "Maybe you have something, Cook. Something to make these guys play like they care." He looked at the sweaty faces around the room. "You have to want this with your whole heart, men. Your whole heart."

Dexter turned to Nolan. "Tell them about the kid."

Nolan grabbed a towel from a stack on the closest bench and rubbed his neck. "The boy's name is Gunner. He's got terminal leukemia, a few months to live, maybe less." He moved to the front of the group, next to Coach. "The kid's lifelong dream is to play ball for his high school. His second is to be here tonight."

The sobering reaction in the eyes of his teammates was undeniable. No one had to point out the fact that the boy's first dream wasn't going to happen. "I told Gunner we would win this game." Nolan paused. "For him." The Scripture came to him again, screaming through his mind. "My dad died when I was a kid. Most of you know that." He looked at the faces of his teammates, and the intensity in his voice grew, his tone more passionate. "But when I started playing ball, he would tell me this: 'To whom much is given, much will be expected.'" He stared at them. "That's in the Bible." He waited again. "Look around this locker room. No matter what you believe, the truth is this, guys: We have been given so much." He didn't move, didn't blink. "I think of Gunner, believing that we're playing this game for him." His voice rose once more. "So let's give something back! Let's win tonight. Let's do this!"

The fire was back in his teammates' eyes. A chorus of shouts rose from the group, and the team came together in a huddle. The coach stepped back and watched, nodding, satisfied. Nolan put his hand in the middle, and the others did the same. The energy had completely changed, the electricity ten times what it had been coming into the locker room. "Beat Boston!"

A chorus of voices echoed the shout.

Nolan felt more on fire than at any time all season. "Gunner, on three. One . . . two . . . three."

"Gunner!"

And with that, they took the floor a different team.

In the third quarter, the Hawks forced four turnovers in the opening couple of minutes, and Atlanta took a two-point lead. They played defense with a frenzied aggression, stunning Boston. A few minutes more, and the Celtics began to unravel. Even Boston's leading scorer fell apart. The guy couldn't hit a shot the rest of the quarter. At one point, he drove in for a dunk and missed it. The arena flew to its feet, celebrating the moment. Later, the announcers would peg it as the turning point. The contest was over after that. Long before the Hawks notched an eighteen-point win and a place in the NBA finals.

As the buzzer sounded at the end of the game, Nolan jogged with the game ball over to Gunner, sitting courtside with his parents and Molly and Ryan. Nolan was sweaty and out of breath, but he handed the ball to Gunner and leaned close so the boy could hear. "We won it for you, Gunner!"

The crowd missed the exchange. The fans were on their feet, shouting for the Hawks. A horde of media filed onto the court, surrounding the players, while police officers kept fans back. Little Gunner didn't notice any of it. He took the ball and hugged Nolan's neck, not minding the sweat or the circus atmosphere.

Nolan nodded to Ryan. "Meet you here in half an hour."

He joined his teammates, chest-thumping and high-fiving and hugging. Dexter came up and slapped his arm. "We did it, man! It was that halftime speech."

"You know what it was, Dex?" Nolan looped his arm around his friend's sweaty neck. Then he pointed up, and for a full couple of seconds, he stared toward the rafters. "It was God Almighty . . . meeting us here. Because maybe we finally got it." He winked at Dexter. "You know, as a team."

"He was definitely with us!" Dexter laughed and raised both fists in the air. "I didn't think I'd ever know this feeling. It's amazing!"

"Nolan . . . over here, Nolan!" A group of sportscasters approached them. Dexter was a phenomenal swing man, but they didn't want him. Nolan's friend patted his shoulder. "Go get 'em."

They shared a quick smile, and Nolan turned his attention to the reporters. Ten minutes later, as he headed for the shower, he looked back one more time to the place where Gunner sat with his family. The craziness around them was finally lessening a little.

Gunner sat between his parents while the adults talked around him. Even from across the court Nolan could see that the boy was in his own world. He had the game ball on his lap, staring at it, running his hand over it. Nolan knew what the boy was thinking, what he was feeling. Despite his losing battle with cancer, in this moment—even for a fraction of time—the boy had won. He was a Hawk and he was a champion.

Nolan blinked back his tears and joined his teammates.

Gunner's dream came true: And that made tonight's victory the greatest of all.

❧ ❧

The dots needed connecting.

That was all Ryan Kelly could think as they sat down with their ice cream on the suite level of the Philips Arena that night. Even with courtside seats, he couldn't stop thinking about the last things Nolan had said before the game, how he'd grown up in Savannah, same as Caroline Tucker. And how the girl he was going to marry had moved away to San Diego when she was fifteen. A girl who would be about the same age as Nolan. Caroline's daughter—Ellie, if he remembered right—had moved with her dad to San Diego when she was fifteen, too. He could picture the sad blond woman, wringing her hands, trembling, her only prayer that she might reconnect with her daughter.

Hadn't she said something about a basketball player? Ryan stared at his ice cream. Nolan had arrived, showered and changed, a few minutes ago. He chatted with Gunner and his parents, and beside him, Molly touched his shoulder. "They've made a new batch." She nodded to the sundae bar. "Hot fudge."

"What?" Ryan caught the glances from Gunner's parents and even from Nolan. "Sorry . . . I was distracted." He stood and nodded to the ice cream bar. "I'll be back."

The others laughed lightly, and even Gunner smiled. Still lost in the details, Ryan found the hot fudge and returned to the table. He took a few bites of his ice cream, then he set his spoon down. "Nolan, can I ask you something?"

Nolan leaned his forearms on the table. "Sure."

The question might be crazy, but he had to ask. Ryan's heart slammed against his ribs as he looked straight at Nolan. "Does the name Caroline Tucker mean anything to you?"

Nolan Cook had a reputation for being poised and easygoing, whatever question came his way. But here, in light of Ryan's question, he simply froze. The color left his face, and he seemed unable to respond. Ryan wasn't sure how much time went by. It didn't matter.

THE CHANCE 193

He had his answer.

Gunner's parents seemed to sense that something had changed around the table. They used the moment to take the boy to the restroom. Molly looked confused, but she slid closer to Ryan.

Nolan found his control. He uttered a single laugh. "How do you know Caroline?"

"She's an old friend of Peyton's." He could feel Molly grasping the situation beside him. "I met with her when I was in Savannah."

"Caroline Tucker and Peyton Anders? They were friends?"

"A long time ago." Ryan couldn't say too much.

Nolan flexed the muscle in his jaw, and again he seemed to struggle to find his next words. "What made you ask?"

Since Gunner and his parents weren't back yet, Ryan shared what he could. "You mentioned the girl, the one you were going to marry. She moved to San Diego with her dad when she was fifteen."

"Caroline told you about that?" His eyes looked sad. The shock seemed to make its way from his mind to his heart.

Suddenly Ryan remembered the basketball detail. "She told me her daughter had to leave with almost no notice . . . and that she left behind her friend, a high school basketball player."

"She didn't mention my name?"

"No." Ryan pictured Caroline sitting across from him at the coffee shop, the way she had hesitated at that part of the story. "The girl you were going to marry . . . is her name Ellie?"

Slowly, gradually, tears appeared in Nolan's eyes. He massaged his temples with his forefinger and thumb. Then he sat straighter, his determination evident in every movement. He dropped his hands to the table and nodded. "Yes. Ellie Tucker."

Ryan felt for the guy. Nolan hadn't moved on. He might've been only fifteen back then, but Nolan obviously cared for her still. "I'm sorry. I had to say something."

"Thank you." Nolan glanced toward the restroom. Gunner and his parents were still nowhere in sight. "Has her mother heard from her?"

"No. She's sent letters—one a week, I guess. But she hasn't heard anything."

Nolan absorbed the blow. "She doesn't want to be found. I've tried everything." He closed his eyes briefly. "So what's it mean?" He looked at Ryan. "You talked to her mom last week? Why would God put us together?"

"From the minute I went on tour, I felt the Lord was up to something." Ryan looked at Molly. She knew better than anyone how strong the feeling had been. He turned to Nolan again. "Maybe this is it."

"I have to think it through." Nolan tapped his fingers on the table, his eyes narrowed, moving from one spot to another, as if trying to see through the thickest fog. "Caroline wants to see her, right?'

"Desperately. We prayed about it, that they would find each other . . . that God would bring healing."

The news sparked something in Nolan. "She talked about her faith?"

Ryan felt tenderness in his smile. "Very much. She's raising her son by herself and praying for her daughter. She hasn't heard from Ellie or her husband since they moved."

"So Caroline's not married."

Again Ryan was careful. Nolan was close to figuring out information that Ryan wasn't privy to share. "She's a single mom."

"Hmm." Nolan looked off, lost in thought again. "I have to find her. For me and for her mom."

Ryan didn't say anything. Molly reached for his fingers, and the two of them were quiet. Gunner and his parents were taking a long time. The boy mustn't feel well. "Well . . . let's pray. For Caroline and Ellie." He looked toward the restroom. "And Gunner."

"Yes." Nolan Cook raked his fingers through his hair. He looked like nothing more than a college kid trying to figure out life. He bowed his head. "Ryan . . . please."

Ryan breathed deep and held tighter to Molly's hand. Then for the second time that week, he prayed for a young woman he'd never met, and that the two people who missed her so much would find her soon. And he prayed for Gunner, that memories of this day would get him through whatever was ahead. "We pray believing . . . we pray trusting. Thank you, God. In the powerful name of Jesus, amen."

When he opened his eyes, Gunner and his family stood close by. Gunner's dad had his arm around the boy's shoulders. "We need to go."

"Guess what?" Gunner looked pale, his cheeks sunken even as his eyes sparkled. "That's exactly what happened. What you prayed about. I was sick in the bathroom, and all of a sudden I remembered playing that game with Nolan." He stopped and grinned at his basketball hero. "And I didn't feel sick!"

Ryan smiled. "Prayer is powerful." He looked at Nolan. "Maybe that's what God wants us to remember after today."

"Definitely." Nolan held his gaze for a few seconds. He stood and went to Gunner and hugged him one last time. While the boy was in his arms, Nolan peered at him and then

Ryan. "Our mighty God still hears us . . . and He still answers prayers."

Ryan and Molly waited until after Gunner was gone before turning to Nolan. "We should probably go, too."

"Wait." Nolan looked from Ryan to Molly and back. "You didn't tell me your story."

"Oh, that . . ." Ryan laughed lightly and looked at Molly. "Molly and I were very close when we were younger. We hung out at a bookstore called The Bridge, but then Molly moved away and we lost touch. It wasn't until something crazy and nearly tragic happened to the old bookstore owner that we wound up in the same place again."

"I knew the minute I saw him. Like no time had passed." Molly tilted her head, her voice pensive. "If there's ever a reason you and Ellie might wind up in the same place at the same time . . . be there. Don't miss it." She slipped her arm around Ryan's waist and kissed his cheek. "That's my advice."

"Yes." Ryan turned to Nolan. "Don't miss the chance."

Long after they said their good-byes and reached the car, Ryan still thought about it, replaying the impossibility of the connection. "God's doing something big. I'm absolutely sure."

"Mmm." Molly watched him from the passenger seat. "Wouldn't it be something? Healing and restoration, brought about by God because you took this tour? Because you talked to Peyton?" She smiled. "I'm proud of you for contacting Caroline Tucker, for putting it together tonight. You're showing everyone what Romans 8:28 looks like."

Ryan smiled. "'All things work to the good for those who love God.'"

"Exactly."

A reverent quiet fell over them the rest of the short ride

back to the hotel. Were they front row to what could be a miracle? Healing from brokenness? Whatever God was up to, Ryan had the feeling as they drove down Jefferson Street that they were no longer in their old SUV, no longer participants in any ordinary moment.

They were on holy ground.

Chapter Twenty

Nolan was the last one to leave Philips Arena. He found the spot—left side, three-point line—and sank the shot on the first try. *For you, Dad. Make sure he knows, okay, God?* He grabbed his bag and headed for his car. The day had been emotional enough, with Gunner's visit and the Hawks' comeback win. The way the team rallied around the sick little boy.

But the rest of the night was nothing short of a miracle. What if Molly hadn't come along for the visit? What if her husband had been on the road tonight? How was it possible the man had been chatting with Caroline Tucker just days ago?

Nolan drove slowly, barely aware of streets and stoplights. When he got home, he went to the hutch in his bedroom again and stared at the photograph. Nolan and Ellie, frozen in time. Her mom had written her a letter every week and never heard a single thing back. Fear sliced through him and filled his blood with adrenaline. Didn't that terrify her? Didn't she wonder if Ellie was even alive? He opened the cabinet and took the photo from its place on the shelf. He ran his thumb lightly over the frame, over the place where she looked back at him. "You would've found me, Ellie . . . I know you."

His heart flip-flopped inside him. It was like Ellie had disappeared completely. What if she was no longer alive? Dead from a car crash or sickness? *Please, God . . . not Ellie. Please let her be alive somewhere. Help me find her.* Nolan took the picture to the edge of his bed and sat down. What hadn't he tried? He had called the base years ago, trying to find Alan Tucker. But maybe . . . maybe Ellie's father had a new position or a new job. Maybe if Nolan made a few phone calls tomorrow, he could figure out where the man worked and call him. If anyone knew whether Ellie was alive, it would be her father.

The man who had taken her away.

Calling her dad was something he could do, something other than thinking about her and missing her and counting down the days until June first. Only five days remained now. Five days until the date that, eleven years ago, had seemed a lifetime away. Molly's words came back to him. If there was a reason to be in the same place at the same time . . . don't miss the chance. It was as if she could read Nolan's deepest thoughts. He breathed in slowly, his eyes on Ellie's. *What happened to you, Ellie. . . . Why don't you want to be found?*

He wasn't sure if it was his imagination, but something deep within his being told him she was alive. Alive and hurting. A spark of concern became a sense of real and pressing alarm. He thought about Ellie often and prayed for her always. But now the urgency was different. *God? Is Ellie in trouble?*

Pray, my son . . . pray without ceasing.

The message seemed to come from a voice deep within his soul. It was too real, too profound, to ignore. Wherever she was, whatever was happening in her life, Ellie needed prayer.

Nolan couldn't wait another minute. Holding her photograph to his heart, he slid down onto his knees and bowed his head.

For half an hour—as if his next heartbeat depended on it—Nolan did the only thing he could do.

He prayed for Ellie Tucker.

〜〜 〜〜

Twenty-nine letters into the box, Ellie wasn't sure how much more she could take. She hadn't been able to bring herself to open the box last night, but she hadn't slept either. This morning she had called in sick, and after taking the girls to school, she came home and started reading. Now her eyes were red and swollen, and her heart would never be the same again. On top of that, the sky had been overcast all day—the June gloom typical for the West Coast had come earlier than usual. She was home alone, Tina at work, and the girls at school. A cool breeze sifted through the open living room window.

A shiver came over Ellie, and she wondered if she was getting sick. Maybe she would die from a broken heart. Literally too much pain all at once. Her fingers were cold and stiff, but she managed to open the next letter. The motivation to read another of her mother's messages was too great.

She pulled out the single piece of paper and read the date. Her mom always included the date. Almost as if, deep within, she knew Ellie wasn't getting her letters, and that if there ever came a day when she did, that detail would be important. The way it was now.

October 17, 2006.

The date jumped out at Ellie and took her breath. The day before Kinzie was born. Ellie had been alone and in labor until Tina rushed home from beauty school to be with her. At the same time—the exact same time—somewhere in Savannah, her mother had been writing her a letter. Fresh tears flooded Ellie's heart and spilled into her eyes. She blinked a few times so she could see the words.

> *Dear Ellie,*
>
> *You're on my heart so much today. I could barely concentrate at work, hardly focus when I was reading John his bedtime story. I have to think that wherever you are, something is wrong. You're hurting or lonely . . . like it's a very difficult day for you. I don't usually feel this way. Call it a mother's intuition, but I'd give anything to know what's happening in your life right now. To hear your voice.*

Ellie brought the paper to her face and let the tears come, let the sobs shake her body and take the air from her lungs. *Mom . . . I wanted you to be there. You should've been there.* She closed her eyes, and she was in the hospital bed again, in the throes of labor. Her body racked with pain and Tina holding her hand. And all Ellie could think, all she could do as Kinzie came into the world, was pretend that the hand she was holding wasn't Tina's at all.

But her mother's.

If you only knew how much I wanted you there . . .

The paper was wet with Ellie's tears. She set it on the floor. Someday she would show the letters to Kinzie. They were all she had of her mom and the years they'd missed. She couldn't afford to lose them. Not one of them. Especially not this one.

Her body needed air. She breathed in and fought for clarity, for focus so she could know what to do next. How could her father have hidden them from her? Letter after letter after letter. More words of love and encouragement and desperation than any mother would usually speak to a daughter in a life-time.

And not one word, not one page had ever reached her.

It was the most horrific thing her father could have done. He must have hated both of them to keep her mother's words from her. To deny her the right to know how much her mom loved her. How much she had always loved her. Ellie held her breath, grasping for any sense of normal.

Ellie felt sick. Sicker than she had all day. She stood, and a wave of dizziness slammed against her. She ran to the bath-room and barely made it before losing her breakfast. When her body stopped convulsing she stayed on her knees, her head in her hands. Her mother's aching tone in the letters and her consistent declarations of love, her undying determination on every page that they would be together again. No wonder she was sick. The truth was that hard to take.

When she was finished, when her stomach ached from the heartbreak and her mouth was sour from the awful reality, she went to the computer and Googled her mother's name. Caro-line Tucker, Savannah, Georgia. No contact information came up. Her mother probably didn't have means for more than a cell phone.

The letters in the other room called to her again. Never mind how sick she felt, she had to get back to them. She read another one and another one and another one after that. Gradually, the pieces of her mother's lonely life began to come together. The letters were full of details and apologies and mentions of God and prayer. Never mind that Ellie never wrote back. Not once in any of the letters had she even hinted at feeling angry with Ellie or bitter or forgotten. She would simply wait a week, take out another piece of paper, another envelope, and try again.

Every week . . . every month . . . for eleven years.

In one of the letters her mom mentioned that she had celebrated her ten-year anniversary working at the new doctor's office. Which meant that even with the time difference Ellie could make a few phone calls and probably reach her mother today. She worked at a doctor's office in Savannah. That was the only information she needed.

Something sad occurred to her. She could've called doctor's offices in Savannah their first year in San Diego. Only she'd been fifteen back then. And until this morning, she'd believed that her mother didn't care about her at all. Why go search for someone who didn't want her? Until a few hours ago, Ellie's mom had been dead to her.

Tina came home for lunch, and Ellie brought the box to the kitchen. "Look at this." She opened the box, and the story poured out. "She wrote all of these."

"Every week? He hid your mother's letters to you all those years?" Tina quickly grew angry. She didn't have a relationship with her own dad, a guy who hadn't been in her life since she was a baby. "That's against the law, I'm sure it is. Hiding mail? Seems like he could be arrested."

Ellie hadn't considered that. For the most part, she hadn't thought about him at all. She was better off not to. The image of him weeping as he stood against the brick wall outside Merrilou's left her torn between hating him and pitying him. What could have possessed her father to hide these letters from her all this time? And what had changed that he would bring the box to her work yesterday?

She pushed the thought from her mind.

Action. That's what she needed. A plan. Tina had to get back to work. When she was gone, Ellie took the box back to the living room. The letter on the floor called to her, the one damp with her tears. The one her mother had written the day before Kinzie was born. She read it once more and then tucked it into the back pocket of her jeans. With all the pain of missing her mom, with all she'd lost over the years, Ellie couldn't help but feel a little better. Her mother had been praying for her the day she went into labor.

No time or distance could change the bond between them.

She bundled the other letters she'd read and set them on top of the mass of envelopes in the box. It would go in the hall closet for now. Kinzie was very perceptive and if she saw a collection of hundreds of letters, she would have another full day of questions.

Questions Ellie wasn't ready to answer.

The box fit on the floor at the back of the closet, where it couldn't be seen.

That much was done, so what next? She could call around and find the doctor's office where her mother worked. But the idea felt wrong. Anticlimactic. Her mother had loved her so well for so long, she deserved to hear from Ellie in person. Yes, that was it. She would go to Savannah. A plan took shape quickly and gave her a break from the tears. She hurried to the computer. Her eyes stung, and her head pounded, but she didn't care.

She would call Merrilou's tomorrow and tell the owner she needed two weeks. She hadn't taken more than a couple of days' vacation since she was hired. Whether they paid her or not, she needed the time. This was a family emergency. She searched the map once more, planning how far she would get the first day.

She would take the I-8 east to Arizona, and connect with Interstate 10 all the way to Las Cruces, New Mexico, before getting a hotel. A ten-hour drive. That would be easy, knowing what she knew now. The day after she would reach the I-20 and take it to Dallas, and on the third day, she would stop in Birmingham. That would leave seven hours before she reached Savannah.

Before she was home.

She would find her mom easily, because she had her address. None of this stalking her just outside work, the way her father had done. Ellie printed out the directions and closed Google. Her mind was made up.

She would talk to Kinzie tonight while the two of them packed. Very early tomorrow morning they would set out and be halfway to Phoenix before she called to say she wasn't coming in to work. It would be an adventure. Kinzie would think a road trip was the best thing since going to church. They would pack light—a couple of duffel bags full of clothes, some basic toiletries, and the letter.

The one her mom had written to Ellie the day before Kinzie's birth.

An hour later, as Tina got off work and picked up the girls, Ellie put together carrot sticks and graham crackers for Kinzie's afternoon snack and thought about the incredible timing. Her father knew nothing about June first and her promise with Nolan, nothing about the tackle box buried beneath the old oak tree. Yet after all these years, he had given her more than a box of letters. He had given her a reason to go back to Savannah.

Days before her long-ago promise to meet up with Nolan.

He was dating Kari Garrett now, but that didn't change the facts. If everything went the way she planned it, she would pull in to Savannah on the last day of May.

Twenty-four hours before the time they had promised to meet.

She dismissed the thought. Crazy timing. A coincidence. How could it be anything more than that?

Chapter Twenty-one

Sleep wouldn't come.

Every time Ellie drifted off, the face of her father came to her. She had every reason to hate him. Tina was right—Ellie had checked online, and stealing mail was a federal offense, punishable by time in a penitentiary. Not that she would press charges, but she certainly had a right to be angry.

So why couldn't she stop thinking of him, standing there and crying? Apologizing to her? Something must've happened. Maybe he'd lost his job or someone in his life had died. Or he'd witnessed a tragic car accident. Something. He had mentioned God, so that could be it. Maybe he looked in the mirror one day and recognized the awful darkness of his heart. Or how far removed he was from his supposed faith. Maybe he'd seen how ugly his Christianity had been. The faith he'd tried to control them with.

She flipped onto her other side, but sleep wouldn't come, and Ellie knew why. Her heart was struggling to hate him. There lay the problem. She could see the pain in his expression, feel the hurt in his eyes when he begged her to forgive him.

She opened her eyes and rolled onto her back. The street lamp shone into her room enough that she could see the ceiling. What did she teach Kinzie about forgiveness? How many times had she come home sad because other little girls on the playground had laughed at her shoes or refused to include her in their games? Inevitably, the next day the same girls would be sorry and want her to be part of their group.

Ellie could hear herself. *Kinzie, if the girls are sorry, you need to forgive them. Forgiveness makes you feel better. As soon as you forgive, you're free. Hurt people actually hurt people.* How many times had she said that to her little girl? She closed her eyes, but she could feel them fluttering open again.

Like at the zoo, this would've been the perfect time to pray. But she didn't need to talk to God. She had to talk to herself. Her father had done the meanest thing possible. He'd stopped her from having a relationship with her mom for a crazy amount of time. Just trying to grasp all she'd lost was enough to send her back to the bathroom. She should hate him and never talk to him. Ever.

Holding on to her anger and unforgiveness would be completely justified. But she would feel sick all the time, and she certainly wouldn't be free. With the clock counting down the minutes until their road trip, an idea began to form. Maybe before they hit the highway, they could stop by his house. She could knock on the front door, tell him she forgave him, and then spend the next three days behind the wheel, trying to convince herself it was true.

There. If that's what she was supposed to do, then sleep should finally come. Instead, the list began to run on repeat through her mind. Every reason she shouldn't forgive him, the sensible facts that would make her feel like a crazy person for stopping by his house for any reason. Her father had been cold and unforgiving, holding Ellie and her mother to an impossible standard. His meanness had pushed Ellie away, just like it had pushed her mother away all those years ago.

She wouldn't stop at his house any more than she would drive to Savannah with four flat tires. Absolutely not. The finality in her decision gradually gave way to sleep. She wasn't sure how much time had passed, but the next thing she knew, someone was shaking her. Ellie put her hand over the smaller one on her shoulder. "Kinzie?"

"Mommy, wake up!" She sounded worried.

Ellie opened one eye and looked at the alarm. "What?" She shot up. The alarm hadn't gone off, or she'd forgotten to set it. They were supposed to be on the road by seven o'clock, but already it was ten after eight.

"You have to see this." Kinzie pointed to her own bed and bounced a little. "Hurry, Mommy."

"Just a minute." Ellie rubbed her swollen eyes and looked at Kinzie. She peeled back the covers and eased her feet onto the floor. "We have to hurry. Today's our—"

"Wait . . . first come here!"

Kinzie never acted like this. Ellie stood and crossed the room to her daughter's bed. It took a second or two to realize what she was looking at, but in a rush, every awful thing about yesterday came back. Scattered across Kinzie's bed were dozens of letters.

The letters from her mother.

"Where did you get these?" Ellie didn't want to sound mad. None of this was Kinzie's fault.

"I opened one." Kinzie bit her lip, and her head dipped a little. "Sorry, Mommy. I thought they were a present."

"Kinz . . . you should've asked." Ellie sat on the edge of her daughter's bed and searched the child's eyes. "How did you find them?"

"Remember that old dolly I didn't want anymore and we were going to give it to a girl who didn't have any dollies? Remember that?"

"Yes." Ellie gave Kinzie a look that said she'd better tell the truth. "We gave that box of old toys away two months ago." She put her hand on her daughter's shoulder. Actually, the doll was in one of Ellie's bedroom drawers. Kinzie had sworn she was finished with it, that she was too old for dolls. Even if that were true, Ellie would keep it forever. A reminder of Kinzie's little-girl days.

"Yeah, but I was thinking maybe the dolly spilled out onto the floor in the closet. And if she did, then maybe she was sad and alone in the closet, and she could move back in here with me again. Because she never really wanted to leave our 'partment, Mommy. That's what I was thinking." Kinzie stopped for a quick breath. She swallowed, nervous. "So I tippy-toed real quiet to the closet to find her, and instead, I found this!" She held her hand out toward the display scattered across her bedspread. "I did make my bed first." She smoothed out the comforter. "See?"

"Kinzie . . ." Ellie didn't want to be angry. She felt sick again. The reality of what her father had done was impossible for her to understand as an adult. Kinzie wouldn't stand a chance. "Come here." Kinzie came closer, and Ellie pulled her into a gentle hug. "You know better than to open Mommy's mail."

"I know." The girl peered up, her blue eyes enormous. "I was curious like a cat, Mommy. I couldn't stop myself." She blinked a few times. "Did you know that every letter in that box is from Caroline Tucker in Savannah?"

"Yes, baby. I know that."

"She's your mommy, right?"

"She is." Ellie sighed. This was the last thing she expected to be doing this morning. "My dad came by the salon and brought me the letters."

Kinzie thought about that for a few seconds. "Did your mom write all those letters last week?"

"No, sweetie. She wrote them ever since my daddy and I moved to San Diego."

The wheels in Kinzie's mind were clearly spinning. "But why didn't you open them sooner?"

"Well, that's just it." She smiled, hoping Kinzie couldn't see the hurt and pain in her eyes. "My daddy was mad at my mommy. So he didn't give them to me until now."

Her daughter's eyes grew wide, so wide Ellie could almost see the whites all the way around them. "What if your mom had something important to tell you?"

"She did." Ellie refused the tears. "Every letter was important, and I never knew about them, so I never wrote back to her."

Kinzie drew in a slow gasp. "That wasn't very nice of your daddy, right?"

"Right." Ellie needed to change the topic. She didn't want to talk about her father. Not when they were about to set out on the biggest adventure of their lives. "Guess what?"

"What?" Kinzie pressed in closer to Ellie, probably glad she wasn't in trouble.

"Today's our road trip! An adventure, just you and me." Ellie looked at the envelopes scattered on the bed. "This is why we're going. After I read some of my mom's letters, I decided we would drive to Savannah. So I can tell her in person that I finally opened my mail."

"Really?" Kinzie's excitement was tempered with concern. "What if she's mad at you?"

"Baby, why would she be mad?"

Kinzie ran her hand over the letters. "You didn't read what she wrote . . . and you didn't write back."

Ellie's heart sank to her knees. "I didn't know her address. And I didn't know she wanted to talk to me."

Kinzie looked at the floor, the reality overtaking her. "That's so sad, Mommy. In the letter I read, she told you she loved you very much. She wanted to see you really bad."

"I know." Her daughter had always been an advanced reader. Who knew what all she'd read in the last hour. Ellie kept her smile, even as her eyes welled up. "See? That's why we're going there."

Kinzie nodded slowly, but she was distant, as if the information was more than she could process all at once. Finally, she came closer and put her hands on Ellie's knees. "Are you mad at your daddy?"

"Yes." There was no point in lying. "He hid the letters from me. That was the wrong thing to do."

"Yes." Kinzie thought some more, her eyes on the letters. When she looked at Ellie, her eyes were desperately sad. "Did your daddy tell you he was sorry? Was that why he gave you the letters now?"

"He did." Ellie could hardly believe she was having this conversation with her daughter.

"So did you forgive him, Mommy? Because remember you always tell me forgiving people makes us free?" Kinzie hesitated. "And remember you say how hurt people hurt people?"

"I remember." Ellie ran her hand down her daughter's hair. "Sometimes, with something like this, forgiveness takes a long time."

Kinzie looked worried. "It doesn't have to." She reached up and patted Ellie's cheek. "I don't want you to be hurt, Mommy."

The crazy plan from last night came back all at once. Something Ellie had to do, given the situation—not for her father but for Kinzie. "Maybe we could stop by his house on the way out of town." She couldn't believe the words had come from her mouth. She wouldn't be able to forgive him. But she could go through the motions for her daughter. Otherwise she would look like a hypocrite, and Kinzie would spend the whole road trip worrying about her.

"Really?"

"Yes. We'll stop there first."

Peace flooded Kinzie's face. "That sounds good." She stood on her tiptoes and kissed Ellie's cheek. "You'll feel better, Mommy." The comment was almost exactly what Ellie had told Kinzie so many times. *Forgive someone . . . you'll feel better.* Kinzie's smile came easily now. "When are we leaving?"

Ellie's stomach was in knots. Was she really going to do this? The idea made her sick. She remembered Kinzie's question and answered it. "We'll leave soon. As soon as we eat." She stood and walked to her dresser. "You still want your baby doll? The one from the closet?"

"Yes." Kinzie's face fell again. "But I think she stayed in the box, Mommy. She wasn't in the closet at all. Now she has some other little girl to love."

"She still has you, Kinz."

"She does?" Kinzie blinked a few times, surprised.

"Yes. Because she's in here." Ellie opened the second drawer and found the doll. "I couldn't give away your baby doll. Even if you were done with her."

Kinzie breathed in loud and long. She ran to Ellie and carefully took the doll into her arms. "Thank you, Mommy . . . thank you. I wasn't done with her. I thought I was too big for baby dolls, but I'm not that big at all. Right?"

Ellie thought about Kinzie's insistence that she forgive her father. "Sometimes you are." She bent down and kissed the top of the child's head. "But never too big for your baby doll."

For a few seconds, Kinzie danced around in arcs and circles. "You know what I think, Mommy?" She held the dolly out, dancing with her. "I think this is going to be the best 'venture ever!"

The sick feeling became an anxiety that spilled into Ellie's blood and worked its way through her body. The road trip would be amazing, and seeing her mother after all these years would be a highlight of her life. Ellie had no doubt.

If she could just get through the next hour.

Chapter Twenty-two

Alan Tucker was dead. Never mind that his heart was still beating. He had died the moment Ellie took the box and turned away from him. He sat on the edge of his bed that Sunday morning and thought about the past week. His predictions about giving Ellie the letters had been right on. She hated him. She would hate him as long as she lived for what he'd done. He had pushed away the people he loved most in life, and that could mean only one thing.

He was dead.

No matter how long it took his body to catch up.

Still, as dead as he felt, he was also convinced of something else. He had done the right thing. The letters were hers, and she deserved to have them, to read them. If she could find her mother after all these years, she needed to do so. He might never find healing, but there was time for Ellie. Time for Caroline.

The thought of Caroline weighed heavy on his chest. She should've received the letter yesterday, if his calculations were right. That meant by now she might've had time to forgive herself. He knew Caroline—no matter how long they'd been apart, he knew her. She hated the fact that she'd had an affair. He could still see the desperation in her face when she begged him to forgive her the night she told him the truth. Never would she have turned to another man if he hadn't destroyed her first. He had tried to be clear about that in the letter. So she could let go of her own guilt, forgive herself, and move on. She would hate him because of the letters.

Same as Ellie.

But that was a small price for finally doing the right thing.

Alan slipped into shorts and a T-shirt. He needed to work out, needed to push his body past feeling comfortable. He might be dead, but he still had to move. Blame it on the marine training. Physical exertion had a way of taking his mind off his broken heart.

The house was painfully silent. Music. That would help. Matthew West's latest CD was in the player. He skipped to his favorite song, "Forgiveness." The song was about realizing that, ultimately, all anyone ever needed was the Lord. Alan could relate.

With the music on loud, he dropped to the floor and did fifty push-ups, slow and methodical. He loved how exercise made his muscles burn, how it punished him the way he deserved. He turned onto his back and powered through fifty sit-ups and fifty squats. Then he repeated the routine.

If he was honest with himself, Ellie hadn't started hating him yesterday. She'd been angry with him since she was nineteen and came home pregnant, since he called her names and accused her of terrible things. Or maybe since the move to San Diego. Yes, she had probably hated him for a long time.

After his third round of calisthenics, he turned off the

music. *You're with me, God . . . I know that. I'm not really dead.*
He'd met with the chaplain again on Friday, the day before he
took the letters to Ellie. The man had said something that
stuck with Alan. As long as he was breathing, God's greatest
task for him was not yet finished. His highest purpose in life
was still unfulfilled. It was why he would attend church that
Sunday. The six o'clock service, same as always.

Because God had plans for him.

Alan found his running shoes. He ran five miles on the
weekends, more than the usual three he logged every night
after work. Today he might go seven or ten. However long it
took so he'd be too tired to feel his aching soul.

He finished tying the laces and headed to the kitchen for
water when he heard the doorbell. *Strange,* he thought. Solici-
tors didn't usually canvas neighborhoods on Sundays. His
mother's house was a simple ranch in an older well-kept neighborhood five miles from the prison. Without stopping to look
out the window, Alan walked to the front door and opened it.

What he saw nearly stopped his heart for real.

"Ellie?" His voice was a whisper, all he could manage. She
stood on the front porch with a little girl, a blonder miniature
of her. The child had her arm around Ellie's waist, her eyes on
Alan's.

His mouth was instantly dry, but he opened the door wider.
"Come in. Please."

"We can't stay." Ellie didn't sound warm, but the anger from
before seemed gone from her voice. For a few seconds, she
didn't say anything. She looked down at her daughter. "This is
Kinzie." She sucked in a long breath. Something about her
tone told him this was one of the hardest things she'd ever
done. "Kinzie, this is your grandpa Tucker."

"Hi." Kinzie waved a little. She was beautiful, big blue eyes and the same innocence that once defined Ellie. And Caroline before her.

Tears blurred Alan's eyes. He didn't come closer, wasn't sure he should. But he crouched down so he was on her level. "Hi, Kinzie. Nice to meet you."

"Nice to meet you, too." She kept her arm tightly around Ellie's waist.

Alan stood and looked at his daughter, too shocked to speak. Of all the things he figured Ellie might do today, this wasn't on the list.

"You said you were sorry . . . for what you did. For the letters." Her voice broke, and she hung her head. Now Kinzie wrapped both arms around her waist and buried her face in her mother's side.

"Ellie . . ." In the awkward, painful silence, Alan had to clarify something. "It would take me all day to tell you everything I'm sorry about. The list is too long. I . . . I loved your mother so much. I still do." He moved to put his hand on her shoulder, but he stopped himself. His words sounded as broken as his heart. "I ruined everything. I'll be sorry every day, for the rest of my life."

Alan could only imagine the battle raging inside his daughter. She had every reason to hate him. Yet she was standing in front of him, which had to mean something. She looked at him, right through him. "I'm here because I forgive you." She lifted her chin, holding tight to the walls around her emotions.

The shock working its way through him doubled. Forgiveness? That was the last thing he deserved or expected.

Ellie hesitated. "I've been teaching Kinzie about forgiving.

So"—she sniffed, barely keeping her composure—"if you're sorry, I forgive you."

For a few seconds, she didn't move, didn't speak. Slowly, tears trickled down her face, and Kinzie noticed. She leaned up and wiped Ellie's cheeks. "It's okay, Mommy. You did it. Now you can feel better."

The child's words cut Alan to the core. Ellie looked at him, her gaze deep and intent, as if she were trying to see into the mean and calloused places where he had been capable of destroying the people he loved.

"I'm sorry, Ellie." He took a few steps back and leaned against the entryway wall. The pain in his daughter's eyes was more than he could take. "If I could do it over again . . ."

Something inside Ellie broke. Alan watched it happen. As if the walls could no longer contain her tears. They didn't fall all at once, but they crumbled a little at a time. And as the walls seemed to fall, almost in slow motion, Ellie came to him. She eased her arms around his waist, pressed her head to his chest, and let the sobs have their way with her.

Alan couldn't breathe, couldn't believe this was happening. His daughter was here, and she was in his arms. He brought his hand to her back and hugged her. Tentatively at first and then with more certainty. Deep down, Ellie was still a little girl like Kinzie, a girl who needed to know she was loved.

Especially since she had doubted that fact most of her life.

The hug didn't last long. Ellie seemed to realize what she was doing and where she was. She gathered her emotions and stepped back. "We're leaving, me and Kinzie." She narrowed her eyes, seeing through him again. "I'm taking her to Savannah."

Alarm pressed in around him. She had just found her way back to him. Her forgiveness felt like a start. A new beginning. "For how long?"

"Two weeks." She shrugged. "I'm not sure."

"We're going to see my grandma." Kinzie found her place at her mother's side again.

Alan nodded. "Good. I'm glad." He was, truly. He only wished he was going with them. "Can you . . . tell her I miss her?"

"Maybe you should do that." Ellie's response was quick, and in it was the anger that remained despite her forgiveness. An anger she would probably always struggle with.

"I wrote her a letter. She should have it by now."

The shock of that relaxed Ellie's features. That was obviously the last thing she had expected him to say or do.

"I wrote you one, too. It's in the box." He put his hands in his pocket. "I left it on top."

Ellie looked puzzled. "I didn't see it."

"Maybe it slipped to the bottom." He prayed she would see how different he was, how his heart had changed. "It's definitely in there."

"Okay. I'll find it." She took a step back. "We . . . have to go."

Alan looked from Ellie to Kinzie and back. "Thank you for coming, for bringing her."

The beautiful picture of the two of them here at his front door was one Alan would keep. No matter what happened after this.

Kinzie smiled at him. "Maybe we'll come over after the trip. We could eat dinner with you." She looked up at Ellie. "Right, Mommy?"

Ellie moved closer to the door. "Maybe." She smiled at her daughter.

Kinzie took a step toward Alan, her eyes still on Ellie. She cupped her little hands around her mouth and whispered out loud, "Can I hug him, Mommy? Since he's my grandpa?"

"Yes, baby. Of course." Ellie crossed her arms and waited by the front door while Kinzie ran to him. Her hug was quick and certain, free from the baggage that stood between him and Ellie. "Nice to meet you, Grandpa."

Again his tears made it tough to see. He pressed his fingers to his eyes and gave a quick shake of his head. "Thank you, Kinzie. You and your mom come for dinner anytime."

"Okay." She returned to Ellie.

Alan wasn't sure what to say. They were leaving, and there was nothing he could do to stop them. If Ellie found her mother, then there might not be any reason for her to come back to San Diego. This could be the last time he would see either of them—for a very long time, anyway.

"Bye." Ellie was the first to speak. She kept her arm around Kinzie, and the two of them turned and headed down the steps.

He followed them to the door and watched them go. "Ellie."

She stopped and looked over her shoulder. Kinzie did the same.

"Thank you. For coming by."

Ellie didn't smile. The sadness emanating from her was too great. Instead she nodded and their eyes held. Kinzie waved once more, and with that they walked to their car, climbed in, and drove away.

As they disappeared down the road, Alan realized something had changed. He no longer felt like a dead man walking.

Their visit had breathed life into him the way nothing else could. He hung his head. *God, You are amazing. So faithful. I didn't deserve her forgiveness and yet . . .*

She was Caroline's daughter. Nothing else could explain her ability to come by on her way out of town and tell him she'd forgiven him. He got the impression that she wasn't walking close to the Lord or even believing in Him, necessarily. Something in her tone yesterday when he tried to bring up God. Even so, she was her mother's girl—kind and compassionate, gentle in spirit.

Kinzie was another one.

A feeling started in his chest and spread through his soul. It reminded him of a video he'd seen on the Weather Channel. The image showed a tornado not bearing down on a house but starting there. A foggy, twisting piece of cloud seemed to grow from the ground and connect to a piece of the sky overhead. The birthplace of a tornado.

He felt that way now as he thought about how much he'd missed with Kinzie. His heart and mind were spinning counterclockwise like the beginning of an F5 twister. His stubborn self-righteousness had cost him almost seven years with his only granddaughter. He hadn't been there for her birth or her first steps, not for her first words or first birthday. He had missed watching her learn to ride a bike and learn to read, and he had lost out on six Christmas mornings.

The child had no father in her life; the soldier had been killed in action. The only father figure she might've had was him. Alan Tucker. But he'd been too busy being right to notice. Too set in his ways to grab the box of letters and get it to Ellie years ago.

Eleven years ago. When it wasn't a box of letters but just one.

If tornadoes came suddenly and left, this one was different. The damage of his actions would tear him up with every reminder of what he'd missed, all he'd lost. The cost of it was more than he could comprehend and here was maybe the greatest cost of all.

The sight of Ellie and Kinzie driving away.

Caroline needed to get to yesterday's mail, but not yet. Bills and advertising could wait. For now, she and John were eating lunch and talking about this morning's sermon.

"I liked what the pastor said." John's words were thoughtful. "We should be different than the world."

"We should." A flicker of guilt seared Caroline's heart. A real Christian never would have had an affair. She dismissed the thought and smiled at her son. "That has to be our goal."

John ate quickly, and after a few more minutes of conversation and a quick hug, he grabbed his basketball and ran out the door for the park. Only then did Caroline pick up the mail at the end of the counter.

She flipped past the electric bill and the Shell statement and two pieces of advertising, and suddenly she stopped cold. The next piece was a white envelope with her name written across the front. Her breath caught in her throat because at first she thought maybe it was from Ellie. Hundreds of times she'd sent a letter to her daughter without ever getting a response. If this were the first time, Caroline would have to go outside to catch her breath.

Just as quickly, she flipped it over and caught the name on the back. Alan Tucker. San Diego. Her heart flip-flopped in her chest, and she slowly found a spot at the kitchen table. Why would Alan write to her now? After all this time? A cold chill came over her. Was this the divorce paperwork she had expected back when he first moved away?

She had never considered remarrying, never dated. She refused to contact a lawyer, unwilling to admit that she and Alan were really over. If there would be a divorce between them, Alan would have to make the move. Caroline dreaded the day divorce papers might show up in the mail. She would certainly lose Ellie forever—in a custody battle. But the papers never came.

Her fingers shook as she held the envelope, staring at her husband's name, his handwriting. The papers hadn't come until now. Alan had probably fallen in love and now he was ready to remarry.

She slipped her finger beneath the envelope flap and opened it. Inside was a card, one with a beautiful photograph of mountains and a stream. What was this? She leaned back, desperate to calm her racing heart. Inside, the card was covered in Alan's handwriting, and it seemed to continue onto a folded piece of lined paper. Whatever Alan wanted to tell her, the message wasn't brief.

The card contained no divorce papers.

Her eyes found the beginning of the letter.

Dear Caroline,

I should've written this letter a long time ago. But lately . . . well, lately, God has changed me on the inside. Changed me so that now I can see what a wretched man I've been, how terribly I treated you, and how I pushed you away.

Caroline felt the room start to spin. What in the world was happening? Was she dreaming, or was it a trick? A prank? The Alan Tucker she knew never would've written a letter like this. She leaned one arm on the table to support herself. No matter how badly he had treated her, Caroline had never stopped praying for her husband—at least every now and then—that God would get ahold of his heart and remind him of the man he used to be.

The one she had fallen in love with.

But she'd never expected this. She struggled to believe Alan had written it. She found her place and continued. He went on to talk about how he must have been a monster to destroy the joy in her eyes and heart. He admitted that he was wrong to berate her and control her.

Then he talked about her affair.

Caroline felt sick to her stomach, waiting for the condemnation and accusations. But they never came. Instead, he took full blame for what had happened. Gradually, a feeling of release washed over her, and she stopped dreading each sentence.

I knew it was happening. You were gone so often, home late at night . . . Now I can't believe you didn't leave me sooner.

He talked about being angry when he heard she was pregnant and wanting to do whatever he could to get back at her. Shame made Caroline's cheeks hot. His feelings weren't a surprise. There was no other explanation for his decision to pull up stakes and move without even a weekend to prepare. Of course he wanted to get back at her.

He wondered who she might be now and whether time away from him had helped her. He explained that he was leaving his contact information for her—just in case—and he asked for her forgiveness.

> *I wish I still lived in Savannah. I'd come find you and look you in the eyes and tell you how sorry I am. I'd take you in my arms and try to love you back to the girl you used to be.*

The years of losses piled up and brought life to her tears. Tears she had stopped crying over Alan Tucker long ago. She couldn't imagine being in his arms again; the thought was too frightening to consider. No one had ever talked to her with such venom as the man she had married.

She took a deep breath and finished reading. Her heart skipped a beat when she reached the part about him having an awful confession, something he could barely tell her. Even so, she never expected what came next. Three times she had to read his words to believe what had happened.

Alan had kept the letters from Ellie? All this time? She pictured herself sitting at this table early in the morning and late at night, on afternoons like this, with John outside playing basketball. Year after year after year. So many letters, so many words of love and hope and explanation.

Not one of them had actually reached her.

Caroline pushed the card away and covered her face with her hands. The devastation of that, the weight of it, crushed in around her chest and made her feel like she was underwater. Her poor daughter, all this time believing that her own mother didn't care enough to contact her.

Dear God, why? She couldn't cry, couldn't move. The idea that Ellie hadn't heard from her since moving to San Diego was more than she could bear. *Lord, help me . . . I don't think I can take it. I'm not strong enough. Please, Father . . . help me.*

I am with you, daughter. You will not fight this battle alone.

The words sounded so loud that she peered through the cracks between her fingers and looked around. As if maybe a burning bush had sprouted in her apartment living room. *If you're with me, then help me, Lord. My daughter must think I hate her. All this time . . . Father, all this time. What am I supposed to do next?*

The suffocating feeling remained, but a thought occurred to her. One that brought hope. Ellie hadn't responded because she'd never gotten the letters. But Alan said by the time Caroline was reading his letter, her daughter would have them. Once and for all, they'd be in her hands.

Two things sparked life in Caroline's soul.

First, Ellie hadn't been ignoring her letters the way she'd thought. She hadn't been reading letters from Caroline and tossing them in the trash. And second, she was finding out that she'd been loved and cared for, no matter what she'd come to believe over the years.

She went to the window and watched John drive to the basket and make a layup, watched him celebrate with his friends. How much she had missed with Ellie. So many years. But maybe everything was about to change. The fact that Alan was sorry was already more than Caroline had ever imagined.

The bigger issue was Ellie. Caroline spread her fingers on the warm window. If Alan had given Ellie the letters, then he knew where to find their daughter. *Wherever she is, God, let her*

know how much I love her. Help me reach her. Until then . . . I
trust you, Father.

When she finished praying, she didn't hear a response, like
she had earlier, but she had a sense that hadn't occurred to her
for many years. As she missed Ellie and loved her and wished
for the two of them to reconnect, one thing was true, especially in light of this bittersweet news.

God loved her more.

A little over a week ago, Peyton Anders's guitar player had
shown up out of nowhere and prayed for Ellie. And now, after
so many seasons of heartache and loneliness, something mirac-
ulous had happened.

Ellie had gotten her letters.

Chapter Twenty-three

The timing was too crazy to be a coincidence.

That was all Nolan could think as he threw a bag of clothes together in his Atlanta house. They had two days off before they needed to be at the Hawks' facility every day, leading up to the finals. Two days—the last day of May and the first day of June. If the front office had given him a calendar this year and asked him to pick two days he absolutely had to have off, those would be the days.

Nolan had talked to Ryan Kelly again, and the man had given him Caroline's work number and address. Her office was the first place Nolan planned to go tomorrow once he arrived in Savannah. She might not know anything, but it would be good to see her. Good to let her know how badly he wanted to find Ellie.

Of course, he still had no way of knowing where Ellie was or what she was doing. Whether she was out of the country or married or no longer alive. But if he had the next two days off, this much was certain: He was spending one of them at Gordonston Park, beneath an old oak tree.

Just in case she remembered.

❧ ❧

They were an hour away from Savannah, and Ellie was exhausted. Kinzie slept seatbelted in the backseat, the way she'd been sleeping since they left Birmingham at six that morning. Ellie's shoulders ached, and her eyes burned. The drive had been harder than she thought. So many hours, so many miles. But she wouldn't trade it. The time with Kinzie had been wonderful. They listened to her *Adventures in Odyssey* CDs—something her daughter had been given at church. The stories were nice. Ellie couldn't count the number of times her daughter had laughed out loud.

As she drove, time and again Ellie had been struck by an undeniable truth. Kinzie was a truly happy child, undamaged by the world around her. No telling how long that would last, given her family tree. But for now Ellie was grateful. In the rearview mirror, she watched Kinzie stretch and turn one way, then the other. A yawn came over her, and she sat up and opened her eyes. "Are we there yet?"

"Not quite." Ellie laughed quietly and glanced at her daughter again. It was easily the most asked question of the trip. "Another hour."

"That's all?" Kinzie blinked, still sleepy. "An hour's nothing, Mommy. That's how long church lasts, and that always goes by really fast."

"Well, then, we'll be there really fast."

Kinzie giggled. She looked out the side window. "It's different here. More greener."

That had been true for most of yesterday and all of today. The feel and sight of the South made Ellie realize how much she'd missed it. How had she waited this long to follow her heart? To get in a car and simply erase the distance back home? "How was your sleep?"

"Good." Kinzie yawned again. "Know what I dreamed about?"

"Tell me." Ellie focused on the road.

"Okay." Kinzie sat a little straighter and took a big breath. "It was a long dream, and you were in it, and I was in it. We were in Savannah, and my grandma Tucker was there, and all three of us were going to church together." She smiled at Ellie. "Isn't that the best dream?"

It wasn't the first time Kinzie had talked about church since they started the road trip. She had talked about Jesus and a happy-ever-after, and she'd talked about at least eight Bible stories she was learning. Some of them took an hour to tell. Ellie remembered the stories from when she was a little girl. The stories of Noah and Moses and Joseph. Jonah and Daniel.

Hearing Kinzie retell the stories touched Ellie's heart. Made her less angry at God and more curious. Now she kept both hands on the wheel, thinking about Kinzie's dream. Her daughter seemed to sense what she was thinking. "You love God, right, Mommy?"

"Well . . . I haven't thought about it." She could hardly tell Kinzie that she no longer believed. The news would shatter her.

"Think about it now." Her happy tone was upbeat, matter-of-fact. "Do you love God?"

"God gave me you, Kinz." She smiled in the rearview mirror. "So of course I love Him."

She could feel the girl's scrutiny, sense her trying to look more deeply into the answer. "So would you go to church with me sometime, Mommy? Since you love God?"

Again Ellie wasn't sure what to say. She had expected these questions earlier in the trip, but now—an hour before they reached Savannah—she didn't feel prepared. "Would that make you happy, baby?"

"Yes, it would." Kinzie nodded, emphatic.

"Then I'll do it." Ellie glanced at her daughter. The answer seemed to satisfy her. She closed her eyes, and in a few minutes, she was asleep again.

Well before Kinzie's birth, Ellie had stopped believing in God. If He was real, then how could He let her father take her from Savannah? How could Nolan's dad have died so young? And how had everything become so broken? Still, there was no denying the fact that Kinzie had been going to church and praying for her. And now, without warning, her father had given her the letters from her mom. A few days before the first of June. She had forgiven her dad—at least in action—and she was almost to her mother's house.

So was God behind all this?

Ellie let her head lean back against the seat rest. The reason she'd stopped believing in God had everything to do with her life after moving to San Diego. Her father would accuse her and doubt her and tell her that God didn't want her to hang out with her friends. He would shout Bible verses at her and tell her she wasn't following God's word. Ellie thought about the years after they arrived in San Diego, the years she'd lived with her father.

He used God to justify his awful behavior back then. *The Lord doesn't want you out late, Ellie . . . God can see through your lies . . . Jesus warns people of the narrow way.* On and on and on, as if he were only passing on orders from his heavenly Sergeant.

It was never really God who had doubted her and accused her, right? The thought hadn't occurred to her until now. No wonder she'd stopped believing. And now he blamed himself for his actions, so what did that say about God? If He was real, then maybe He was working a miracle in her life. A miracle that was half an hour from becoming a reality.

She focused on the road again. A real miracle would've been finding Nolan.

She let that thought stay for a while, but it didn't ring true. It was her own fault she hadn't connected with Nolan. He wasn't missing. She could've reached out to him at any time. The truth was, she didn't want him to see how she'd turned out. How she hadn't graduated from college or written the great American novel or waited for the right guy, the way she'd told him she would that last time they were together.

A slow sigh came. So many mistakes over the years. The fact that God had blessed her with Kinzie was proof that maybe He was real after all. The child was the single ray of light in what had been a whole lot of dark years.

Some of the places were starting to look familiar. A picture began to form in Ellie's mind: the house she had shared with her parents back on Louisiana Avenue. If only her dad had loved her mom back then. If only he hadn't forced her away.

She had been the happiest woman. Ellie remembered the two of them playing at the park and her mother pushing her on the swings. She could hear her again, the joy in her voice when she used to talk about the weekend. *Daddy will be home on Friday, and then we'll have a special dinner. We'll come to the park and play together. The three of us.* Funny. Ellie could remember her mother talking about that, but she couldn't recall one time when the three of them actually went to the park together.

One memory after another settled on the screen of her heart like a slide show from a different life. One she never had the chance to finish living. If her father had been there, if he hadn't chosen a life where he spent all week at the base, they could've been a real family. They would've played together and shopped for groceries together and done chores together on Saturdays. Sundays would've been for church, and her mother never would've felt alone. And Ellie never would've lost Nolan Cook.

She glanced again in the rearview mirror at Kinzie sleeping.

Things had a way of working out. She would never regret the path of her life, not when it had resulted in this precious daughter. Still, she couldn't help but wonder at the cost, the price life demanded, all because her father had been unbending. Controlling and heavy-handed. He was mean in the name of Jesus—something that could never be from God.

If God were real.

One more turn, and suddenly she was back in her old neighborhood. She slowed and checked her mirrors. No one was behind her. She drove at a crawl until she reached Kinzie and Louisiana, the corner where she and Nolan had met more times than she could remember. She pulled over and put the car in park. It looked different. Older, a little more run-down. But it was familiar enough that she had only to look around, and she was back again. Fifteen again.

As if just being here could take her to the day before her father moved her to San Diego.

She didn't want to wake Kinzie. Not yet. She eased the car back onto the deserted street. People would be getting home from church and making Sunday dinner. Families laughing together and catching up on the week. Here in the South, the streets were empty. No one was out running errands or getting to work. Chick-fil-A was closed. Ellie looked at the people sitting on their porches with pitchers of iced tea perched between them. The kids playing on the front lawns. Savannah and San Diego might as well be different countries.

A little way down, and she turned left onto Kansas Street. She kept her pace slow. This was the very street she had ridden her bike down on the way to see Nolan. She stopped again at the corner. She could see his house, the one where he lived back then. The new owner had painted the place yellow. But a coat of paint couldn't take away the memories.

She and Nolan sitting on his front porch or walking across Edgewood to Gordonston Park. The talks about his science class or her biology exam. The laughter over something someone had said at lunch.

Their last night together.

That memory more than any other. The way he'd held her in his arms and his desperation before he'd come up with the idea of writing letters. The tackle box and the old oak tree.

She could see it all again from behind the wheel of her car.

Tears blurred her vision, and she blinked them back. *Enough.* She would come here tomorrow, back to the park. That was something else she'd decided while they were driving here. She wanted her letter. Maybe if she came here on June first and dug up the box, if she took her letter and read his, she'd have closure. Fully and finally.

Nolan was probably gearing up for the first game of the NBA finals. He and his teammates. If he had a day off, he was probably spending it with his girlfriend. His life had been so golden lately that he probably didn't remember anything about the tackle box and the tree. She didn't blame him. Kids didn't keep promises they made that many years ago.

She began driving again, and this time she used the GPS on her phone and the address she had memorized three days ago. The apartment where her mother had settled in once her baby was born. Three and a half miles. A few major city blocks and a handful of stoplights, and she would be at her mother's house. She pictured her raising a son on her own, scraping together coupons and living with the heat on summer days in order to cut corners. Week after week after week.

So many lives changed.

Another few turns and she was on Whitaker Street, across from Forsyth Park. The biggest park in Savannah. Ellie checked the addresses of the apartments with the one in her phone until she was directly in front of it. She made a U-turn and parked along the curb adjacent to the unit. The place was more of a condo than an apartment, and her mother's was on the first floor. It included three stairs and a porch not quite big enough for a rocking chair. The paint was peeling off the walls, but the neighborhood felt safe. The park looked just like Ellie remembered it. She stared at the open field and watched a mom and dad playing with their little girl.

The memory she never made.

She took a deep breath and rolled down the windows. It was just after noon and cooler than usual, only sixty degrees or so, according to the panel on her dashboard. She would get Kinzie up in a minute, but first she wanted to see if her mother was home. Her knees shook as she stepped out and walked around to the sidewalk. She stopped and stared at the door and breathed. Just breathed.

So many years without her mom. Every weekend in high school when she needed someone to talk to, when kids started drinking and trying drugs and having sex. Even if she couldn't admit it then, all Ellie ever wanted was her mother. Her mom to pour her heart out to. The way other girls did. Through every dance and every lonely summer and so many Christmases and birthdays and her high school graduation.

She would cry herself to sleep, missing her mom and hating her at the same time. Hating her for not caring that somewhere in San Diego, Ellie was growing up and graduating and hanging out with a soldier who wasn't good for her. Her mother had a calendar, but year after year on her birthday Ellie would ache at the knowledge that her mother hadn't tried to contact her.

And the whole time—through every moment of missing her mom—Ellie hadn't thought once that her mother even cared. She pictured the box of letters. The reality was so different. While she was missing her mom, her mom was missing her. The two of them both wishing for a way back to yesterday.

Ellie breathed in sharply through her nose, walked up the stairs, and knocked on the door. The sound was nothing compared to her pounding heart. Sunshine baked down on her shoulders, but her nerves left her shivering. Would her mother recognize her? Ellie, a woman now, all grown up. Seconds felt like hours as she waited. Maybe she had the wrong address . . . or possibly her mom was out for the day.

Ellie was about to turn around when the door opened. And there she was, as beautiful as Ellie remembered her. "Mom?"

Her mother's hand flew to her mouth, and tears flooded her eyes. "Ellie?" She didn't need to ask how or why; her eyes made it clear. All that mattered was that Ellie was here. She had come. "Ellie." She ran to her and hugged her, held her the way soldiers held their loved ones when they returned from war.

Like she'd come back from the dead. "You're here. You're really here."

"Mama. I got the letters." Ellie savored the feeling, being in her mom's arms again. She treasured it and let it replace all the times when her mother hadn't been there. "I missed you."

"I missed you, too. Every day." She held Ellie, rocked her. "Thank you, Lord. She's home. Thank you!"

And there in her mother's arms—for the first time since Ellie was fifteen—the thought occurred to her that God might be real after all. Because she could feel His love in the person of Caroline Tucker. The mother who had prayed for her and missed her and loved her since the day she left.

Ellie stepped back a few inches and studied her mom's face, the familiar curve of her cheeks, the depth in her eyes. Eyes like Kinzie's. "Mama." She wiped at her tears, but they still came. More and more they came. Ellie looked back at her car and then to her mother again. "I have someone I'd like you to meet."

Chapter Twenty-four

It was a miracle. Caroline Tucker had no other explanation for how it felt to have her daughter in her arms again. She hadn't seen her since she was a teenager, but she would've recognized her anywhere. Her eyes, her pretty face, her graceful way. She had grown up. The teenage girl was forever gone.

But she was still Ellie.

Caroline's tears came despite her joy. Her daughter was home! After eleven years she was here, and Caroline was never going to lose her again. She shaded her eyes and checked on John, at the park again, playing basketball with his friends. She would introduce them later. For now she watched as Ellie jogged back to the car and opened the back door. She bent down and seemed to talk to someone.

A few seconds passed, and as Ellie backed up, a little blond girl stepped out. Caroline's gasp was silent. Ellie had a daughter? She had missed knowing her grandchild? What was Alan thinking, keeping her letters from Ellie? More tears rushed from the depths of her tortured soul. The girl wasn't a baby. She was older than kindergarten. The losses piled up.

Ellie held the child's hand and walked her to where her mother stood. "This is Kinzie."

Kinzie? Caroline met Ellie's eyes. The street where Ellie and Nolan met so often. Her daughter might've been gone for over a decade, but their ability to communicate remained. Caroline put her hands on her knees and looked at the little girl. "You have very kind eyes, Kinzie. They're beautiful."

Ellie's daughter was still partly asleep. But at the sound of the compliment, she opened her eyes a little wider. "Thank you." She looked intrigued. She batted her eyelashes a few times. "You're my grandma Tucker, right?"

"Yes." Caroline wiped her cheeks, knowing that her tears would only confuse the child. "Looks like we have a lot to catch up on."

Kinzie nodded and leaned against Ellie. "My mommy says you used to take her to the park to play on the swings."

Her words wrapped themselves around Caroline and told her something she was desperate to know: Ellie remembered. She remembered, and she had missed Caroline and her growing-up days in Savannah as much as Caroline had. Caroline lifted her eyes to Ellie's, and again the look they shared held years of loss, but an even greater hope. She found her voice and put her hand on Kinzie's shoulder. "It's been a while . . . but I definitely like playing on swings."

"Can I have a drink of water, please?" Kinzie peered past Caroline into the apartment.

"Of course, honey." Caroline opened the door and ushered Ellie and Kinzie inside. She helped the child with a glass of water and gave her a plate of graham crackers, and then she and Ellie took a spot in the adjacent room.

"Dad gave me the letters. A few days ago." Ellie reached for

her hand. "I thought you didn't want to find me. Like . . . "
She looked out the window for a long time, as if trying to see
into the past. "Like you forgot about me."

"Never, Ellie." Caroline looked deep into her daughter's familiar eyes. "I've been here the whole time. Praying, believing.
Knowing that somehow you'd find your way back."

"You wrote once a week." She covered her mother's hand
with her own. "When I realized that, I left the next morning."

Ellie told her about the letter she'd opened the night before
she left. The one Caroline had written the day before Kinzie was
born. Caroline remembered it well. "I felt like you were hurt or
in trouble. Like something was wrong. I couldn't shake it."

"Grandma?" Kinzie had gotten down from her chair and
joined them in the living room. "Can I sit by you?"

"Yes, sweetie." Caroline released her daughter's hands and
patted the place on the couch next to her. "We three girls can
sit here and catch up. How's that?"

Kinzie smiled. "I like that." She hesitated and patted Ellie's
shoulder as she walked by and took the spot beside Caroline.

There was no way to describe the fullness in Caroline's
heart. Her daughter and granddaughter on either side of her,
the walls that had stood between them, forever gone. They had
so much to talk about, so many moments to catch up on.

Ellie told Caroline about struggling with her father and
never feeling good enough; she told her about C.J. Kinzie
hung on every word, so Ellie's expression told Caroline there
were details she would have to share later. "He was very kind
and very handsome." Ellie smiled at her daughter. "Kinzie's
laugh sounds a little like his."

Kinzie leaned in to Caroline's arm, saddened by the story of
her father, though she had clearly heard it before. Caroline's

heart filled with pride over the way Ellie had raised the girl. She was well-behaved and clearly very close to Ellie.

Carefully, again seeming to take note of Kinzie's presence, Ellie explained that her dad hadn't been in favor of her relationship with C.J., so when she'd gotten pregnant, she'd moved in with a friend. Ellie's eyes held Caroline's for a long moment. "We didn't talk until the other day. When he brought me the box of letters."

Caroline had always figured Ellie had a wonderful relationship with her dad, that the two of them had connected to the point where he filled her need for both parents. Instead, Ellie had been alone in the world, raising Kinzie, since she was nineteen. Anger and sorrow and helpless frustration fought for first position in Caroline's soul.

"I have a question." Caroline didn't really want to ask. Especially when she had a feeling she already knew the answer. "Have you talked to Nolan Cook? Since you left Savannah?"

"No, Grandma." Kinzie popped her blond head closer so Caroline couldn't miss her.

Caroline put her arm around the girl's shoulders and turned to her. "You know him?"

"Mommy and I watched him on TV when we had lunch at the zoo." She smiled at Ellie. "He's very nice. That's what Mommy said."

"He is, baby." Ellie acknowledged Kinzie, sharing the moment with her before lifting her eyes to Caroline's. "We haven't talked." She looked unsure whether she should say the next part. "I changed my name. After I moved out of Dad's house."

Caroline wondered when the parade of surprises would end. "What'd you change it to?"

"Ellie Anne." She didn't look sorry about the fact. "I dropped the Tucker."

An understanding filled Caroline. "So he couldn't have found you if he'd tried."

"Right." She glanced at Kinzie. "Everything's different. He found his dream." She paused, and this time she locked eyes with the child for several seconds. Her smile was as genuine as summer. "He found his, and I found mine."

Caroline could feel Kinzie beaming beside her. "That's my name, too, Grandma. Kinzie Anne."

Who could blame Ellie for no longer wanting the name Tucker? After how Alan had treated her? She cringed on the inside, imagining what it must've been like for Ellie, coming home and telling her father that she was pregnant. After what had happened with Caroline and Peyton? He must have called her unthinkable names, accused her of the worst possible things.

Again, they could talk later. For now Caroline put her hand on Ellie's knee and gave her a look that said how very sorry she was. Her other arm was still around Kinzie, and she leaned close and kissed the top of the girl's head. "I think your name is beautiful, baby girl."

"Baby girl!" Kinzie giggled. "That's what my mommy sometimes calls me."

Caroline looked at Ellie, drinking in the reality of her presence, trying to believe it. Her daughter was here, and she was home. "I used to call Ellie that when she was your age."

Kinzie's eyes grew wide, and she made a quick gasp. "That 'splains it then."

"Yes, it does." Caroline listened for the sound of the basketball across the street. She could hear it, but she needed to check on him. Every half hour or so she would catch a visual of him at the window or walk over to the park to watch him play. "I have an idea." She tried to look excited, despite the gravity of Ellie's story. "Let's walk to the park. That way you can meet John."

Caroline felt Ellie stiffen a little, felt a cooling that had not been there in this fresh new season. Kinzie blinked twice. "Your son?"

"Yes." Caroline ran her fingers through Kinzie's hair. "John's my little boy. He's ten. Going into the fourth grade."

Kinzie looked around, slightly uneasy. "Is he hiding?"

"No." Already Caroline felt a connection with her granddaughter. "He's playing basketball at the park across the street. We'll go watch, okay?"

"Okay."

"But first . . . can we do something together?" Caroline looked from Ellie to Kinzie. "Yes! What do you wanna do, Grandma?"

Caroline was still grasping the idea that she was a grandmother and that her granddaughter had gone six years without her. Ellie looked slightly skeptical. Though they could read each other, time had placed a complicated distance between them. Distance they would have to work through, no matter how long it took.

Caroline took a breath and pushed ahead. "I was thinking maybe we could hold hands and pray." She smiled at Kinzie and then lifted her eyes to Ellie's. "Would you mind?"

Ellie hesitated. "It's fine." Her smile looked slightly forced. "Go ahead."

A rush of emotion caught Caroline as she gently took Ellie's and Kinzie's hands. She closed her eyes and bowed her head, her heart too full to speak. God had already answered so many of her prayers. She ran her thumb along the hands of her daughter and granddaughter and finally found her voice. "Father, You have heard our cries, and You have brought us back together. It's more than we can believe right now. But I have the sense You're not finished. Please have Your way with us as the hours and days unfold. Whatever miracle You are working in our lives, help us not to stand in the way of it. In Jesus' name, amen."

"Amen!" Kinzie's response was upbeat and certain as she grinned at Caroline. "That's how the pastor prays at church." She raised her eyebrows, as if a possibility had just hit her. "Do you and John go to church, Grandma?"

"We do." Caroline hesitated, not sure she should have this conversation with Kinzie before she had it alone with Ellie. Her daughter had agreed to the prayer, but again Caroline had felt her hesitation.

Ellie released Caroline's hand and stood. "I'll get our bags." She didn't look angry or upset. Just uncomfortable. She smiled at the two of them and then patted Kinzie's arm. "You go ahead and talk to Grandma, baby."

"Okay." When Ellie was out of the room, Kinzie lifted her eyes to Caroline's. "I go to church with Tina and Tiara. Mommy stays home and cleans the apartment."

"Tina and Tiara?"

"Tina's my mommy's friend from work, and Tiara is her little girl. They're like our family, kind of."

"I see." The picture was clearer all the time. The lonely life with Alan, his controlling ways, her own affair . . . everything that had happened since the move to San Diego. No wonder Ellie didn't go to church. Caroline silently grieved her part in harming her daughter and in the losses that had stockpiled since.

"Are you sad about that, Grandma?" Kinzie took her hand again. "About Mommy not going to church?"

"I am sad." She smiled for Kinzie's benefit. Ellie would be back any second, so the conversation couldn't get too involved. Not now, anyway.

"I pray for her. Every night." Kinzie pointed to the floor. "On my knees by my bed."

"Thatta girl, Kinzie." Once more Caroline felt an uncanny connection to the precious child. "Keep praying. God hears you, baby girl."

"I know. And Pastor says that some people take longer to find their happy-ever-after in Jesus."

"That's right." A new layer of tears formed in Caroline's eyes. "Some people take a little longer."

Kinzie leaned closer and rested her head on Caroline's arm. "I'm glad we found you, Grandma. My mommy's really happy about that."

"Well." She struggled to find her voice, her emotions too many and too great. "I'm really happy, too."

Ellie returned with their things, and the three of them walked across the street to the park. Caroline called to John, and he grabbed his basketball and joined them. They all seemed to connect well, but Caroline had to keep forcing herself to listen to the conversation. She was too busy survey-ing the scene, taking it in. Amazed by it. Ellie was home! Seeing her and Kinzie and John talking together was like a scene from her dreams. The greatest answer to prayer she could imagine.

Now she would have to change her prayer. That the broken

things would get fixed, and that one day soon Ellie would find among the ashes of the past what Caroline had already found.

Her happy-ever-after in Jesus.

❦ ❦

Caroline had only just sat down at her desk at work that Monday morning when Nolan Cook walked in. Again she wondered if she were dreaming. The basketball player had been on her mind since Ellie arrived yesterday. She and Ellie talked about him late last night, and only then did Caroline understand the gravity of his absence in her life.

"I'll never see him again; I already know that." Ellie sat with her knees pulled up to her chest, her shoes off. Despite the years they'd lost, she looked like a teenager again. "He's famous now. The guy everyone wants." She laughed, but only to hide her obvious sadness. "There's no way back. Even here in Savannah."

Then Ellie had told her about the buried tackle box beneath the oak tree in Gordonston Park. About the letters inside. The date they had set to meet was tomorrow. Ellie was convinced that Nolan had forgotten the meeting and the chance it represented for the two of them to find each other.

Which was why as Nolan walked into her office, Caroline had to discreetly brace herself to keep from falling out of her chair. He wore dark blue jeans and a white V-neck T-shirt. She was the only one at the front desk that early, and the waiting room held just one older couple. She was trying to figure out what to say as he walked up and stuck his hands in his jeans pockets.

"Mrs. Tucker." He nodded, humble and polite. Much like he'd been as a kid. "It's been a long time."

"Nolan." Caroline stood and looked over her shoulder

toward the business office. "Hold on." She found a coworker to cover for her at the front desk, then she joined Nolan in the waiting room. "Can we talk outside?"

"Yes. Please."

The older couple didn't seem to recognize Nolan, so they could have these few minutes to themselves. Nolan motioned to a metal bench just down from the office door, and the two of them sat facing each other.

"I won't take your time." The morning was warm and cloudy. Neither of them needed sunglasses to look at each other. "I'm here because of Ellie."

Caroline wasn't sure what to say first. "How did you find me?"

"The short answer?" His eyes held an unmistakable kindness. "The Lord answered my prayers." He managed a slight smile. "Ryan Kelly? The guitarist for Peyton Anders?"

Hearing the name changed her expression. Caroline could feel it. There was no way to stop the shame she felt whenever the country singer's name came up in conversation. She nodded, fighting her way back to the moment. "Ryan stopped by here not long ago."

"He and his wife came to one of my games. I was talking about my childhood. How I lost my best friend when she moved to San Diego the summer we were fifteen."

Caroline felt her heart skip a beat. "That's crazy."

"Exactly." He ran his hand through his still-blond hair. "He asked me if I knew a Caroline Tucker. We figured out the rest pretty fast." The look in his eyes grew deeper. "I came as soon as I had a day off." He folded his hands, and for a long time, he stared at the ground. When he looked up, his eyes were damp. "Ma'am, I've looked for Ellie since the day she left."

Caroline's mind began to spin. Nolan had been looking for

Ellie all this time? Was this really happening? She wanted to interrupt him, to tell him that she'd found Ellie, but Nolan was talking, and the shock was too great.

Frustration and intensity darkened his expression. "It's like she fell off the face of the earth." He leaned his forearms on his knees, as if he believed he was out of options. "Ryan said you haven't seen her. But if you have any hints, anything that would point me in the right direction, please . . . I have to know."

The wind felt like it had been knocked from Caroline's lungs. The young man sitting beside her didn't only remember Ellie. He was consumed with her.

Her silent prayer came with her next breath. *Dear God . . . thank you.* "Nolan . . ." She smiled, trying to figure out where to start. "You won't believe this."

"Yes?"

Caroline didn't know what to say first. For a few seconds she could only bask in the reality that God was here. His Spirit hovered over the place where they sat. There was no question that God was working out a miracle.

Any other explanation was impossible.

Chapter Twenty-five

She knew something. Nolan could tell. Long before she began to speak, he felt the blood drain from his face, felt his heart kick into a rhythm harder and faster than anything he was used to on the basketball court. "Mrs. Tucker?"

"I'm sorry." She laughed, but tears filled her eyes at the same time. "Ellie . . . she came home last night."

The news grabbed Nolan's whole world and literally crashed it to a halt. All of life from that moment on would be defined as *before* this conversation with Ellie's mother and *after* it. No matter what came next, he had the main thing he needed to know, the thing that had troubled him every day as long as he could remember.

Ellie was alive.

He closed his eyes and exhaled. She was alive. As the revelation became reality, he had more questions than he could ask at one time. "Did she call? I mean, what . . ." His thoughts ran together. Ellie was alive! He forced himself to concentrate. "What made her come home?"

Caroline sighed. "Another long story." She put her hand on

Nolan's shoulder for a few seconds. "God's working a miracle. For all of us."

Nolan learned the other details in a matter of minutes. The letters from Caroline to Ellie, the change of heart in Caroline's husband. How the letters had triggered Ellie's road trip. Her mom didn't mention the meeting at Gordonston Park tomorrow, so Nolan didn't, either. But whether Ellie remembered or not didn't matter. If she was here in Savannah, he was going to find her.

His heart felt lighter than it had since his dad died.

"Can I see her?" Nolan pulled out his phone. "Please, give me your address and I'll go right now."

Something changed in her eyes. She sat a little more stiffly and shook her head. "How about this evening? Around five?"

Nolan studied her. She was hiding something; at least it looked that way. Details about Ellie, maybe. Something she didn't want to talk about. "I have all day."

Her pained smile begged him to understand. "She might be asleep. She drove four straight days."

Disappointment tried to crowd in, but Nolan refused it. He'd waited eleven years to see her. He could wait another eight hours. "Okay." He clenched his jaw. She was here. He still couldn't believe it. "I'll find something to do. Head down to the river, maybe." He stood, and she did the same. They hugged, the way he might hug his own mom. "Five o'clock?"

"Yes." She paused. "While you're at the river today . . . pray, Nolan. Just pray."

Again he sensed something cryptic in her tone. Whatever it was, he would find out that evening. When he would see Ellie for the first time since they were fifteen. Something he never

252 @ KAREN KINGSBURY

dreamed would come from this conversation. He nodded as they parted ways. "I'll pray. Definitely."

"See you, Nolan."

"Five o'clock." They both waved. She returned to the office as he headed for his SUV. Was Ellie sick? Or had she grown to despise him somehow? Was that why she'd never contacted him? Why she hadn't wanted to be found? Fear tried to consume him, but he took even the thought of it captive.

The trick was something he'd learned a long time ago in the battle of living a Christian life. The start of sin and destruction, discouragement and darkness, always happened with a single thought. He couldn't stop that. Wrong thoughts were like billboard signs on the highway of life. They were bound to come. Victory or defeat depended on how he handled the thought. "Take every thought captive to the obedience of Christ." The Scripture from 2 Corinthians 10:5 came back to him now, the way it had countless other times.

He grabbed the wayward thought and pushed it from his heart and mind. He wouldn't be afraid. Whatever had happened with Ellie, whatever her mother wanted him to pray about, God was in control. He had nothing to fear. The Lord had worked a miracle to this point. He wasn't finished yet.

Nolan was convinced.

Ellie had to leave in a hurry.

Her heart raced in time with her thoughts as she paced across her mother's kitchen. Kinzie and John were in the other room, watching a *Veggie Tales* movie about Jonah, but all Ellie could think was the obvious. She needed to run.

"Honey, I don't get it." Her mom spoke in little more than a whisper. She sounded practically desperate. "You told me how much you've missed him, how you wish the two of you never would've lost touch."

"Yes." Ellie worked to keep her voice down. "Because I'd be a different person if Nolan and I had stayed close. But now . . ." She held out her hands. Why couldn't her mother understand? "Look at me. I'm not the same girl. He'll be . . . he'll be disappointed, Mom. Nolan Cook wouldn't want me." She didn't want to spell it out, how she was a single mom with few accomplishments, but the facts remained. "I don't want to see him."

Ellie hadn't realized how true that was until her mother came home from work early and told her what had happened. That Nolan had come looking for her was shocking enough. But now that he was only a few miles away and headed for her mother's apartment, Ellie couldn't get around the panic.

It was one thing to be curious, to want to dig up the tackle box and read what Nolan had said about her all those years ago. But facing him here in her mom's living room? Introducing him to Kinzie and trying to explain away the last decade? The thought was more than she could take. Better to remember Nolan the way she knew him when they were fifteen than to see him pity her.

"Honey." Her mother tried again. "I told him you'd be here." She leaned on the kitchen island that separated them. Her tone was a mix of frustration and fear. "He's looked for you since you moved."

"I'm sorry." Ellie walked around the counter and gently put her hands on her mother's shoulders. "I need to go. I'll explain later." She grabbed her keys from the counter and hurried into the living room. Kinzie couldn't know her frantic resolve. The child was too perceptive, too able to tell that something was wrong. It was already a quarter to five. No time for explanations. She came up behind her daughter and touched her blond hair. "Kinz, we need to go shopping. Mommy has to get something at the store, okay?"

Kinzie looked at her mom and back at the TV. "But the movie's almost over."

"We can watch it later."

"It's okay." John stood and stretched. He was tall, with dark hair and eyes as blue as Caroline's. As blue as Ellie's and Kinzie's. John patted Kinzie on her head. "We can finish when you get back. I need to shoot hoops."

"Okay." Kinzie's shoulders dropped a little. "I guess."

John grinned at her, then walked down the hallway toward his bedroom.

"You ready?" Ellie tried to keep her calm. The minutes were falling away.

Her daughter patted out the wrinkles in her sundress. "Right now?" She picked up her dolly off the floor.

"Yes, baby." Ellie fiddled with the car keys. "You ready?"

"I have to use the restroom." Kinzie moved slowly, probably tired from sitting. "Here, can you hold her?" She handed over the doll.

"Yes." Ellie reminded herself to be patient. None of this was her daughter's fault. "Hurry, okay?"

"Yes, Mommy."

The clock screamed at her, taunting her. She checked her phone. Seven minutes. That was all the time she had until Nolan Cook pulled up out front. Her mom came to her. "You're really leaving?"

"I am. Tell him . . . I had things to do." She turned and the two of them hugged. "I can't see him. I just can't."

"He won't believe that." A slow sigh came from her mom. "It's been so long, Ellie."

"Exactly." She smiled, willing her mother to understand. "Kinzie?" She kept her tone friendly. "Baby, we have to go."

"Just a minute." The little voice came from down the hall-way.

"Can I say one more thing?" Her mom still faced her. "Don't you think the timing is a little strange for all of this to be a coincidence?" She seemed less determined, more accept-ing of the reality: Ellie didn't want to see Nolan. Period.

"It's not that strange. This Ryan Kelly guy talks to you and then . . ." Ellie stopped cold. All she had focused on earlier was that Nolan had come by Caroline's office, that he was coming here. But now the other details of her mother's explanation screamed through her mind. "Ryan is Peyton Anders's guitar player? And he came because he knew you and Peyton used to be friends?"

"Yes." A depth came over her mother, both in her eyes and in her tone. "Peyton and I were friends."

"When?" Ellie's heart pounded faster, and she felt sick to her stomach.

"I met him thirteen years ago. We were friends for two years."

"So . . . that's . . ." Her voice trailed off. She couldn't form the words, couldn't imagine them. Instead, she searched her mother's eyes as the blood drained from her face. If her mother had something to tell her, she could say the next words.

"What you're thinking . . . you're right. He's John's father." Caroline dropped her voice to a whisper. "John doesn't know all the details. Just that his dad was a singer who wasn't ready to be a dad."

Her mom was a groupie? The picture was so awful, Ellie couldn't believe it. "I always . . . pictured you had been with someone . . . normal. Someone who loved you."

"I thought he did." Caroline's tone said she wasn't going to defend herself. But at the same time her eyes said there was more to the story.

Of course. Ellie caught her breath. There had to be more to the story.

Kinzie came bouncing down the hall, a grin on her face. "Let's go. I decided a trip to the store will be fun."

They had maybe three minutes. Nolan could pull up any moment. "Yes." Ellie looked at her mom and felt her expression soften. "We'll talk later." They had both made decisions they weren't proud of. Whatever had happened, her mother must've had a reason, an explanation.

If she'd known him for two years, she must have been more to Peyton Anders than a groupie.

They said good-bye, and Ellie put her arm around Kinzie's shoulders. "Let's race to the car!"

The little girl's giggles made the world feel right somehow.

A minute later, they were out of the neighborhood, and Ellie noticed something.

She could breathe again.

❦ ❦

Nolan could hardly wait for five o'clock. After a day at the river, he wasn't sure he had ever prayed more intensely for Ellie Tucker. Whatever the situation, however she felt about him, and whichever way the past eleven years had played out in her life, he couldn't wait to see her. Just knowing she was here in the same city made this one of his best days ever.

A day he wasn't sure he'd have.

He pulled up outside her mother's apartment and double-checked the address. He felt more nervous than he'd been back in middle school when he came to Ellie's house, or when they'd meet at the park. He understood why. He was no longer sure of Ellie's feelings or who she'd become.

Her mother answered the door seconds after he knocked, and from the moment their eyes met, he knew there was trouble. "Nolan, come in."

The living room was quiet except for a boy sitting at the dining room table. He had a basketball on his lap, and he stood slowly when Nolan walked through the door. Nolan smiled at the kid and looked around, intent on getting answers. He kept his tone polite, but his panic must have been evident. "Where is she?"

"She left." Her mother looked like she'd aged a year since that morning. Her voice held an apology. "She had a few errands to run."

Nolan didn't speak, didn't move. In college he'd taken a biology class in which he learned about cortisol. The death hormone, it was called. A substance that the body released into the bloodstream upon suffering stress or hearing bad news. He was pretty sure he was experiencing an overdose of it now.

"I'm sorry." Mrs. Tucker crossed her arms, clearly embarrassed. "I don't understand her, Nolan. I told her you were coming, how you'd looked for her since she moved away."

"Did she say if . . . Will she be right back?"

"No." Caroline sighed and shook her head. "She doesn't want to see you. I can't explain it. I'm so sorry."

The boy came closer, the ball still under his arm. He stood by Ellie's mom, and Nolan understood. This was the child she'd been pregnant with; he was the result of the affair that had caused Ellie's father to move to San Diego. Nolan felt compassion for the child. None of the heartache and loss surrounding his birth was his fault. "Hey." He held out his hand, and the kid shook it. "I'm Nolan Cook."

"John, sir." The boy clearly knew who Nolan was. "My friends aren't going to believe this."

"Nolan and I need to talk for a few minutes." Ellie's mother looked nervous.

"Yes, ma'am." John returned to the other room and sat at the table, watching them from a distance.

Once he was out of earshot, Ellie's mom lowered her voice. "I don't know when she'll be home. I'm not sure what to tell you."

"I'm not going anywhere." Nolan was at peace about that much. "She has to come back eventually."

"I just . . . I don't think she'd like that. I'm so sorry."

"I'll let her tell me." Nolan smiled, despite the way his heart had fallen to his feet. Ellie Tucker, avoiding him? The reality confirmed every painful possibility he'd considered over the years. She was alive, yes. But she didn't want to see him. Now he had to figure out why. He wouldn't leave until he had the answer.

Nolan had an idea. He took a few steps toward the kitchen. "Hey, John, I stopped by Savannah High earlier today. The coach has the gym open for me tonight. Sort of a private thing."

"Really?" John was on his feet in a flash. The kid seemed nice, and judging from his Hawks T-shirt and the basketball in his hands, he was crazy about the sport.

"Maybe we should go shoot around. What do you think?"

Nolan looked at Caroline. "Would you mind? For an hour or so?"

"Please, Mom." John hurried over to her.

Nolan watched the woman consider. She had known Nolan since he was a kid, and she trusted him. But letting John go meant that Nolan would have to bring him home later. Another chance to see Ellie. He tried to put her concern to rest. "Ma'am." He kept his tone polite. "I can tell you this. Either way, I'm not leaving until I see her."

"Well," Caroline hesitated, losing her fight. "John would love it." She smiled at her son. "As for the rest . . . I'll pray."

That was all Nolan needed to hear. He nodded to the boy to follow him. John kissed his mom on the cheek and hugged her, and with that, the two of them left for the gym. The place where Nolan and Ellie had spent almost half their teenage years. The court where he could feel his father again, see him coaching from the sidelines. God had brought him this far. He would play basketball with the boy, take him home, and do what he'd dreamed of doing since his last hour together with Ellie. He would hang out with Ellie and figure out an answer to the question that had parked dead center in his heart.

Why was she avoiding him?

Chapter Twenty-six

Ellie figured she'd wait an hour before she called her mom. She and Kinzie had gone to the closest market and bought ingredients for chocolate chip cookies. Her daughter was in a delightful mood, completely unaware of what Ellie was feeling. Kinzie liked Savannah, she thought John was funny, and she wondered when they could come back. "Or maybe we could move here, Mommy? Because then I could be near my grandma. Little girls should have their grandmas close by, right?"

Ellie wasn't sure why, but she pictured her father alone in his house with no family. If she and Kinzie moved to Savannah—something she'd been thinking about since she first hugged her mom—that's how his life would be. How it would probably end. Alone and without the people he really did love. The image brought no satisfaction.

"Well, Kinz." Her heart ached, but she smiled at her daughter. "Families should be together. Moms and dads and grandmas and grandpas." She walked alongside Kinzie down another aisle, the two of them taking their time. "So, yes, little girls should be near their grandmas."

Kinzie seemed content with that explanation. She launched into a description of the *VeggieTales* movie. Ellie tried to listen, but she couldn't stop thinking about Nolan. Why was he in town? It had to be a coincidence. He was about to start the NBA finals. That and he was dating someone. If he had come looking for her, it was only because he happened to be here and he was curious.

Right?

She couldn't quite convince herself. The timing was uncanny.

All the way here, every long mile between San Diego and Savannah, Ellie had told herself Nolan wouldn't come to the meeting at the old oak tree. At the same time, she had allowed herself to dream. If he did come, she would hold on to the moment like the most beautiful treasure. It would be a last time to say good-bye. Closure. If he met her at the park, the minutes with Nolan Cook would be theirs alone. Outside of time.

But never along the entire drive had she thought it would happen.

Kinzie switched topics and began remembering out loud every special thing they'd seen on the trip to Georgia. Ellie nodded and said what she needed to say in order to remain part of the conversation. The imagined moment with Nolan had only been a fantasy.

All that changed the moment her mother mentioned Nolan's name. Fear had seized her in a vise grip. She didn't want to see Nolan Cook, didn't want to stand across from him, so close she could touch him. Couldn't bear to see him disappointed in her. Not now and not ever. Of course she couldn't get out of her mom's house fast enough.

If she let him see her now, he would never again know her as the fifteen-year-old girl she had been. He would see who she was today. Who she had become. He would see her place in life and the consequences of her actions, and he would see Kinzie. In as much time as it took to blink, he would shift his emotions from curiosity to compassion.

And just like that, Nolan Cook would feel sorry for her.

Something she could never let happen. Partly because she was happy with her life—especially now that she'd found her mom and her heart was beginning to let go of the anger she'd felt toward her father. She had a job she enjoyed, even if someday she still wanted to write her novel. And she had Kinzie.

Kinzie most of all.

If Nolan felt sorry for her, then it would mean he didn't understand her or know her whatsoever. No, the only way their memories of yesterday would remain untouched was if they left the past back on Edgewood and Louisiana and Kinzie streets. Back in Gordonston Park.

"Mommy?" Kinzie tapped Ellie's hand and stopped walking. "Can we get Grandma some of that tea? Because I saw it by her sink, and I think she likes it."

"Hmm?"

"This." Kinzie picked up a red box of Tazo Awake tea. "I saw it on her counter."

"Yes, baby, we can get it."

"You look funny. Were you listening to me before?" Her eyes had a teasing look. "Are you thinking about making cookies?"

"Yes, baby, that's right." She put her arm around Kinzie's shoulders and hugged her. "I can't wait to make cookies with you."

"Me, too, Mommy. Because you and me and my grandma are making cookies for the very first time."

Ellie smiled at her. "Kinz, I have to call Grandma real quick, okay?"

"Okay." She skipped ahead a few feet. "Tell her about the cookies."

The number had been in her address book for a day, but already Ellie had it saved as a favorite. She touched the button, and it began to ring.

Her mother answered quickly. "Ellie . . . you're okay." She exhaled. "I was worried. You left so fast."

"I'm fine." Her daughter was close enough to hear the conversation, so she didn't want to mention Nolan. "Kinzie and I are going to make chocolate chip cookies with you when we get back."

Her mom hesitated. "Nolan came by. You know that."

"You told him I was out, right?"

"After eleven years?" Her mom made a sound that was more cry than laugh. "He won't give up now, honey. You have to know that."

It wasn't something she had considered. She figured if her mom discouraged him, if he thought she didn't want to see him, then he would give up. Especially if he was only curious. Another ribbon of concern wrapped itself around her. "What did he say?"

Kinzie skipped in circles, singing a song. Something about cucumbers. Ellie worked to hear what her mom was saying. "He took John to the gym, to Savannah High. To shoot around for a few hours."

"Wait . . . what?" Ellie's panic hit a new level. "Nolan has John?"

"He won't leave, Ellie. He wants to see you."

She was about to argue, about to beg her mom to make him understand. But suddenly, she understood what she needed to do. Even if she didn't want to. If he was going to hang around, if he wouldn't leave until he saw her, then she had just one choice. She needed to go to him.

Yes, it would change things between them. It would alter the memories of yesterday. But at least they would both have their answers, and he could leave her alone. The first of June would come tomorrow, and after that she could move on. Once and for all.

"Fine." Resignation sounded in her voice. She wasn't upset with her mom, just steeling her heart. "I'll bring Kinzie home, and I'll go talk to him."

Her mother hesitated. "Thank you." She sounded beyond relieved.

"One question, Mom." She still couldn't believe she'd found her mother. "Did you tell him about . . ." She glanced at her daughter. Kinzie was closer now, dancing not far from the shopping cart. "You know."

"About Kinzie. No. I didn't tell him anything. I thought you'd like to tell him."

"Thank you." Ellie let that sink in. Her mom was so kind, so understanding. Ellie thought again about all that she'd missed without her mother. They had so much to talk about, a lifetime to catch up on. They could start tonight, making chocolate chip cookies with Kinzie. One conversation at a time, they would catch up and find their way back. Ellie could see great things ahead.

If only she could get past Nolan Cook.

⟨⟩ ⟨⟩

Ellie dropped Kinzie off at her mom's and headed for Savannah High. Now she paused just outside the gym door, and there, in the humid late-May air, she listened. Just listened. The slap of the ball on the wood floor and Nolan's still-familiar voice filled her ears.

"Thatta boy . . . now you've got it!"

Ellie stepped into view and held her breath. It was one thing to see him on TV, to watch him tearing up an opposing defense, to see him interviewed by ESPN. But to see him here at the Savannah High gym? Her heart was instantly full, her resolve to say a few words and be on her way sorely shaken. If only she could stand here unnoticed for an hour and just be with him, here, where they'd spent so much time together.

John cut one way and then the other, dribbling the ball toward the basket. She needed to hurry, no matter how she felt. Before she left, Kinzie and her mom were pulling together ingredients for the chocolate chip cookies. Ellie wanted to be back before they put them in the oven.

But now . . . now she couldn't do anything but watch him. His kindness toward John, his graceful, artful way of driving to the net and scoring. He had been destined for basketball greatness since he was in middle school.

"You're doing great, buddy. Get some water." Nolan gave John a quick pat on the back.

The boy noticed her first. He headed toward the water fountain, did a double take, and then stopped and looked straight at her. "Hi, Ellie."

"Hi." She could feel Nolan's eyes on her before she turned

in his direction. Feel them drawing her in the way a magnet drew steel.

John jogged off to get a drink, and almost in slow motion, with eleven years wrapped up in the moment, Ellie looked at Nolan. Like something from a dream, she let her eyes find his, and everything around her faded. Everything except Nolan Cook. She didn't breathe, didn't notice her heartbeat or John walking back from the water fountain.

Because in all the world, there was only her and Nolan.

She caught herself just in time, before she said something or did something that would've tipped her hand to how she was feeling. How, for the first time in all those years, her heart felt like it was finally home. *Walls,* she ordered herself. *We're not fifteen.* She stood a little straighter and walked toward him. "Nolan."

"Ellie . . ." He looked like he couldn't decide whether to run to her or stop and drink in the sight of her.

She came all the way to him. His skin was dry. Clearly, he'd been letting John do most of the playing.

"You know each other?" John came a few steps closer. He looked like he was facing Christmas morning.

"We do." Nolan kept his eyes on Ellie. "It's been a long time."

She didn't turn away, either. Her words came slow and measured. "We were fifteen last time we saw each other."

"Wow." John's mouth hung open. "That's a long time ago."

"I have an idea." Nolan turned to John and passed him the ball. "How 'bout you go to that hoop over there and make a hundred free throws." He winked at John. "Would you mind, buddy?"

"Sure." John grinned. He dribbled to the far end of the court, and like that Ellie and Nolan were alone.

"Why?" Nolan's voice was pained, beyond hurt. He searched her eyes more deeply. "Why didn't you want to see me?"

"I'm sorry." *Keep the walls up, Ellie. You can do this.* "It's complicated." Ten minutes. She would talk for ten minutes, then take John and leave.

"Ellie . . . it's me." He reached for her hand. "What's wrong?"

The feel of his fingers around hers sent electricity through her body. His skin against hers. Nolan Cook, standing in front of her, holding her hand. *Breathe . . . you have to breathe.* How could she keep her distance if their brief reunion began this way?

"Talk to me." He moved a few inches closer, his eyes never leaving hers. "Please, Ellie. What happened?"

"I'm fine." She stood a little taller, using all her strength to appear sensible, in control. "Nolan . . . it isn't anything personal."

He looked almost frantic. "I said . . . this is me." Almost without moving, he came still closer. He kept his voice low, though John was too far away to hear them. "Why are you doing this?"

"I have to say something." She gave his hand the gentlest squeeze. "I'm sorry about your dad. I didn't know until a few years ago. I'm so sorry, Nolan." She felt him take her other hand. The feeling was heaven. *Hurry, Ellie, get out of here. Don't let your heart go.*

"Thank you." He ran his thumbs along hers. "I miss him still. Every day." For a few seconds, it looked like he might add that he missed her, too. Instead, he narrowed his eyes. "You're so . . . so completely beautiful, Ellie."

"Thank you." Her cheeks felt hot, her heart basking beneath the attraction he still had for her. How was this happening? When she was sure he'd forgotten her?

"But," his eyes still held hers, still searched deep inside her soul, "you're not the same."

She smiled, and she could feel how forced it must have looked. "No. I'm not." This was her moment. If she didn't say it now, she might never have the chance. He would understand better as soon as she got the words out.

"Why, Ellie? Talk to me."

Somehow, the warmth of his hands made her hesitate. As if she could hold on to this feeling, memorize it, and pretend they were fifteen again. One last time.

"Is there . . . someone else?" He ran his thumb over her ring finger. "It's the first thing I noticed. You're not married."

"I'm not." *Say it, Ellie.* Her determination was fading. She had no choice. *Stay strong. Get it over with.* She wouldn't deny Kinzie. Not even here, with Nolan Cook. "Things are different." A strange mix of joy and sorrow colored her tone. "I'm a mom now. My little girl . . . she's six."

His expression softened the moment her words were out. "I'm . . . sorry. I didn't know."

Suddenly Ellie felt strange holding hands with him. What they'd had was over. It had been over for a long time. Ellie eased her fingers free and crossed her arms. His apology grated on her soul. Already he pitied her. "Don't be sorry. She's wonderful."

"I didn't mean it like that. I just . . . I didn't realize." His voice trailed off, but his eyes remained kind. Maybe more than before.

Ellie felt sick to her stomach. "Don't do that."

"What?"

"That look." She took a step back. Her anger brought her back to reality in a hurry. "Don't feel sorry for me."

"I'm not." He was frustrated, no question. "If you're happy, then I'm happy. I'm sure she's beautiful. How could she not be?" He looked across the court at John. "I was thinking about her dad. Whether maybe you were living with him. Or if you were divorced."

"I never married." Ellie thought about his words, and she took a step back. "You thought I'd just live with someone?"

"Ellie." His stare cut through her. "That's not fair."

He was right. She had a child, after all. She hadn't waited until she was married, like she had planned to do when she was fifteen. "Okay." She found a hint of the polished smile once more, the one that wouldn't let him get anywhere near her heart. "But you get it. See, Nolan? Our lives are different now." She didn't waver, didn't look away. He needed to really hear her. "I'm happy for you. Your success. Your dreams." She allowed her sincerity to show. "You did it all."

"You make it sound like you're done. Like we're finished talking." He looked baffled, as if she were speaking Russian. "Ellie, tell me about it. About your daughter and your life."

"It's not what I planned, but it's good. Just different. That's all." She took another step away from him and looked over her shoulder at her brother. "John, we need to go." Again she smiled at Nolan. "I can't stay. I promised my daughter we'd make cookies tonight."

"You can't be serious." His words were more shocked than angry. "I spend a decade looking for you, and this is all I get? A few quick lines? Like I'm some acquaintance you barely know?" He closed the distance between them. "Ellie, I haven't changed. I want to know about your life, your past."

She looked at him for a long time. "No, you don't." They were out of time. *Run, Ellie. Don't let him close.* He wouldn't want her, not after he had time to comprehend how she'd changed. If she didn't leave now, she might fall for him again. And when he knew her whole story, when he politely moved on, her heart would never heal. She couldn't stand here waiting for that to happen. *Run now . . . go!* The rest of her answer came slowly. "Really, Nolan, just let it be." She put her hand on his arm and hesitated. Everything in her wanted to hug him, feel his arms around her.

Especially standing this close.

"I have to go." She held up her hand, waving to him as she walked away. "It was good seeing you, Nolan. Really."

John was out of breath when he met her near the half-court line. He looked from Ellie to Nolan and back. "We have to go?"

"We do." Ellie barely knew the child, but she felt a connection. It was another loss that she hadn't calculated. The fact that she never knew her brother until now.

John looked at Nolan. "Wanna come? I mean . . . if you want a snack or something back at the house."

Ellie could feel it again. Nolan's eyes on hers. She couldn't stop herself from looking at him one more time. "Nolan's busy."

"That's true." Nolan looked like he was fighting tears, and once more his eyes stayed locked on hers. "Maybe some other time." He tore himself away from her long enough to smile at John. "Next time I'm in town, I'll call, okay?"

"Okay." John couldn't have looked happier. "See you then." He dribbled his ball toward the door.

"You can't run, Ellie." Nolan looked at her once more. His eyes could still find their way through her walls. "I'll find you again."

"It's too late." Her whisper proved she couldn't last much longer. She could already feel her tears. "Good-bye, Nolan."

She didn't stay around to argue. There was no debating where the two of them went from here. They were two old friends who no longer stood on common ground.

Her tears came before she reached the door, so she didn't look back. That was the thing about Nolan Cook. Now that she'd seen him, she couldn't look back. Not ever. And as she walked alongside John to her car, as she listened to him chatter about the thrill of getting advice from Nolan, she assured herself she'd done the right thing.

Nolan might seem interested and not completely shocked by the fact that she had a child. But the truth came from what he *hadn't* said. He hadn't brought up the one thing that would prove he still cared, the one thing that would make her believe he still longed for yesterday.

The fact that tomorrow was June first.

Nolan wanted to run after her, but this wasn't the time.

Ellie was crazy if she thought he was giving up this easily. Quitting wasn't in him. Not on the basketball court, not in life. And not when it came to Ellie Tucker. He sat on the edge of the nearest bench and hung his head. Her daughter wasn't the issue. Nolan could sense it. Something else was wrong, something she wasn't saying. Maybe she was still involved with her daughter's father. Still in love with him.

His heart hurt at the possibility. That had to be it.

Even so, he wasn't moving on until he did the one thing he had come to do. If she didn't show up, fine. But if she was remotely the same Ellie he had looked for and longed for and loved all these years, then they had at least one more meeting. He looked for a long time across the court at the bleachers, at the place where a pixie-faced Ellie would cheer for him like her life depended on it. He had never felt so desperate in all his life.

Help me, God. . . . Seeing her again . . . it only confirmed how I feel. I need to talk to her. So what is it? What's happened to her heart?

Be still, my son. Be still, and know that I am God. I will never leave you nor forsake you.

The answer came from his Bible reading that morning. But in that moment they didn't seem like thoughts in his head. Alone in the gym where he'd grown up, where his father had taught him the game, God might as well have been standing across from him. The words were that powerful. Nolan checked the time on his phone—8:37. He had a little over three hours.

June 1st started at midnight, after all.

No matter what Ellie said or how strangely she was acting, when midnight hit, there was only one place he could be. He stood and dribbled the ball to the opposite basket, left-side three-point line. *Focus, Cook. You gotta focus.* He took aim and shot. The ball went through the net so cleanly it never even touched the rim.

For you, Dad. He pointed up, jogged to the door, flipped off the lights, and locked up behind himself. He would head back to the hotel and order room service. Lots of it. Then he would head to the all-night Walmart and get a small shovel, a sweatshirt, bug spray, and a blanket. And a little before midnight, he would set up camp for the next twenty-four hours. As long as the calendar said June first there was only one place he would be.

Gordonston Park.

Caroline had toyed with the idea ever since Ellie left. Kinzie had kept her busy while they made cookie dough, but the first batch was in the oven and Ellie and John still weren't home. Now she was practically compelled to take action. Alan had written the letter from a full heart, a repentant heart.

His letter hadn't brought about her forgiveness. She had forgiven the man she was still married to a long time ago. The week he moved away. It was either that or let the brokenness destroy her. Very simply, God had forgiven her, an unfaithful woman. Amazing grace was something Caroline knew personally. The only right response for the rest of her life was to extend that grace to others, to forgive the way she had been forgiven.

Kinzie was washing her hands, so Caroline opened the drawer next to the silverware in the kitchen and pulled out Alan's letter. She had prayed about reconciliation for so long, but always the prayer was for her and Ellie. Not for her husband. The man she assumed hated her.

His letter cracked the door open to all sorts of possibilities. Or maybe that was only her optimism. Either way, Ellie belonged to both of them. Kinzie, too. The situation with Ellie and Nolan was serious enough that the call was warranted. Especially now. She picked up her cell phone and dialed the number Alan had provided in his letter.

Her husband—the man she hadn't spoken with in over a decade—picked up just before the call went to voice mail. "Hello?"

"Hello?" Her voice trembled. "Alan?"

"Yes." He hesitated. It was after six o'clock there, and he

sounded winded, like he might have just gotten home. Still, his tone told her he was listening. "Caroline?"

"It's me." She closed her eyes. Hearing his voice took her back to the beginning. Back when she was sure love would live forever. "I'm sorry for calling like this. I got your letter. We . . . can talk later." She rested her head in her hands. "I'm calling about Ellie."

"What about her?" The concern in his voice reminded her of the old Alan. "Is she okay?"

"Nolan found her. He still cares for her, it's obvious." She rushed ahead, not sure she was making sense. "But Ellie doesn't want to see him." Tears filled her eyes and the sadness spilled into her voice. "Our problems . . . they've cost her so much, and I just thought . . . I mean, you said you'd found a closer walk with God, so I figured . . . maybe if we both prayed for her."

"Definitely." Alan's hesitation didn't last long. "Go ahead, Caroline. I'll finish."

And with that, Caroline and Alan did something they hadn't done together since Ellie was very young.

They prayed for her.

Chapter Twenty-seven

In the end, Ellie decided she didn't need to wait until the first of June had passed. Her dream of seeing Nolan in Gordonston Park was over. He clearly hadn't remembered the date or that this was the year. He might've forgotten entirely about the tackle box beneath the oak tree. Otherwise he would've said something.

It was okay. She wasn't upset with him. She would remember the feel of Nolan's hand in hers forever, but she was ready to move on. She had a plan now. She would go back to San Diego, wrap up her life, and pack her things. She would rent a U-Haul and move to Savannah as fast as she could. She still didn't like the idea of her dad living alone. But maybe someday he'd find his way back here, too.

Her mother loved her after all. San Diego could never be home now that she knew the truth. She had her mom, and Kinzie had a grandma. Nothing else mattered. Yes, she would miss Tina, but her friend would find another roommate. Maybe someday Tina and Tiara would come visit. But whether they did or not, Ellie couldn't worry. Savannah was her home.

Her mom stood a few feet away sipping a cup of tea. Watching Ellie. "You're sure you want to leave now? It's three in the morning, Ellie."

Ellie zipped her bag the rest of the way and moved it near the door. Kinzie lay asleep on the couch. "She won't wake up until we get to Birmingham. We can have breakfast and make it to Dallas before tomorrow night." She went to her mom and smiled. "It'll cut a day off the trip."

"And make for a sixteen-hour drive before you get any sleep."

"Don't worry." Ellie hugged her tenderly, careful not to spill her mother's tea. "I'm wide awake. I can do this."

"Tell me your time frame again?" Her concern remained.

"I'll get back to San Diego late on the third, work another two weeks, and give notice. Collect my last paycheck and get my things together. That'll give Tina a month to find a new roommate."

"She'll be okay with that?"

"I texted her earlier. She's happy for me." Ellie hoped her smile would ease her mother's fears.

"Okay." Her mom put her hand alongside her face. "I can't wait till you get back."

"Me, either." She hugged her mom and held her gaze, grateful again that they'd found each other. "Don't worry. I'll be safe." Her joy was genuine. Never mind the date or the disappointment with Nolan. What she'd found with her mom was more than she could've imagined.

"Do me one favor, Ellie, please. With all this driving."

"Okay." It had been so long since anyone cared whether she came or went, whether she arrived safely or not. She took her mom's hands and looked deep into her eyes. "What would you like me to do?"

"Pray." Her mom's eyes, her smile—they were the way Ellie remembered them, the way they'd been before Peyton Anders. "Ask God to make Himself known to you. He doesn't mind when we ask Him things like that. Please."

Ellie nodded slowly. "Okay." She thought for a moment. Faith had helped her mother survive. It had given her a quiet strength, the same one Kinzie carried with her. Ellie might not believe, but she respected the fact that they did. "I'll ask Him. Really."

"Thank you." Her mom leaned in and softly kissed her cheek. "I'll help you get Kinzie."

Moving quietly, Ellie brought their bags to the back of the car while her mom woke up Kinzie and took her to the bathroom. Together they helped the girl to the car and belted her into the backseat. She looked so little, sleeping there.

"She's an angel." Her mom leaned into the car and kissed the top of Kinzie's head. Then she stood and took Ellie's hands. They kept their voices to a whisper. "I can't think about the years we missed."

"No." Ellie's eyes teared up. They walked around to the driver's door, and she leaned against it, facing her mom. She hated leaving so soon. But now that she'd found her way home, she couldn't wait to be back for good. "Let's only think about the ones we have ahead."

Her mom studied her, as if trying to see her at seventeen as a high school girl, and at nineteen as a young mother. Then at twenty-two, self-sufficient, and raising her daughter on her own. And at every stage in between. Then suddenly her eyes lit up. "Wait!" She motioned toward the apartment. "Be right back!"

"Okay." Ellie stayed there, leaning against the driver's door as she watched her mom run lightly up the steps and back into the apartment. How could she ever have thought her mother didn't love her? She remembered a time when the two of them had walked to the park when Ellie was maybe seven. A storm had come up, and they'd been forced to run all the way home, breathless and laughing. When they reached the house, her mom wrapped her in a towel and held her close for a long time. "You're my greatest gift, Ellie. You'll always be my little girl."

The memory dissolved. Of course her mom had loved her. Every hour of their years apart. Ellie was crazy to have thought otherwise, no matter what the silence suggested. Her mom appeared at the door and hurried to the car, carrying a small brown bag. "I found this in the laundry room while you were at the store." She handed it to Ellie. "In case you need it."

Ellie opened it, and again she felt a connection with her mother that time hadn't touched. "A garden shovel."

"I used it to fill a pot once." Her eyes locked on to Ellie's and she hesitated. "In case you need it before you get on the highway."

She held her mother's eyes for a long moment. Then she opened the car door and set the bag on the floorboard, before turning back to her mom. "How can you know me so well?"

"I'm your mother." She put her hand lightly on Ellie's shoulder. "Ellie, I didn't finish the talk earlier . . . about Peyton."

"That's behind us. Your heart was involved; I don't need to know anything else."

"Still." Caroline studied Ellie, looking deeply to the private areas of her soul. "I'm sorry. I have no excuses. What I did . . . it destroyed our family. It changed everything." Tears made her eyes shine in the light of the street lamp. "Nothing was the same again for any of us. Not for you or your dad or me." She paused. "Not for you and Nolan."

"Mom, you don't need to—"

"Ellie . . ." She gently touched a finger to her daughter's lips. "I need to say this." She wiped at a tear on her cheek. "If I had known I would lose you . . ." She trailed off, overcome by the emotion of the moment.

Ellie hadn't expected this. Seeing her mother break down. It was one more picture of how much the missing years had cost them. She wanted nothing more than to stay here with her mom and spend the rest of time catching up.

"If I'd known he would take you from me . . . I never would've left the house." Her shoulders shook. "I could've lived alone without love for a hundred years. I would've done anything to keep you."

"I know." Ellie wiped her own tears. "If only I'd gotten your letters."

Her mom pressed her fingers to her eyes and tried to collect herself. "There's something else."

Ellie was grateful that, despite the years, there was no awkwardness between them. She waited, watching her mom, loving her for being this brave.

"I called your father. I've forgiven him."

"You did?" It was the last thing Ellie expected her to say. "He wrote you a letter, right?" She'd forgotten about that. They'd been so busy talking about the past that it hadn't come up.

"He did, and he apologized." Caroline caught a few quick breaths, and her eyes filled with compassion. "Unforgiveness is the worst kind of sick. I taught you that when you were growing up." She hesitated, looking for Ellie's reaction. "Do you remember?"

"Yes . . . it's how I've raised Kinzie." She blinked so she could see through her tears. "She reminded me of that before we left San Diego." She paused. "His house was our first stop as we left town."

Her mom exhaled, obviously relieved. "So we have no more reasons to hate, no more bitter roots to feed."

"No." Ellie appreciated her beautiful mother more than ever. "I don't know what happens from here. But we have forgiveness. At least that."

"God knows." Caroline smiled, and they hugged one last time. "Ask Him to show Himself, Ellie. Promise?"

"I will." The coming month couldn't go fast enough. "I don't want to say good-bye."

"Me, either."

Ellie caught a quick breath. "I'll call."

They waved good-bye, and Ellie climbed into the car. Even with the gift of her mother's shovel tucked against the seat, Ellie was pretty sure she wouldn't go by the park. Nolan didn't remember, so why bother? What point was there in digging up the old letters now? Whatever he had written to her no longer applied.

But as she crossed town and headed for the freeway, she felt a pull toward the park. She'd waited too long for this moment *not* to dig up the box and take her letter. After all, she had planned to do that much even before she saw Nolan. The closure would be worth the time it took. Then, as she'd planned from the beginning, she could put Nolan Cook out of her life for good. With every mile, the feeling grew stronger until she was certain it would consume her if she didn't stop.

It was only three thirty in the morning. But it was June first. If she didn't go now, she'd regret her decision forever.

Chapter Twenty-eight

Ellie parked adjacent to the entrance and cut the engine. The stop wouldn't take long, but her daughter couldn't stay in the car. She grabbed the paper bag and tucked it beneath her arm. Then she stepped out, closed her door, and opened Kinzie's. She put her hand carefully on Kinzie's shoulder. "Baby girl . . .wake up." Her whisper cut the quiet night air. "You need to come with me. Mommy has to do something."

Kinzie took a few seconds, gradually blinking her eyes open. "What . . . what are we doing?" She rubbed her hands over her face, her light blond hair matted to her cheek.

"We're headed back to San Diego like we planned. I just have to do something real quick first."

"Oh." Kinzie squinted as she stepped out of the car and took Ellie's hand. "Why?"

"Well, this is the park. The one I used to come to when I lived here."

"A park?" Kinzie looked confused. She blinked again, trying to wake up. "It's too late to go to the park, Mommy."

"We won't stay." Ellie smiled. Kinzie was awake enough to

walk. The two of them headed for the park's entrance. "I left something here. I need to get it."

"In the park?" A hint of a grin tugged at Kinzie's lips. "That's funny, Mommy. If you left it here when you were a little girl, someone probably already found it."

Her daughter had a point. "Maybe." She smiled again at her daughter. At this hour, even the crickets and bullfrogs from the nearby pond were silent, and no breeze stirred the Spanish moss overhead. Ellie used her phone's flashlight app to navigate up the curb and through the gate. As she walked, Ellie remembered what her mother wanted her to do. She didn't believe, didn't really see the point. But she had promised. *God, if You're real . . . please show Yourself to me. It matters, God. Thank You.* They walked into the darkness toward the big oak tree.

"Is it okay to go in?" Kinzie stayed close, holding tight to Ellie's fingers.

"Yes, sweetie. We're fine." It felt right to make good on her mother's request. She had few expectations that anything beyond that would come from the prayer. But she had kept her word.

The pathways beneath the trees had grown over with weeds and brush, and the park looked different. But Ellie could still navigate her way to the largest tree. The changed look of the place only added to the sadness of the task at hand. The closure it represented. A closure that the fifteen-year-old she'd been had never wanted or expected. As they came closer, Ellie's heart pounded in her throat.

"Are you scared, Mommy?" Kinzie whispered. "'Cause I am." She was jumpy for sure, walking so close she was practically attached to Ellie's hip.

"Not at all. This is a safe place, sweetie." Ellie realized her words weren't entirely true. Her heart was breaking in half. Nothing safe about that.

A few more yards and they rounded a cropping of bushes, and there, behind another section of brush growing tall and wide from the ground, was the tree. The tallest one in the park. The spot where she and Nolan had practically grown up together.

"Are we close?" Kinzie was concerned.

"Yes, baby girl." A series of sobs rushed at Ellie as the tree came into view. She stopped and choked them back. "Almost there."

Kinzie stayed close as Ellie started walking again and the entire tree came into view. The canopy of branches and the moss that hung from them, the width of the trunk and—

"Mommy!" Kinzie whispered, loud and frantic, as she threw her arms tight around Ellie's waist. "Someone's there!"

Ellie turned off her flashlight and slipped her phone into her jeans pocket. She stroked Kinzie's back and peered into the darkness ahead of them. Kinzie was right. A person was sitting against the tree trunk. From here, it looked like a man, but it was impossible to tell. Probably a homeless person, someone like Jimbo, down on his luck. Homeless people didn't scare her. She bent low and whispered to Kinzie, "Stay here. I'll take a look."

"No!" Kinzie held tight to her arm. "Don't go. Please, Mommy!"

Ellie was stuck. She had to get the box. She hadn't come this far to turn around and walk away without her letter. "Baby, it's just someone trying to get some sleep. Let's go a little closer."

Kinzie was hesitant, but she whispered loudly, "Stay with me!"

"I will, baby. I will." They walked slowly, hidden by the shadows. Closer and closer until they were within ten feet of the tree and suddenly . . . the image of the person became clear.

Ellie gasped and then slapped her hand over her mouth. *Nolan Cook?* The person sitting propped against the tree trunk was sound asleep. He had a blanket around his shoulders, and it looked like the tackle box was on his lap.

"Mommy!" Kinzie clung to her. "What's wrong?"

"Shh, baby. Nothing." They had to leave. There was no understanding why he had come and why he was here. Especially at this hour. But Ellie couldn't see him again. Life had moved them past this place, past all it had meant to the two of them. He must've wanted to read her letter—curious, probably.

But then he'd fallen asleep, strangely. Maybe he had set up camp just in case she came by? Could that be it? The idea seemed impossible. She had been convinced that he didn't remember the significance of the date. "We need to go," she whispered close to Kinzie's ear. "The man's sleeping. We shouldn't wake him."

"Okay." Kinzie sounded grateful, as if she couldn't get out of the dark overgrown park fast enough.

Moving as stealthily as she could, Ellie turned around and flicked her flashlight back on. Quietly, slowly, they began to leave Nolan behind them. But after only a few steps, she heard something behind her. She stopped and again flipped off the flashlight app.

"It's too late, Ellie." He was coming closer, making his way along the overgrown path. "I see you."

She froze, and once more Kinzie grabbed on to her. "Mommy!"

"It's okay, baby. I know him." Ellie faced Kinzie and dropped down so she could speak straight to her daughter's eyes. "It's my friend Nolan Cook. Remember him?"

Kinzie relaxed a little. "Nolan?" She stepped away and turned to face him. "You're Nolan?"

"I am." He was stepping carefully along the dark narrow pathway. When he reached them, he crouched down next to Ellie and faced her daughter. He held out his hand. "You must be Ellie's little girl."

Kinzie grinned, tucking her chin close to her chest the way she sometimes did when she felt shy. "That's me." She shook his hand. "I'm Kinzie."

"Well," he waited a few heartbeats, "hello, Kinzie." He shifted his eyes briefly to Ellie's, then back to the child's. "I like your name. Nice to meet you."

Ellie's world began to spin. Had that really just happened? He still knew her so well. In the space of a few seconds, he knew exactly where Kinzie's name had come from. She wanted to run, wanted to protect her damaged heart before there was nothing left of it. But she couldn't move. Not with him this close.

Kinzie looked from him to Ellie and back. "Did you mean to meet here?"

"Sort of." This time Nolan kept his attention on Kinzie alone. "We made a plan a very long time ago."

"Oh." Kinzie stared at Ellie. "Why didn't you tell me that, Mommy?"

"Because." Ellie finally turned to Nolan, wondering if he could see her heartache, her determination to keep this short. "I wasn't sure Nolan remembered."

Slivers of moonlight were enough that she could see his expression fall, and his voice with it. "Of course I remembered."

Kinzie yawned. "That's a ginormous tree." She looked all the way up, taking it in. "Can I go sit on the blanket?"

They'd come this far. He'd already dug up the box, so if she was going to see the contents, she needed to take a few more minutes. "Yes, baby. Go ahead." She turned her flashlight on once more and walked beside Kinzie to the tree trunk.

Her daughter curled up in the thick blanket and closed her eyes. "I'm not really tired. I'll just rest here. Tell me when it's time to go."

The adventure had probably exhausted her. She'd been woken out of a deep sleep, after all. Ellie adjusted the blanket so part of it covered her daughter's shoulders. The trunk was wider than three of the other oak trees. With Kinzie resting, Nolan picked up the tackle box and motioned for Ellie to follow him around the other side. Two oversize roots made for perfect benches. They sat facing each other.

"She's perfect." He looked through Ellie, as if searching for the familiar connection. "She looks just like you."

"Thanks."

For a long time he only looked at her, as if he wanted to understand her but wasn't quite sure where to begin. Again, Ellie felt her anger rising. If he was going to sit here and judge her, try to figure out the reasons why she'd run or the reason she hadn't lived up to her plans, then she and Kinzie could leave. "Why are you looking at me like that?"

"Why are you angry?"

His question caught her off guard. She leaned her shoulder into the familiar rough bark. She worked to keep her voice low so Kinzie wouldn't hear her. "Because . . . you feel sorry for me."

"For you?" He rested his forearms on his knees and studied her again. "Not at all. I feel sorry for *me*."

"What?" Confusion slammed her heart around. The moon shone just enough so she could see the hurt on his face. "What do you mean?"

"It took eleven years to find you." He shrugged, his eyes never leaving hers. "And now you treat me like this." He lowered his voice. "I would've found you sooner if I could've, Ellie. I never stopped trying."

Ellie could feel her arguments unraveling, feel everything she'd believed about Nolan turning upside down. His eyes were so deep that here in the dark of the oak tree, it was hard not to feel fifteen again. Her walls began to crumble. Was she wrong about him? About who he had become and how he would judge her? Could that be possible? The kindness in his eyes was the same as it had been the last time they were together.

He opened the tackle box and pulled out the first folded sheet of lined yellow paper. "Maybe if you read this." A depth rang in his voice, his words quiet and sure. He handed the letter to her. "Go ahead."

She didn't want to read it, not here in front of him. They'd written the letters back when they were kids. How could they possibly apply here, now? But he wasn't going to change his mind. She felt herself losing the fight. "Okay." Maybe if she read it, they could remember the past, acknowledge it for what it had been, and finally move on. She held the letter in one hand, her phone in the other. The flashlight app lit up the entire page. She opened the paper and found the beginning.

My best friend, my girl, my everything . . . my sweet Ellie.

She got only that far before the tears came. He had thought

of her as his girl back then? He'd never said that to her, so the wording took her by surprise. She brought the hand holding the letter to her face and used her wrist to dry her eyes. He was watching her, caring for her. She could feel it. *Don't break down, Ellie . . . just read the letter.* She found her place and continued.

> *I can't believe your dad's moving you to San Diego to-morrow. I feel like this is some crazy, terrible nightmare, and any minute my mom's going to wake me up and it'll be time for school. But since I can feel the tree beneath me, I know it's not a dream. That's why we had to write these letters.*
>
> *I'm only fifteen, Ellie. I don't know how to drive, and I don't know where you're going exactly. That pretty much terrifies me. So we definitely had to do this. In case we don't find each other, we'll have at least this one chance.*

More tears, but this time Ellie didn't try to stop them, didn't bother to dab at them. They slid down her cheeks, a constant reminder of the sadness of the situation. Not for a minute did either of them think back then that eleven years would go by before they saw each other again. His letter wasn't long, just one page. She kept reading.

> *Here's what I have to tell you. You think I'm kidding when I say I'm going to marry you. You always laugh. Only I'm not kidding. I love you, Ellie. I'll never love any girl like I love you.*

Quiet sobs came over her, and she wondered if her heart would ever be the same. She had never expected this . . . this beautiful letter. Not even back then. And why did he want her to read it now? When they had gone and grown up and their feelings had long since changed? She blinked a few times so she could see through her tears.

See, Ellie? That's how I feel, but I can't say so right now, even though you're leaving tomorrow. Because I don't want you to laugh this time. That's why I had to write it in this letter. Oh, and don't worry about the eleven years. I'm sure by then we'll be married and living in a big house near the Atlanta Hawks. You know, 'cause I'll be playing for them. But just in case, I couldn't let you leave without telling you how I feel. I'll love you forever, Ellie.

Love, your guy,
Nolan Cook

She closed her eyes and pressed the letter to her chest. For a long time she hunched over the piece of paper, desperate for a way back to then, a way to know how he had felt for her. She heard him moving, felt him take the seat beside her, but it didn't fully register until she felt him put his arm around her shoulders.

Instead of saying anything, he let her cry. Let the losses of a thousand yesterdays have their way with her. In the recesses of her mind, the feeling of his arm around her only made her more upset. Because this was a last time, a final good-bye. And what if she never had anyone again in all her life who loved her the way Nolan Cook had loved her the summer before their sophomore year?

Finally, she folded the letter and set it carefully on the ground. She covered her face with her hands and dried her eyes. She had to look a mess, eyes and nose red and swollen, but she didn't care. She had to tell him how much the letter meant. "I never knew." She angled herself so she could see him. Their knees touched in the darkness, and her eyes stayed on his. "That was beautiful, Nolan. Sweetest letter I've ever read."

"Thanks." He didn't look different. If she didn't know about his fame and success, she could've believed he hadn't changed at all. He allowed a slight grin, just enough, given the gravity of the moment. "I already read yours."

"Can I see it?" She remembered what she'd written, sort of. But she wanted to see the words again.

He took the second letter from the box and handed it to her. "It's not as good as mine."

"Fine." She sniffed and took the paper from him. His teasing disarmed her, made her wonder again if she'd ever left for San Diego at all. She tried to stay in the moment, in the current year, where they belonged.

> Dear Nolan,
> First, I'm only doing this because you won't read it for eleven years. Ha ha. Okay, here I go. You want to know how I feel about you?

He was still beside her, still watching her, and again her tears came. These were her words, the ones she'd penned that awful night. And every syllable reminded her of the truth, of how much she cared, how much she'd missed him ever since. She told him how she loved that he was her best friend, and she loved the way he stuck up for her when Billy Barren made fun of her pigtails.

A half smile came over her when she read the next line.

> *Sorry you got in trouble for tripping him, but not really. I love that, too.*

She went on to tell him how she loved that he came to the aid of a kid being bullied, and how much she loved watching him play basketball. Ellie wanted to go back in time and hug the girl she'd been then, tell her to guard her heart, because after that night nothing would ever feel like this again. She read the rest of her letter slowly, each word finding its rightful place in her heart.

> *Here's the part I could never tell you right now. Because it's too soon or maybe too late, since I'm leaving in the morning. I loved how it felt earlier tonight when you hugged me. It never felt like that before. And when you took me into your garage and then over here to the park, I loved how my hand felt in yours. If I'm really honest, Nolan, I love when you tell me you're going to marry me. What I didn't really understand until tonight is that it isn't only those things that I love.*
>
> *I love being here, just me and you, and just hearing you breathe. I love sitting beneath this tree with you. So, yeah, I guess that's it. If we don't see each other for eleven years, then I want you to know the truth about how I really feel.*
>
> *I love you.*
> *There. I said it.*
> *Don't forget me.*
>
> *Love,*
> *Ellie*

Again the sorrow was so great she couldn't lift her head. Her tears didn't come with sobs, like before, but rather, like a slow leak in her heart. Like a safety valve making certain she wouldn't drown in the endless rushing river of sadness. She folded the paper and set it on top of the other one near her feet. It was all such a waste, the feelings they'd had, their friendship. The way they'd loved each other back then. How could eleven years have come and gone? After this, she would have to forgive her father all over again. How could he move her away from Nolan and her mother? The two people who loved her most in all the world?

She covered her face once more, grieving losses too great to measure. Eventually, she felt Nolan's hand on her knee. "Ellie . . . you okay?"

She pressed her back against the bark as she sat straighter, as she allowed herself to look at him. "It's just . . . so sad. You and me." She felt safe saying it. After all, he had wanted her to read his letter. He had to know how it would make her feel. "Eleven years. We can't ever get that back." Ellie realized something that hadn't hit her before. Nolan's eyes were dry. She tilted her head, trying to read him. "You aren't sad?"

"No." He drew a full breath and released it slowly. His eyes never left hers. "Can I ask you something?"

"Sure." She couldn't convince herself that he didn't care. He was kind, and he was here. This was more than a chance to pity her. He wanted this trip back to who they'd been as badly as she did.

The distance between them wasn't great, but he slid a little closer. He held both his hands out and slowly, tentatively, took hold of hers. With their hands joined, he showed the first signs of concern, of fear, even. "Are you seeing someone?"

She was confused again. "You mean . . . dating?"

"Right. Dating, engaged. Involved." He ran his thumbs along the sides of her hands. "Is there anyone else, Ellie?"

"No." Her broken heart couldn't take this, not if his questions were merely surface talk. But they weren't. She still knew him that well. The depth in his eyes was absolutely intentional. "Kinzie's dad . . . he left me after she was born." The shame was there, the same as it had been when she was nineteen. "A few months later, he died in Iraq, in battle." She shook her head. "There hasn't been anyone since."

Again he inched closer. He didn't say he was sorry about her past or comment on it at all. Instead, he brought her hands to his lips and did something that nearly stopped her heart. He kissed her fingers. The whole time he kept his eyes on hers. "Me, either." He let go of one of her hands, picked up the letters, and held them up. "Not since this."

Ellie felt her head begin to spin, her heart racing wildly one more time. What was he saying? Was she dreaming? "The news . . . they said you and Kari Garrett . . ."

Nolan smiled. "The news? Come on, Ellie. Last week they said I was quitting basketball to take up singing."

She laughed out loud, and the feeling was wonderful.

"I went out with her once." His smile faded. "I bored her. Only talked about one thing."

She didn't look away, didn't do anything to break the moment. "What did you talk about?"

"How much I missed this girl I knew when I was fifteen. A girl I was going to marry."

It had to be a dream. In her wildest imaginings, she'd never dreamed Nolan felt this way. She held on to his hands and closed her eyes, and she was eight or nine again. The two of them had gone to Forsyth Park, and Nolan had pushed her on the merry-go-round. Faster and faster and faster he spun her until she had to close her eyes so her body could catch up with reality.

Exactly how she felt now.

Before she knew what was happening, he helped her gently to her feet. She opened her eyes and looked at him, at the face she had loved since she was a little girl. For the first time tonight, tears shone in his eyes. "Come here." His voice was a whisper, and slowly, so slowly, for the first time since that long ago summer, he pulled her into his arms. For a long time he just held her, rocked her to the beating of their hearts. After a while he framed her face with his hands. "I told you, I'm not letting you get away again."

"But . . ." Doubts crowded in around her, trying to steal every good thing about the way she felt. "You don't know anything about me. You don't know where I live or where I work . . ." Her voice fell. "Or what I believe."

"Ellie." He didn't waver, didn't blink. "I know you. That's all that matters." The concern in his eyes gave way to love. A love she had never felt or known or imagined. "We can figure out the rest. God brought us this far."

God.

A chill ran along Ellie's arms and legs and turned her stomach upside down. Her mother's words came back to her all at once. *Ask God to show Himself to you . . . He wants His people to ask Him.* Ellie's knees felt weak. She put her head on Nolan's chest and felt his pounding heart. He was real and he was here. She held on, warm in his embrace. Yes, this was really happening! After all this time, the two of them were here together, and Nolan still cared about her. Which could only mean . . .

Ellie tried to catch her breath. Half an hour ago she had asked God to show Himself to her, and now Nolan Cook was holding her and saying he had never loved anyone else. She let that thought surround her, let it wash over her. If that wasn't God showing Himself to be real, she didn't know what was. After all this time, Nolan Cook still loved her, still wanted her! Which could mean only one thing.

God was indeed real. Not only that, but like Nolan, God still loved her.

He loved her more than she could comprehend.

Chapter Twenty-nine

Nolan had more to say, and Kinzie needed somewhere to sleep.

That was how he came up with the plan to head back to her mother's home. Ellie could wait and leave in a few days. Or a few weeks. There was no way he was letting her go tonight. Caroline answered the door in her bathrobe, and though she clearly had countless questions, she asked none of them. She hesitated, but only for a few surprised seconds. "Ellie. Nolan. Come in. Please."

Nolan smiled; he hadn't been able to stop smiling. "Thank you." He held Kinzie in his arms, and now he laid her on the sofa near the front window. Out of the corner of his eye, he watched Caroline and Ellie hug. For a long time. When he returned to them, Caroline turned to him and hugged him, too. As she pulled back she met his eyes. "I'm so glad you're here."

"Me, too." Nolan hoped his next question wouldn't be awkward. "Ma'am, it's late. Do you mind if I stay on the sofa? So Ellie and I can talk?"

"Not at all. Please." Her mother's eyes grew teary. She smiled at Ellie for a long moment. "You did what I asked you to do." It wasn't a question.

"I did." Ellie hugged her mom again. "I have my answer."

"Yes." She looked at Nolan and back at Ellie. "I believe you do."

After that, she bade them both good night and headed back to bed. When they were alone, Nolan turned to Ellie. He took her in his arms again. "Where were we?"

"Dreaming." Her expression was a mix of shock and joy. A joy that reminded him of the girl he had grown up with. She searched his eyes. "I keep asking myself . . . is this really happening?"

Relief continued to make its way through Nolan's soul. This was his Ellie, the girl he remembered, the one he had missed and searched for. "It's real. I'm not going anywhere." He wanted to kiss her so badly, but not yet. They had more to talk about. Like a pair of middle-school kids slow dancing to the last song of the night, neither of them wanted to let go. Their faces were inches apart, both of them swaying to the feel of their beating hearts, lost in the moment. "You really thought I didn't remember?"

"You didn't say anything." Her words came easily, her expression open. She was even more beautiful than he remembered, and now that she wasn't pretending to be someone who didn't care, her laughter, her words, the way she spoke all went straight to his heart. All of it was familiar, as if they'd never lost a day.

He put his hand alongside her face and ran his thumb along her cheek. "You acted like you didn't know me."

A soft bit of laughter came from her. "I'm sorry. I didn't know."

"Tell me everything, Ellie. All of it." He breathed in the sweet smell of her perfume, the hint of jasmine in her hair. All the years of searching and wondering and missing her. Now he wanted to know everything he'd missed. "Please."

She searched his eyes. "Where do I start?"

"June second, 2002. The day you left Savannah."

She laughed again, careful not to wake Kinzie. "All of it?"

"Okay." He grinned at her. "How about the main points." His smile held her, captured the feel of her in his arms. "We can talk details tomorrow. And the next day."

They kept slow dancing, but slowly, gradually, the story began to pour from her. She told him about moving to San Diego, and together they remembered her frantic call to him from the grocery store.

"You were going to send me your address."

"I did. Three times." A look of resignation filled her eyes. "I figured it out a few years ago. My dad always sent postcards instead of letters. The three times I sent you a letter, I used the stamps from his bedside table. I never put a return address, because . . . well, I didn't want anyone to return the letter to me. Besides, we didn't have our permanent address then. But since I was sending a letter with a postcard stamp, I never had enough postage. When they didn't come back to me, I didn't know you never got them. I never dreamed the letters wouldn't make it to you."

Nolan struggled for a moment with the anger he sometimes felt toward Ellie's father. The man's control of Ellie back then had been complete. He worked to keep his tone even. "I waited every day. And when your letter didn't come, my dad wanted to help me figure out how to find you. But then . . ." He took a long breath, a fresh sadness grabbing at his heart.

He struggled in silence for a long moment. "I miss him. The pain of losing him . . . it never really goes away."

"I'm sorry." Her eyes searched his. "He was a wonderful man. A great coach."

"He was such a great dad." Nolan felt his expression grow more intense. "I would give up playing basketball for one more day with him, one more hour." He touched her cheek. "It's why I'm glad you forgave your dad." She had told him that much back at the park. "He made terrible mistakes over the years. But he gave you the letters." He felt intoxicated by her, holding her this way. "Otherwise I wouldn't have found you."

She kept her arms looped around his neck. "I can't hate him." A sad sigh came from her. "That's what I meant back at the tree." She framed his face with her hand. "It's all so sad. My mom was fighting her own battle. My father was acting crazy. We were just a couple of kids, Nolan. No wonder we lost touch."

"But at some point . . ." His words came slowly, marked by a sad truth he was still trying to understand. "You didn't want me to find you."

"True." Guilt darkened her eyes. Her tone spoke volumes about her regret. "I . . . I changed my last name. Legally." She waited, as if she could only hope he would understand. "I'm Ellie Anne now. My middle name."

"Ahhh. No wonder." Nolan hurt for her, for what she'd been through. He hoped she could see the understanding in his eyes. "I hired a private investigator. As soon as I signed my first pro contract. Didn't help, obviously." He touched her hair and ran his fingers along the back of her head. "The guy guessed you might have changed your name."

"You did that?" Her shock was genuine.

"Of course. I told you, I missed you." He brushed his cheek against hers. "I never stopped trying to find you." He ran his knuckles lightly against her shoulder. "What happened next?"

"After I sent the letters . . . you didn't write to me. I thought . . . I thought you moved on. You know, busy with high school and basketball." She looked ashamed by her long-ago assumptions. "I didn't know about your dad."

"I mean after high school. What happened after that?" He led her to a smaller sofa across from where Kinzie was sleeping. They sat facing each other, and again he took her hands in his. He couldn't get enough of the way he felt alive just being with her again. "Tell me, Ellie." There was no judgment or condemnation in his voice. "What was his name?"

Her hesitation didn't last long. "C.J. Andrews." There wasn't much to the story. Ellie explained that at a time when her father suspected her of doing any number of sinful things, C.J. was a ray of light. A reason to laugh again. "I never loved him. But, I don't know, he made me feel good about myself. After years with my dad, I guess that was enough."

The truth hurt more than Nolan had guessed it would. If only he'd been there, if only he'd found a way to reach her sooner. "I'm sorry."

This time she didn't get mad at his apology. She smiled and looked briefly at her sleeping daughter. "I have Kinzie. I'll never be sorry for that." She told him how she'd earned her cosmetology license and started cutting hair for a living. "Kinzie . . . she's been everything to me. I love her more than life."

Nolan looked across the room at the girl. "She looks so

much like you." He hesitated. "Her name? The street where we always met."

"Yes." She didn't waver. "Happiest times of my life."

He touched her hair again, still trying to believe she was here with him. "Having Kinzie . . . It's like the Bible says. God works everything to the good for those who love Him."

She was quiet at that. He might've imagined it, but her expression seemed a little more closed off. It was something else they hadn't talked about—her faith. His was public, of course. People knew him as much for the way he gave credit to his Savior after every game as for his basketball skills. But she hadn't mentioned God since they found each other at the park. "Ellie . . . do you still believe? In God . . . in His word? His plan?"

"I've struggled." Her eyes had been dry since they walked into her mother's apartment. Now they grew wet again. "My mom told me to ask God if He was real." She sniffed, and the heartache she'd lived with was evident again. "I think . . . finding you tonight, knowing how you feel, how you've always felt . . . that was God's way of telling me that He is real. He loves me no matter what I've done. And . . ." She paused, her voice strained by the depth of her emotions. "Even when I felt most alone, He was there."

"He was." Nolan pulled her close again, running his hand along her back. "He is real. He's here now."

"Kinzie . . ." Ellie leaned back so she could see his eyes. "She prays for me all the time. That I'll find my happy-ever-after in Jesus."

Nolan smiled. He loved Ellie's daughter already. "Not a lot different from my prayer for you." He grew more serious. "That and my constant prayer that I'd find you. I never stopped asking God for that."

The sky was getting light, the sun coming up. "I have today. But after that I report back to the team." He hesitated. "We fly to Los Angeles on the third."

"The Lakers." She already knew. "They clinched it yesterday."

"They did." He grinned, proud of her. "You still love basketball."

She smiled, their eyes connected again. "I still love watching *you* play basketball."

He pictured her over the years, cheering him on from a distance while she hid from him. Something he would probably never completely understand. "Anyway." He eased the two of them to their feet again and slipped his arms around her waist. "I can't leave without telling you something."

She looked unsure. "Okay."

He pictured the tackle box with both letters in the back of his SUV. Before leaving the park, they had filled the hole again. They would have anyway, but something about the act felt like closure. The search was over for both of them. He looked deeper into her eyes. "It's about my letter."

"Your letter?" She didn't ask more than that. Her eyes showed a hint of the fear she'd brought with her to Savannah.

"Yes." He paused. How he loved the feel of her in his arms. "Ellie . . . I still mean every word." He moved one hand softly to her cheek, looking into her heart. "Do you understand?"

She searched his eyes, clearly confused. "Not really."

He felt his smile start in his heart and work its way to his eyes. "I want to marry you. I still mean it."

"Nolan . . ." She gave the slightest shake of her head. "You only just found me."

"It doesn't matter." He held her face tenderly with both

hands. She was the rarest gift, his Ellie. "I've wanted to marry you for as long as I can remember."

She looked like she might disagree with him, but after a few seconds, she let her forehead rest on his chest. "Nolan, I'm not laughing now." She seemed to summon all her strength to lift her head and look at him again. "Please don't tease about this."

He couldn't wait another minute. If she was going to doubt his feelings even after all he'd told her, there was only one way he knew to convince her. He drew her close, and slowly, as if all of his life had led to this moment, he brought his lips to hers. The kiss started like a slow burn, but after a few seconds, he was struck by the passion between them, how badly he wanted her.

"Mmmm." He stepped back, forcing himself to keep at least a little distance between them. He felt dizzy, his body screaming for her. He could feel the smoke in his eyes as he looked into hers. "I'm serious, Ellie." Each word was measured, rich with the fullness of his love and desire for her. "I want to marry you. I don't have a ring, but I'll get one." He smiled at Kinzie, tuckered out across the room. The little girl with no father in her life. "I'll be her daddy, Ellie. No one could ever love your little girl more than me. I want you both. For the rest of my life."

Her smile mixed with happy tears, her own passion giving way to the childlike joy he had always loved in her, the one he would never tire of, for the rest of his life. She wrapped her arms around his neck and rocked with him. "It's more than I can take in." When she pulled back, her cheeks were wet, but her smile remained. "Like I might need a lifetime to believe this is real."

"Fine with me." Once more he kissed her, not as long this time. He wouldn't put either of them in a situation they'd regret. He'd waited all these years to find her. They would honor the God who had brought them together by waiting until their wedding. "I love you."

"I love you, too. I always have."

"Can we pray?" He looked at her, into her soul. "Do you believe enough to pray?"

"I do now." She smiled as if just saying the words brought her more peace than she could contain. "After this week, I'll believe in God as long as I live. He didn't need to prove Himself to me." She seemed to understand at a deep level. "But He did anyway. Because He loves me."

"So much, Ellie." Nolan bowed his head so that their foreheads touched. He thanked God for letting him find her, and for helping Ellie believe again, and for Kinzie. "The prayers of children are sometimes the strongest of all. Thank you for the faith of Ellie's daughter. Help us always have faith like a child, Father. In Jesus' name, amen."

"Amen."

He needed to get some sleep at the hotel where he was staying. But he promised to come back as soon as he woke up. They could spend the day together, and at night he would head back to Atlanta. She promised to stay at her mom's until the play-offs were over. Until they could make a plan. They hugged again for a long time, and finally, he pulled himself away. On the drive back to the hotel, he did the one thing he hadn't done when he was with her.

He let the tears come.

Tears for all they'd lost, the seasons and years. And for the way they'd almost missed each other even at their eleven-year mark. But most of all he broke down because of God's faithfulness. The Lord had prompted him to head to the oak tree at midnight instead of waiting for daytime or the evening. The Lord who had helped him survive his dad's death and the years of missing Ellie had faithfully brought the girl he loved straight into his arms.

God had moved all of heaven and earth to see that the impossible might happen tonight. On what had been their last chance to find each other. And as Nolan's tears dried, he was consumed by gratitude for his Lord. For the one who loved so much that He didn't only die for him. He had brought him Ellie Tucker. Not only yesterday and today.

But forever.

Chapter Thirty

It was the sixth game of the NBA finals.

Atlanta was up three to two games over the Lakers, and the Hawks could clinch it with a win at home tonight. Caroline had prayed for Nolan since she woke up that morning. She and John and Ellie and Kinzie were supposed to meet him at the Hawks' arena ninety minutes before game time. He'd given them specific directions about where to park and where to find him.

Caroline couldn't put her finger on it, but Nolan seemed to be up to something. He had already asked for Ellie's hand, but he planned to propose to her at Gordonston Park after the play-offs. Not here, in front of thousands of people.

Still, judging by the way he'd acted that morning when he came by for breakfast, she was almost sure he was up to something, some kind of surprise for Ellie.

"You ready, Mom?" Ellie was driving. She parked the car in the garage VIP section, like she'd done at the previous recent home games, and the four of them headed into the arena. "They're going to win tonight. I can feel it."

"Me, too." Kinzie pumped her fist in the air a few times.

"I thought they'd clinch it last week." John was bursting with excitement. "Nolan said he was distracted, thinking about Ellie." He grinned at his sister.

"I'll take that as a compliment." Ellie held Kinzie's hand, and the two of them led the way into the elevator and got off at the top floor. "He's in the executive dining room. Down this way."

Caroline studied her daughter. She, too, seemed a little antsy tonight. If Nolan were cooking up a surprise engagement, Ellie wouldn't know. Caroline was still trying to figure it out when they reached the dining room.

"Here we are." Ellie grinned at Kinzie. Then she looked back at Caroline. "Ready?"

"Of course." Caroline laughed, slightly baffled. Whatever was happening, she felt like she was the only one out of the loop.

John linked arms with her as they walked inside, and there was Nolan standing next to . . . "Alan!" Caroline whispered his name as her hand flew to her mouth.

"Dad." Ellie walked over and hugged him. Kinzie did the same. The two of them stood beside Nolan. Ellie smiled at her father. "Thanks for coming."

Caroline couldn't believe her eyes, couldn't remember how to speak or breathe. Alan was here? After all this time?

That was when she noticed his face, the tears on his cheeks. Alan looked from Ellie and Kinzie to Caroline. "You can thank Nolan." He looked at the young man next to him. "It was his idea. He flew me out."

"Well . . ." Nolan's eyes looked damp. He held Ellie closer, his arm around her shoulders. "I can't have my dad here." His voice was strained. "So having you here . . . to watch us win the championship . . . that was the next best thing."

Caroline wasn't sure what to do first. John had his arm linked through hers. Before she could close the distance and introduce John to Alan, her husband made the first move. He walked over and held his hand out to John. "Hi. I'm Alan."

"Sir." John shook his hand, unaware of the drama playing out around him. "Nice to meet you. My name's John."

"Nice to meet you, too." Alan wiped at his cheeks and smiled. "I hope I have the chance to see you more often."

"Yes, sir." John smiled shyly and then headed over to Nolan. Ellie and Kinzie were already in conversation with him, and John joined in.

And like that, Alan came to her. It was the first time Caroline had seen Alan Tucker since he kicked her out of her own house two days before he and Ellie moved. But that man might as well have been a different one altogether. The man before her exuded a kind humility. His posture and demeanor, the light in his eyes. This was the Alan she had fallen in love with.

Not only that, but his transparent heart shone in his expression so she had no doubt. His letter was absolutely true. He looked broken, no question. Repentant and desperate to make things right. He stopped a few inches from her. "I'm sorry, Caroline. I can't say it enough."

"I forgive you." Her words came slowly, soaked in a lifetime of meaning. "It was my fault, too. I'll be sorry as long as I live." She studied him; he still looked young and fit, but more than that, he looked gentle and compassionate. Like he cared about how she felt and what her life had become. "I can't believe you came."

"I've wanted to see you for years. But I thought you'd refuse me." His eyes were dry now, more serious. "Like I deserve."

"You know what I think?" She reached slowly for his hands, her heart full.

He seemed to feel the shock of her touch to his core. As if he'd never expected her to care about him again. His words fell to a whisper. "What do you think, Caroline?"

"I think tonight we'll leave the past in the past." She smiled at him. "We've all lost enough without looking back."

He nodded slowly, almost in a daze. Like he was seeing something in her from decades ago. "You have it again."

"What?"

"Your innocence. Your joy." His eyes welled up one more time. "I thought I killed it."

"It isn't me." She put her hand over her heart. "It's Him. God almighty." She looked around the room at Nolan and Ellie, Kinzie and John. Then she shook her head as she found Alan's eyes again. "None of us would be standing here if it weren't for Him."

"So true."

"You know what else I think?"

"What?" He looked a little more lighthearted now, if still cautious.

"I think after eleven years . . . I'd like to give my husband a hug."

And for the first time in far more than eleven years, distance and anger and emptiness didn't stand between them.

And maybe—if God let the miracle of grace continue— nothing ever would.

Nolan had never let go of her heart.

That was the only way Ellie could explain what had happened since June first. Nolan had won her heart when he was a boy, and he had never once let it go. She understood that now. In the meantime, in the years they'd lost, God had been shaping and growing him into a man who could love her and lead her. A man who was ready to share his whole life with her and Kinzie.

If only she'd known sooner.

Ellie took her place in the fourth row, center court, between Kinzie and her mother. On the other side of her mom was her father, and next to him was John. It would take time for the boy to get to know him, but what Ellie could see so far looked amicable. No telling where God would take her parents.

As if, suddenly, anything was possible for all of them.

If Ellie hadn't believed in God after the first of June, watching her mom and dad hug in the executive dining room an hour ago was absolute proof. Grace and forgiveness like that weren't possible in human strength.

The game started, and like old times Ellie couldn't take her eyes off Nolan. The way he played the game. Even with all the hoopla and packed stands she had to remind herself that she wasn't back at Savannah High.

They had a plan now, she and Nolan. She had called Tina and given a thirty-day notice, and she had found a salon in Savannah in need of a stylist. Tina had been thrilled for her. "Remind me to ask Kinzie to pray for my Prince Charming." She had laughed, purely teasing. "No, really, Ellie. I feel like I'm watching the best ending to the best movie ever."

Ellie smiled now, even in the midst of the frenzied game, remembering how true her friend's words had felt.

On the court, Nolan hit a jumper from fifteen feet out. Atlanta by two.

"Go, Nolan!" Kinzie jumped to her feet and clapped big. She screamed over the roar of the crowd. "He's amazing, Mommy!"

"Yes, baby." Ellie had to yell to be heard. She gave her daughter a thumbs-up. "Very amazing!"

L.A. called a time-out, and Kinzie scurried down the row to talk to John. Her parents were laughing about something, tentative, cautious. But more together than Ellie had seen since she was very young. She let her mind drift again. Tina had offered to box her things and FedEx them to her mom's apartment. There wasn't much, really. Clothes and some photo albums. And the box of her mother's letters. The furniture was all Tina's except Ellie's and Kinzie's beds, which would cost more to move than replace.

In little time, the decision was made. Ellie and Kinzie didn't ever need to go back to San Diego. They were home. Which was why, since the first of June, Ellie had spent every possible spare moment with Nolan. Not nearly as much time as either of them wanted—but then these were the NBA finals.

And Nolan wanted badly to win.

The Hawks stayed even with the Lakers through the third period, while Kinzie and John cheered at the top of their lungs. Time seemed to fly off the clock, and all at once there were two minutes left, Lakers up by four. *Please, God . . . let him do this. Give him Your strength. You know how much he wants this for his dad.* She smiled. Now that she had found her faith in God again, she was remembering how to pray. How she could talk to God as a friend. The way she had when she was Kinzie's age.

Fifteen seconds ran off the clock while L.A. passed the ball, and this time the Hawks called a time-out. Again Ellie prayed for Nolan, for his dream to be fulfilled. But in a much bigger way, they had already won. All of them. She no longer allowed herself to be constantly consumed by how much they'd lost. The years apart. Instead, she found herself grateful for what they'd found. What they'd all found.

Once in a while, she could still hear Nolan's voice the way it had sounded that summer when they were fifteen. He had the tackle box, and they were about to write their letters, and she had just told him that eleven years seemed like a long time. His eyes had shone in the moonlight. For a single moment she closed her eyes, and she could hear him even now in the deafening arena. They had to write the letters, had to bury them in the tackle box.

Just in case. We'd still have this one chance.

That was where Ellie kept her mind these days. Not angry about what they'd lost but grateful. Because through the love of Nolan Cook and God Himself, they'd all been given exactly what they needed—one last chance. A smile filled her heart and spread to her face. This much was certain, no matter what happened as the rest of their lives played out. Her heart was healed and whole. And she knew something else as well.

She would never, ever doubt God again.

❧　❧

Nolan could feel the victory; he could taste it.

Not because of his own abilities but because he could sense God's spirit moving in him as tangibly as he could feel the ball in his hands. The sounds of the arena, the shouts from the players, the ball against the floor. None of it could touch the quiet in his soul. The peace and certainty there.

One of the Lakers had cussed out the ref and gotten a technical foul with a little over a minute to play. Nolan sank both resulting free throws. Hawks down by two. A turnover at the other end, and this time Nolan spotted Dexter streaking down the floor. His bounce pass landed perfectly in his friend's hands. Dexter palmed the ball with one hand and crashed it through the net with a dunk that brought the entire arena to its feet.

Time-out Lakers. But nothing could stop the momentum. *Let us shine for You, Lord . . . I don't want it if it doesn't glorify You.* They ran down the floor, and Nolan could see the ball with crazy clarity. He stole it from the Lakers' famous guard and threw it almost full court to Dexter again.

The top of Dexter's head reached the rim. Another resounding dunk. The crowd exploded, the noise deafening. Atlanta had the lead for the first time in five minutes. The final minute passed in a blur. But in that time, Nolan hit four more free throws. He watched the last seconds fall off the clock, watched it wishing only one thing.

That his father could have seen him win this game.

Maybe he has a way, Lord, a place where he can see this. If so, please . . . could you give him a front-row seat?

The buzzer sounded and Atlanta's fans went crazy. They were the NBA champions. Nolan pointed up and held his hand that way, peering into the rafters of Philips Arena, looking for a glimpse of heaven. *All for You, God . . . all for You.* In a rush, the players joined at center court and began celebrating, chest-thumping and grabbing each other around their necks. This was what they had set out to do at the beginning of the season. NBA champs in God's strength, not their own.

Nolan looked up at Ellie. She was watching him, smiling at him, both fists raised in the air. The way she used to cheer for him back in high school. He waved at her, and fifteen minutes later, when he was awarded the series MVP, Nolan took the microphone and did what he had longed to do since the game ended.

"First, I'd like to thank my Savior for letting me play basketball. I also want to thank my coaches and teammates. I'm nothing without them. And, of course, my family." His mom and sisters had flown in for the games in L.A., but they couldn't make it to Atlanta tonight. One of his sisters was graduating from nursing school tomorrow morning.

Nolan's voice stayed strong. "Thanks also to my second family." He pointed to where they were seated. Then he paused and held tight to the trophy. His voice filled with passion. "I'm dedicating this game, this series, to two people. My father, a man who was my mentor and friend. My first coach. Dad, I hope you're watching from heaven." He paused, struggling, his heart bursting.

"And second . . . I dedicate this to Ellie Anne Tucker." He smiled up at her, and for a few seconds, they were the only people in the arena. "I told Ellie when we were fifteen that I was going to marry her. And that's exactly what I'm going to do." He held the trophy in her direction. "I love you, Ellie."

He saw her mouth the same words to him from her place in the stands. Nolan could picture the couple from the Dream Foundation—Molly and Ryan Kelly. Somewhere, if they were watching, Ryan had the answer to why he was supposed to go on the road with Peyton Anders this year.

Another miracle.

Nolan stepped back and gave the platform to his coach. When the celebration died down, Ellie and her family joined him on the court, and he whispered close to her, "Now the whole world knows."

"I love you, Nolan Cook."

"I love you. That's all I want to do the rest of my life. Love you."

When they went to leave that night, for the first time since his father had died, Nolan didn't take the shot from the left-side three-point line. He didn't have to. The championship he had promised his father was finally his. Promise fulfilled. Instead, he left the arena the way he hoped he would leave it as long as he played the game.

With his arm around the only girl he'd ever loved.

Ellie Tucker.

Acknowledgments

No book comes together without a great and talented team of people making it happen. For that reason, a special thanks to my friends at Howard Books and Simon & Schuster, who combined efforts to make *The Chance* all it could be. Your passionate commitment to Life-Changing Fiction™ leaves me beyond grateful for the chance to work with you. A special thanks to my dedicated editor, Becky Nesbitt, and to Jonathan Merkh and Barry Landis and my talented team from Howard Books. Thanks also to the creative staff and the sales force at Simon & Schuster, who worked tirelessly to put this book in the hands of you, my reader friends.

A special thanks to my amazing agent, Rick Christian, president of Alive Communications. Rick, you've always believed in only the best for me. When we talk about the highest possible goals, you see them as doable, reachable. You were the one least surprised and most grateful when I hit number one on the *New York Times* bestseller list last year. You are a brilliant manager of my career, an incredible agent, and an encouraging, godly friend. I thank the Lord for you. But even with all you do for my ministry of writing, I am doubly grateful for your encouragement and prayers. Every time I finish a book, you send me a letter worth framing, and when something big happens, yours is the first call I receive. Thank you for that. The fact that you and Debbie pray for me and my family keeps me confident every morning that God will continue to breathe life into the stories in my heart. Thank you for being so much more than a brilliant agent.

Thanks to my husband, who puts up with me on deadline and doesn't mind driving through Chick-fil-A after a soccer game if I've been editing all day. This wild ride wouldn't be possible without you, Donald. Your love keeps me writing; your prayers keep me believing that God is using this Life-Changing Fiction™ in a powerful way. Thanks as well for the hours you put in, helping me. It's a full-time job, and I am grateful for your concern for the readers. Of course, thanks to the rest of the family who pulls together, bringing me iced green tea and understanding my sometimes crazy schedule. I love that you know you're still first, before any deadline.

Thank you also to my mom, Anne Kingsbury, and to my sisters, Tricia and Sue and Lynne. Mom, you are amazing as my assistant—working day and night to sort through the e-mail from my readers. I appreciate you more than you'll ever know. Traveling with you these past years for Extraordinary Women, Women of Joy, and Women of Faith events has given us time together we will always treasure. The journey gets more exciting all the time!

Tricia, you are the best executive assistant I could ever hope to have. I appreciate your loyalty and honesty, the way you include me in every decision and the daily exciting changes. This ministry of Life-Changing Fiction™ has become something bigger than I ever imagined, and much of that is because of you. I pray for God's blessings on you always, for your dedication to helping me in this season of writing, and for your wonderful son, Andrew. And aren't we having such a good time, too? God works all things for good!

Sue, I believe you should've been a counselor! From your home far from mine, you get batches of reader letters every day, and you diligently answer them using God's wisdom and His Word. When readers get a response from "Karen's sister Susan," I hope they know how carefully you've prayed for them and for the responses you give. Thank you for truly loving what you do, Sue. You're gifted with people, and I'm blessed to have you aboard. And Lynne, your help this past year has made a difference in my ability to adjust to life in Nashville. Thank you for that!

I also want to thank Kyle Kupecky, the newest addition to the Life-Changing Fiction™ staff and to our family. Time and again, you exceed my expectations with business and financial matters, and in supervising our many donation programs. Thank you for putting your whole heart into your work at Life-Changing Fiction™. I'm blessed to have a front-row seat to watch your solo Christian music career take wing. One day the whole world will know the beauty of your heart and voice. In the meantime, know that I treasure having you as part of the team.

Kelsey, you also are an enormous part of my team, and I thank you for loving the reader friends God has brought into our lives. This past year we've all discovered another talent of yours—cover design. The hours you've spent conveying my heart to the talented team at Howard have netted the gorgeous cover on this book and the last. And I hope for many more to come. What a special season, when you and Kyle are married and working together at our home office. God is so creative, so amazing. Keep working hard and believing in your dreams. I expect everyone to know your gift of acting someday soon. Along the way, I love that you are a part of all that God is doing through this special team.

Tyler, a special thanks to you for running the garage warehouse and making sure our storage needs are met and that we always have books to give away! You're a hard worker—God will reward that. Thanks also to my forever friends and family, the ones who have been there and continue to be there. Your love has been a tangible source of comfort, pulling us through the tough times and making us know how very blessed we are to have you in our lives.

And my greatest thanks to God. You put a story in my heart and have a million other hearts in mind—something I could never do. I'm grateful to be a small part of Your plan! The gift is Yours. I pray that I might use it for years to come in a way that will bring You glory and honor.

Turn the page for an

extract from

Fifteen Minutes

Chapter One

Chandra Olson made the trek every July.

She inked it on her calendar and told her manager and staff so that everyone in her camp knew she was off-limits. For two days midsummer, nothing was more important to America's premier black vocalist than leaving Los Angeles, flying to Birmingham, and driving out to the old country cemetery where her parents were buried.

Nothing.

She would spend the day here, same as she did each July for the last four years. No driver or entourage or fanfare. Just Chandra Olson, a fold-up camping chair, a cooler of smartwater, and a journal. Always a journal.

That way Chandra could write her parents a letter they would never read, and express in words her thanks for their support and her regrets at the cost of fame.

The very great cost.

She parked her rental car in the corner spot and surveyed the area. Oak trees dotted the couple acres of grass and tombstones that made up the graveyard. A few worn-out bouquets and the occasional American flag pressed into the earth over the grave of a soldier's sacrifice. A quick look around confirmed what she hoped to find. She was alone. Except for her, the place was empty.

Chandra stepped carefully through the freshly mowed grass, between markers, to the place where her parents lay. She set down her cooler and opened her chair. For a long moment she simply stared at the etchings in the modest gray stones, letting the truth wash over her once more. Martin and Muriel Olson. Young and vibrant and full of life. Her dad, forty-eight. Her mother, forty-four. Weddings, grandbabies, retirement—all of life ahead of them. Shot down just when their beautiful story was at the best part.

Tears blurred Chandra's eyes. Their death dates were the same: May 15, 2009.

A song burned in her heart this morning, a lyric that had been swimming to the surface for weeks. It would come together here, Chandra was sure. Here, close to the bodies of her parents and with the auditions for season ten of *Fifteen Minutes* set to begin later in the week. The song would be a ballad. A warning to be careful what you wish for, be careful what you dream.

In case it actually happens.

Chandra took her seat and studied the gray clouds slung low over the cemetery. She'd been part of the audition process in seven cities across the country over the last two months. Atlanta would be the last one, and the contestants who moved on would go straight to New York.

Yes, somewhere in houses across America, they were getting ready. Thousands of them. Saying good-bye to family and friends and heading off for a weekend of auditions in the heart of the South. Looking for a shot at fifteen minutes of fame.

Six years ago, Chandra was that wide-eyed singer, working at a state-subsidized day-care center and taking college classes at night. Nineteen years old with a dream bigger than Texas. What did she know about *Fifteen Minutes* or where it might lead, where the journey would take her?

Chandra closed her eyes and saw herself the way she was back then. No one had been more excited about her audition than Chandra's parents. They were longtime hard workers, both of them office managers for sales firms in downtown Birmingham. Martin and Muriel grew up in the projects, too poor to eat some days. They spent their lives trying to give their kids—Chandra and her brother, Jalen—everything they never had. Jalen's dream had been soccer. He was playing now, a senior at Liberty University in Virginia. But only because her parents had worked years of overtime to pay thousands of dollars in club soccer fees and private coaching and gym memberships. It was the same for Chandra—only her passion wasn't soccer, it was singing.

She opened her eyes and looked at her mother's tombstone. *You used to tell me I was born humming. Remember that? You gave me every advantage, Mama.* It was true. Chandra took voice lessons from the best teachers. She'd attended a private arts school on the south side, and when she wrote her first song, her parents took her to Atlanta and had it produced by a legend known for turning out R&B hits.

Nothing opened the door to her singing career the way *Fifteen Minutes* did. Chandra blazed through the audition process; even with the show's manufactured drama, there was never really any contest. On the show's finale, when dapper host Kip Barker smiled at the cameras and rattled off the famous line "The next fifteen minutes of fame go to . . . Chandra Olson!" there wasn't one surprised person in the audience or at home.

"You might be the best singer to ever grace the *Fifteen Minutes* stage." That's what longtime judge Cullen Caldwell had told her, and the comment was plastered across the Internet, everywhere from the *Today* show to *People* magazine.

Chandra remembered a private moment with her mother a week later. "You realize how big this is, baby girl?"

Beneath the warmth of her mother's words, Chandra's heart swelled. She hugged her mama for a long time. "It's big."

"It's more than that!" Her mother put her hands on either side of Chandra's face and looked deep into her eyes. "*Fifteen Minutes* is the biggest show on television, baby. And you're the best singer they've ever seen! God's gonna use you, child. He's gonna use you like none of us can begin to imagine."

Her mama was right about *Fifteen Minutes*. The show had been on the air for ten years, and though other voice talent programs competed for a share of the market, nothing compared to *Fifteen Minutes*. Between the judge's comment and her mother's praise, the future seemed brighter than the sun, Chandra's potential unlimited.

Anyone could see the success ahead.

But none of them saw coming what happened two years later. The second autumn after Chandra's win—with her first album topping the charts and her fame far surpassing what even Cullen Caldwell expected—an Alabama stalker stepped into the picture. He found Chandra on Facebook and asked for a loan. Money to help him and his mother buy a house. Chandra let the comment pass.

The request quickly became harassment, with the guy posting daily demands for money. His most chilling post was also his last. *What if something happened to your parents, Chandra? Maybe that would get your attention!*

Chandra blocked him from her Facebook page and filed a report with the Birmingham police.

"The guy's annoying," the Birmingham officer told her. "But anyone can make a Facebook page. We can't even prove he's a guy or that he lives in Alabama. People like this are rarely serious." The officer added that there wouldn't be enough hours in the day to investigate every crazy threat made against a celebrity. "It comes with the territory."

Yes. It came with the territory. Another aspect of being in the public eye. Chandra tried to believe the officer's words. The threat was nothing. Her concert schedule rolled on, and Chandra talked to her mother every night before she took the stage, same as always. Once she even shared her fears about the guy.

"I should get you a bodyguard, Mama. I have one."

"Don't be silly." Her mama's calm never wavered. "God's in control, baby. Me and your daddy are fine."

"I wish you were with me." Fear made the drafty wings of the arena colder than usual. "You and Daddy could come out on the road."

"Aww, Chandra." Her mom's smile rang through her words. "When we retire we'll be front row at every show."

Chandra had two minutes before her first song. "I love you."

"I love you, too. Do me a favor, baby."

"What?"

"Out there tonight, picture me and your daddy in the front row. We're with you, baby girl. We're always with you." Her emotion got ahead of her. "I'm so proud of you, Chandra."

Her mama's confidence kept Chandra sane, helped her forget the stalker's awful comment. But one warm night later that week, her parents pulled into their driveway after a church service and climbed out of their car. One of the neighbors was outside getting her mail and saw everything. Chandra's parents were laughing and talking, full of life. Her father had just taken her mother's hand when a spray of bullets exploded from the front porch, ripping through their bodies and dropping them to the ground. They were dead before the neighbor could call for help.

The man turned out to be certifiably insane, an escaped patient from a mental hospital. He waited on the Olsons' front porch until the police arrived, at which point he handed himself over and readily admitted to the killings. "I wanted Chandra's attention," he told police.

It worked.

Life would forever be measured as before and after the shootings. No question, a part of Chandra was buried right here with her parents. In the wake of their murders, she took two months off and became a recluse, handling her parents' affairs, afraid to leave their house. Eventually she hired two additional bodyguards and returned to the limelight.

She had no choice. The stage owned her now. It was where she belonged.

Questions plagued her then the way they did four years later, here at the cemetery. What was the point of fame and celebrity? All the record sales and accolades and awards? The money and houses and vacations? None of it could take her back to that moment, her mother's hands on her cheeks.

Her parents' faith had been strong and foundational, a key to Chandra's life before *Fifteen Minutes*. Now only one Bible character allowed Chandra a sense of understanding, a point of relating.

Solomon.

The king who had everything but finished his days believing the most desperate of thoughts—that all of life was meaningless. A chasing after the wind. Chandra had read the book of Ecclesiastes again on her Bible app during the flight here, and once more she had found her life verse, the only one that applied, Ecclesiastes

2:17, a nugget of sad truth tucked in the mix of a host of depressing Scriptures. She remembered the verse word for word.

So I hated my life, because the work that is done under the sun was grievous to me. All of it is meaningless, a chasing after the wind.

Her newest album was number one on iTunes, and she'd been asked back to *Fifteen Minutes*. This time as a judge. She had ten million Twitter followers and daily requests for movie and book deals. But here, in the warmth and quiet of the cemetery, she could only agree with King Solomon. Where were the real winners? Life was meaningless . . . a chasing after the wind.

All of it.

She opened her journal and began to write. The lyrics came easily, pouring from the gaping holes in her heart. It would be a hit, she was sure. Even that was meaningless. Only one thing kept Chandra going, kept her engaged in the daily trap of celebrity and fame, through concerts and autograph seekers and handlers and bodyguards. It wasn't her new role as judge on *Fifteen Minutes* or the countless hopefuls heading out to audition this week.

It was the twenty finalists.

The ones whose lives were about to change forever. The unsuspecting contestants who would never be the same, who could never go back to life the way it had been. Just maybe among them was a singer like she used to be, someone with faith and family and a quiet, happy life.

If she could warn just one about the false illusion and prison of fame, she would do it. In the process she might find something she'd lost four years ago with the death of her parents. The one thing celebrity could never give her. The one thing worth chasing.

Meaning.

This book and other **Karen Kingsbury** titles are
available from your local bookshop or can be
ordered direct from the publisher.

Fifteen Minutes	978-1-47113-136-3	£12.99
The Bridge	978-1-84983-961-7	£8.99

These titles are also available in eBook format

IF YOU ENJOY GOOD BOOKS,
YOU'LL LOVE OUR GREAT OFFER
25% OFF THE RRP ON ALL
SIMON & SCHUSTER UK TITLES
WITH FREE POSTAGE AND PACKING (UK ONLY)

How to buy your books

Credit and debit cards
Telephone Simon & Schuster Cash Sales at Sparkle Direct
on **01326 569444**

Cheque
Send a cheque payable to Simon & Schuster Bookshop to:
Simon & Schuster Bookshop, PO Box 60, Helston, TR13 0TP

Email: sales@sparkledirect.co.uk
Website: www.sparkledirect.com

Prices and availability are subject to change without notice.